BORN OF
LIGHT
AND
SHADOW

RYAN KIRK

OLIVER HEBER BOOKS

BORN OF LIGHT AND SHADOW

RYAN KIRK

.

OLIVER HEBER BOOKS

Published by Oliver-Heber Books

Cover design by Covers by JV Arts

Copyright © Ryan Kirk

0 9 8 7 6 5 4 3 2 1

❀ Created with Vellum

PROLOGUE

Elian ran through the fields of wheat as Gabe's heavy footfalls slowly faded into the distance. The sun had already set behind the tall canopy of the grove to the west, but their game wouldn't end until their parents called them home for supper. Elian crossed paths with Sara, who laughed with delight as he dodged past her. He heard a muffled *thump* and a loud curse as Gabe tripped over his feet.

Elian seized advantage of the moment. He took a few steps to the side, then crouched in the wheat and quieted his breath.

Gabe grunted as he pushed himself to his feet. He followed in the direction he'd last seen Elian running. Of the youth in the village, they were the fastest, and Gabe wanted to prove he deserved sole possession of the title. He couldn't admit what everyone else in the village already knew: no one could outrun Elian. He beat his way through the wheat, approaching close to where Elian had changed directions.

Elian tensed his legs and leaned forward, ready to sprint if Gabe spotted him. The chase, if there was one, would be decided by who ran first. He didn't worry. Gabe was almost as fast on his feet, but he lacked Elian's cleverness. The older boy wouldn't think to look down.

Gabe walked within six paces of Elian, then passed without slowing. The sounds of laughter and running feet to the east drew Gabe's attention away, and he sprinted after the other children, settling for easier prey.

Elian let out the breath he'd been holding, a little disappointed he hadn't had the chance to run. Gabe would call him a coward for hiding, and Elian had no defense except that he was winning.

He stood and hoped that Gabe might yet see him, but the chase had moved to a different part of the field, and he was alone. A cool breeze blew from the northwest, rippling across the endless expanses of wheat and causing Elian to shiver. Winter was at least a month away yet, but the chill in the air reminded him autumn wouldn't last forever.

Nothing did.

The moon formed a sharp crescent, a bright scythe working its way across the darkening sky. Elian watched it, wondering what the view of his world was like from there. Would he and his neighbors look like ants? He considered the question, then decided they wouldn't even be seen. The moon was too far away. At that distance, a single human was as small as a speck of dust.

The thought brought him comfort, though he couldn't say why. It felt good to be small.

Voices called out from the village, summoning the children and farmers from the fields. Elian's stomach rumbled at the thought of warm stew. He turned toward home, then saw a group of farmers to the north gathering their tools for the night. He ran over to them.

One farmer stood a head above the others, and he gave Elian a weary smile as he approached. "How were the games?" he asked.

"Gabe never caught me," Elian proudly announced.

"Good for you! Did he tire you out so much you can't help me carry some baskets to the house?" Father asked.

Elian grinned. "That's why I'm here."

"Thank you." Father handed Elian four empty baskets stacked together. He carried the scythes himself.

"Jace!" One of Father's friends shouted.

Father nodded at the other farmer. "Yes, Henk?"

"When are you going to let Elian carry *my* baskets home?"

"Maybe when you're too old to carry them yourself."

Henk adopted the gait of one of the village elders, rounding his shoulders and shuffling forward. "Day's coming soon, then!" he laughed.

Father chuckled and turned his attention back to his son. "How was the day?"

Elian squared his shoulders and pretended he was a veteran adanist giving a report to his clan leader. "We pulled most of the carrots and some potatoes."

"That's good progress. If you and the other children keep up your pace, you'll be done within a few days."

Elian had been thinking much the same. "If we finish early, could I help you in the fields?"

He'd expected an outright refusal, so he was surprised when Father considered the question seriously.

"I don't think so. We still haven't received any word this season from the wandering clans, and I'd prefer you stay closer to the village for now. I'm also certain your mother is already planning a great number of chores to keep you occupied after the garden is harvested."

"I'm old enough to help, and you could use more hands," Elian pouted.

"Both true," Father acknowledged, "but my decision stands. It's more important to me that you're safe. The lack of word from the clans worries me."

"I can fight! Master Heinrick says that I'm a natural with the sword, and I'm one of the best archers in the village."

Father raised a skeptical eyebrow at that claim. "Are you, now?"

"At least among the children," Elian added. He'd seen Father bring down a running deer without problem at more than thirty paces. Elian couldn't do that, yet.

"Have you mastered any bindings yet?" Father asked.

Elian looked down at his feet. "No, but I will soon, I'm sure of it."

Father put his free hand on Elian's shoulder. "I'm certain you will, and I'm grateful for your offer. I know you're eager to help, but for this season, I'd prefer it if you stayed closer to the village. Then we'll see what the winter brings, and if you master the basic bindings before the snow melts, I'll allow you to help me in the fields, though you might regret offering your help after."

Elian nodded. "By spring, my bindings will be greater than Abram's!"

Most parents would have laughed at such a claim, but Father didn't. "If you mean that, you'll need to study more than you have. Your mother would be an excellent teacher if you'd listen to her."

"Why don't *you* teach me? Mother always says your bindings are stronger than hers."

Elian meant the question as a compliment, but Father's eyes went distant and his face fell. The reaction was as familiar as it was mysterious. Father never shared where his thoughts went in these moments, and all Elian knew was that they arose whenever he asked too much about the distant past or about Father's bindings.

Father's expression passed, but his smile looked like it held back a bushel of sorrow. "That's kind of her to say, but trust me, she's the one you want teaching you."

Elian was sensitive enough to Father's moods to know he

shouldn't pursue the matter any further. Fortunately, they'd reached the outskirts of the village, and the smell of roasting pork banished all thoughts of more serious questions. Elian's stomach rumbled again, so loud that Father heard it and grinned.

They'd only passed three houses when Father was ambushed by a mess of unkempt hair with legs. It leaped into his arms, heedless of the two scythes he carried.

Elian saw the way Father shifted his weight, positioning his body between Samora and the dangerous tools. He caught her with his left arm only and swept her up into a powerful embrace.

Elian had become more aware of the way Father moved since he'd started daily lessons with Master Heinrick. He wasn't like any of the other farmers. He never tripped, never stumbled, and was never caught by surprise. Elian hadn't yet worked up the courage to ask why.

"Did you miss me, Father?" Samora asked.

Elian rolled his eyes. Every day, they went through the same routine, but neither Father nor Samora ever seemed to tire of it. Samora acted as if they'd been gone on an epic quest of legend, and Father pretended Samora had grown into a woman in the time between dawn and dusk.

"Of course I missed you. It was of you and no one else I thought about all day," Father said.

Samora hugged Father tight around the neck. "If you wanted to think about Mother, too, I'd allow it."

"I appreciate your generosity." Father put her down and she walked between Father and Elian. "Tell me, what did you do today, and why does your hair look like you've been outside in a windstorm all day?"

Samora chose not to answer the question about her appearance, though both Father and Elian knew the answer. Every day, once his younger sister's chores were done, she'd run off to the nearby grove of trees and play. She always came back scuffed, dirty, and with torn clothes, much to Mother's dismay. Father allowed it but was always encouraging her to take better care of her possessions. Samora was only a year younger, but sometimes he wondered if she would ever grow up and take more responsibility for herself.

"Mostly I cleaned carrots, but Mother did give me some binding lessons. Do you want to see?"

"Please."

Samora scrunched up her face and held out her hand, palm up. Elian didn't want to watch, but he couldn't resist anything that had to do with adani, even if it was his younger sister showing him up. He couldn't sense her weaving strands of adani into a binding, but the sweat beading on her dirty brow told him she was trying. They walked several steps without anything happening, but then the air twisted above her palm and ignited, turning into a loose ball of light about the size of a potato.

The light only lasted a moment, but the grin on Samora's face looked like it would last all day.

"Very impressive. You just learned that today?" Father asked.

"Yes, Father."

"That looks like a flame binding, so where's the fire?" he asked.

"I didn't want to burn anything, so I made a change to the binding, and this happened."

"You made the change on your own?"

Samora nodded.

Their father grunted, impressed.

Elian sneered at his sister, who was oblivious. Father always acted impressed by every minor achievement she shared.

They reached their home, and Father opened the front door and placed the tools inside. He thanked Elian for his help, then shut the door and led them to the village square. Their family had been one of the first to settle in the village, so they were only a few small homes away from the square.

Most of the village had already gathered, including Mother.

She wore her light hair short these days, and her sharp blue eyes reflected the glow of the fire. She was almost of a height with Father, making her by far the tallest woman in the village. Father reached around her waist and greeted her with a long kiss, prompting eyerolls from both son and daughter. Long tables and benches encircled a large cookfire, and the square buzzed with conversation as neighbors gathered.

Mother shooed them toward the food line, and before long they were seated at a table enjoying the long-awaited roast pig and stew. Eighthday feasts were always the best part of the week, and he dug into his food as if his parents had forgotten to feed him since the last eighthday.

Henk and his family sat beside them. Their glum expressions stood in stark contrast to the smiles at the other tables. Henk leaned over and murmured to Father. "I just checked with my wife, and there was still no word today. Do you think we should send out a scout?"

Elian stopped eating as he watched Father. Whenever Henk, or anyone in the village, suggested they send a scout, it always ended up being Father who went. They never ordered him, but he always left without question.

Father chewed his food slowly while he considered. He wasn't a man who rushed to decisions, a trait that often drove Elian to distraction.

"What do we know, and how much is just rumor?"

"It's mostly rumor, but we don't have any news. I don't think any of the other outer villages have heard word from the front in weeks, either."

"If the front had fallen, we'd know," Father said.

Henk acknowledged the point with his spoon. "I'd still feel better if we knew more."

"If it's as bad as you fear, would you rather have me here or away?"

Henk swallowed hard at that. Now it was his turn to think. "Here."

"Then there's your answer. There are plenty of reasons we might not hear from the front. Let's not wildly speculate."

Henk nodded, though he hardly looked reassured.

The feast wasn't as boisterous as usual. After he finished his second bowl of stew, Elian leaned across the table so he could whisper to Father. Fortunately, Henk was speaking with his wife and was distracted. "Do we need to be worried?"

Father glanced to the west. "It's good for us to be cautious, but there's little use in worrying. The world will move as it will."

It was a favorite saying of Father's, but it always irritated Elian. Father spoke often of seas, of waves and currents that could only be ridden and never controlled. Elian had never seen the sea, and in the legends, Abram had bound even the waves to his will, so Elian didn't put much stock in Father's willingness to be carried about by strong currents.

A real fighter, like Abram, would take on the entire world and win.

After the meal was over and they were safely back in their house, Elian listened to Father and Mother speaking while he played with Samora.

"Do you think I should go?" Father asked.

"No. Even in good conditions, it'll take you days to get to the front and days to return. I'd rather you not be gone for so long, given how little we've heard."

"How are the bindings?"

Elian's ears perked up at that, wondering what bindings they spoke about.

"I've been maintaining them. Nothing short of a Vada will break through."

Father leaned over and kissed her forehead. "And if we encounter one of those, we'll have bigger problems on our hands."

"Indeed. Now go play with your children. They're both listening."

Father did, joining them on the floor. Mother stood and finished tidying up the house for the night.

"What are we playing?" Father asked.

Before Elian could answer, Father and Mother both suddenly straightened and twisted their heads. They looked at one another and Mother nodded. Father swore, which he never did in front of the children, and Elian's heart raced.

"How strong, do you think?" Father asked.

"Moka, at least. Maybe Belog," Mother answered. The Debru titles sent a shiver down Elian's spine.

Father cursed again. "A mile out, still?"

Mother nodded, and Father turned to Elian. "Debru are coming with otsoa. We need to warn the village and get as many people into our home as possible, but we don't have long. I need your help, but you need to listen and obey every word I say."

"Yes, Father," Elian said.

"I want you to run to the east side of the village and shout 'Debru!' Run to every home you can, but as soon as you leave our house, I want you to count to sixty. As soon as you reach sixty, you run back home as fast as you can, no matter what you see and hear."

"Jace—" Mother began.

"He's old enough, and he's the only one."

"You want me to go outside as the Debru approach?" Elian asked.

Father squatted and met Elian's eye. "We don't have the time to discuss this. We need to save as many as we can."

Suddenly, the legends Elian was always imagining himself a part of lost their luster. Home was warm, comfortable, and safe. Beyond its walls, terror awaited. He forced himself to nod.

Father kissed Mother deeply, but Elian didn't roll his eyes this time. When they separated, they stared at each other for a moment. "I love you so much," Father said.

Mother's back straightened. "Not as much as I love you."

"We'll argue about it when I come back."

Father pulled Elian out of the house. Elian looked back to see Mother in the doorway, eyes closed. A translucent dome of golden light appeared over their house, an intricate binding Elian couldn't unravel with his crude senses. He stared. Adani, the life force that ran through every living creature in the world, was available to all, but to weave it and bind it into something so powerful should have been impossible to the untrained villagers. Mother spent all day in her garden, and this was the work of a warrior of the wandering clans.

Father pushed Elian east and shouted, "Count!"

Elian stumbled forward a few paces before the weight of the situation fully landed on his shoulders. He almost cried, but he looked to the west, which was covered with a shadow darker than the night sky. Father ran toward the danger, shouting "Debru!" loudly. Elian watched for a moment, then started counting in his head as he shouted the same. He ran from house to house, pounding on the doors as he yelled.

His feet felt heavy, and when he reached sixty, he was near the outskirts of the village. He shouted one last warning, then turned to run home.

A sound from the wheat behind him chilled his heart and froze his feet in place. The wheat swished back and forth and rustled, as if a dozen children sprinted through the harvest.

No child was so fast, though.

Elian listened a moment longer, unable to place the sound that grew louder than the pounding of his heart. Too late, he realized his danger, and his feet churned. He slipped and almost fell. Then he was running, faster than he would have if Gabe was only a pace behind him.

The wheat exploded with dark fur and sharp teeth, and a pack of otsoa burst into the village just as neighbors ran from their homes.

Elian had heard otsoa described as Debru wolves, but he'd never seen a wolf, so the comparison did him little good. They were almost as tall as him, but they raced forward on four powerful legs that ended in short, sharp claws. Their fur was darker than a moonless night, streaked with blue. Their eyes glowed a soft green, and Elian thought he saw blood dripping from their long fangs.

He leaped to the left as the village blacksmith stumbled into his path, an otsoa biting through the back of his neck with a single, bone-crunching *snap*.

His house was up ahead, a glowing refuge from the nightmare that enveloped him. His legs churned, burning from fear. Every breath came up short. Home seemed miles away.

A growl to his left was the only warning he received. He slid, more by instinct than by reason, the grass scratching and cutting the side of his torso as it pulled his tunic up. A shadow passed overhead, smelling of blood and bile.

Elian scrambled to his feet and ran, never looking back. Others ran beside him. The golden safety of home was only a few dozen paces away when three otsoa appeared from the west, emerging from the village square.

The monsters had encircled them.

Elian skidded to a stop, looking left and right for an escape, but he couldn't see past the press of bodies.

The otsoa charged, snapping and snarling, and there was nothing Elian could think to do. His thoughts were as frozen as his limbs. The farmers and villagers surrounding him held scythes and digging forks like they were swords, but Elian's hands were empty.

Light flared behind the otsoa, briefly illuminating Father's face as he flung three bundled spears of blue light. The spears flashed like lightning, passing through the otsoa as though they were mist and vanishing before they struck the villagers.

The otsoa collapsed like limp dolls, skidding to a stop only paces away. The green light of their eyes had gone out, and they seemed suddenly insubstantial, as though he'd been terrified of mere ghosts.

"Run!" Father shouted. "Get to my home."

He advanced as the crowd charged at him. They broke around him as though he were a boulder in a stream. His measured pace never slowed.

Unlike the others, Elian couldn't bring himself to run. He stood, open-mouthed, as he stared at Father. Father shook his head as he stopped beside Elian. "You need to run, too."

Another bundle of spears appeared in Father's hand, and Elian turned as he flung them. The otsoa chasing the villagers from the east fell as the spears pierced them.

"I'm safer with you," Elian claimed.

Father crouched down. "You were brave to help me. But sometimes, it's better to run. These otsoa aren't the real danger. That's still approaching, and I'll fight better knowing you're safe behind Mother's bindings."

"But—" a hundred questions demanded answers.

"There will be time to explain later. For now, just run."

Elian shook his head, but Father embraced him, then pushed him toward the house. Once moving, he began running, the golden dome of protection almost close enough to touch.

He felt the dark presence before he saw it, an oppressive weight that made drawing breath difficult. It came from the sky and landed hard behind Elian. The impact lifted him off his feet and he flew headfirst at the binding. He closed his eyes and brought up his hands for protection, but he passed through without slowing. He hit the ground a moment after he expected. His shoulder popping out as he tumbled, but such was his fear that he didn't notice. He spun, right arm limp, to see what had happened.

The figure that had landed was cloaked in swirling shadow, revealing little of the monster within. Flashes of blood-red light from inside the shadow allowed Elian to glimpse a long arm and sharp claws.

The monster stood between Father and the safety of the dome. Elian stepped forward, not because he had a plan, but because Father needed help and he was closest. He stopped when a slim, chilly hand wrapped around his wrist. He looked back and found Samora holding tight. She shook her head, driving reason into him. He couldn't fight an otsoa, much less whatever that was.

A spear of red light darted toward Father's heart, faster than the blue spears he'd used to kill the otsoa moments ago. Elian screamed, but the light skipped harmlessly away from Father, deflected by an adani shield Elian couldn't sense.

A dozen pinpricks of blue light appeared in the air around Father, each a powerful enough binding that even Elian's crudely developed senses noticed them. They sped into the shadow, attacking it from different angles. That much adani should have been enough to destroy every home in the village, but the shadow swallowed the light whole, churning as it struggled to digest the attack.

Father leaped at the shadow, a long blade of light in hand. When he cut down, the shadow coalesced into a sword of swirling blackness, revealing the monster within. It was a skinny giant, nearly twice as tall as Father. The swords met, and the impact almost knocked Elian off his feet.

What happened next was faster than Elian's eye could track. Father and the giant traded blows, their swords and bodies inhumanly fast. The ground rumbled with their battle and Elian stumbled backward to keep his balance. The fight didn't last long, and it ended with the monster's head falling from its shoulders and Father shuffling toward Mother's dome, clutching his side.

In the distance, otsoa howled and bounded into the village. Father took a faltering step forward.

Elian wouldn't wait any longer. He ripped his hand out of Samora's grip and left the safety of the dome. He reached Father as he was about to fall forward, then supported Father's weight with the uninjured side of his body. His gritted his teeth against the fiery pain in his loose shoulder. His vision swam, but they remained upright. Together they stumbled toward the dome, but the howls of the otsoa told Elian they wouldn't make it to safety in time. Father's weight grew heavier, and Elian's weary legs nearly buckled under the load.

He screamed for Samora to help, but her eyes were focused on something distant and she didn't hear. She raised her hand.

The howls of the otsoa suddenly became cries of pain and agony. Elian looked back, and there were three that had emerged from the village square, eager to devour the last unprotected citizens. Fire had erupted from their cores and burst out their backs, though, and now consumed both their bodies and their attention. They jerked and twisted, convulsing in an animalistic effort to put out the flames, but they died long before they succeeded.

The sight gave Elian the strength to push forward, and another dozen steps carried them over the boundary and into safety. Elian helped Father onto a bench outside the house. He was alarmingly pale. Blood soaked the side of Elian's tunic, and he realized how deep Father's wounds were.

"I'll get bandages," Elian said. He turned toward the house, but Father caught him with his cleaner hand and shook his head.

Elian tugged, not understanding, but he wasn't strong enough to break free of Father's grip. Samora sank to her knees and put her head on Father's lap. Tears ran down her face, and Elian wanted to shout at her. Father needed help, not tears!

Mother came out of the house, and even Elian's rough sense

of weaving was blinded by the adani radiating from her. It wasn't weighty like the monster's had been, but something light, reminding him of a summer breeze. She maintained the dome without apparent effort as she knelt in front of Father. She gently pried his hand away from the wound and her breath caught at the sight. "My love," she said.

Father smiled, though the effort clearly cost him. His breathing became labored, but he seemed at ease. He looked up at Elian, down at Samora, and some of the light returned to his eyes. "My steps are light," he said.

Mother nodded, tears running down her cheeks as she leaned forward and kissed him.

Father leaned his head back against the house he'd built with his own hands, closed his eyes, and went still, the lopsided smile never leaving his face.

Samora squatted in the long grass and put her hand to the ground. It wasn't necessary, but it was a habit she'd picked up from Mother that helped focus her attention. She extended the adani that flowed through her body until it merged with the currents running through the world. It spread outward, and so long as she kept her mind empty, it returned with all the knowledge of her surroundings she could wish for.

It pulled toward Elian, as it always did, but she nudged it around him and pushed it farther out. The land they stood on had once been a field, but it hadn't been planted for years, and now wheat battled native grasses for dominance. Every year the elders decreed less land be planted. Otsoa roamed more freely than when they'd been children, and the elders demanded the farmers stay closer to the relative safety of the village. It meant less food both for the villagers and the wandering clans, but they rarely lost farmers to attacks. Only arable land.

Samora pushed her worries aside as adani coursed through her limbs. The land was alive, though, dancing with the flow of adani. On those days when she allowed herself free rein, far out of the sight of others, it made her want to dance as well.

Others never understood, though they shared the same ability. The other adanists in the village nodded along with her when she asked about the intricate web of life and the unspeakable beauty of the world, but they never added their own observations, nor did they encourage her to ask deeper questions.

She knew the extent of her abilities was unusual. Most adanists could only extend their adani for a few hundred paces at most. Mother could send hers for about a mile, but Samora could go farther yet. To this day, she wasn't sure what her limit was.

She listened for a few moments longer, then stood. A part of her didn't want to share the knowledge she'd acquired, but the lives of villagers were at stake. She raised three fingers and pointed north.

"Deer?" Elian asked.

She nodded.

Elian set a demanding pace in the direction she'd pointed, but with adani flowing through the soles of her feet, she had little problem keeping up. Though it was nearly harvest, the air was hot and sticky, which meant the deer would rest in the shade.

Samora was surprised they'd found any so close to the village. They were only a couple of miles east of the village, and anything that served as prey for the hungry villagers had long since learned to roam elsewhere. She wondered at the reason but didn't question their good fortune. Elian would harvest the deer and they'd return to help the farmers by mid-afternoon at the latest.

Twice more she stopped and put her hand to the ground, but the deer remained at rest. A copse of trees grew near the bottom of a draw, providing the shade the deer craved. Elian saw it, too, and guided them in that direction. They stopped long before the deer had a chance of noticing them.

"Top or bottom of the draw?" Elian asked.

Samora didn't bother placing her palm on the ground. She closed her eyes, then pointed up.

Elian studied the draw, then pointed to the top of the ridge that formed its south side. "The view looks most favorable up there, and the wind is from the north, so they shouldn't smell you. You can catch them if they bolt over the ridge. I'll wait until you're in position, then approach from the bottom."

Samora completed her own study and agreed with Elian's assessment. He'd likely kill two of the deer before they sensed him, but three would be a stretch, even for his considerable skills. She stole a glance at him. In the twelve years since Father had died, he'd grown as tall as Father had been, and he'd developed a lean musculature ideal for long days of hiking. The never-ending struggle to grow enough food meant he always had a hungry look in his eyes, but when it was just the two of them, he was always quick to smile.

She thought Father would be proud of the man he'd become but didn't dare say so. Anything about Father struck a raw nerve, even after all these years. No one understood as well as Samora because she felt the same.

She turned away before he noticed her looking and nodded. Elian shared a few sips of water from the skin he carried and then she made her way toward the ridge, taking a longer route that would keep her out of sight of the deer. They were always alert to motion, and if she spooked them early, their hunt would take much longer.

It didn't take her long to hike to the top of the ridge, and from her elevated position, she could watch Elian as he neared the draw. Long experience had taught her that he would approach slowly, then sprint when he thought they were close enough to catch. She'd partnered with him for dozens of hunts, and he never failed to impress. He was the best hunter the village had seen in a generation. Better event than their father, some said.

Samora extended her adani once more to check that the deer hadn't moved without their knowledge. The deer remained where they were, but an unusual sensation caught her attention farther to the east. She narrowed her eyes as she looked in that direction.

Unfortunately, the rise in the hill that formed the top of the draw blocked her view.

She pushed more adani in that direction, but it reported... nothing. It was as if her adani either bounced off a wall or flowed around, and she hadn't believed either was possible without her intent.

Indecision seized her. The village needed the venison, but she was concerned by what she didn't feel. Whatever was happening was only a few miles from the village. Her thoughts ran immediately to the Debru, but the sensation could have come from anything.

She needed to explore. The potential danger of the unknown sensation was greater than her and Elian not bringing back venison today. She backed slowly down the hill until she was hidden from sight and gathered adani to her.

Elian lacked the talent to push his senses out like she could hers, but he wasn't blind. She bound adani into an enormous sphere of light, then cast it gently into the air. A moment later, she felt him change his direction, altering his path so that he followed the approximate route she'd taken up the hill.

Soon, he sat down beside her. "What's wrong?"

She cleared her throat, preparing her voice for its rare use. "Something mysterious to the east. I can't feel it with my adani."

It was more than she'd said in several days, but it was enough for Elian. He glanced east. "Probably makes sense to find out what it is, then. Debru?"

She shrugged.

"I suppose it's pointless to say that if something happens, you should run?"

She grinned and nodded.

"Figured." He stood, then offered his hand to help her up. "Lead the way, but let's stay out of sight of the draw. Assuming all goes well, the deer might still be here when we're done."

Samora took the lead as they walked over the hill and dropped to the other side. She paused just past the summit, but her eyes couldn't pick out what her adani had sensed.

Though the disturbance felt like it was at least a half-mile away, she proceeded cautiously. If it was related to the Debru, there was no telling what nasty surprises they might stumble upon if they weren't careful.

At one point, Elian drew close to her and whispered, "Not many animals around. I haven't seen so much as a bird pass near."

With her so focused on adani, she hadn't noticed the lack, but once he drew her attention to it, she observed it as well, and it set the hair on the back of her neck on end. It wasn't just a lack of birds, but a lack of everything. She felt no birds, no gophers, no rabbits. Ants still roamed around, but they weren't as sensitive to adani as most animals, and they couldn't escape even if they wanted to.

They climbed another rise, and Samora stopped. The place she sought wasn't as large as she'd imagined, but it was clear to the eye. Elian stopped beside her and grunted.

A small valley lay below them, with a spring-fed pond at the bottom. A loose ring of oak trees had grown around the pond, and Samora guessed it was a common refuge for many species.

At least, it had been. All the oaks had lost their leaves, but not through the annual autumnal ways. The leaves were all withered and brown, lacking any of the brilliant greens and yellows that decorated the few trees farther away from the pond. The bark had turned a darker shade than Samora had ever seen on a healthy tree, looking almost as if it had been burned. Gnarled branches stabbed at the blue sky.

Beyond the line of trees, the grass was dead, too.

The sickness was sharply demarcated, forming a nearly perfect circle around the pond. Elian rubbed at his bare chin. Samora kept arguing he should grow a beard, but so far he'd refused. "Any ideas?" he asked.

She extended adani, but the area was as impenetrable up close as it had been by the deer. It pulled at her adani and started to unravel it the moment it came in contact.

He understood her expressions well enough to know her answer. She always appreciated that about him. Everyone else wanted her to explain or elaborate, forcing her to speak. Elian had learned to pay closer attention, able to decipher the most subtle changes in her expression and bearing. "Is it safe to approach?"

Samora wished she had a more certain answer to that question. She weaved a spear of blue light in her hand and flung it toward the circle. It passed through without a problem, so the area wasn't shielded, but as it flew across the barren land, her weaving unraveled the same way her questing thread of adani had. By the time it reached the pond, it was gone.

Elian swore under his breath. "I take it that's a no, then."

Samora wasn't so sure. The weaving hadn't unraveled immediately, nor had it broken as it passed the barrier of the disturbance. She considered other tests, but nothing seemed as informative as exploring more closely.

Elian took his pack off and removed some of the rope he'd planned on using to tie their harvest of deer to one another. He wrapped the rope around his waist, but Samora put her hand out to stop him. He looked up, then shook his head. "If it affects adani, you'll be more sensitive to it than I am."

She met his gaze. *Exactly*.

Elian was always the one protecting her. Always the one charging into danger to protect her. She was strong enough to protect herself, and here, she was the only one sensitive enough to understand what was happening within the circle. It had to be her. He had to see it.

He sighed, then looked between her and the disturbance. "I don't like it."

Samora attempted a reassuring smile, but it failed to convince him. She reached for the rope, and he relented, allowing her to pull it from around his waist. She wrapped it around her own and tied the end tight. He pulled on the rope a few times to test it. Then she started toward the circle, Elian keeping pace a few steps behind.

She paid careful attention to the flow of adani and was surprised that her ability to sense it ended before the dead grass began. She gestured for Elian to stop advancing, then took a couple more steps toward the circle.

The effect was subtle enough she might not have noticed if she wasn't searching for it. Even before her feet reached the dead grass, her adani behaved in unusual ways. She was used to its ebbs and flows, leaving her body and returning in time, but now it was as if it was pulled away from her.

Was she growing tired, or was that simply her imagination?

She studied the effect before advancing, searching for some understanding of what was happening. Her observations didn't unveil the secret, so she took another two steps forward. She stopped just outside the circle and crouched down, feeling the grass between her fingers.

It wasn't dead yet, but it was dying. Like with her body, adani disappeared and never returned, and the grass couldn't pull more from the land. The flow was broken, seemingly beyond repair. She wove a sliver of her strength into a blade of grass, granting it a brief reprieve. As she watched, though, it faded again.

The circle was expanding.

Only one test remained. She stood but hesitated to step forward. This close to the circle, the air felt different. It carried a weight similar to one she'd felt before.

The night Father had died to save them.

She reached out with her hand, breaking the imagined barrier. At first, she felt nothing out of the ordinary. Slowly, her hand and arm felt heavy, and she sensed adani fleeing from her body faster than before, though she still had plenty to draw on.

She tried a weave she'd always found simple, but adani unraveled faster than she could gather it, and her own reserves depleted quickly. She stopped after a few moments of failure.

As a last test, she stepped through the barrier completely. Her strength waned quickly, but so long as she paid careful attention to her reserve, she had little to worry about. The air here reeked of Debru influence, though she didn't sense any of the monsters nearby. She squatted and placed her hand against the dead land, pushing adani into it.

The consequences struck faster and stronger than she was prepared for. A twisting, writhing shadow formed over the pond and shot toward her, stretching smokey tendrils around her face and waist. Before she could scramble backward, they closed tightly, and her vision went black.

She released a wave of adani, which gave her space for a moment, but the shadow closed around her again before she could escape. It drew adani from her as though she had filled a bucket and turned it upside down. She lost all strength and flopped to the side, and as she fell, the darkness before her assumed new shapes.

Samora blinked to clear her eyes, but the sights persisted whether her eyes were open or shut. She wasn't in the valley any longer, but standing upon a tall mountain peak, frigid winds tearing through her cloak as though it was silk. Chanting filled the air as dead-eyed men and women stood in a circle, arms outstretched to a bleak sky that rumbled with distant thunder.

The only meaningful light came from a glowing sphere in the center of the ring. It was the only warmth for miles, and the gaunt figures kept shuffling closer, desirous of the warmth but still afraid of stepping too close.

That light was life and death, wrapped up in one shining star.

She wanted to run to it, to embrace the paradox and see which fate this cruel world had in store for her, but her limbs were weary. She'd walked weeks to get here and sacrificed so much, but she failed at the very doorway to her destination. Her hand, or a clawed version of it, stretched toward the light, but the small star grew more distant as some force pulled her away.

She screamed, and her voice wasn't her voice, and even so, no one paid her any mind. They chanted, oblivious to the suffering of the one who'd journeyed so long with them. They were together only because the pilgrimage couldn't be made alone, but at the end of the road, each stood separately, praying for their individual deliverance.

The darkness grew lighter as she slid away, pulled by a force not of this world. Her companions and the mountains they had braved returned to shadow, then faded away. A tight belt around her waist made it difficult to breathe. The sun burned her face and she wished for the comforting shadow again. Voices called out in the distance, and she saw a familiar face, though the name attached to it escaped her.

Samora's memories returned with a physical force.

Elian crouched beside her, his strong hands surprisingly gentle as he forced her eyelids open and pressed his wrist against her forehead. She couldn't remember the last time she'd seen him so worried.

"Samora, can you hear me?"

She nodded, and the relief that passed over his face made her feel sorry for worrying him so. She flopped onto her back and basked in the sun's warmth. Elian, who always understood, didn't bother her with questions. She was fine, and they had time.

She let her head fall to the side. The shadow had disappeared, leaving no physical trace of her encounter. She felt the scars it had left across her heart, though, and suspected her recent memories would haunt her dreams for some time. It wasn't just the sights which confused her more than frightened her. It was the feeling of the place.

A place of shadow, darkness, and stone. Without light and warmth, and at least in her brief brush with it, a place without affection or compassion. She crossed her arms tightly over her torso to hold the heat of the sun in.

"Bad?" Elian asked. He split his attention between her and their surroundings, but he missed little. It always surprised her how relatively blind he was to adani when he was so sensitive to so much else.

She nodded.

"Better now?" He tried to keep his voice light, but his worry seeped through.

She pulled adani from the land, filling her reserve. This close, she suspected even Elian noticed. The psychic cold of the shadow lingered, but she sensed nothing out of the ordinary in her body. She sat up and nodded. Then she inclined her head toward the dead grass, made a circle by pressing her thumbs and fingertips together, and expanded it.

His face fell and he turned his attention to the barren area. "How fast?"

She held her thumb and forefinger close.

Elian thought in silence, then stood up. "Mother?"

Samora nodded.

"Your story can wait until then. You're convinced you're uninjured?"

He held up his hands as she glared. "Had to check. Do you mind if we harvest the deer on the way back? The village still needs the food."

She was grateful to focus on something besides the shadowy vision, and she enthusiastically agreed. They made haste away from the area.

Samora glanced back before it passed out of view, and the sight raised goosebumps down her arms. She couldn't help but think, as she looked at the dead land, that the shadow had claimed it for good.

2

The rope that had pulled Samora to safety now tied the harvested deer together, which allowed Elian to carry them both to camp. The third had escaped thanks to an uncharacteristic miss from Samora's adani spear, a failure that still irritated him. Venison, like wheat, was an increasingly scarce resource. Every scrap mattered.

He bit his tongue, though. Samora's gaze had wandered in and out of focus since that shadow had ambushed her. She'd only been under attack for a moment, but she'd collapsed without putting up any fight that Elian could see or sense. Whatever had happened to her lingered, despite her continued insistence she was fine.

He wanted to hound her with questions, but he held his peace. She would tell him what had happened in time.

The children raced to meet them as they neared the village, and Elian forced a wide smile onto his face. Samora drifted a few paces further back to avoid the coming commotion. The children soon circled around Elian, sometimes coming so close he had to pause so he didn't accidentally walk over them. Mother had once compared them to a pack of predators surrounding a wounded animal, and on days like today, Elian found the comparison apt. They showered him with questions, which he answered patiently.

The children ignored Samora, having learned long ago she wouldn't answer their questions. Elian glanced back and tried to keep the worry off his face. She walked even further away than usual, lost in her own thoughts.

He stopped by their neighbor's house to drop the venison off. Normally he would prepare the animals himself, but it was best if they didn't delay long, and they'd be talking for a while. His gift was welcomed with open arms, and by the time he reached the village square, the children had all been shooed back to their chores by watchful parents. They complained but reluctantly obeyed, trickling away in ones and twos.

Elian felt for them. Villagers rarely let their children wander far, and no small number of them dreamed of exploring the world beyond the closest fields. He'd been much the same as a child, even when the rules hadn't been so strict.

Once the last of the children scampered off, he asked Samora if she wanted Henk present as well. He'd become the unofficial leader of the village years ago, and he'd want to hear their tale. She nodded and they parted ways. Elian fetched Henk as Samora returned home. Henk wasn't pleased to be pulled from the fields, but a look from Elian was enough to silence his complaints.

Mother had poured four cups of water by the time Elian arrived with Henk in tow. Henk bowed in thanks, and they took seats around the family's small table. All eyes turned to Samora, but she inclined her chin in Elian's direction, and he took his cue. He briefly spoke of their hunt and Samora's discovery that something was hidden from her adani. Throughout his retelling, he kept most of his focus on Mother, as she was the one most likely to understand what they'd experienced. She looked as confused and concerned as he felt, though.

After he'd told most of the story, he turned the tale over to Samora. His sister bowed her head in acknowledgement and cleared her throat. She told them of her vision and how it had made her feel.

Elian clenched his fists under the table. Ever since they'd been young, Samora had been far better at binding, which was why it made sense for her to explore the circle first. If he'd just been more capable, he could have assumed the risk in her place. But because he was weak, he had no choice but to put his sister in danger.

He forced himself to exhale slowly and stretch his hands. Anger wouldn't help him. It never had before. And if he let it get out of control, the adani that raged in his body would make him act in ways he'd soon regret.

Samora ended her retelling quickly and she folded back into herself. She spoke only of the experience, saying nothing of the effect it had on her. Elian knew the brief experience had wounded her, but she refused to share her pain.

The memory of Father rose unbidden: of him stumbling forward, covering his mortal wound with his hand, as if he just needed a brief rest before heading back into the fields for another day of harvesting.

Elian promised himself he'd ask her later, but for now, he finished the story. He looked at Mother expectantly.

She leaned back in her chair, rubbing her chin. In the years since Father's passing, she'd adopted some of his habits, including his tendency to think carefully before speaking.

Her light hair still hadn't faded to gray, a point of minor contention among some of the older women of the village. Her sharp gaze missed little, and her ability to bind adani had only grown with every passing season. Elian didn't know who was capable of more, Samora or Mother, but if they were ever to fight, he wouldn't feel safe until he was in the next village over.

Mother's first question was for Samora. "Debru?"

Samora's shoulders rose a fraction of an inch, then she gave one nod. *Likely.*

Mother wrapped a braid of her hair around a finger as she stared out the window. She thought for a moment more, then sighed. "I don't think I've ever heard of anything like it. The Debru often leave dead ground behind them, but that doesn't sound like this."

"A new weapon?" Henk asked.

Elian hadn't even considered the possibility.

"It's possible, but I'm skeptical. New Debru weapons and techniques tend toward more dramatic results."

"Hardly reassuring," Henk said drily.

"I'm not trying to be. I'm trying to seek the truth," Mother said sharply.

The two elders stared at each other, but Henk broke first. He knew well enough his leadership relied on Mother's implied approval. She was, without question, the most respected person in the village, and that respect only grew the closer the Debru advanced. The only reason Henk enjoyed his status as the village leader was because Mother wanted nothing to do with the role.

It frustrated Henk, but they usually got along well enough. Henk looked down. "Sorry, but everyone is already nervous. I fear how they'll react when they hear about this."

"How they react will be up to them. Don't you dare consider hiding this. If that circle is only a few miles away, it's very possible someone weaker than Samora wanders in there and never leaves," Mother said.

Henk held up his hands in surrender. "Of course."

Silence settled over the gathering for a moment, but Henk kept them focused. Mother and Henk didn't always agree, but Elian considered Henk a well-intentioned leader. He lacked courage, at times, but he did his best by the people who called the village home. "What are we going to do?" he asked.

The same question had troubled Elian most of the way home. The circle wasn't immediately dangerous, but Samora was strong, and it could have killed her easily. That shadow might have caught her by surprise, but Elian didn't think the result would be much different if she'd been prepared.

Some powers were simply too great to resist.

Henk's question only had one reasonable answer, but that answer was unacceptable, so Elian hoped Mother had a different plan.

Mother considered the question, but when her gaze settled on Elian, his stomach knotted.

"If there is an answer, it will lie with the masters closer to the front. I wouldn't even know where to begin," Mother said.

Elian clenched his fists again and fought to keep his voice even. "Do you think it would be worthwhile to examine the circle yourself?"

Mother didn't even consider it. "No. Samora's ability with adani is greater than my own. If she couldn't discover more, I couldn't either."

Henk turned to Elian. "Will you go to the front and seek out a master?"

Elian looked between Henk and his hopeful gaze and Mother with her sorrowful countenance. Adani rushed through his limbs, and he knew if he wasn't careful, he'd destroy the furniture Father had made them. He stood slowly so as not to knock the chair back. He stared at Henk, causing the elder to scoot his own chair away. The coward looked about ready to beg, so Elian cut him off. "Not a chance."

The house closed in on him and the air grew thick. He spun on a heel and walked toward the door, careful to open it with a fraction of his typical strength. He grabbed an ax leaning against the wall, then he strode into the open air and turned west, toward the grove that bordered the village.

By THE TIME Mother found him, he'd felled several large trees. The first few had fallen to his fists, and after he'd bled off the greater share of his frustration, he switched to the ax, expelling the adani that strengthened his limbs and poisoned his mind.

She made no secret of her approach, but he finished trimming the branches off a fallen log before he acknowledged her. He set the ax down and stretched, feeling better than he had since returning home. Mother eyed the work he'd done. "I haven't seen you this frustrated since the last time I tried teaching you to bind a spear," she said.

The memory had once been a bitter one, but time had dulled its sharp edges. The failure still stung, but it no longer drove him out here with an ax in hand, as it had for almost a week after. That had been the last time he'd tried a basic binding, and Mother had never pressed him to learn one since.

He wiped the sweat from his brow. "Probably right. There was the time I found out Gabe had taken Sara out here."

Mother laughed at the memory. "I'd forgotten about that. For a while, I was worried you were going to cut down the entire grove, so they'd have nowhere to hide. Walk or sit?"

"Walk. I think I've endured enough sitting for the day."

She shook her head and smiled faintly.

"What?" he asked.

"You've saved your sister, hunted and carried two deer home, and cut down enough lumber to light our fires for a month. Most would be in bed, unable to move for a week."

Elian looked down at his hands and shrugged. "But I still can't complete the simplest bindings."

Mother ignored the comment, avoiding the argument that had colored their relationship for years.

"A walk it is, then." She took his arm and together they meandered through the well-worn trails that crisscrossed the grove. She said nothing, but her presence alone soothed the raw emotions no amount of tree cutting could bury.

"How much is adani, and how much is your own emotion?" she asked.

"I don't honestly know anymore."

"It was flowing strongly through you even before Henk's request."

He didn't bother denying it. No doubt both she and Samora had felt it building within him. They were sensitive enough they probably would have felt it if he'd been out in the fields. "It was Samora's story. She hasn't said anything, but she carries wounds from the attack."

"She's strong, though, and the hurt is in her memories. It will fade in time."

"I should have been the one to enter."

Mother squeezed his arm. "I know you know that's not true. You were there for her and did exactly what was required. You saved her."

Elian broke from her grasp and turned so he stood in front of her. "And she never should have required saving."

They threaded their way between some close trees, and then Mother lifted her hand to his cheek. "I think you should go."

He shook his head. "Never."

"Do you still think I am so weak? You have all my love, but it is past time for you to move on. I can protect myself better than most."

"But I would never forgive myself if something happened to you while I was gone."

She patted his cheek. "That's kind of you, but silly. And besides, though you may hate to hear it, I'm still more capable than you."

Elian looked down at his feet. Mother was right, but reason couldn't change the way he felt. "I don't think I can. What if—" he couldn't even bring himself to finish the thought.

"Life is what it is. You can't control what happens."

"I hate that saying."

Mother grunted. "Your father was fond of it, though I preferred a different saying."

"What's that?"

"Let go."

The words hit him like a hammer. "But what if I lose you, or Samora?"

"You can't lose what you never had. We're your family, not your possessions."

Elian felt emotions building in his chest. He looked up at the sky and calmed himself with the breathing exercises Mother had taught him when he was younger. "I don't want to go."

"I know, but you will."

"You're ordering me?"

Mother chuckled. "No, but Samora wants to leave. She told Henk she would go with or without you."

Elian thought he'd misheard. Samora was so kind she gently carried spiders out of their house instead of killing them. Why would she want to go toward the front, where violence ruled both day and night? "She wants to leave?"

"For someone who pays such close attention to her, you seem surprised."

Elian scratched his head. "I thought she didn't want to leave, either."

"Only because you don't want to, so it never occurred to you. There's a valuable lesson there. Don't let the stories you surround yourself with blind you to reality."

"She wants to leave?" Elian repeated, still not quite believing.

"Yes. We reached the limit of what I could teach her months ago. Samora wants to learn more, and the only place for that is with the wandering clans. The Bears should be close this time of year, and they're a worthy clan."

Elian felt his heart being torn in two. He couldn't be with both his mother and sister, unless, "Why don't you come with us?"

"I've considered it but won't. You and Samora need to find your own way, and I promised Henk that I'd protect this village. It's a good place, and one I'm happy to call home."

Mother wrapped him up in an embrace, her arms still strong enough that it was harder for him to breathe when she squeezed. "You'll go?" she asked.

He wiggled out of her grasp. "I suppose. It sounds like you and Samora conspired to not give me a choice."

"There's always a choice, but I think you're making the right one. You both need to learn to control your abilities, and I don't think either of you will be satisfied living all your days here."

They returned to where Elian had left his ax. The sun neared the horizon and it was almost time to eat.

"Aren't you nervous? You and Father left the wandering clans when you were pregnant with me because you wanted a safer place to raise a family. And now you're sending us back?"

Mother took his arm again. "Honestly?"

"Of course."

"I'm terrified. Sending you two will break my heart, but that's part of being a parent. If you raise your children well, someday they'll leave you behind."

"The world is what it is, eh?"

Mother snorted. "That it is. But I wouldn't trade my years with you and Father for anything. Hopefully, when you're my age, you'll feel the same about the choices you've made."

Elian patted her hand, trying to be reassuring. But when he looked back at the grove, he had a feeling, deep in his gut, that after he left this village, he'd never see it again.

3

Samora thought Elian had always been strong, even when he'd been younger. When they had worked in the gardens together, he often carried enough stone and tools for two children.

It was no different now. His pack was nearly twice as heavy as hers, but the added weight didn't trouble him. He shouldered it with a smile after every rest and only stopped when she called for a break. She suspected he would have made this journey twice as fast alone, but he never would have left if she hadn't led him away.

She didn't regret leaving, although abandoning the village and Mother worried her. Mother didn't need their protection, but Samora felt more secure when all three of them were together. They'd been separated that fateful night and hadn't been whole since.

She and Mother had spoken at length in the past about Samora leaving the village to find a suitable master, but it wasn't until her and Elian's discovery that she had sufficient reason to leave. She'd long since exceeded Mother's ability to instruct her, though Mother's experience proved invaluable as Samora explored her growing strength.

Elian needed a master, too, though of a variety Mother was less familiar with. A few legends spoke of warriors who'd mastered the art of directing adani through their bodies, but Mother had never known one in her years along the front. Everyone bound adani now, he alone seemed to lack the ability.

Samora extended her senses toward Elian. Adani gathered to him without apparent effort, his body pulling it from the land and roughly cycling it. She knew if she asked, he would deny doing anything, and she believed him. He possessed some limited control over his ability, but it mostly manifested without his intent. Mother had offered to teach him the basics of looping adani through his body, but he'd been so single-mindedly focused on binding adani after Father died, he refused her lessons. Eventually, he swore off adani all together, relying only on the limited abilities that came naturally to him.

Elian didn't realize how remarkable he was, no matter how many times she told him. He blazed brightly against her senses, but through no effort of his own. He saw only what he lacked.

Samora sensed the presence of others well before Elian. Adani informed her of a handful of bright figures wandering to the northwest. She pointed it out to Elian.

"A wandering clan?" Elian asked.

She shrugged but nodded. The size of their party and their individual strengths almost certainly meant they were warriors, though she and Elian hadn't expected to encounter a clan for at least another day or two. The front was still roughly a week of travel away.

At least, that was what they had believed. If a clan wandered here, the front might be approaching closer to their village than anyone realized.

"Do you want to meet with them?" Elian asked.

She nodded. What information they had was likely long out of date. Before they'd left, Mother had told them all she knew and had given them a list of names to inquire after. If they were lucky, some of those names could be found among this clan. If not, perhaps the clan could direct them onward.

Elian altered their path so they angled toward the clan. As they neared, Samora's imagination wandered. After Father's death, Mother had told them about their past, how they'd been part of a wandering clan before she'd become pregnant. Mother claimed most who expected children didn't leave, but she and Father had other plans. She'd answered every question Samora asked about the wandering clans, but Samora had little direct experience with the clans. The messengers they sent to the village met only briefly with the village elders before leaving, and Samora had never joined the farmers as they carried provisions to the front. The clans were more rumors, stories, and legends to her than flesh and blood. The thought of meeting them in person made her heart race.

She suspected Elian felt the same. He'd subtly quickened his pace, adani rushing through his body faster than before.

They were sensed by scouts well before they came within sight of the main clan, and Samora used hand gestures to warn Elian of their impending arrival.

The scouts rode horses, so they towered over the two travelers. Elian bowed to them as they slowed to a stop.

One of the riders was a woman considerably shorter than Samora. Her hard gaze and steady grasp of adani marked her as a considerable warrior. The man riding beside her had a vicious scar running down the left side of his face and more weapons on his person than Samora thought were in the entirety of her village. Most adanists traveled without weapons, content to bind what they used out of adani when needed. Metalwork was rare enough in the villages, but this scout looked like he was in danger of stabbing himself with a knife no matter what way he moved.

Neither of the scouts were anything like the neighbors she'd known her entire life. Samora saw it in their eyes and in their bearing. They were hard, and knew it, and she was a spoiled brat from the villages. She wasn't sure they were wrong. Hard as farm life could be, it paled beside the duties of the wandering clans.

Both were strong adanists. Samora could probably bind more raw adani than either, but guessed it wouldn't make a difference. Experience had taught them to wield adani in ways she couldn't predict. Mother had always told her she was strong, but being in the presence of these two made her wonder if Mother had been too generous with her praise.

The scouts were wary of the new arrivals, but not overly concerned.

The woman spoke for the scouts, and she kept an eye on Elian. She no doubt sensed the unique flow of adani around him and wondered what it meant. "Who are you and why are you here?"

She'd directed the question at Samora, but Elian answered. "My name is Elian, and this is my sister Samora. We're from one of the outer villages, and we come with news and questions for the wandering clans."

"What news?" the woman asked.

"We discovered a growing circle of dead grass and trees outside our village. Bindings unravel within its boundaries, and any binding performed within it results in a shadowy attack. We've observed no Debru, but it has their feel."

Samora had worried how their news would be taken, and if they would be believed. Mother said that many in the wandering clans looked down on the villagers, but also assured Samora that she and Elian would be of interest. Samora was a capable adanist and Elian, well, no one with any sense of adani could miss how unique he was.

The scouts debated and questioned them less than Samora expected. The woman looked over to her companion, who nodded.

"That is concerning. We'll escort you to the clan. Our leader, Harald, will want to hear more," she said.

"Harald?" Elian asked. "*The* Harald who singlehandedly fought a Belog and lived to tell about it? The leader of the Bears?"

The corner of the female scout's mouth turned up in a smile. "The very one."

Elian looked eagerly at Samora. He'd pried every story out of wandering warriors since he'd been little, so she wasn't surprised he recognized the name. It wasn't one that had been on Mother's list, though.

The scouts turned their horses around and rode at an easy pace Elian and Samora had no trouble matching. After cresting a small rise, they caught their first glimpse of the full might of a wandering clan.

A long line of horses and warriors stretched through the rolling hills and prairie. Many of the horses pulled sleds filled with the supplies needed to build a home wherever they settled. Samora estimated the clan was somewhere between a hundred and fifty and two hundred strong. What surprised her most were the children running freely around the column.

She'd known what to expect, but seeing children still threw her off-balance. These were the wandering clans of legend. Parenting seemed too mundane a task for their strength and growing up along the front too dangerous for children.

The scouts gave her little time to observe from a distance. They aimed for a group of horses near the head of the line, where one of the largest men Samora had ever seen made the horse he rode upon look like a foal.

The clan welcomed the scouts with warm shouts, reminding Samora of the excitement she'd felt after seeing Father returning from one of the distant tasks Henk assigned him. She'd wait all afternoon, peeking through every window to find Father's tall silhouette on the horizon. When it finally appeared, all chores were forgotten in her rush to greet him.

Presumably, the scouts had only been gone for some small part of the day, but their welcome was no less heartfelt. Samora revised her first impression of the pair as they broke out in wide grins and loud shouts.

She and Elian were ushered into the group of horses and warriors. Elian once again introduced himself and his sister, and the enormous man dismounted so he could walk beside them. "My name is Harald, and I have the honor of leading this mighty clan of Bears," he said.

His voice carried as though he'd shouted his introduction, and more than one shout went up in reply from further down the line.

Samora didn't know if it was the man's incredible adani or his overwhelming presence, but the world spun around her. Elian, always alert, took her arm and supported her. The dizziness passed after a moment, but she didn't let go of Elian.

"What brings you to our fair hunting lands today?" Harald boomed.

Samora wondered if Harald was limited to shouting only. His voice rang in her ears long after he'd stopped speaking.

Elian told their story again, filling in many of the details he'd omitted from telling the scouts. Harald listened closely without interrupting. They walked as Elian talked. By the time her brother finished, the clan had reached a small draw with a stream running down the bottom of it.

Harald raised a finger above his head and twirled it. The nearby riders broke off in all directions, shouting orders and leaving him alone with the siblings. He laid one massive hand on each of their shoulders. "There is much to discuss, but we've reached camp. Wander about as you like, lend a hand if you wish, and join me for supper tonight. We'll talk then."

Harald rode off before Samora could object. She looked over to Elian, curious about his reaction.

He stared at Harald's departing back as if the man was Abram in the flesh. After a moment, he caught Samora studying him, and his cheeks turned red. "He's impressive. I've never met anyone like him."

Samora supposed that was true enough. Their village didn't produce much in the way of fighters. Gabe had styled himself as one when he was younger, but after encountering a Debru in person, he'd changed his tune. Master Heinrick's lessons had gradually gone from being full of eager young children to nearly empty, and eventually he'd left for another village where he could do more good. Thankfully, he'd taught Elian as much as he could before he'd left.

So it was little surprise Elian looked upon Harald as a legend, even though all they'd seen him do thus far was crush a horse as he rode.

The Bears fell to their tasks with an easy familiarity that spoke of long years of routine. Everyone from child to elder knew their role, and for a while, Elian and Samora watched with wonder. In the course of an evening, the draw transformed from unoccupied wilderness to camp for the clan. Elian helped the warriors cut down wood for cookfires while Samora hauled supplies from the sleds to their temporary destinations.

It wasn't long before Samora was no longer needed, so she used the opportunity to rest her weary feet and observe the final stages of the camp's construction. She'd grown up in a home built with Father's sweat and blood, a gift to his family and a monument to his life. At a glance, the tents that now surrounded her were nothing like it. They felt soulless.

As she watched families settling in, she changed her mind. These tents lacked the sturdy walls of Father's house, but they were no less a home for the families that slept within.

Several Bears started fires near the center of the camp, and the promise of warmth and food called Samora that way. She volunteered to cut vegetables for a stew while others butchered the game hunters had harvested earlier that day. Samora lost herself in the work, grateful to take part in a routine that reminded her of evenings at home.

As night fell, the clan gathered for the meal. Elian and Samora sat near Harald, but he made it clear the meal was to be enjoyed, and their discussion would come after. The siblings ate eagerly, grateful for a warm meal that hadn't come straight from their packs.

The meal was as raucous as Samora had ever known, putting the village's eighthday feasts to shame. Warriors traded joyful barbs with one another while onlookers celebrated any particularly sharp witticism. The pots of stew emptied until the last warriors were scraping out the bottoms with their ladles. Out of the corner of her eye she noticed two children punching each other, but no adult stepped in to intervene.

Samora took it all in, not even trying to comprehend. She'd always imagined the wandering clans as somber guardians, sacrificing their own lives and comfort for the villagers who lived farther from the front. There were stories of epic feasts, of course, but nothing, not even Mother's warnings, prepared her for this.

She noticed that some warriors finished their meals early and vanished into the night. As they did, others appeared to take their place. Even at supper the clan had duties to fulfill.

Once most of meal was finished, families wandered back to their tents, and Harald revealed a small skin hidden somewhere near his chest. He pulled the stopper out, took a swig, and passed the skin to Elian. "A brew made by one of the villages. Have you had it?"

Elian shook his head, and Samora almost warned him against it. She could smell it from here, and it burned the hairs inside her nose. Elian didn't hesitate to take a swig, then coughed as the liquor burned down his throat. His eyes teared up, and he handed the skin back to Harald. The clan leader extended it toward Samora.

"She doesn't drink," Elian said.

"She can also speak for herself," Harald said. There was an edge to his voice that hadn't been there before.

"But she doesn't like to," Elian argued.

"Is that true?" Harald asked Samora.

She nodded. After watching her for a moment, Harald nodded. "So be it."

The leader whistled. Several of the warriors scattered around the fire answered the call, sitting in a loose circle. Most were older, and all carried scars. Harald leaned forward. "You've told me your story, but I'd appreciate it if you shared it one more time with us all. This is my war council, and I decide little of import without their wisdom."

Samora figured the request was double-edged. Harald wanted the story told to his council, but he would listen closely to see if their account differed in the telling. He was no fool, and although he welcomed them, he didn't blindly trust them.

With that one request, phrased in such a way no reasonable person would question it, Samora understood how different the wandering clans were from her village. Back home, Henk was well-meaning, but he was as subtle as Elian excising his anger in the grove.

Elian recounted their story again, then answered their questions. The warriors listened to every word with an attentive silence that lasted even after Elian's story ended.

Harald said, "I've heard no such tale in my travels, and I confess the matter beyond my knowledge. Have any of you heard something I have not?"

Heads shook around the circle. A stout man with a beard that reached almost to his belt said, "Tiafel and the Hounds are only two clans to the north. If anyone would know something, he's the one."

Samora recognized the name. It was one Mother suggested they find.

Harald tugged at his own beard. "True. It's a dangerous journey, though, and the Crows haven't been welcoming as of late. Does anyone have any better suggestions?"

Silence greeted his question. He waited, but when no answers were forthcoming, he said, "Very well. I'd thought much the same, but hoped there might be another way. Get your rest. We'll pack up camp tomorrow and lead them north for a day or two. We might as well protect them while we can."

Samora caught the way the warriors glanced at one another.

"The clan's tired, Harald. We were looking forward to the rest," said a tall woman who sat beside him.

"True, but if the circles are something the Debru have created, I fear they've found a way to break through our lines without us noticing. Understanding what Samora found may be a matter of our survival. We'll rest as soon as we're able."

None of the warriors looked pleased by Harald's decision, but no one argued openly against it. The circle unraveled as the warriors returned to their families. Harald gestured that the siblings should remain, and once his council had dispersed, he asked, "I'd hear your history." He pointed at Samora. "You possess an untapped gift that would make you valuable among any of the wandering clans, and as for you," he looked at Elian, "I don't know what's happening with you, but adani favors you, as well. We haven't seen any like you two from the villages in years."

Elian said, "Our parents used to be Spiders. They chose the villages when Mother became pregnant with me."

"Spiders?" Harald asked.

Elian nodded, and Harald's face fell.

"I'm sorry to tell you this, but they were destroyed in an attack several years ago. This actually used to be their land. The Debru came in force. Many of the clans were sorely tested that night, but none like the Spiders. A small handful survived and have scattered to other clans, but the rest died as heroes. Only a few Debru broke through to the villages, thanks to their sacrifices."

Samora lowered her head. She'd often imagined meeting grandparents and cousins, relations many of the other children in the village had that she didn't, but Harald crushed that dream.

She dug her nails into her palm. It didn't matter. She shouldn't grieve over what she'd never had.

"Tell me of your parents," Harald asked. "Were their names known?"

"I'm sure you would have heard of my father," Elian said, nearly bursting with pride. "His name was Jace."

Harald searched his memories, then shook his head. "I'm sorry, but I don't think I've heard the name."

Elian folded in on himself as though someone had punched him in the stomach. Harald moved the conversation along quickly. "Why are you two here instead of your parents?"

"Father died defending the village from a Debru attack several years ago," Elian said without looking up. "We tried to convince Mother to come, but she believes the village still needs her protection, and that we need proper instruction from the wandering clans."

"She was wise to do so. We're in desperate need of strength. I'm sorry to hear about your father. He sounds like a brave warrior, and there are never enough of those."

Elian leaned closer to Harald and spoke low, as though they were confidants. "How bad is it out here? Back home we know that we're losing territory, and the Debru strike at the lines more than before, but we don't hear much beyond that."

"It's bad. We're losing warriors too fast, and the Debru are growing stronger. We've been surrendering ground that's been ours for generations. If we keep losing ground as we have, the outer villages will be near the front in a year or two."

Samora's head shot up, her eyes wide. She'd known the situation was bleak, but hearing Harald speak of it with such certainty made it real, and she already had memories of the Debru attacking to keep her up at night.

Harald noticed and offered her the skin of liquor again, but she shook her head. Dulling her senses was tempting but unhelpful. He offered it to Elian, who accepted it gladly and took one long pull and then another.

The sight returned a grin to Harald's face. "It's not so gloomy as all that. We have young warriors, about your age, who have started to master their incredible powers. I can't tell you why, because I don't know, but as the Debru have pushed us back, our children have grown stronger."

Harald noticed Samora's doubt and grinned wider. "Ask any of the council. They lack the experience needed to make the most use of their raw ability, but our children are stronger than us. You two are little different. You'd lose in any fight you picked tonight, but with some proper training, you'd be among the best warriors in the clan."

Elian took another long drink and handed the skin back to Harald. The giant man shook the skin, which barely sloshed at all. "You can even hold your liquor better than the adults."

Harald stood, and he was once again the leader they'd first met. "Have no fear, friends. The days have never been darker, but our strength has never shone brighter. We'll get you close to Tiafel, who will have answers if there are any. And while we travel, we'll train you with our best, so you can lend us your strength in return."

With that, he strode away from the fire, leaving Elian and Samora alone.

Elian tried to stand, but he almost crashed into the fire at the attempt. His face was flushed and his eyes were glazed.

Samora's heart went out to him. They both considered Father a hero, but in different ways. She respected Father's sacrifices and his kindness, qualities that remained unchanged regardless of his fame among the wandering clans.

Elian viewed him more like a legend from the tales he'd grown up on. Father had become larger than life, and in so doing, became something to Elian he hadn't been in truth. Harald not knowing Father had cracked the illusion, and then he'd offered Elian a way to forget the crack existed.

Samora stood and offered Elian a hand. He slapped weakly at it.

"I don't need your help," he slurred.

He tried to rise again, and when he stumbled, Samora was there to catch him. She positioned herself under his arm and helped him away from the fire. They'd set up their bedding in a different part of camp, and she guided him between the tents so he wouldn't trip and fall.

"I should be the one protecting you. It's not right, you protecting me all the time," Elian said.

She wished Elian saw himself the way she saw him, but he considered his uniqueness a failure. He wanted to wield and bind adani like Father, but some cruel twist of fate had so far denied him the opportunity.

There was little point in saying anything tonight. He would likely not remember much beyond the council meeting. She embraced him tightly before helping him lay down. "We protect each other," she whispered.

Then she made sure he was laying on his side and covered well before she attended to her own sleep. If Harald had spoken true, and she believed him, tomorrow she'd begin learning binding from the best in the clan.

She didn't want to learn how to bind a better spear, as it seemed such a crude use of adani. But there were other methods and techniques, skills her mother had spoken about but never learned. Here, among the wandering clans, she might finally find the teachers she'd always wanted.

She couldn't wait.

4

Elian woke the next day feeling as if Harald played an enormous pair of war drums on his head. He rolled over and groaned, sensing Samora beside him. She placed a skin of water in his hands and he sipped from it. The cool water settled his stomach and quieted the drums. Instead of playing on his head, it felt as though Harald had retreated a few paces. Regardless, he had the feeling it was going to be a very long day.

He cracked one eye open and almost screamed at the sudden agony. The sun shot its cleansing light straight into his head, unleashing a piercing pain in his skull. He closed his eyes, then rolled over so that his face was buried in the folded-up clothing he used as a pillow.

When he found his voice, he croaked, "I regret nothing."

Samora patted his shoulder, somehow both comforting and condescending at the same time.

It was the worst headache he'd ever endured, but he deserved no less. Harald's liquor had burned with every sip, but he'd paid no attention. He remembered Harald saying he didn't know who Jace was, but that was his last clear memory of the night before. He'd been upset that Harald didn't know his father, but with the benefit of hindsight, he couldn't think of a reason why Harald would have known a warrior from another clan. Especially not one that had retreated to the villages to raise his family.

Elian squeezed his eyes shut and wondered if he could jump back in time and introduce himself to Harald again, this time without making a damned fool of himself. No matter how hard he wished it, though, he remained where he was. After a while, guilt at moping around overwhelmed his desire to dig a hole and bury himself within it. Harald's clan pulled down tents, loaded sleds, and sharpened weapons, filling the air with a cacophony that constantly reminded Elian he wasn't helping.

He was finally among the wandering clans, and his very first act had been to get drunk and embarrass himself in front of a living legend. Sometimes, when he wondered why he couldn't bind adani, he looked at his failings and wondered if it was his own fault.

He recognized the familiar pattern of his thoughts and shoved them down. No one knew why he couldn't bind adani, but if the answer existed anywhere, it was here. And he was still laying down, moping.

When he sat up, he realized he had absolutely no memory of making it to his bedding or laying down for the evening. His last vague impressions were of attempting to stand and failing. He ran his hand through his hair and looked down so he wouldn't have to meet his sister's gaze. "You helped me last night."

Out of the corner of his eye, he saw her nod.

He wasn't sure he could remember a time when he'd felt lower than he did at that moment. "Thank you."

Samora stood and offered him a hand, which he eagerly accepted. He found the courage to look up and saw that she had a hint of a smile on her face.

He didn't deserve her forgiveness, but he was grateful for it all the same. They packed their bedding and cinched the straps on their packs tight, then they searched for ways to help the Bears prepare for their journey.

Elian remembered the objections the council had raised when Harald made the decision they would travel farther north, and he feared that disagreement would make he and his sister pariahs within the wandering clan. Their hosts dispelled his worries quickly. Friendly smiles, bows, and enthusiastic greetings welcomed him in every corner of the camp, and he returned the welcomes with as much grace as he could while enduring the drums relentlessly pounding in his head.

He'd just finished loading a sled when a young man about his age greeted him. They exchanged bows, and the man introduced himself as Alec. He stood a little shorter than Elian, the top of his head only reaching Elian's nose, but he was heavier, laden with muscles that Elian's body refused to grant him. Alec's arms were as big as Elian's thighs, and when he clapped Elian on the shoulder, Elian feared the bruise would last a week.

"Thanks for the help with the sled. How are you finding it here so far?" Like Harald, Alec wore a smile as a nearly permanent expression.

"You're welcome, and everyone is far kinder than I expected." He regretted the words as soon as he said them, afraid that his new host would interpret them to mean he'd expected the clan to be rude.

Fortunately, the smile never left Alec's face. "No reason to be surprised. Can't say we're happy to be wandering when we should be resting, but it's hardly the first time. Besides, word about you has already spread throughout the camp."

Elian's eyes darted left and right as though he'd walked into an ambush. "What word?"

Alec's grin grew even wider. "Friend, you drank almost all of Harald's remaining liquor last night. The last time someone tried that, it was a war leader from another clan, and the rumors claim he *still* doesn't walk straight after Harald's beating."

Elian froze like a deer startled by a loud noise. Alec laughed. "There's nothing to fear. If Harald was going to make you suffer for what you did, you would already be suffering, trust me."

When Elian's fear didn't entirely vanish, Alec said, "Anyway, Harald asked me to train you. He said adani flows differently through you, and I can sense that's true."

Alec had the build of a strong fighter, but Elian wasn't sure what Harald expected from someone so young. Master Heinrick's hair had been more gray than black, and he'd dismissed the skills of anyone who wasn't at least as old. "What are you going to teach me?"

"Not sure yet. Harald said you were looking for a master, and I'm afraid I'm not that person. Harald thought I might have something I could teach you though, so we'll give it a try. Later, once we're walking, I'll test what you're capable of, and we'll decide then. I just wanted to introduce myself now, but I'll find you once we get moving."

Elian thanked Alec and they parted ways.

Elian and Samora helped where they could, and it wasn't long before the camp was on the march. Once they were walking, Samora pointed toward Alec and gave Elian a questioning expression. She'd been helping another family during Alec's introduction.

"He's going to help me learn how to control my adani," Elian said.

She brightened, so much so that it made Elian uncomfortable. "Don't get your hopes up too high. He told me he wasn't a master, but that Harald thought he might be the best in the clan to help me, at least for now."

Samora's expression didn't dim. She grinned wider and looked at Alec again. Elian snorted. "I don't think you should be quite that excited. We'll see. I am very curious to see what he can teach me. Did anyone approach you?"

Samora's face fell, and she shook her head.

"Well, don't worry. I'm sure Harald has someone in mind."

His sister brightened again, and Elian was glad he'd been able to help a little today.

Some of her enthusiasm wore off on him. He imagined making camp this evening and showing Samora some new bindings he'd learned, just like she'd always tried to show Father the bindings Mother had taught her. He knew better than to get his hopes up, but it was hard not to.

Just before last night's campsite fell out of sight, Elian turned back and marveled at the empty grasslands. It was no surprise that the wandering clans wandered, but he couldn't imagine sleeping in a different place every night, never having the familiarity of home to welcome you after a long day in the fields.

He'd always admired the stories of the wandering clans, but now that he was living among them, he realized their lives were more mundane than he'd thought. He wasn't sure what to make of that.

Alec found him soon after, and the two fell immediately to the task Harald had assigned them. They wandered a few hundred paces away from the column so their training wouldn't bother the others. Elian noticed, as they left, that another warrior had taken Samora to the other side of the column.

Elian had higher hopes for his sister than for his own improvement. Her strength, at least, was one they were familiar with.

Alec tested how fast Elian could sprint, how hard he could hit, and how high he could jump, and was repeatedly impressed by Elian's abilities. "You do this all without focusing adani?" he asked.

Elian nodded. "I've never been able to. I understand there's plenty in my body, but I can't complete the simplest binding."

Alec frowned. "Show me."

Elian fought the shame rising in his chest, but he attempted the first binding taught to all children in the village. The adanists

55

described it as simply pulling some of the adani from your body, mixing it with some from the world, and binding it into the desired form. Every adanist found techniques that worked best for them, but the fundamentals were the same for all.

Elian tried to pull some of the adani from his body, but it was like trying to grab water slipping through his hand. Before it all disappeared, he tried to mix it with some of the surrounding adani and bind it into a small sphere of light.

If Elian squinted, he could almost imagine the air above his hand grew brighter for a moment. Then he could do no more.

He stared hard at his feet, the shame rising to his cheeks. Little children learned how to make a light not long after they could walk so they'd always be able to find their way around in the dark. He couldn't even do that, and he thought he deserved instruction from the wandering clans.

He was pathetic.

Alec didn't make fun of him, though Elian was sure the warrior wanted to. He made a show of frowning and considering the problem carefully. Then he asked, "Can you loop it within your body and focus it that way?"

"I don't know what you mean."

Alec held up two fingers. "There are two ways to manipulate adani. The first, as you know, is binding. But there is another aspect, which is focusing it in different parts of your body."

Mother had said something about that once, but Elian had been so frustrated with his lack of progress he'd ignored her. What did manipulating adani in his body matter if he couldn't bind something as simple as a light? If not for his shame, he might have made the same argument here, but his embarrassment rendered him silent and Alec continued.

"I think working with internal adani gives us a promising place to start."

"Do you think it will help me bind something?" Elian interrupted.

Alec shrugged. "Maybe? But even if it doesn't, it'll make you stronger and faster than you already are. You might not be able to bind a spear when I'm done with you, but you might be able to arm wrestle Harald."

Elian blew a sharp breath through his teeth. What did it matter if he could wrestle with Harald? It was binding that altered the course of battles. Father and Mother had proven that beyond a doubt on that night.

But he couldn't show rudeness to Alec, who was only trying to help. And perhaps it would be the missing ingredient that would allow him to bind. He nodded, and Alec's grin grew wider.

"Good. We'll do the exercises my masters taught me when I was young. Take a deep breath. As you do, follow the air. Can you feel the way it travels into your body?"

Elian obeyed and nodded. He felt the way the air flowed into his stomach and expanded upward into his chest.

"Good. And if you want, you can control where that breath goes. You can push it into your chest, you can push it against your spine, or you can make it feel as if it fills your entire torso, right?"

Elian practiced with a few deep breaths and agreed.

"Focusing adani is much the same. Can you feel the way it moves through your body?"

"A little."

Alec frowned at that, but then the smile returned to his face. "Start there. Sense it as well as you can and think of it like the breath. Once you think you have that, focus it into your legs, then jump."

Alec made it sound simple, but Elian was skeptical. Manipulating breath came naturally but manipulating adani felt like trying to control a slimy fish squirming out of his grasp. After a few tries, he thought he succeeded, so he jumped.

To his surprise, his feet almost reached as high as Alec's ears.

The extra height caught him so much by surprise that he landed hard and had to roll so that he didn't hurt himself.

"Impressive," Alec said.

"It didn't feel that way," Elian replied. "It barely felt like I focused adani at all."

"Take heart. You've been used to adani doing one thing for your entire life, and now you're trying to teach it to do another. It will take time, but with practice, it should become as natural as breathing. And if you jump that high doing very little, it's no wonder Harald thought you had such promise."

That also caught Elian by surprise. "He thinks I have promise?"

"It's why I'm here. I might not look it, but I have the most control in the clan over adani in my body. He wants to see if I can make you stronger than me." Alec's smile grew. "Though I'd say you've got a fair way to go."

Elian laughed, and for the rest of the day, Alec did just as he'd promised Harald. He taught Elian to focus adani in his limbs and proved to be a patient teacher. That patience became important as Elian struggled with developing the skills Alec used naturally.

Elian's progress was uneven. Sometimes, he grasped adani exactly the way Alec told him, and when he did, he performed feats that he hadn't known he was capable of. But then on the next attempt he'd fail terribly, and he wasn't sure what separated the two. Complicating the matter was the fact that the practice brought up the familiar frustrations he'd known back home, and the more adani ran through his body, the more frustrated he became. He had to take frequent breaks to calm his temper, but when he returned to the practices Alec assigned, it felt like he had to start over from the beginning.

Still, at the end of the day, he was training with the wandering clans, and he had achieved something. It felt like a small, insubstantial step, but it wasn't nothing.

Maybe, just maybe, he could someday be useful to the people he loved.

5

Samora watched Elian train with undisguised interest as she walked amidst the rest of the Bears. She'd lived with him her entire life, and although she thought she understood him, he continued to surprise her. The brief glimpses she caught of him revealed little about his new training. He jumped higher and ran faster, but it wasn't until she extended her adani that she understood the subtle changes happening within him. Alec was helping Elian learn how to manipulate adani within his body.

She resisted the urge to shake her head. Mother could have taught him that years ago, but Elian had dismissed the possibility. He saw only what he lacked, so anything that wasn't binding was thrown to the wayside. Watching him now made her remember a conversation between her and Mother about Elian's refusal to learn the one skill that would most benefit him.

"Why don't you *make* Elian learn?" Samora had asked. She'd been frustrated with Elian, because all knowledge appealed to her, so she never refused Mother's offer to teach anything, no matter how meaningless it might have seemed.

"It's not for me to say what he'll learn and what he won't. All

I can do is make my best arguments for why he *should* learn something. Whether he chooses to or not is up to him."

"You could bind him to a chair and make him learn! It would be good for him."

Mother had chuckled at that. "There are days when I feel as you do, trust me. But I also believe that learning can't be forced. Sometimes life itself teaches us what we most need, but otherwise, the student must be willing. It was the way I was raised, and I think it's for the best."

"But he's weaker than he could be, and he's been wandering farther away from the village."

"All good points, and ones I've made to him. The choice is still his, and he's made it clear what he wants. If he ever changes his mind, I'll be glad to help him however I can."

Samora had been unsatisfied by the exchange, but Elian had inherited his stubbornness from Mother, so there was no point in arguing once Mother had decided something.

Now he'd finally changed his mind, but from what her adani told her, the process of learning the basic techniques was proving challenging. That didn't surprise her. Personal history guided the shape of the future, and Elian had spent years firmly denying anything about adani that wasn't binding. Hopefully he was willing to pay the price for his ignorance now.

She wished for his sake that the price wasn't too steep. Adani was easier to learn about in childhood. There was less of it to work with, but children also hadn't yet determined their relationship to adani. They could more easily learn new techniques and bindings because they weren't used to anything yet. As ways became set and a person grew up and acquired more adani, new techniques became much more difficult to master.

Samora pulled her attention away from her brother and Alec to the line of wandering Bears. She gave her adani free rein and basked in all it taught her about her new allies. There were fewer Bears than there were people in her village, but their effect on her adani was completely different. Partly it was due to their physical closeness. Outside of the eighthday feasts, the villagers were never all in the same place. The closest they came was when they all slept in their houses at night, but even then, they were separated by the wide streets.

Most Bears walked no more than a pace or two away from their neighbors, which made the whole column glow like a bright line of life to her adani-aided senses. The web they formed was brighter and more beautiful than any other she'd seen.

The other part of the explanation was that the Bears, almost to a person, were far more gifted with adani than any villager. Looking at most with adani was like staring into the heart of a fire, and there were a few, like Harald, that glowed as bright as a sun. Even the children, running freely along the column, glowed brighter than all but the strongest farmers in the village.

Samora wondered what caused the difference.

As they walked, adani flowed toward the column. It was a subtle effect, but clear once she recognized it. As always, adani moved back and forth, exchanged across a vast, intricate web that always inspired her. But here, more of it flowed toward the clan than away, which was something else Samora had never sensed except around her brother. She wasn't sure if the adani flowed this way because of specific individuals, or if it was because of the gathering.

If so, it meant the Bears were literally stronger together than apart.

She sensed the approaching warrior with her adani before she saw her. The adanist was one of those that burned like a bright fire, short of Harald's strength, but not by much. Samora sensed a link of adani between them as the other woman focused on her.

Samora forced a smile to her face when the woman came into view. It felt uncomfortable, but she was already grateful for all the Bears had done and she didn't want to be rude. The woman stopped in front of her and offered the barest hint of a bow. "My name is Rakella, and Harald has asked that I train with you today."

Samora returned a deeper bow.

"Harald tells me that you prefer not to speak, which is fine by me. I've taught many who could learn from your practice."

Rakella led Samora away from the main column, though they continued to keep pace with the Bears' slow march. "Show me what you know."

Samora nodded, quickly demonstrating the wide variety of bindings that she knew. She presented them to Rakella in turn, who ran her adani across each. Rakella said little after each inspection, and Samora couldn't tell if she was pleased or disappointed. She finished her demonstration and bowed.

"That is all you know?" Rakella asked.

The Bear didn't bother to hide her disdain.

Samora frowned. Those were all the techniques Mother had taught her, as well as those she had taught and developed herself. She was likely the strongest adanist in their village and any that neighbored it. How had she already disappointed Rakella?

"All those techniques, and the only one you know that's worth the time you spent to learn it is your basic spear. What was your instructor teaching you?"

Samora's anger kindled at Rakella's dismissal of Mother's teachings. Back home, she had healed sick animals, helped the crops grow, and expelled coughs and colds from farmer's lungs. Why did she need to fight? A bound spear was enough to help Elian on his hunts, but even that was rarely needed.

She kept her lips sewn shut. Regardless of the slight, there was no doubting Rakella's strength, and what did it matter if her instructor was rude? Mother had taught that knowledge and wisdom came from places both pleasant and not, and if she closed herself to those she disliked, she lost valuable opportunities to learn.

Rakella had expected a response, but when it became clear

Samora wasn't going to speak, she nodded with a self-satisfied air. "Well, no matter. You should have had a better master in the village, but you're with us now, and we'll get you caught up to us in no time. You've got the potential, you just need a proper master."

Every word Rakella spoke grated against Samora's nerves, but she kept her mouth shut and her senses open.

"Let's start by improving one of your existing bindings. Those spheres that you can make dance around like fireflies—make those again."

Samora did, pleased that Rakella had recognized the binding. It was one of Samora's own, a modification of the light-globe most learned as their first binding. She wove the adani tighter, but then duplicated the feat until a dozen small lights danced around her head. Mother had also been impressed with the technique, and though it wasn't good for much more than entertaining children, she had told Samora to use the technique to practice manipulating several bindings at once.

Mother had always found Samora's ability to juggle the bindings incredible, but it had always come naturally to her.

"You make that look easy," Rakella observed.

Samora bowed her head, never losing control of the globes.

Rakella duplicated one of the globes with ease. "Drop yours so you can study this," she said.

Samora obeyed, using her adani to sense how Rakella modified the binding. The Bear twisted the adani, tightening the weave until the light shone bright against Samora's senses.

"By focusing the adani, you can make it much more useful. You try, and if one is easy, see if you can make more."

Samora found herself warming to the judgmental adanist. It had been some time since she'd been given such a unique challenge. She began with her original binding, then twisted and tightened it until it matched what Rakella had created. Focus made the binding more powerful. Her original one wasn't much more than a light in the dark, but this focused adani would hurt if it hit someone.

"How difficult was that?" Rakella asked.

In answer, Samora formed another globe of light, this time starting it even smaller. A third and a fourth followed the first pair. Before long she had eight points of light dancing around her head, each more powerful than her dozen original globes combined. It was easy.

Rakella gave a satisfied grunt. "Harald was right when he said you had promise. Can you form two spears at once?"

The spears didn't come as naturally as the points of light, but Mother had made her practice. The otsoa and the other creatures like them that the Debru commanded hunted in packs, and a single spear was rarely sufficient. Samora formed two spears, one appearing in each hand.

"Now do six."

Samora raised her gaze. She'd never done more than four, but there was no harm in trying. The process took her much longer than the globes, but eventually she had six floating before her. Their bindings were weak, but they held.

Seeing so many glowing blue spears in front of her made her think of the night of the Debru attack. She'd seen Father launch this many spears and more, slaying otsoa wherever he struck.

The bindings on the spears unraveled. She wiped the bead of sweat from her forehead.

Rakella's satisfaction vanished. "The spear is a simpler binding than the globes you just made. Why do you struggle?"

Thankfully, Samora didn't feel like Rakella expected an answer from her, so she remained silent. Rakella thought for a moment, then turned an eager eye onto her new student. It made Samora want to find cover.

"There's a technique that I've been working on, but I haven't been able to master yet. You might be able to, though. You seem to have a gift for the tighter weaves."

Rakella formed Samora's original globe, then twisted and folded it until it was just a point of light. Having attempted the weave herself, Samora thought hers had actually been more focused.

Rakella explained as she wove adani tighter and tighter. "The point would be to make the adani as focused as possible, into such a tight weave it could punch through any defense."

She bunched the adani up even tighter, but her efforts felt crude to Samora. Instead of weaving a neat knot, she bunched it all together. Her strength was such, though, that it worked. It could have worked better, but Samora continued to observe without comment.

Rakella launched the point of adani, which started unraveling the moment it was outside her control. "Then, after it penetrates a shield, or even once it enters a body, you do this."

She pulled on a weave Samora had noticed but hadn't understood. The point of light rapidly expanded, exploding in a flash of heat and light. Samora jumped at the suddenness of the reaction and Rakella smirked. "Put one of those in a Debru, and they'll never know what hit them. A one-hit kill."

Samora stared at the place where the adani had exploded. She'd never seen anything like it before.

"Unfortunately, the problem is getting that initial weave tight enough. It might work on your average Debru, and maybe even a Moka, but it's not strong enough to slip past a Belog's defenses. You, though, might be able to accomplish what I can't."

Samora shook her head.

"Don't sell yourself short. You're already capable of tighter weaves than most adanists. It's just a matter of developing that skill further."

Samora had little choice but to break her silence. She cleared her throat, then said, "I don't want to."

Rakella's eyes narrowed. "What do you mean?"

Samora bit her lower lip. The only person she'd ever spoken

about this with was Mother, and even she'd been skeptical. She didn't think Rakella would understand, and she wasn't inclined to attempt to persuade her.

"What do you mean?" Rakella demanded.

"Adani is a force of life, not death," Samora said.

Rakella stared hard at her, as though trying desperately to define words she didn't know. Her jaw worked, but it took several long moments for words to emerge. When they did, they were laced with disbelief. "You don't want to use adani *to fight*?"

Samora shook her head.

For a moment, she thought Rakella was frozen solid. The only signs she was alive were the blinking of her eyes and the burning fury of the adani within her. Her jaw hung slightly open, and her stare was sharper than a razor. She took a step toward Samora so that they were face to face. For the first time since their training had started, Samora realized there was nothing protecting her from Rakella except Harald's implied promise of safety, and she didn't know how much faith she could put in that.

"Do you have any idea how many of my friends and family have died to keep you villagers safe from the Debru?"

Samora thought of her father and almost answered, "Not enough," but she kept her thoughts to herself.

"I've left more loved ones behind than you can imagine, all so you could live in peace. And now here you are, clearly gifted, yet you refuse to use that gift. Just what do you think is happening out here against the Debru? Do you think you can *talk* to them? We've been fighting them for generations, and we've never heard them utter a word. All they do is advance and kill, and you're not even going to fight?"

Samora didn't have an answer, or at least, not one that would calm Rakella. She didn't want to fight. She didn't think it was right, but she wasn't a fool. The wandering clans had sacrificed more than she could imagine. And she wasn't under any illusion of what would happen if the clans stopped fighting.

Still, there had to be a better way.

She just didn't know what it was. Not yet.

"Well?" Rakella leaned in, her breath hot against Samora's cheeks.

Samora bowed her head.

Rakella's fists clenched, then she swore and stomped away.

Samora kept her head bowed, heaving a long sigh of relief. Her knees trembled, and when she turned around, her steps were shaky. Their argument had attracted some attention, and no one seemed that eager to be seen near her. When she rejoined the column, it spread apart near her, so that it felt as though she walked alone.

She felt like she deserved no less.

6

Elian noticed Samora sitting alone that evening, but was too busy being introduced to the other warriors to visit with her. She'd always been eager to find space, and this was more people than they usually saw in a day, so he assumed she sought the solace of solitude.

His own day of training had been long, but he was slowly learning Alec's new concepts. He couldn't control the adani within his body often, but when he did, the results were encouraging. He succeeded just often enough that his motivation never waned.

The meal was heavy with game the scouts had brought back, and Elian ate almost as eagerly as he listened to the warrior's campfire stories. Back home, such stories were of faraway lands and people they'd never meet. Here, the stories were personal, told by those who had lived them.

It was only near the end of the meal that he realized Samora had never approached the cookfires and hadn't eaten. He watched her out of the corner of his eye. It was hard to tell with his sister sometimes, but she didn't look pleased.

He took some of the last food from the pots, selecting some of the game he thought she would like the most. Then he left the warmth and camaraderie of the fire to sit next to her. He offered her the bowl of food and she took it eagerly.

He didn't ask. If she felt like telling him, she would when she was ready.

The bowl was halfway empty before she spoke. "Training didn't go well."

Elian had seen her walk off with one of Harald's warriors, but he'd been so wrapped up in his own training he hadn't paid her much attention. "Want to tell me?"

She did, and ended with, "You probably think I'm wrong, too."

Elian didn't answer right away. "I do, but I admire your ideal."

She looked up at that. "You do?"

Elian nodded. "The world is a violent place, and even more so with the Debru in it. But I don't think that means everyone needs to fight. Isn't that why the villages were established in the first place? The wandering clans needed a steady supply of food, so the villages were built to farm the land and share the bounty with the wandering clans. Some fight while others grow, and I don't think you should be ashamed that you want to grow."

It looked like she might tear up, and he turned away so that she wouldn't have to be ashamed.

They went to sleep soon after, and he was reassured when she drifted off quickly. He lay awake a while longer, attempting to loop adani through his body one last time before going to sleep. He was still practicing when his eyes closed, and he lost consciousness.

The next morning dawned bright and clear, and he and Alec began their training early. The rest had done Elian good, and it wasn't long before he felt like he was once again making progress. The path ahead of him was long, but at least he was traveling the right direction.

Their training abruptly ended at the sound of a horn from the west. "What was that?" Elian asked.

Alec's smile vanished, a feat Elian hadn't been sure was possible.

"Debru. But don't worry. We'll return to the column, and you'll be protected."

Elian's insides turned to water. He hadn't seen a Debru since that day. He'd dreamed of killing them hundreds of times, but now that one was near, his eagerness vanished. A part of him wanted to say that he would help. How could he get revenge if he didn't fight? But the greater part of him, still guided by reason, recognized that idea was foolish. It yelled at him to return to the column, where he could enjoy the protection of the entire clan.

More horns sounded, still to the west, but farther north and south. Elian looked to Alec for an explanation and saw that the additional horns had turned his training partner's face pale.

"What's happening?" he asked.

Alec tried to sound nonchalant, but Elian didn't believe his new friend.

"A lot of Debru, it seems."

Elian's knees threatened to give out. One had come close to destroying their entire village. What chance did the Bears have against many?

Alec hurried toward the column, and Elian was only too happy to follow him. Alec dropped him off with a group of children, then left to find his fellow warriors.

Elian's cheeks flushed with shame at his new companions, but he didn't raise his voice to protest. Whatever strength he possessed, he hadn't tested it against the Debru. Until then, he was no better than a child. As much as he hated it, this was where he belonged. He watched other warriors form a defensive line in front of him and the children, and his cheeks burned even brighter at the fact they considered him so helpless.

He was grateful to be behind them, all the same.

He looked for Samora, expecting her to appear among the children, too. As the horns grew closer, there was still no sign of her. He looked and found her near the rear of the column to the south. She was in one of the defensive lines with the other warriors, ready to fight. Their eyes met and he didn't think he'd ever seen her so scared.

Elian took a step toward her, but no more. His feet refused to carry him further. He called out, but the words stuck in his throat.

She should be with him. Why hadn't they decided to protect her, too?

Scouts on horses charged over the horizon, followed by a small horde of dark creatures. A chill shot down Elian's spine. He knew kettu, but he'd never seen so many in one place. Small packs of them frequently roamed near the village. They were short four-legged creatures that only came up to Elian's knee. They were about as long as his arm and had narrow heads and jaws full of sharp teeth. Like otsoa, dark fur covered them from nose to tail, though they were streaked with silver instead of blue. Also like otsoa, they were creatures of shadow commanded by Debru. One *could* kill a human, but they were most dangerous in packs of five to ten.

They came in the hundreds.

The horde of kettu would be a challenging enemy on their own, but they were nothing compared to the billowing clouds of shadow that followed them.

Elian couldn't see how many Debru were cloaked by those clouds, nor could he sense them with adani. Judging from the expression on his guards' faces, though, the number was too high.

Dozens of glowing bound spears appeared in hand as the clan prepared for battle. Others bound knives, and at least one warrior bound a flaming spear. They flung as one, obeying some command Elian couldn't sense. As the adani fell, shadows raced forward from the advancing clouds like thousands of dark strips of cloth caught in a gust. They covered the kettu before the adani arrived, hiding the result of the attack from Elian's gaze.

The warriors paled and shot nervous glances at one another. The scouts were almost to the lines, but the kettu covered in shadows weren't far behind.

Harald strode forward and stood near the center of the line with his hands on his hips. He stared at the advancing shadow, then raised one hand high above his head. When he began the binding, even Elian felt its power. A spear appeared in his hand, glowing with the golden light of the sun.

Harald heaved the spear into the shadow, which pulled back as though afraid.

The flight and impact happened so fast Elian only glimpsed it. The spear blasted past kettu, crushing them underneath with the force of its passing. Many of the shadows shrank and became a solid black shield protecting a lone Debru, but the spear punched through the shield and impaled the dark warrior.

The Debru crumpled, but the spear remained. Harald flicked his wrist, and a blinding light erupted, brighter even than the morning sun that had pierced Elian's alcohol-addled vision the morning before. When he could see again, the shadows had coalesced into a dozen small clouds, and dust filled the sky as dirt and kettu bits rained down on the attackers.

Ellian gaped at the small crater that was evidence of Harald's binding.

This was the power of legends made flesh. The Debru stood no chance.

Someone had forgotten to tell them, though. Their charge never faltered. Hundreds of smaller spears and other bindings took to the air, and now that the shadow didn't race forward to protect them, kettu died wherever the spears landed. The small monsters paid a steep price for every pace they advanced, but their numbers were so great it didn't matter.

Walls of light appeared in front of the line, and the kettu slammed into them. They scratched, bit, and clawed at the linked shields. Harald's adanists groaned against the effort of maintaining the wall, and the light dimmed as the assault intensified.

Elian looked for Samora and found her with other adanists. She appeared to be binding a shield, aiding those adanists that were near her. For the moment, they held, though Elian wasn't sure how much longer they would last. The kettu piled high against the shields, heedless of the dangers.

As the kettu attacked, the clan defended with shield and spear, and though the shield wall flickered and dimmed against the assault, the kettu died faster than reinforcements could arrive from the rear.

Harald stood on the other side of the wall, sweeping kettu away with a pair of enormous bound swords. Elian didn't know why he risked himself against such meaningless enemies. The clan's spears were plenty strong for the task.

Then the Debru arrived and taught Elian why. In their hands they carried dark reflections of the bound weapons adanists used. Most preferred a shadowy sword slightly shorter than the adanists'. When they reached the wall of bound shields they raised their weapons and struck.

The wall of adani didn't even flicker as the Debru smashed their weapons against it. The adanists' shields simply collapsed against the strength of the assault, and every kettu still alive scrambled over one another to be the first to sink their jaws into the exposed flesh of the nearest human. Elian watched in horror when one woman fell to the ground as four kettu tackled her and bit at her face.

The line of Bears still held, but when the Debru fell among the adanists, what shreds of order that still remained disappeared. Every warrior fought for themselves, and when they fought a Debru alone, they lost more often than they won.

The Debru seemed smaller than the one in Elian's memories, but that didn't make them any less dangerous. Their dark swords cut through bound shields with the ease of Elian slicing bread at the dinner table. Only Harald and his chosen few strode among the creatures without fear, but they could only be in so many places at once, and the kettu slowed them at every turn, nipping at heels and leaping for throats.

Elian and the children remained safe, but even their defenders, those safest from the bulk of the fighting, started to buckle under the unrelenting pressure. He clenched his fist at the sight of yet more warriors fighting and dying for him, but he couldn't convince his legs to move. It was as if an invisible rope had been tied around him and staked to the ground.

He twisted his head and searched for Samora again. His eyes went wide when he couldn't immediately find her. She and her shield had vanished and four of the Debru were where she had once stood, hacking through the few defenders that still remained. Two pounded their swords against a shield of adani on the ground that refused to break.

The rope that held him tight shattered. Adani pooled in his legs, and he leaped forward, one jump carrying him halfway across the battlefield. As he fell, adani gathered in his fist and he brought it down on one of the Debru assaulting the shield.

The monster sensed his arrival a moment too late. It turned, but Elian punched before it could complete the action. His fist went through the monster's head, and he landed hard against it. They went down in a tangle of gore, limb, and claw, but Elian's momentum carried him away from the monster.

Samora had been under that shield. He'd just saved his sister.

He couldn't believe it.

He sat in the grass, dazed, as the three remaining Debru turned toward him. Voices in his head shouted at him to run, but he was comfortable right where he was. The Debru closest to him raised a dark sword, but before it brought the sword down, a dozen tiny spherical bindings attacked its decaying flesh. It stumbled forward, dazed, but still eager to bring its bound sword down on Elian's skull.

Elian's hand found a steel sword in the grass, dropped by one of the fallen defenders. He clutched it tightly. Strength returned to Elian's limbs, filling them in less than a heartbeat, and he raised the sword.

He knew it for a hopeless gesture. He couldn't defend himself with one hand against a powerful overhead cut. But when the Debru's bound sword struck his steel one, it stopped in place. Elian felt like he was holding back a child's attack.

He swept the bound sword aside and rose to his feet, bringing his sword back and hacking at the Debru. It was an ugly cut, one that Master Heinrick would have punished him for back in the village, but it cut through the Debru without resistance.

The Debru collapsed and Elian held the sword before him, wondering what strange powers its previous owner had imbued it with.

The remaining Debru took offense at the loss of their companions and attacked him. He tried to summon the strength he'd used to leap to Samora's aid, but he felt no stronger than usual. One Debru clawed at him and he retreated. Its claws cut through his shirt and drew blood, but the injury barely slowed him.

His retreat brought Samora into the corner of his vision. Dozens of globes of light surrounded her, and she flung them at the Debru that attacked him.

Samora's bindings drew the Debru's full attention. She launched the small suns, but the Debru she targeted had already raised a dark shield. The light struck the shield and ran off like water running off the roof of a house.

The dark shield became a sword, and the Debru struck at Samora. Elian cried out. The sword bounced off Samora's hastily formed shield, but she winced at the impact and retreated a step. Both Debru turned to pursue her, Elian forgotten.

The sight of his sister in danger filled him with a familiar rage. Adani rushed through his limbs like water crashing down a waterfall. The Debru ignored him, as though he was a small child trying to play an adult game. Adani filled his arms and hands, and he swore he felt the sword absorb some as well. He swung the sword at the back of a Debru's neck right as Samora hurled another dozen globes of light at it.

Elian didn't know if the Debru hadn't sensed his attack or if Samora's assault distracted it, but it didn't make any effort to avoid Elian's sword. Once again the sword went straight through, slicing the Debru's spine as though it were butter.

That was enough to earn the attention of the final Debru, who threw a pitch-black spear at Elian. Samora knocked it aside with one of her bindings. Elian thought there were even more swirling around her than he'd ever seen before.

The Debru struck out at both of them, sending two spears at Samora for every one it threw at Elian. Samora blocked or deflected them all while Elian steadily advanced. He stabbed at the Debru, who slid easily to the side, but Samora used the moment of distraction to strike with her bindings. The Debru stumbled back, not hurt but off-balance. It turned its shield toward Samora, leaving it defenseless against Elian's wild kick.

His boot landed hard, and the Debru skipped across the ground. Before it could rise again, Elian raced over to it and stabbed the sword straight through its chest and into the ground below. To ensure it died, he pulled the sword out and stabbed again, and then again. Only when it was completely still did he stop.

Elian twisted around, expecting to find another Debru some-where close, but the battlefield surrounding him was quiet. Down the line, Harald and his strongest warriors were dispersing the last of the kettu and killing the final Debru.

His knees suddenly went weak. He looked around and found a place on a rise to rest. He stumbled there and flopped onto his bottom. His hands shook, so he gently put his sword down and pressed them against his knees to still them.

Samora sat beside him. She stared at nothing in particular, and he took her hand in his own, wondering if he was comforting her, or if it was the other way around.

7

Samora walked across the battlefield with Brittany, one of the young adanists in Harald's clan, searching for survivors. Though she appeared to be a few years older than Samora, she only came to Samora's chin. Even so, she bound adani with an effortlessness that Samora envied, and she suspected that if they were to duel, Brittany would beat her with ease.

"Where did you learn those healing bindings?" Brittany asked.

Samora stepped closely from one patch of clear grass to another. Dead kettu lay everywhere, and she didn't want to embarrass herself by rolling an ankle and requiring care for an injury sustained *after* the battle was over.

"Almost everything I know I learned from my mother. She and Father used to fight for a wandering clan, but they retreated to a village when she was pregnant with my brother."

"What clan?" Brittany asked.

"Spider."

Brittany squatted next to a corpse and placed the tips of her fingers against its neck. "That explains why I haven't seen it before."

Samora passed Brittany and mirrored the action on another corpse. When Harald had first given them this task, she'd wondered why Brittany checked for a heartbeat on every corpse they passed, but when she'd discovered a pair of warriors who looked dead that were actually alive, Samora understood.

Appearances and truth were not always the same.

She pressed her fingers against another corpse's neck. The skin was cold to the touch and still. To be sure, she held her hand under the young man's nose. He was as dead as he looked.

"Do you know healing bindings from several clans?" she asked.

After the argument with Rakella, Samora hadn't expected to train with any other Bears. But then the Debru had attacked, and Samora's healing abilities became far more useful than the day before. Harald had paired her with Brittany, and Samora was cautiously optimistic about what she could learn from the young healer.

Brittany was far kinder than Rakella, and her curiosity almost matched Samora's own.

Brittany stood and nodded, tucking a loose strand of brown hair behind her ear. "We've met with most of the wandering clans over the years. Whenever we do I seek out their best healers to learn their bindings. I don't know every healing binding, but I would bet that I'm close."

"What made you decide to collect them?"

"I'll tell you if you tell me why your parents left the wandering clans."

Samora followed Brittany east, to where the next pile of corpses waited. She found the task grisly enough, though necessary. But these were strangers to her and Samora had to keep reminding herself that these were Brittany's friends and family. However difficult this was for her, it was much more so for her companion.

"I wish I knew, but it's not something they talked about. Mother told us it was because they wanted to raise a family, but now that I've seen a wandering clan, I'm not sure why they didn't raise us with the Spiders. My father didn't like to use adani, though, so I wonder if something happened that made them want to leave."

It wasn't much of an answer, but Brittany kept her end of the bargain regardless. "Not long after my husband and I were bonded, he was wounded in a Debru ambush. It wasn't that deep of a wound, but it became infected, and none of our poultices pulled it from him. Fortunately, we were close to another clan at the time, so he and I rode there and begged for help. The healers there thought we were joking. They pulled the infection out with barely a thought, and I insisted they teach me."

They checked a couple of corpses in silence, and then Brittany said, "I like Harald's clan. He's strong and a capable leader, but he trades lives away too cheaply."

"Are all clan leaders like him?"

"Some, but not all. I believe Harald is a good man and a good leader. He's held us together in circumstances that would have broken a lesser leader. He's just single-minded, is all. He believes we'd be better served attacking the Debru than patrolling and waiting for them to attack us. He used to give me grief about collecting healing bindings, until he was poisoned by a bad piece of food, and I saved his life. He hasn't complained once, since."

Samora smiled at that. "Have you taught others?"

"I would, but few in the clan are interested. Harald's beliefs trickle down to the others."

"I'd like you to teach me what you can, if you would."

"I'd be happy to."

Samora grinned. Here was an adanist she could learn from.

SAMORA WAS DISAPPOINTED they didn't find more survivors than they did, but Brittany didn't seem surprised. The numbers of kettu had been such that when a warrior fell, they were often overwhelmed. The others in the clan helped load the wounded onto sleds, and Brittany taught Samora what she knew as they continued their journey north. The wandering clan didn't stop wandering, not even to bury their dead.

The battle and its aftermath cast a pall over the clan. Even Harald, who'd been shouting one thing or another all morning prior to the attack, was silent. They'd lost more than two dozen warriors, enough that everyone in the clan had lost someone close. In one poor child's case, his entire family had been killed.

Grief slowed the clan's pace but didn't bring them to a stop. Elian had convinced Alec to continue training him, which Samora worried was a request that rubbed salt in the clan's open wounds. She caught many staring in the pair's direction as they punched and kicked at one another. No one said anything, though, so she let the matter drop.

Brittany had just shown her a new healing binding to use on broken bones when a warrior approached from the front of the line. He bowed to Brittany and Samora, then told Samora, "Harald wishes to speak with you."

She ensured that Brittany had all the help she needed, then made her way to the front of the column. Harald walked beside his horse, maybe two dozen paces ahead of the rest of the clan.

She cleared her throat and wished that more people understood her the way Elian did. She'd spoken more in the past two days than she had in the previous two months, and knowing Harald, there would be more conversation to come.

Harald acknowledged her with a nod. "Thank you for helping Brittany. You two have saved several lives today."

Samora bowed.

"Your brother, is he a great warrior in your village?"

Samora shook her head.

"Many saw the leap he made to come to your aid in the battle. Not even I could have done the same, and I have more adani flowing through my blood than anyone here."

From anyone else, it would have sounded like an empty boast, but he'd shown his true strength in the battle, and she couldn't deny it.

"He's never fought before," she said.

Harald stared thoughtfully toward Elian. He tugged on his beard.

Eventually, he said, "You two fought well, especially given your lack of experience. Those Debru may have lacked a Moka, but we would have been far worse off without you. You two held a flank that might have otherwise collapsed. You're both welcome to join my clan if you're so inclined."

Somewhere behind them, Samora swore she felt Rakella gathering her adani in surprise.

The request caught her by surprise, too. After her fight with Rakella, she assumed Harald would be more than eager to drop them off with the Crows as soon as his honor allowed.

"That is very generous. Once we've aided my village, we will discuss it. You've shown us nothing but kindness since we've arrived."

Harald raised an eyebrow. "You can string more than one sentence together."

Samora nodded.

"Yet you don't often. May I ask why?"

"You may."

Harald waited for her to continue, but when she didn't, he laughed. She was glad he wasn't offended, because she didn't know how to explain well. She believed Elian and Mother understood, though they'd never asked directly.

"You're an interesting one. Maybe there's something I'm supposed to learn from you," Harald said.

Samora didn't believe that, but it was kind of him to say.

"That binding you used against the Debru, that's one of your own, isn't it?"

Samora nodded.

"How do you keep track of so many bindings at once?"

Mother had often asked her the same question, but Samora didn't know how best to answer. They'd started with a single small binding, then moved to two and three. Mother could do no more than six, but Samora could juggle a dozen with no difficulty. She'd never seen how many more she could do.

"I never found it particularly difficult. I do not know why."

"It's an impressive skill. Someday, I would like to see what you do with it."

Samora gave a short bow. It sounded as though he was pressuring her to accept Rakella's modification to her technique, but she never would. Or he could be as genuine as he sounded. She could never tell if there were layers to Harald's personality or if he was as simple as he sometimes seemed.

"I'm sorry to ask so much of you but thank you for indulging me. You and your brother served me and mine well today, and that will not be forgotten. Please continue to help Brittany in caring for my wounded. By tomorrow, we should be in the land of the Crows, and we'll part ways, at least for a time."

Samora bowed deeply, then left him to his thoughts and his mourning.

THEY STOPPED EARLIER that day than they had the day before, but no one rushed to throw up tents. The sky was clear, and Brittany reminded her they only set up the tents if they expected to stay a while, or if a storm was on the horizon.

The clan threw the excess effort that would have gone into the tents into the fire and the feast. They'd left the fallen where they died, their flesh exposed to the carrion eaters that roamed the land. Tonight, Samora finally worked up the courage to ask Brittany why.

Brittany was confused by the question. "It's the way of all things. Our bodies become food for creatures, little different than a deer becoming venison after a successful hunt. It's the least we can do in return, after hunting as much as we do to survive."

Samora scrunched her face at the comparison, which made Brittany smile. "You do it differently in the village?"

"We light the bodies on fire."

"Seems like a waste of a perfectly fine body."

"I don't think I want a wolf gnawing on my bones," Samora said.

"Why would you care? You'll be dead."

Samora supposed Brittany had a point, but the thought of it still sent a shiver down her spine. The wandering clans and the villages were all descended from the same people, but the more she learned about the wandering clans, the more different they seemed.

"How do you honor your dead, then?" she asked.

"You're about to find out," Brittany answered as she pointed to the central cookfire.

The clan slowly gathered around, sitting down in such a way that Harald was at the center. Samora and Brittany joined the others, and she saw Alec and Elian on the other side of the fire.

Harald waited until everyone had settled, then said, "Eleven generations ago, Adanias was born. He was a poor hunter, a terrible craftsman, and a slow speaker. His friends and family expected little of him, as he spent more time staring at the grass and the trees than he did helping the clan."

The story was familiar to Samora, as she assumed it was to all who were gathered. But Harald was a natural storyteller, and as he recounted the legend of Adanias, she leaned forward as though she was hearing it for the first time.

"We know now that Adanias wasn't helpless but was deeply

immersed in our world. He discovered the force we now know as adani, named in his honor, and learned how to shape it. The bindings he created are nothing to us now, but it was those first steps that set our people on the journey we walk to this day."

Samora was surprised Harald took Adanias's techniques so lightly. In the village, his bindings were still taught to anyone interested. Many were useful in the growing of crops, as they strengthened the adani flowing through a field.

Harald continued, "His discoveries came just in time. Less than a generation after he taught the use of adani to the rest of his clan, the Debru arrived. Moka struck at the clans, leading their frightful gathering of dark creatures. If not for Adanias's discovery, humanity's story might have ended then."

Harald paused and let his gaze travel across the assembled warriors.

"We defended ourselves that day, though the cost was high. And we've defended ourselves every day since. A blade can only be forged in a fire, and our skills with adani have been forged in the endless conflict with the Debru. Their attacks grow fiercer every year, and I know that for many of you, hope feels like a distant shore."

Several heads nodded around the gathering.

"But I tell you this: as we gather tonight to honor our dead, my hope has never been stronger!" Harald's voice boomed into the night, daring any Debru to attack.

Again, Samora thought to herself that if it was anyone else, she would have called them a liar, but Harald's voice rang with conviction.

"The Debru fling themselves against us because they sense their end is near! I have seen into the future, not in a dream, but in the strength of our young. Once, there was no one who could match my techniques, but we all know there are at least six young warriors in our midst whose promise is greater than my own. Today we survived an attack from a dozen Debru, and I watched as a stranger to our clan, who isn't even a warrior, leaped halfway across a battlefield to help his sister."

Harald paced back and forth, the fire casting his shadow over the gathering. He met the gazes of all, lifting their spirits with his own optimism.

"We all know that night is darkest just before the dawn, and I am certain we are about to wake up to a glorious morning!"

Samora was about ready to stand up and shout when Harald suddenly stopped pacing. When he spoke again, his voice had returned to its normal volume. Still as loud as a shout for most, but quiet for him.

"I mourn the loss of our friends and family. They died so that we may live, but their loss is especially bitter today, because I know how close we are to the end of our trials."

Harald made a fist with his right hand, then brought it to his navel, where adani was strongest. "Mourn, friends, but do not let your thoughts turn in too bitter a direction. The end of our suffering is near."

Harald turned to look at the fire, ending his part in the evening.

Samora couldn't help but look at the giant warrior in wonder. The mood among the clan had been dark all day, and the suffering remained, but it had taken on a different flavor. Families cried as they mourned those they'd lost, but Samora knew, as certain as she was that the sun would rise in the morning, that tomorrow they'd walk to the next battle without question.

She'd never met anyone like him before, and wondered if the other clan leaders were the same. If so, the villages would have nothing to worry about. What could Debru do to break the spirits of leaders like these?

Brittany excused herself and Samora didn't try to follow. Their welcome had been warmer than she'd expected, but she was a stranger here, a guest without a room.

Elian soon sat in the empty space. She questioned him with

her gaze, and he said, "Alec wanted to be with his family. He invited me, but it didn't seem right."

Samora understood that feeling, too.

Elian didn't look well. His eyes were sunken, and even in the firelight, he looked pale. She put her hand on his shoulder and gave him a concerned look.

"I'm fine," he said. He watched the others for a bit, and Samora noticed his gaze lingered on Harald. "At least, I'm not hurt. But being here, it's not like the legends, is it? Alec's cousin died today, someone he's known his entire life. It's like losing Father, except that it happens all the time for them."

Samora thought again of Rakella's outburst at her refusal, her words and logic cutting deeper every time she thought of them. She nodded. She'd never held the same reverence for the legends that Elian had. Before Father's death, he'd sometimes dreamed of running away and joining the wandering clans. Most boys did, at least for a while. Anything seemed better than the daily monotony of farming. But even after, he'd turned to the legends to help him understand the father he'd not known as well as he thought he did.

"Harald found me earlier today and told me we'd be welcome in the clan if we wanted, once we made sure our village was safe. Did he ask you that, too?" Elian asked.

Samora nodded.

"I'm not sure what I want," Elian confessed.

As well as she knew him, she was still surprised. He might have stopped planning to run away to join the clans but fighting against the Debru had always been what motivated him most.

He saw her surprise. "I know. It's just... different seeing the war in person."

Elian stared into the fire, and Samora watched him. He'd saved her today, impressing the entire clan with an ability none of them understood. But that wasn't what impressed her most. She'd always known he'd risk everything to keep her safe.

When she saw him staring at the fire, it wasn't with the naive optimism of a child, but with the considered gaze of an adult, weighing both sides of his potential futures carefully.

8

Elian didn't consider himself as soft as Samora. Ever since Father had died and she'd turned inward, she'd possessed a sensitivity and awareness about her surroundings Elian couldn't match. She said little, but her words were carefully chosen and carried a weight others' ramblings didn't. It wasn't just a sensitivity to adani, though Mother had praised her for that. She sensed moods, too.

He wondered what she thought of the Bears, one day after tragedy had struck the clan. He would have asked, except she was away with Brittany, training new skills just as Elian trained with Alec.

The normalcy of the next day's march confounded him. The Bears had lost a significant number of their friends and family the day before, but he never would have guessed if he hadn't been present. He sometimes caught a glimpse of a few puffy faces, and the column was a bit quieter than when they'd first joined, but that was it.

The whole clan reminded him of a fighter who'd just taken a nearly lethal blow, only to rise to their feet and prepare for the next exchange.

They'd reminisced last night about the lost, but their grieving seemed incomplete, an open wound left to fester. He didn't mourn over their losses as they did, but he understood their pain.

When Father had died, he'd been torn to shreds for weeks. He moped around the house for days, despite both Samora and Mother pleading for him to go outside. When he finally charged out the front door in a fit of despair, he spent as much time alone in the grove as he could, taking out his anger on innocent trees.

Mother still claimed he'd brought down enough wood to keep the village warm all winter, but he was sure she exaggerated.

He didn't know what to make of the Bears, and his attitude toward them changed course more often than a swirling wind. At times, he looked upon their relentless march as a sign of their strength. The Debru might kill their friends and rend their flesh, but the invaders couldn't extinguish the spirit of the clan. Then, a moment later he would see a mother drying her tears, and he thought that Harald was a broken and cruel leader who denied his people a proper chance to grieve.

Alec did little to help him sort through his emotions. During their first break, Elian tried to bring the subject up, but Alec only grunted, mumbled something about "the way of it," and cut their break short.

Elian supposed he was grateful Alec continued to train with him. It was hard to be too judgmental about the march when he was asking Alec to teach him fundamental techniques he should have learned years ago. But if there was one thing he'd learned from the Debru assault, it was that he needed to be stronger.

The Bears were more impressed by him than he was of himself, but there was no denying Alec's training helped him slowly gain more awareness of the flow of adani through his body. Shifting it around at will eluded him, but he enjoyed enough small successes that he kept at it.

Sometime before lunch, Alec decided there was little more he could teach until Elian had practiced longer, so they separated.

Alec returned to his family, where he embraced his mother and walked by her side. Elian felt guilty he'd kept Alec as long as he had.

With little else to do, Elian continued practicing Alec's techniques.

The Bears stopped briefly by a creek to let the horses drink, fill their waterskins, and eat a light lunch. Then they were moving again.

Not long after, Harald wandered by and watched Elian as he completed one of Alec's exercises. "How's the training?"

"Slow, but Alec has taught me well. Mastering what he's taught me is difficult, though."

"Don't be too hard on yourself. It can take a long time to master the basics."

"We don't have a long time, though."

Harald conceded the point. "I wanted to ask, because I didn't when you first joined us: were we the first clan you encountered after your village? Did you see any sign of any other?"

"No. We weren't expecting to find you as soon as we did, honestly. We thought the front was farther west."

"Until last year, it was. The Debru have been pushing hard lately, though. But you're sure you didn't see any sign?"

Elian shook his head. "Samora didn't sense anyone until we ran into your scouts, but I don't think we saw a single horse track. Why?"

"Given where you came from, I would have expected you to come across some evidence of the Crows. The fact that you didn't is slightly concerning."

"They're the clan we're about to meet?"

"If all goes as planned, yes. They control the territory between us and the Hounds, which is bounded by the next creek we come to. My hope is to hand you off to them, and they can escort you to Tiafel."

Elian's face fell.

Harald noticed. "As much as I'd like to join you all the way, my duty is here, and as you've seen, we're pressed harder than ever before. The Crows are as good a group of warriors as you're like to meet. Just remember that when you've gotten what you need from Tiafel, you're always welcome among the Bears."

"I won't forget, thank you."

"There's something else, too," Harald said. He reached behind his back and pulled out a sword and sheath. "Our swords are valuable, but one of our warriors died without an heir to pass her weapon to. After seeing how you put it to use against the Debru, my council decided to gift it to you."

Elian's breath caught as Harald held the sword out to him.

He reached out and took the weapon. "I shall strive to be worthy of it."

"See that you do." Harald smiled, but it lacked the warmth it usually possessed. "Though I think I have little to fear in that regard."

Harald nodded, then continued down the column, stopping to speak with every family. Elian watched him, noticing how grim expressions softened after Harald passed. He couldn't take their grief away, but he could share the burden.

It was good he was as strong as he was, because he was carrying the heavy spirits of the clan on his broad shoulders, lifting them up as he passed.

He was so focused on Harald he didn't notice Samora standing next to him until she purposefully bumped his shoulder with her own. It startled him out of his reverie.

Samora tilted her head toward Harald, unspoken questions in her gaze.

"He said we'll be entering Crow territory soon, and he's going to leave us with them."

She didn't look pleased, but she kept her focus on him, inviting him to share his feelings.

"I know it's silly, but I'd hoped we could stay with the Bears longer. Alec has been a good teacher, and Harald is something else."

How so? Her look asked.

"Look at how he leads. People stand straighter when he passes, despite their losses."

Samora joined him in watching Harald walking down the line, then she said, "He looks sad."

Elian shot his sister a questioning look, but she didn't feel the need to elaborate. Had the claim come from someone else, he would have laughed, but Samora had a way of seeing deeper into people than he did. He didn't see whatever she saw, but he extended her the benefit of the doubt.

They came to the next creek by mid-afternoon, and Harald once again called a rest. He conferred with his council, and a handful of scouts were sent across the creek while the rest of the clan rested. The scouts returned before long, and the council again convened.

Elian didn't know why such a small creek resulted in such an enormous delay, so he walked up to Alec to ask.

"The wandering clans are bound by strict traditions. Long ago, the clans were as likely to fight each other as they were Debru, and so at a great gathering, rules were created to guide the clans. Scouts and messengers can cross borders without worry, but leading an entire clan across a territorial line is considered a terrible aggression. I suspect Harald sent the scouts to find some sign of the Crows, but if they came back with none, then Harald will have to decide what to do," Alec said.

"That rule is foolish. Clans should be allowed to wander wherever they need to," Elian said.

"If clans wandered haphazardly, there would be gaps in the front the Debru could walk through. It's because we have our assigned territories that we can keep a protective net around the villages. I'm sure it's one of the questions Harald is wrestling with. If we keep escorting you north, not only do we risk trouble with the Crows, but we'll be abandoning the defense of the land assigned to us."

When Alec explained it like that, Elian felt like the fool for first disagreeing. He only wanted the Bears to stay with him.

Not long after, word traveled down the line. The Bears were going to enter Crow territory. Elian endured several long stares, but no one spoke out against the decision. The column advanced over the creek and continued north.

Elian rejoined Samora near the middle of the column, and soon Harald was once again walking down the line. He was stopped more frequently this time, and Elian saw the effort he had to expend to keep the clan in agreement.

Eventually Harald reached them, and he looked tired.

Elian didn't want to make the offer, but it seemed only right. "You don't have to bring the entire clan to escort us. We're certainly grateful, but I know how tough of a decision it was."

The corner of Harald's mouth turned up in a smile. "Not that difficult, actually. Your story has me worried, and it's important you get to Tiafel. I can't imagine it will take us more than a day to find some Crows, and then we'll return to our land. The Crows will be furious, but I think I can convince them to see reason."

Elian bowed deeply. "Thank you, then. It's more than we ever would have asked for."

Harald dipped his head, then continued down the line.

He didn't make it far before a group of scouts returned from the north, riding their horses at a full gallop. They sped down the column until they found Harald, then dismounted. Elian saw it was the same man and woman that had found them. They spoke in hushed tones away from the column, but Harald kept glancing toward him and Samora.

Harald dismissed the scouts and rejoined the siblings. "Our scouts have found something up ahead. It's not a pleasant scene, but it's important you two be there. Do you know how to ride?"

Neither did, so Harald ordered two scouts to let Elian and

Samora climb up behind them. The rest of the column halted, and it was clear Harald expected trouble. The column became more of an oval, and they set up a thick perimeter, with horses and scouts riding in wide arcs around the others.

Elian's mouth was dry, and he didn't think it was because of the dust the horses kicked up. He wanted to ask what was ahead, but Harald had already ridden away. Once he and Samora were set on their horses, they too rode north.

It wasn't Elian's first time mounted, but he hadn't ridden anything since he was a child, and for a while he lost himself in the joy of the ride. But when they crested a small rise and saw what was before them, the joy vanished like a candle snuffed out.

The field was a mess of corpses, and none had died peaceably. Few were even whole. Whatever battle had taken place here had been brutal, and then the scavengers had fallen upon the remains. Elian's stomach churned as he witnessed half-eaten intestines, clawed faces, and severed limbs. One arm had landed in such a way that the grass supported it, a hand outstretched toward a sky it would never seize.

He'd seen the results of the first battle, but this was so much worse. Rider and horse had often fallen together over a stretch of nearly half a mile. The scout Elian rode with stopped and forced him to dismount, though the last thing he wanted was to be closer to the destruction.

If anyone else in the clan felt the same, they didn't show it on their faces. Harald and the others moved among the corpses, squatting and studying them for long periods of time. They turned bodies over and examined wounds from different angles. At times, they'd gather over a specific corpse and confer, reminding Elian of farmers gathering to look over a field, discussing a grotesque harvest.

Worse was watching Samora join them. His little sister moved among the corpses, her gaze focused.

Let them call him a coward. He backed away until he was

beyond the immediate field of battle. He pretended to watch while he thought about anything else.

Samora joined him before Harald had finished his own study. She looked him over, and it felt like she was staring straight into his heart.

"Why did Harald want us here? There's nothing we can do to help," Elian asked.

Samora turned and pointed. Elian followed her direction, and his knees went weak. The spot wasn't as obvious, because there were no trees marking the death of the land, but perhaps a mile away there was a circle of dead grass, several times wider than the one they'd discovered.

"Does it feel the same?" he asked.

She shook her head. "Stronger. It's even pulling adani here."

Before he could ask her to explain that cryptic remark, Harald whistled, summoning them all together. It required Elian to walk across the battlefield, so he kept his eyes turned up, only glancing down on occasion to ensure he didn't trip.

"What happened here?" Harald asked.

One of the scouts spoke first, the shorter woman who'd escorted them to the Bears. "They were lined up against the circle, but whatever killed them, killed them fast. They didn't even have time to scatter."

Her partner added, "Most of the wounds are from Debru techniques. There's a handful I don't recognize, though. They look more powerful than most."

"Are we dealing with a Vada?" Harald asked.

The scarred man wasn't sure. "I've never encountered one, so I couldn't say."

Harald listened to the reports, running his hand through his beard as he did. He glanced back toward the circle. "How strong are your techniques against that?" he asked.

A few of the scouts formed spears and threw them at the circle. Elian saw no more than he expected—the spears hit the circle and slowly unraveled. Everyone else looked more concerned than him, though. "Weaker," one scout said, and the others nodded.

The leader of the Bears turned to Samora. "How does this compare to the circle you saw?"

Samora had little choice but to speak, but her voice was loud enough for all to hear. It was the most people she'd spoken in front of in years.

"Similar. The effects within it seem the same, but this one is much bigger, and ours wasn't pulling in so much adani."

Harald dipped his head in thanks. "The question is, did the Crows lose because the circle pulled too much adani from them, or did they lose because they fought something bigger than they could win against?"

"Could be a bit of both," one scout said.

"These are the Crows?" Elian asked. He felt silly for asking the question as soon as it left his lips. Of course these were Crows. This was their territory.

No one mocked him for the question, though. "All of them," Harald said. He looked to his scouts for confirmation and received nods in return.

Elian didn't believe them. An entire wandering clan, wiped out in one battle? It had to be a twisted joke, but no one was laughing.

Harald gestured with his hand, encompassing the entire battlefield. "Anyone else notice anything?"

His question was met with confused gazes.

"There's not a single Debru corpse."

As if on cue, a sharp wind cut across the field from the north, chilling Elian to the bone.

The scouts turned pale as the weight of the observation settled on them. The scout with the scar on his face said, "The Debru must have done something with them. The Crows might have numbered less than us, but they were no less powerful."

"Maybe, but did you see any Debru blood? I haven't."

The scouts passed looks around, but no one stood up to say that Harald was wrong.

"What do we do?" one asked.

Samora surprised them all by answering before Harald. "I want to go into the circle."

"No!" Elian shouted.

Harald cut him off with a look, then turned his full attention to Samora. "Why?"

"We need to know more about them."

Harald didn't consider nearly as long as Elian thought he should have. "Fine. We'll wrap rope around you like Elian did."

"Who is most sensitive to adani?" Samora asked.

Every eye turned to Harald, who said, "Me."

"I expect that if this circle is anything like the one by our village, I'll provoke the shadow. Don't pull me out right away. Leave me in until it's about to kill me."

"You can't do this!" Elian shouted. He pushed his way through the circle so he could reach Samora. Harald's giant arm came down and blocked his way, and when Elian looked up, Harald's gaze was sharp.

"I won't let her die."

Elian cursed, but his words didn't move Harald's arm. He felt adani pooling in his limbs, and he imagined what would happen if he leaped up and punched the look off Harald's face. The warriors around him tensed as they sensed the shift in the flow of adani.

Then Samora was there, her hand on his arm. "I'll be fine. Trust Harald."

"Not all wounds are physical. What if it hurts you worse than last time?" The haunted look in her eyes was still too fresh in his memory.

She acknowledged his point, but he saw he wouldn't convince her of her foolishness.

"Be safe," he said.

She nodded, and the scouts proceeded to tie a rope around her waist. Once she was secure, she gave the group a quick bow, then walked toward the circle. Harald held the other end of the rope loosely in his hand, letting it out as she advanced.

Elian almost ran in after her, but he was needed here. If Harald lost focus for even a moment, Elian would be there, ready to pull his sister to safety.

Samora reached the edge of the circle and stepped in without a moment of hesitation. Elian waited for the shadow to attack, but there was none. She turned, waved, then continued deeper into the circle.

Elian almost shouted after her but couldn't guess if the sound would carry. All she needed to do was reach the edge. There was no need to explore deeper. But she kept walking toward the center of the circle. At least this time it was all grass instead of a pond.

Samora waved again, which Elian took to mean she was still unharmed.

"Breathe, Elian," Harald said.

Elian did, only realizing after Harald spoke that he'd been holding it since she'd stepped past the circle. He glanced up at Harald, who was focusing on Samora as if he hadn't eaten for a week and she was a deer wandering in front of him.

She reached the center of the circle and looked around. She squatted and ran her hand through the grass, then dug into the dirt. Finally, she began her return. Harald pulled in the rope, keeping it almost taut.

At the edge of the circle Samora stopped and called out, "I'm going to extend adani. That's when it attacked last time."

Harald nodded as Elian bit back his argument. She lay down on the grass, as though she planned to take a nap along the edge of the battlefield's carnage. She placed her hand on the ground, and although Elian couldn't sense her use of adani, the shadow appeared near the center of the circle a moment later. It raced toward his sister, reminding him of the battle against the Debru, when they'd used shadows to cover the advance of the kettu.

The shadows embraced Samora and hid her from sight. Instinctively, Elian reached out, grabbed the rope, and pulled. Harald's firm grip killed his efforts, though. The leader of the Bears never glanced back, but he said, "She's not hurt yet. The shadow is draining her adani quickly, but she's strong enough to endure more."

Elian pulled on the rope again, but his heart wasn't in it. Samora wanted this, and she'd only been able to trust Harald to keep her safe. Elian lacked the necessary strength and skills. As he always did.

The rope tugged suddenly, and if not for Harald, Elian would have been pulled off his feet. Harald gripped the fleeing rope tightly, and the muscles on his arms bulged with the sudden effort. He twisted, wrapping the rope around his own torso and leaning back, using his legs to fight against the otherworldly strength of the rope. Elian lent his own strength to the task, though it was little compared to Harald's efforts.

The rope snapped, sending both Harald and Elian stumbling backward. Harald regained his balance after a step. He stared at the loose rope as though it was an apparition.

"What happened?" Elian asked.

Harald shook his head. "She's losing adani quickly!"

No one took a step forward, either caught by surprise or too uncertain about the circle's effects to risk themselves.

Adani pooled in Elian's legs, and he leaped ahead of Harald. He didn't consider the risks or worry about what was best. Samora was in danger.

He raced at the shadow, hoping he could rescue his sister before it consumed her.

9

Even though she expected the shadow's assault, its speed and ferocity still left her on her back foot. It raced toward her faster than any predator, faster than an arrow launched from a hunter's bow. She barely had time to breathe deep before it surrounded her, wrapping around her like a blanket soaked in a freezing stream.

She didn't fight back with her adani, electing instead to keep it wrapped tightly within. The circle pulled it from her already, and the shadow stole more, sucking it from her the way a leech sucked blood. She held onto what she could, but it wasn't a fight she could win.

All she could do was endure.

The darkness was complete, a deeper black than anything she'd known. It wasn't just an absence of light, but an absence of warmth, of movement, of life. She felt as though she was carried from one place to the next, but she wasn't sure if that was real or illusory.

The shadows took on form, but this time she didn't find herself on a mountain peak. She was on a beach, once again standing among a circle of dark figures chanting at a sphere of light. An endless expanse of water was off to her side, cold waves lapping gently against the sand. The water was as dead as the land, a graveyard that extended farther than the eye could see.

She'd traveled for countless days. Scavenging birds had flown overhead for the last three, waiting for her to fall so they could feast. She'd disappointed them by keeping to her feet. She'd even frightened them away from other carcasses, depriving them of their rightful meals. On hands and knees, she'd torn what meager scraps of meat she could from the bones and shoved them in her mouth. The birds had cawed and hissed, but they shrank from her glare.

They'd eat their fill soon enough. When all else was dead, they would feed until their stomachs burst, the last living creatures on a dead world.

With luck, she would no longer be here.

One last sacrifice, and then salvation would be hers.

In the light was life, a second chance.

She chanted louder, feeling the strength of their gods draw near. Her fervor increased until she shouted at the light. Her voice tore out of her parched throat as she fought to prove herself the worthiest. The others did the same. Its strength was a weight upon their souls, far heavier than the despair each pilgrim already carried.

It dropped among them, dark strength flaring to slow its descent. The Debru landed no harder than a feather falling from the sky. It cast its gaze about and nodded in satisfaction. Her heart pounded with joy. The journey, hard as it was, was almost at an end. She'd done shameful things to survive, but she'd escape this dying world with her life.

And in the end, life was all that mattered.

The Debru stared into the light at the center of the circle and raised its hands. The light grew and hardened as it pulled more strength from her body. Her legs trembled, but she refused to fall. Not when eternal life was only a few steps away. Others in the circle succumbed, but she only chanted louder, the eternal words giving her the strength to endure.

Despite her faith, she grew weaker. She waited for the Debru to turn, to offer its clawed hand to her and escort her through the gate. It wouldn't be long now.

Just a moment longer.

The saying became a mantra, a sturdy tree she wrapped herself around to remain standing. Others in the circle were crying out, knowing they had come this far only to fail at the end. They pleaded for mercy, forgetting in their desperation that the Debru entirely lacked the quality.

Only strength survives. It was the lesson all life needed to learn, and the Debru were master teachers.

She risked a glance around and saw that she was the only one who still stood. Far from being saddened by the loss of the other pilgrims, her heart filled with boundless joy, for now there was no doubt she would be chosen. Any moment now, the Debru would extend its hand and invite her to join it.

It stepped toward the light and vanished.

She blinked at the spot where the Debru had been, waiting for it to reappear. The light lost its hardness and grew more diffuse.

Awareness dawned too late. She stumbled forward, reaching out toward the light that unraveled like a child's first weaving attempt. What had once been warm cooled, and she leaped at the fading gate.

Her feet barely left the ground. She fell forward onto her face, with no strength left to stand. She was no better than any of the others.

Left behind.

The air grew colder and she shivered uncontrollably. She wrapped her arms around herself, but they didn't help.

So cold.

Everything faded to black as ice crawled up her toes, into her ankles, and up her legs.

She closed her eyes and surrendered to its inevitable advance.

Warm arms scooped her up, burning her skin where they touched, but she welcomed the fire. Anything was better than the ice.

The shadow receded and light returned, blinding even though it was hidden by the clouds.

She wasn't she anymore, but Samora, and she was safe in Elian's arms.

Not left behind.

Together.

WHEN SAMORA WOKE, she saw Harald and Elian sitting beside her. She was glad to see them both, but Elian was in a rage.

She couldn't tell from his expression, which he kept carefully masked, but it was plenty obvious from the adani rushing through his body, blindingly intense. For a moment, she thought she caught a glimpse of something else, hidden within the storm of light, but she was too tired to look deeper.

Elian noticed she was awake first. He leaned forward. "Are you hurt?"

She remembered the cold, not as a physical sensation, but something that lingered deep in her bones. But in answer to the question, she shook her head. Her grasp of adani was the same as before, if not stronger, and nothing in her body hurt worse than usual. She feared the nightmares that would result from the vision, but that wasn't the point of Elian's question.

"What happened?" she asked.

Harald's answer was silenced by Elian's glare.

Elian said, "It worked mostly as you expected. When you used adani the shadow appeared and attacked you. According to Harald, you were fine for a bit. Then it pulled on the rope and snapped it. Your adani was being pulled fast at that point, so I rushed in, grabbed you, and carried you out."

"It was brave of him. The attack intensified quickly and most of us were caught unaware. Elian saved you before any of us could even form a plan," Harald said.

Samora sensed how the praise calmed Elian. Furious as he was, he still wasn't immune to Harald's charisma. "What happened to you when you entered?" she asked.

A frown passed over Elian's face. "As near as I can tell, nothing," he said.

She gave him a skeptical look and he held up his hands. "It all happened quickly, but I wasn't attacked. The area leeched adani from me, but it was barely enough for me to notice. When I reached my hand in the dark cloud to pick you up, the shadow retreated."

Samora looked to Harald, who confirmed the story. "The shadow vanished as soon as he touched it. He was able to pick you up and run, and if I had to guess, I'd say he was using adani when he did."

Samora closed her eyes and considered the revelation but didn't know what to make of it. Maybe Elian hadn't been in the circle long enough, or maybe something else had happened. Outside of the second vision, the exploration of the circle had revealed little.

Footsteps pounded against the ground close enough to her head she felt the vibration. She opened her eyes to see the woman who'd escorted them to the Bears standing beside her head. She was looking at Harald. "Sir, we spotted clan scouts to the north."

Harald was on his feet in a heartbeat. "Crows?"

"We don't know. We retreated before making contact. Wasn't sure what you'd want, given we're in Crow land and separated from the rest of the clan."

"Wise," Harald said.

He considered, but not for long. "We'll ride to them."

As the scouts raced to their horses, Harald extended his hand to help Samora to her feet. "Can you ride?"

She didn't want to, but she could. She nodded and took his hand.

It didn't take Harald and the others long to mount their horses and gallop north. Harald spoke with the scouts, and soon called a halt. They stopped on a rise that made them visible for miles. Samora would have preferred someplace hidden deep in a forest, but she trusted Harald.

The other clan's scouts soon appeared, and Harald raised his hand in greeting. A moment later, the leader of the other scouts raised his hand, and everyone relaxed. There would be no ambushes today.

Harald led his adanists forward and they met in the middle.

The scout who had signaled them from a distance had looked formidable at first, but as he pulled his horse to a stop before them, Samora realized he was almost too old to be a useful warrior. Wrinkles lined his weathered face, and his long hair was completely gray and fading to white. His gaze captured Samora's attention, though. It was slow and considered, as placid as a lake on a perfectly calm morning.

"Greetings from the Hounds," the man said. He bowed. "My name is Myril, and it's a pleasure to meet you, Harald of the Bears."

Harald hadn't yet introduced himself, but he didn't seem surprised the man knew who he was. "I've heard word of you, Myril, and I'm surprised to find you out here riding Crow land."

"We heard word of tragedy, but feared to split our forces lest we suffer the same. Tiafel asked me to ride hard and report back."

"You're too late," Harald said, his voice flat.

Myril didn't look surprised, and Samora wondered how he had guessed. "May we see?"

"Of course."

The Bears turned their horses around and returned the way they'd come, this time accompanied by the small group of Hounds. Samora and the scout she rode with ended up near the rear of the loose column, too far away to listen to the quiet conversation between Harald and Myril. Samora was frustrated Harald picked now of all times to keep his voice at a normal volume.

She supposed she should be grateful. Harald recounting her story meant she didn't have to, freeing her to pay more attention to the surrounding land.

Sensing adani was more challenging on a horse, but not impossible, and Samora let hers travel widely. It clumped around the adanists, but enough escaped for her to sense the flows of the life force around her. Adani ebbed and flowed, pulled by the horses and adanists as they breathed in and pushed as they exhaled. All felt normal until she pushed her adani further.

Once it had gone a ways beyond the riders, it was gently pulled away and didn't return. It fled south, in the direction of the circle. At this distance the effect was small, but given they were still almost a mile away, she was concerned. She leaned closer to the scout who graciously ferried her from one place to another. "Could we speak with Harald?"

He glanced back, then shrugged. He urged the horse forward and reached the front of the line quickly. Harald looked surprised to see her, but when he saw the expression on her face, he asked, "What?"

"The circle is pulling adani, even from here."

Harald frowned, then extended his own sense. Most weren't as used to sending adani as far afield as she was, but Harald came close. He sent it out far enough he sensed the same. His frown deepened. "She's right."

Myril leaned forward on his horse so he could look around Harald's bulk. "You must be Samora. Harald has told me about you."

Samora appreciated the recognition, but they had more pressing problems than introductions. The circle wasn't pulling a tremendous amount of adani, but it was more than the smaller circle by her home had done. "It's possible that the bigger the circles get, the more adani they pull and the more dangerous they become," she said.

Harald nodded. "You didn't feel anything like this before?"

"Only in the closest proximity."

They stopped their horses among the dead and Myril dismounted with one smooth motion. He examined several of the bodies, much like they had earlier, then cast his gaze toward the growing circle of decay. Samora watched him with interest. Despite his gray hair, he strode among the fallen with quick, confident steps. His inspection of the battlefield took less time than Harald's, and he only glanced at the circle before announcing he'd seen all he needed to see.

The scout addressed Harald. "Why were you here?"

The leader of the Bears gestured toward Samora and Elian. "They are from one of the outer villages. They discovered a circle like this one close to their home, and we intended to escort them to the Crows, then hand them off so Tiafel could speak to them."

Myril nodded slowly. "He'll be interested in doing so."

The scout took one last look over the field. "I came because we'd heard rumors of trouble among the Crows, though we didn't expect this. Would you gather the Bears and join us? In this time of trouble, wisdom dictates we band together."

To Samora, it seemed like the most sensible idea in the world, but Harald was slow to answer. "What if I sent you the siblings and a scout that I trust?"

Samora was offended on Myril's behalf. He'd extended the hand of cooperation, only to have it slapped away. But Myril didn't seem surprised. "Most days I would applaud your caution, but these are not most days." He inclined his head to remind Harald they were surrounded by the remains of an entire clan.

"We're worried, Harald, and are willing to make any concession that eases your fears. Name the place of meeting, demand hostages, or require whatever else your heart and mind desire. Just bring your clan. We need your strength," Myril said.

The pleas came close to begging, the effect even more pronounced because they came from Myril, a man Samora suspected never bent a knee unwillingly.

Harald looked almost as moved as she was. He reconsidered, then laughed, dispelling some small fraction of the gloom that had settled over the small gathering. "Anything I want, you say?"

Myril grimaced. "Within reason, of course."

Harald made a show of stroking his beard. "Well, it can hardly be anything I want if you expect me to be reasonable. It has to be one or the other."

Myril looked as though he'd swallowed something terribly sour, but Harald just stood there with the stupid grin on his face, waiting for Myril's answer.

Finally, Myril relented. His answer, though, was barely loud enough for Samora to hear. "Anything you want."

Harald slapped him on the back, and Myril winced. Samora was a little surprised his spine didn't break from the blow. "We'd be happy to join you, old friend, but I'll make sure you regret this incredible generosity."

From the look on Myril's face, he already did.

10

E lian's skin itched as if a colony of ants were making their home just underneath. He slapped and scratched at the phantom tickles, gritting his teeth when his new companions looked his way. He walked among the Bears, maybe a third of the way back in the column as it snaked over the land and crawled toward the Hound's territory.

For the moment, he was alone. The recent attacks made the clan skittish, so Alec was needed to help scout. Harald had ordered so many riders out that Elian didn't think a wayward mosquito could reach the column without notice.

When the order had come down, he'd offered to help, but Alec and the other adanists had rejected his generosity. They made excuses about "the way things were done," but they were a weak attempt to avoid saying what they all thought.

He was too weak to help.

His lips curled at the thought. When his sister had been attacked by the Debru, who had leaped across the battlefield to save her? When shadow consumed her, who had rushed into the circle to pull her out?

It hadn't been a Bear, that was for sure.

When Samora offered to help, no one denied her. Even now she rode near the front of the column with Harald and Myril, deep in a conversation both leaders paid close attention to. Somewhere deep in the back of his thoughts he knew they were discussing the visions the shadow had given her, but he was still back here with the sleds instead of up there with her. He'd been in the circle, too, though no one seemed to remember it.

At camp that night he and Samora spoke little. He was tired after a day on the road and fell asleep quickly.

The next morning was cloudy and blustery, portending a storm before day's end. The wind already carried the scent of rain and the Bears rose from their slumbers quickly.

Elian didn't understand the rush. He woke to the sounds of the camp being broken, but his eyelids were heavy. He pulled his covers higher over his head and dozed on and off until someone shook him.

"It's time to get up," Samora said.

"In a bit," Elian answered.

She pulled the covers from his face. "Now. You've already slept too long. The clan is going to be leaving soon."

He tried to pull the covers back over his head, but his sister's grip was tight.

"Are you hurt? I've never known you to want to sleep in so late, especially not on a day you'll get a chance to meet a new clan."

"Leave me alone," Elian groaned.

Samora reached for his forehead, but he slapped her hand away.

She glared at him for a moment, then rose in a huff and walked away. Probably to have another talk with Harald and Myril as they rode toward the Hounds.

He groaned again and pulled himself out of his sheets. He looked around with bleary eyes and saw that Samora was right.

The Bears would be on the move soon, and he wondered if they would leave him behind if he fell back asleep.

He decided he didn't want to find out. He packed up his gear with a yawn and joined the column. Alec and his friends were already mounted and scouting, but Elian didn't offer to help. He shuffled along with the rest of the column.

Samora was also right about him being interested in meeting the Hounds. Of the wandering clans in the area, they were one of the largest and most well-known. Elian hadn't heard of Tiafel before meeting Harald, but the history of the Hounds was littered with heroes of legend. If Harald, the leader of the Bears, was so remarkable, how much greater would the Hounds be?

Maybe there'd even be one among them who could teach him how to truly harness his strength.

He should have been excited, but all he could think about was climbing back under some covers and falling asleep. He could sleep for a day, easily. Maybe two, if they let him.

But they wouldn't let him. They kept waking him up and making him walk across this featureless nightmare, all while mocking him behind his back.

Samora deigned to visit him once, but he couldn't bring himself to do anything more than grunt at her obnoxious and intrusive questions. Finally, she understood he didn't want her pity, and she wandered off.

The itches returned that day, stronger than before but less frequent. It felt for sure as if something was crawling under his skin, and he considered visiting Brittany. Everyone, including Harald, spoke of her skill, but she was also friends with Samora. Elian didn't want his sister looking at him like he'd gone mad.

He endured the itches. If he did nothing for long enough, the feeling would fade, and he could stumble on as before. He decided he preferred the strong, infrequent bouts to the constant annoyance it had been yesterday.

Harald stopped their journey on a broad plain with clear views for miles in every direction. When Elian found the strength to lift his head, he saw there was a camp already here, bigger than the Bears' by far. It was bigger than the village he'd grown up in, more tents than he'd ever seen in one place.

Harald and Myril rode toward the camp together. They were met by a pair of riders from the camp, and from a distance, the conversation seemed friendly enough. Elian noted that Samora had been left behind, which served her right.

She was the problem.

He'd only come out here because of her, and now that she'd pulled him so far from home, he did nothing but save her time and time again. And what did he get in return? A chance to walk next to the children as she spoke with the leaders of clans.

Life would be easier without her.

Elian grimaced, shook his head, and pressed his palms against his eyes. He was too tired to think straight, but he didn't know why. Hopefully, once Harald made peace with the Hounds, they'd camp for a few nights and get some good rest. Samora wasn't to blame for anything, and she'd saved his life, too.

He just needed warm food and rest. Then he'd apologize for being short with her earlier. She'd only been trying to help.

The conversation between Harald and the Hounds went on far longer than necessary. For once, Harald wasn't so loud that Elian could hear every word he said, but of course he'd only discover the ability during the very conversation Elian most wanted to hear. Eventually, though, they broke apart, and Harald strolled back to his clan. He spoke with the commanders near the front, and word came down the line quickly. Harald planned to join the Hounds in their camp.

It seemed a foolish amount of trust. The Hounds already outnumbered them, so why make an ambush even easier? They'd be wiser to set up camp far, far away from the Hounds.

Elian's head started to pound in time with his heart, and he was surprised to find it beating so fast. He'd been tired all day, but it wasn't as though today's walk had been strenuous. It was only a fraction of the distance he and Samora had covered each day on their own, and that had been with her holding him back.

He looked around to see if other Bears shared his concerns about being so close to the Hounds, but they all looked eager to join the other clan.

Was he the only one who understood?

He considered hurrying up to the front of the column and calling Harald a fool to his face but decided against it. Not because he was uncertain of his conclusions, but because he knew Harald wouldn't listen. Fools never listened to the wise.

The Bears hurried to join the Hounds, almost as if a distant enemy pursued them. Harald chose their campsite, a flat stretch of grassland on the southern edge of the Hounds' camp, and the clan fell to their tasks. Unlike the nights before, the clan pulled all their supplies and tents from the sleds.

Elian could take no more. After he hauled the frame for a tent for a nearby family, he found Harald and his sister. They worked with others to set up Harald's tent, a monstrosity at least twice as large as any family's.

Samora noticed him first, and she warily watched his approach. She nudged Harald, who turned and greeted Elian with a wide grin. "Your sister and I were just speaking of you. She said you both are familiar with some of the legendary Hound warriors. Tonight, Tiafel has invited a group of my choosing to feast with his Hounds. I would have you join us, and if fate smiles upon you, you'll have the opportunity to meet some of your heroes in the flesh!"

The greeting was so far removed from how Elian had imagined the conversation that he found himself at a temporary loss for words. Harald misinterpreted the silence as some form of nervousness and leaned in close, placing his hand on Elian's shoulder. "They'd be pleased to meet you. No doubt, some tales of your deeds have already spread among the Hounds."

At Harald's touch, Elian's exhaustion and headache fled as though routed. He remembered coming here because he thought Harald was a fool, but his conviction disappeared along with his weariness. Some of his doubts remained, even if they lacked the fire they'd once possessed. "Are you sure it's safe to camp so close to the Hounds? You were wary when you dealt with Myril before."

Now that he stood before the giant, he worried his question might be considered rude, but Harald took no offense. "A wise question, young friend. Samora has spoken often of your observant nature, and I see she speaks as truly of this as she does everything else. Interactions with other wandering clans are always fraught, and history is always ready to rear its ugly head and pull us back to a more brutal time when our greatest enemies were one another. But Tiafel is wise, and Myril's willingness to sacrifice anything to have us here convinced me of their honesty."

Elian saw the reasoning, but he asked, "Even so, wouldn't it be wise to set up our own camp farther away?"

"Some would say so. But the Hounds are a much larger clan than the Bears, so even if we put some distance between us, it would hardly matter once a battle began. More than that, though, I don't believe in half-measures. If I'm going to trust, I'll trust completely. It's why you two found a ready ear and a welcome among my clan, as well." His answer was sharper than it needed to be.

Now Elian felt foolish for having asked the question, and ashamed Harald had to remind him of the generosity they'd been shown. He swallowed his bitterness and said, "Thank you for your patience in answering my questions. I'd be honored to join you in the feast tonight. Until then, I'll help the other families set up their tents."

He spent the rest of the afternoon fulfilling his half-hearted promise to Harald. He helped unload the sleds, raised tents, and hauled supplies for anyone who could use a hand. When he grew tired, he tried to focus adani the way Alec had taught him, but the technique made his stomach churn and the feeling of things crawling under his skin return. He grew weary and was considering backing out of his promise to join Harald and Samora at the feast. What he needed was rest.

He couldn't, though. He'd already promised, and he considered his word ironclad. He found some water to clean his face and hair with, and then he sought out the rest of the Bears invited to the feast.

Once among them, he was glad he'd made the decision. All the Bears' strongest warriors were present and in high spirits, and some of that enthusiasm rubbed off on Elian, too. The itches had disappeared, and his headache faded. Harald soon wrangled them all and said, "We don't receive invitations like this very often, so try not to make fools of yourselves tonight."

Behind Elian, one of the warriors said, "Speak for yourself!"

Harald grinned, then led the party through the Hounds' camp. The scale of it was no less impressive from within its well-protected boundaries. Tents were crowded, breaking the wind for those fortunate enough to be protected within. The camp couldn't have been here long, as the grass wasn't yet trampled down by the clan.

Elian tried to imagine all the effort it must take to move the Hounds from one camp to the next. Though the tents were little different than those of the Bears, he couldn't imagine these grasslands empty and the Hounds on the hunt.

Before they reached their destination, Harald spoke to the siblings. "You may be tempted to bring your troubles to Tiafel tonight, but I would urge you to refrain. Tiafel is a man who prefers quiet and slow deliberation over hasty action, and he'll not want to discuss our concerns in front of so many. The matters that concern us will likely be discussed tomorrow morning among a select few. Tonight's gathering is a celebration only, and it will be taken poorly if the spirit of the evening is ruined."

Elian bit back his retort when Samora nodded. He glared at her, but she pretended not to notice. Why meet with Tiafel if not to advance their causes? Too late, he realized Harald was waiting for Elian's acknowledgment. He gave Harald one sharp nod in answer, though he promised himself that if the opportunity arose, he'd speak to Tiafel about the danger near their village.

Their short journey ended in the center of the Hounds' camp. The tents they passed had grown larger, but the center was open, with a healthy fire warming the gathered warriors. His mouth watered and stomach rumbled as he sat down next to Samora.

All his concerns vanished when he was served a large bowl full of roasted meat and a thick stew.

Despite the long day, the meal and the company made him feel better than he had in days. He ate hearty portions of everything that passed in front of him, including dishes he'd never heard of. The Hounds welcomed their guests with open arms, and Elian's greatest disappointment was that they let Harald speak far too often.

It wasn't that Harald's stories weren't interesting, but they were surrounded by legendary warriors Elian didn't know. He wanted to hear their tales, for he was certain they possessed many. Almost all carried visible scars, and there was a sharpness to their gazes that belied their smiles. Elian tried to match faces to the legends he'd heard, but it was a hopeless endeavor.

One man, so large he made Harald look small, shouted across the fire, "Harald! Did I ever tell you of the time I wrestled an otsoa barehanded?"

The woman sitting next to the giant elbowed him in the ribs. "Pay no mind to my husband, friends. The night was a dark one, and though he may weave a tale of mighty deeds, when the sun rose in the morning, all we found was an otsoa pup, so small it would have died if my husband tripped over it."

Her words were sharp, but her grin was as wide as her husband's.

The giant held his arms out wide. "I swear on my life it was as big as a deer, with fangs as long and as sharp as a dagger. The fight lasted half the night."

His wife raised a cup. "I can assure you all, my husband is a great man and warrior, but his 'fights' never last half the night."

Laughter rippled around the fire, and Elian joined in. Despite everything, he couldn't remember a time since Father had died when he'd felt so content. Harald responded to the giant's story with a tall tale of his own, and the banter danced around the circle. Elian's face began to ache from the constant laughing.

He ended the evening not exhausted, but happily tired, and full to the brim. His skin didn't itch or crawl, and he and Samora walked to the tent gifted to them by a generous Bear family. Samora, as usual, was silent, but it was a companionable silence, and Elian thought she seemed just as happy as him. They reached their tent, fell into their bedding, and fell asleep almost as soon as their bodies were horizontal.

Elian had hoped to sleep contentedly through the night, but he woke well before the sunrise in an agony unlike any he'd experienced before. It felt as though an entire colony of ants crawled beneath his skin, from his smallest toe to the top of his scalp. His stomach rumbled, as though the massive amount of food he'd stuffed down his throat earlier that evening had been little more than an illusion. He clutched at his stomach and groaned, rolling back and forth under his covers to squash the ants crawling underneath his skin.

He wanted to groan more loudly and to cry, but he fought against the urge. Samora slept peacefully on the other side of the tent, and he didn't want to wake her.

As the agony continued, his thoughts from earlier in the day returned, and he saw the world and recent events with startling clarity. He'd been a fool to trust Harald, and an even greater one to be impressed by the Hounds and their empty boasts. They gathered to feast while the shadows grew in power, sucking the adani from the world and giving nothing in return. The heroes he thought he'd believed in were nothing more than cowards hiding behind a long list of false accomplishments.

Elian finally groaned out loud, but Samora didn't stir. And why should she? Of all the liars, she was the worst of them all. She was the one who had decided to split apart what remained of their family, forcing Elian to wander with her when Mother needed them at home to protect their village.

And what did he get for her thanks?

She left him behind to cavort with Harald and the commanders of the Bears. She'd always known she'd be welcomed among them with open arms and granted special consideration thanks to her abilities.

He was nothing but a joke to her.

He slid the knife from his pack, the edge sharp and hungry. Once it had been his father's knife, and he liked to imagine it had traveled countless miles at his father's side, keeping him safe through good times and bad. He stood and stretched, the ants underneath his skin finally settling as he set his sights on Samora's sleeping form.

In the faint light that trickled in through the holes in the tent, he saw that she slept with the hint of a smile on her face, no doubt dreaming about the various embarrassments he'd suffered and would continue to suffer.

He squeezed the hilt of the knife tightly in his right hand, comforted by the weight and well-worn grip of the weapon. He was no stranger to its use. He'd skinned deer, fileted fish, and more with this knife. All he needed to do was slide it quickly across her throat and she'd never laugh at him again, not even in her sleep.

Elian took a step forward, intending to finish the deed quickly. He was certain that if he did it, he'd sleep without dreams or pain for the rest of the night.

Something stopped him, froze him in the middle of the tent.

It wasn't adani, nor any wall or force. It was a whisper, soft but urgent, coming from the back of his own mind. He couldn't hear what it said, but it demanded consideration.

The voice was familiar, though he couldn't name its owner. He strained his focus, even as his other thoughts demanded he bend over and open up Samora's throat.

But what was the other voice saying?

The whisper became a sudden shout, and the voice was as clear as if its owner was leaning next to Elian's ear.

"That's your sister!" Father yelled.

He knew that, of course, but it carried a different weight in Father's voice. Elian blinked, shuddered, and then let out a cry.

It woke Samora. She twisted in her sheets and saw him, standing beside her with a knife in his hand.

Elian wanted to run and hide, shame burning deep in his heart. What had he been about to do?

He took half a step back, but his legs felt weak, as though all the strength had been pulled from his limbs. His eyelids felt heavy, and the knife in his hand weighed more than a boulder. It dropped from his hand and fell to the ground. He tried to take another step back, wanting to turn and hide from his sister's confused gaze.

His body refused to answer. He stumbled backward, tripped over something, and fell. He was unconscious before his body struck the ground.

11

Samora woke to a choked-off cry in their tent, her heart pounding as though she'd woken from a nightmare. She twisted in her covers, raising a shield of adani more by instinct than by any intent. Elian stood above her, only a step or two away, but his face was twisted into an expression she couldn't name. In his right hand was their father's old knife.

He'd been acting strangely the past two days, ever since he'd pulled her out of the circle, but she'd assumed it was nothing more than the challenges they'd faced finally catching up to him. Her brother always wanted to carry everyone's problems on his shoulders, and while she loved him for that, he made his life more difficult than it needed to be. He forgot that even the heroes in the stories he obsessed over had the strength of a clan behind them.

She'd been wrong, though, and knew it the moment she laid eyes on the knife. She'd seen the way he'd been glaring at her, revealing the angry thoughts he didn't permit himself to speak. But she hadn't guessed at the depths of his feeling.

Her gaze startled him out of whatever he'd been considering, though. His face twisted in horror and revulsion. He stumbled backward, dropped the knife, and fell across the twisted covers. She threw her own off and came to her feet, prepared for whatever might happen next.

Elian didn't move, and after a few moments, she realized he'd passed out.

But from what? He was as healthy and strong as anyone she'd ever met. He'd complained of weariness earlier but had seemed fine at the feast and after. She extended her adani toward him, expecting it would be drawn to him as it always was.

It circled around her, not pulled toward her brother at all.

Samora dropped her shield and rushed toward him. He looked as white as snow and his breathing was uneven. She pressed her wrist against his forehead and immediately recoiled. Not only was he burning, her adani sensed something foreign in him. She reached out to touch him again, then thought better of it. This was likely beyond her, and even if not, it would be wise to have someone else nearby.

Samora threw on more clothes and stepped into the cool night air. Off in the distance, Hounds and Bears patrolled the perimeter of the camp together, but here everyone was well asleep. Samora worked her way through the tents, careful not to trip over stakes or ropes. She'd walked this route once during the day, but at night she feared getting turned around.

It didn't take her long to find the tent she sought. She undid the strings holding the door closed and poked her head inside. She cleared her throat as she prepared to speak.

Brittany woke and sat up. "Samora?"

"Elian needs help."

Brittany didn't ask any other questions, for which Samora was grateful. She didn't like not being by his side, especially now.

Brittany grabbed a smaller pack that she kept stuffed with all the healing supplies she'd gathered on their journey, and soon they were running back to Samora and Elian's tent. When they barged in, Elian was still there, lying where he'd fallen.

Brittany was at his side in a heartbeat, and she reached out to check his temperature with her wrist before Samora could warn her. She flinched when she touched him, but she didn't draw away like Samora had. Tense moments passed without movement, then Brittany lifted her wrist and looked at Samora. "You felt what was happening within him?"

Samora waggled her hand. *A little.*

"He's safe to touch, but there's barely any adani flowing through his body. It's been pushed out by something darker. I haven't felt anything like this before. I'm going to try healing him and push adani back into him. Do you want to help?"

Samora nodded, and Brittany gestured that she should kneel on Elian's other side. Samora did so, and put her hand on Elian's chest, mirroring Brittany's actions.

They closed their eyes to focus on the flow of adani. The shadow flowing within her brother made Samora's stomach churn, but as she forced herself to confront the darkness, she recognized it. It was a fragment of the shadow that had attacked her in the circle, now growing within her brother.

Guilt threatened to break her heart in two. Was this something Elian had caught when he'd entered the circle to rescue her?

It was a question she couldn't answer now, but she vowed she would once Elian was safe. He always threw himself into danger on her behalf, heedless of the consequences.

Through her contact with Elian, she sensed Brittany's healing efforts. Most healing, Samora had learned, was a matter of returning the flow of adani to its natural paths through the human body. A wound such as a scratch or cut was a trivial matter. Such wounds broke the flow of adani, but the disruptions were small, and the body working in conjunction with adani could heal the wounds on their own in time.

Elian's pathways felt shriveled and brittle to Samora's senses. Brittany sent healing waves of adani into them, trickling the life-giving force through Elian's limbs. The adani had to fight against the shadow, and at first it was overwhelmed, but Brittany was patient, pushing more adani into Elian, a little at a time. Too much might be just as harmful as the lack he currently experienced.

Samora watched the process with her senses, amazed both by Brittany's constant effort and the shattered nature of Elian's body. It was no wonder he'd been weary the past few days. If the shadow had crippled him like this, it was a testament to his strength he'd been able to stand at all.

They were fortunate to have someone like Brittany nearby. She had the strength to match most of the Bears' adanists, but the way she manipulated adani was a wonder. The weavings she ran through Elian's body were so thin it seemed they should unravel immediately, but they were remarkably strong.

The process took so long, though. Once, when Brittany took a break, Samora asked if there was any way to hurry the process.

Brittany gave her a sympathetic look but shook her head. "When it comes to healing, it's best to trust adani. The fact that it isn't rushing through him tells me to proceed slowly."

Brittany returned to healing, and Samora lost track of time. It was still dark in the tent when Brittany's efforts began to wane. Her flow of adani into Elian rose and fell, but every time it rose, it was a little less than the time before. Samora opened her eyes and saw that Brittany was swaying back and forth, nearly as pale as Elian had been when he'd fallen. Samora reached out and grabbed her wrist.

Brittany's eyes shot open, and when she saw Samora's concern, she shook her head. "I know, but he's not healed. If I stop now, the shadow will simply return."

Samora tapped her own chest and nodded.

Brittany didn't seem so certain. "Are you sure?"

Samora nodded. They didn't have many choices, not if they

wanted to save Elian. Brittany quickly decided the same. "You sensed how I did it?"

Samora nodded again.

"Then I'll take a break. Just remember not to push. Let adani guide you. I'll be right here if you need me."

Samora smiled her thanks, then closed her eyes and placed her hand back on Elian's chest. Fortunately, Brittany's technique was a simple one, not all that different from when Samora pushed her adani out to extend her senses. Instead of the land, she trickled it into her brother, driving the shadow slowly from his body. The hardest part was not succumbing to the temptation of pushing all the adani she could gather at once.

Once again, she lost track of time as she worked. All that mattered was feeding a constant stream of adani into his body. That task became her entire world, to the point where she even forgot Brittany was in the tent with them.

When she opened her eyes again, the light coming through the holes and gaps in the tent told her morning was near. She'd lost most of the night but had succeeded in completely driving the shadow from Elian's body. She slumped back, tired both from the sustained effort and the lack of sleep. Brittany was beside Elian in a moment. "I'll take over," she said.

Samora shook her head, then gestured for Brittany to check Elian. It felt to her like the last of the shadow had been banished, but she didn't trust her own senses.

Brittany put her hand on Elian's chest while Samora tried to gather the strength to stay awake. Brittany sent her adani through Elian, but it wasn't long before her gaze met Samora's. "He seems fine to me, now. Adani is flowing smoothly, and he's pulling from everything close to him, just like before. I think he's going to need to sleep for a while. Just like you. I figured that would have taken most of today, too."

Samora hated to ask more from her friend, but she could barely keep her eyes open. She gestured toward her bed, and Brittany nodded. "I'll keep watch over you both, and I'll check on Elian every once in a while to ensure the shadow hasn't returned. You sleep."

Samora bowed deeply to Brittany, then fell into her bed and fell asleep a moment later.

SHE WOKE to a gentle hand on her shoulder. For a moment, she lingered in that comfortable space between sleeping and waking, but then she remembered what had happened to Elian and sat straight up.

The sudden movement surprised Brittany, who hurried to calm her friend. She whispered, "He's fine. He's sleeping well, his breathing his even, and I haven't sensed a trace of shadow since you went to sleep. The sleep is doing him good, too. I suspect when he wakes up, he'll be every bit as strong as you're used to. I woke you because you've both been summoned by Harald. He's going to meet with Tiafel and the Hounds' council soon."

Samora looked down at Elian, then looked back at Brittany with a question in her eyes.

Brittany grimaced. "I think it's best if he keeps sleeping. I don't want to do anything that would slow down his healing."

Samora agreed and was glad to hear Brittany felt the same. She bowed deeply, then left the tent, confident Brittany would care for Elian as well as she could.

The position of the sun told Samora she'd slept almost to mid-day, but she'd needed every bit of it. She suspected she'd sleep well tonight, too. She stretched briefly, then walked toward Harald's tent.

He greeted her warmly, then said, "I haven't seen you or your brother all day."

There was no way of explaining what had happened through

her preferred means of communication, so she was forced to speak, telling Harald of their long night.

Harald listened with a growing concern. When Samora finished, he said, "I'd noticed the changes in him, but like you, assumed it was just from everything you two had been through the last few days. I offer you my apologies, I should have noticed."

Samora was grateful for the apology, but assured Harald it wasn't necessary.

Harald didn't look convinced but told her about the summons. "Tiafel has invited a small group of Bears to today's council. I would have preferred if Elian could have joined us, but if you and Brittany agree he needs to rest, I'll defer to your judgment. Shall we?"

Samora nodded, and she and Harald walked together to Tiafel's tent, which was one of the large ones near the center of the camp where they'd feasted the night before. They were welcomed into the tent, where a number of the warriors from the night before sat in a circle around the perimeter. Harald and Samora took some of the last spaces available.

She ran her eyes over the group, but it was Tiafel who attracted most of her attention. He was easily in his sixties, making him one of the oldest people she'd ever known, but he had endured the march of years better than most. His muscles weren't as firm as Samora imagined they'd once been, but they still possessed a wiry strength that made her certain he could walk twenty miles a day without rest. His thinning hair was white, contrasting with his dark eyes that absorbed everything and reflected nothing back.

She was surprised that his first question was about Elian. "Where's the boy?"

Samora prepared herself to explain the entire story again, but Harald was kind enough to speak on her behalf. He gave an accurate retelling of Elian's suffering, and Tiafel listened with interest. When Harald finished, Tiafel said, "He's a unique one, isn't he?"

"I believe so. It's no exaggeration when I claim I saw him jump over half a battlefield to save his sister."

Tiafel turned his gaze toward her. "And though you were the one saved from the circle, you seem to have suffered no ill effects."

"None that I'm aware of," Samora admitted. The question had troubled her as well, but she had no answer.

"Given what we've heard, would you consent to a check from one of my own healers? I want to ensure nothing spoken here today is influenced by shadow. This is a troubling development."

Harald looked like he was about to protest, but Samora believed in the wisdom of the action. "Of course."

Tiafel nodded to the second oldest man in the circle. He was a solidly built man with long hair just starting to turn gray. He rose from his position with one smooth motion, then stepped across the circle and kneeled in front of Samora. After a quick bow of his head, he reached to her face, pressing his thumb to her forehead and his middle finger near her ear. She felt his adani speed through her as quick as thought but as gentle as a feather.

Brittany would want to meet him. His skill far surpassed hers.

He was done in a moment. He removed his hand, offered another quick bow of his head, then returned to his spot. "There is no shadow within her," he announced.

Samora had been reasonably certain, but it was still a relief to hear it from another.

"Thank you," Tiafel said to both of them. "Now, I would hear the stories you've hinted at, Harald."

"Myril has seen the circle and the remains of the Crows, so I have little more to offer there. The rest comes from Samora and her brother, but she doesn't like to speak, so with your permission, I will retell her story as well as I can. She can correct any mistakes I make."

Tiafel glanced between the two of them, then nodded.

Harald began his retelling, and once again Samora was struck by Harald's qualities as a leader. At home, Henk had always been complaining about her. "It's only talking!" he'd insist, and even though Elian did all he could to defend her, Henk's distaste for her silence had made all their interactions contentious.

Harald didn't try to change her, and because of that, earned a loyalty Henk could never imagine.

Unlike the night before, in which interruptions had been more common than silence, the gathered warriors listened intently to every word Harald uttered, all of which were faithful to Samora's experience. She didn't have to correct him once.

When all was done, silence lingered in the tent as the warriors considered the news.

"Are there any questions?" Tiafel asked.

There were a few, but all were of minor matters. No one questioned the validity of Samora's story or Harald's retelling, which surprised Samora. The growing circles seemed so far beyond their normal experiences, she thought there would be more doubt. Myril hadn't arrived until after Samora had explored the circle, so he'd seen none of her exploration or the attack firsthand.

Once the questions came to an end, Tiafel spoke. "I'm afraid your stories match with others we have heard. The Crows are the first clan to fall, but many have experienced attacks of a scale similar to yours. All were turned aside, but in almost every case, the losses were substantial. I'm sorry for the loss of your Bears, Harald."

Harald bowed. "What other stories?"

"They vary in their details, but they always rhyme. More Debru, more monsters, and strange events. This is the first I've heard of the circles, but others have reported monsters in the sky, making eagles look like ants in comparison. Our clans are weaker than they've been in my lifetime."

"You've thought on this, then?" Harald asked. It seemed half an observation, half a question.

"I see no other option but to retreat. The weaker wandering clans can band together, and we can continue the fight."

Harald's hands curled into fists. "There has to be something more we can do. We've done little but surrender ground to the Debru since I became the leader of the Bears. We have the strength to fight. There are youths among the Bears who will someday put to shame any achievement I could claim."

"All the more reason for us to retreat today, to buy the time our youth need to grow into their strength. I understand and share your frustration, but I see no other way."

For a long moment, Samora thought Harald might storm out of the tent, but he visibly mastered himself. His hands relaxed as he took a deep breath. "Speaking of nurturing the strength of our youth, I would ask a favor on Elian's behalf. His strength is unique among the clans, and he seeks a master who can instruct him. Are there any who might suffice?"

Tiafel considered the question for a long time. "If Loken were still alive, he might be able to guide Elian. He has forgotten more about adani than I've ever learned."

Harald frowned. "Loken is dead?"

"Not for certain, but he joined the Hawks several months ago, and we haven't heard from them since the Debru began their most recent push."

Harald's frown deepened, and Samora sensed a deeper change in his attitude. "What happened to the Hawks?"

Tiafel's eyes fell, the first time he hadn't been willing to meet Harald's gaze. "Kati decided to explore further west. She called upon the Serpents to patrol her land, though I don't know how she convinced them. They left maybe three months ago. She didn't send word to anyone. I only found out when word from the Serpents trickled down to me."

The expressions on Harald's face twisted as he wrestled with the news, and once again Samora feared he would leave the tent with the council unfinished. Finally, he mastered himself and asked, "Do you know why?"

Tiafel shook his head. "The Serpent I spoke to didn't know. It's possible their leaders do, but you know Kati better than anyone else. It's just as likely she left without informing a soul."

Harald nodded. "What happened to them?"

Tiafel shrugged. "We don't know, but I assume that they're lost. Her timing couldn't have been worse. The Debru's first strikes happened less than a month after they left. Given the number of Debru we've seen and the losses we've already sustained, I assume the worst."

"The Hawks are strong," Harald argued.

"Without doubt, but so were the Crows, and you were the one who discovered their fate." Tiafel's face fell, and his tone softened. "I can guess at how you must feel, but I beg of you, don't follow Kati to your doom. We need to retreat, and with you supporting me, the other clans will soon see reason."

Every eye in the tent was on Harald, but he didn't notice. His gaze was fixed somewhere far beyond the walls of the tent, and Samora, for one, couldn't guess at the thoughts that raged behind that distant stare.

Harald blinked, then looked around, seeing the attention he'd acquired. He bowed deeply to Tiafel. "I can't yet give you my answer. There is much I must consider, but you'll have my decision by dawn tomorrow."

Tiafel was disappointed, but he accepted Harald's need for more time. "I understand. Relax and consider tonight, and you and I shall speak again in the morning. But may I leave you with one final thought?"

"Of course," Harald said.

"You've heard Samora's story, seen the circles, and walked

among a fallen clan. Our need for strength is great, and we can't waste it on foolish pursuits, no matter our personal feelings. It isn't just the fate of those we care about, it's the fate of us all that's at stake. Please consider that."

The advice made Harald flinch, as though he was being cut, but he nodded and bowed one last time before taking his leave.

12

Elian woke to the sound of a soft conversation being held on the other side of the tent. Normally he was the type to emerge from sleep fully awake and ready for the day, but today sleep clung to him like the hooked burs from some of the burdock back home. No matter how hard he tried to shake it off, he couldn't quite fully emerge from his slumber. He rolled over onto his side, pulled the blankets higher over his shoulders, and prepared to surrender to sleep.

Fragments of the conversation between his sister and another woman caught his attention and pulled him closer to wakefulness.

"Who is she?" Samora asked.

"The leader of the Hawks, and one of the strongest adanists in all the clans, but even more impulsive and less cooperative than Harald," said the other voice.

"But who is she to Harald?"

"I'm not sure anyone besides Warran would know with any certainty, but the rumor is that he and Kati were lovers for a long time."

"But they're not bonded?" Samora asked.

There was a low and soft chuckle from the other voice. "What you believe there depends entirely on who you ask. Some would say they were bonded in secret. Others argue they had some sort of fight that drove them apart. But I think most, including me, would tell you that although they love one another, their sense of duty to the clans prevents them from swearing their oaths. Harald lives to lead the Bears, and she's no different with the Hawks."

The two voices went silent and Elian slipped closer to sleep.

"What will Harald do?" Samora asked.

The voice chuckled again. "Your guess is as good as mine. He might agree to Tiafel's request. The clan is hurting after the Debru attack, and I don't think anyone would complain about surrendering land if it bought us time to cooperate with the other clans."

"Could Tiafel order Harald to do it?"

"He could try, but chances are the clans would all end up fighting one another before long. According to the promises our ancestors made, the size of the clan has no standing in the relationships between leaders. The Hounds may be a much larger clan, but Harald and Tiafel are peers."

Elian wanted nothing more than to go back to sleep, but he couldn't make sense of what he heard. Not only that, but the sun was out, warming the tent and sending bright shafts of sunlight through the tent's open flaps. How long had he been asleep?

For that matter, *why* was he asleep? Sounds from beyond the tent started to worm their way into his ears, and it was clear the camp was up and busy. So why was he here, sleeping?

The question unlocked a flood of memories that rushed through him like a bitter poison. He'd been so angry at everything. He relived them all, hardly believing them, but knowing they were true all the same. His last memory was the longest and most bitter of them all, standing in the tent with Father's knife, about to use it on Samora.

He curled into a ball, wishing the world would open beneath him and swallow him whole.

He couldn't have done those things.

Yet the memories had the sharp edge of truth, and as much as he wanted to deny them, he couldn't. He'd been beyond terrible the past few days, but then what had happened?

The only way to find out would be to talk to Samora, even if he'd rather swallow rocks. He couldn't bring himself to roll over and face her, though. Thankfully, they must have been observing the flow of his adani closely, because they noticed he was awake without him having to announce it.

Samora kneeled beside his bed. "Elian!"

Elian groaned but nodded. Gathering his courage, he rolled over so that Samora wasn't forced to speak more than necessary. He expected judgment, distrust, and anger, but all he found was concern. He couldn't bring himself to meet her gaze for long.

She reached out and grabbed his shoulder, gently forcing him to look at her. There was a question on her face.

"I feel good," he said, ashamed when she sighed with relief. "What happened?"

The other voice, who Elian now saw was Brittany, answered on Samora's behalf. "You've had quite a rough few days. How much do you remember?"

He almost lied and claimed he remembered nothing. That was about how much he wanted to remember, but he couldn't lie to Samora. Even if he had decided to, he didn't think he could slip one past her. She knew him too well.

Still, he didn't know how much either Samora or Brittany knew, and there were some truths he'd prefer to keep to himself. "Everything up until last night. I was standing over Samora's bed, and then there's nothing."

He caught a hint of wariness in Samora's eyes and his heart broke. She'd caught him standing over her, then, knife in hand.

Blood rushed to his cheeks, and he pulled the covers to his chin. What apology could possibly suffice?

Brittany, though, seemed oblivious to the tension lingering between the siblings. She launched into an explanation of all that had happened since he'd passed out, then explained what she and Samora thought had happened to him. When she was done, she gave him some time to let the story sink in.

Elian's stomach churned, but not like it had the past few days. On the one hand, he was glad that his mood and his actions had an explanation outside himself. On the other, it was too easy an excuse to blame the shadow. What he'd thought about doing was beyond any apology.

Layered on top of it all was the awareness that events were slipping beyond what little control he'd convinced himself he had. He felt like a leaf that had fallen on top of a raging river, tossed around by forces far stronger than those he could summon. Mother had taught him to keep better control of his emotions, but he'd failed.

And Samora had needed to save him again, this time from himself. There was much he was uncertain of, but he could tell that whatever she'd done to heal him had been successful. He felt better than he had, even before the shadow had infected him. Only because she'd been there to save him.

It was all too much, and the walls of the tent felt as though they were closing in. He stood and bowed to both the women.

"I'm sorry. I need to go for a walk but thank you for all you did."

Before they could answer he pushed the flap of the tent aside and hurried away. He didn't have a destination in mind, but he didn't want to be bothered either, so he left the camp and wandered around the outskirts, keeping close to where the Bear tents were. It wasn't that he didn't trust the Hounds, but he felt more comfortable near Harald's clan.

He'd only been gone for a while, his thoughts barely cooled, when he saw the giant warrior himself striding toward him. Harald came from the direction of his and Samora's tent, and Elian stopped so it didn't look like he was trying to run away, no matter how much he wanted to.

"Elian! It's good to see you up and on your feet! I heard the story from Brittany. How are you feeling?" Harald's grin was as wide as his face, and his voice boomed so loud Elian felt it in his bones.

Elian didn't want to talk to Harald much more than he had Samora. He remembered all too well their last meeting and wished that it was somehow possible to erase the past. But Harald was all smiles, freely offering him the forgiveness he didn't deserve. "Much better, thank you," Elian murmured.

Harald's sharp gaze saw through his feeble defenses, but he didn't press the matter.

"I've just come from speaking with your sister, and she wants you to know that no decisions have been made, at least by her. I, however, have to talk to you about my plans."

Elian wasn't ready. He needed time to think, to catch up to everything, but the world kept rushing forward. He couldn't tell Harald to wait, certainly not after all the patience Harald had already shown him. "Brittany told me about the council that took place this morning, I'm sorry I wasn't there."

"Never apologize for taking the time to heal and rest. When it's necessary, it's necessary."

Harald started walking, and Elian joined him. It felt good to be on the move, to burn off some of the emotion that kept welling within him. He wondered if Harald felt the same.

"I've decided to take a small group of Bears and travel west to search for the Hawks. I'll be among them. In my absence, Warran will lead the Bears. They'll join, for a while, with the Hounds, and return in the direction of your home. I don't know if we can do anything about the circles, but we'll be there to do all that we can."

Elian was grateful Harald told him the clan's plans but wasn't sure why he bothered. No doubt, everyone would know by nightfall.

"Tiafel believes that an older healer named Loken might be able to help you. I hadn't thought of him because he isn't a warrior, but Tiafel's reasoning is sound. I know of no one better among the clans when it comes to manipulating adani within a body. He's turned it to a different purpose than you have, but he may be the guide you're looking for. Tiafel tells me that the last time he was seen, it was with the Hawks. So, I'll offer you a choice: if you'd like, you're more than welcome to join me. Otherwise, you can remain with the rest of the Bears and return home, a wandering clan behind you."

Harald stopped suddenly, and Elian noticed he was staring off toward the west. "I want you to come with me, because if we can develop your strength, I believe you can be a strong fighter against the Debru. I've never seen one person kill them so easily with a sword, and I think it's a skill worth developing further. But I won't mislead you about the risks. Kati is an incredible leader and a stronger warrior, but I'm not sure what her odds of survival are. There's a very good chance I'm leading a small group to our own deaths, but if there's a chance the Hawks are out there, I mean to bring them back."

Harald looked down at Elian. "So, what will it be?"

Elian started to answer, then stopped. His first instinct was to say "yes." When a warrior like Harald asked for you personally, there was only one answer. But he couldn't ignore Harald's warning, and he longed for the simplicity of home. He thought about how upset he'd gotten at Gabe taking Sara out to the grove behind their village and longed for a return to such petty conflict.

"I'm sorry, that was rude of me to ask so suddenly after you wake. Of course, you'll have to speak with your sister," Harald said.

Elian nodded too enthusiastically. He didn't know the

answers, but if nothing else, talking with Samora would delay the decision.

Harald nodded, then clapped him on the shoulder. "Don't feel like you need to agree because of me. Whatever you decide to do, I'll understand. But let me know by the meal tonight so I can plan."

Harald squeezed Elian's shoulder so tightly Elian thought it might crack, then meandered back to camp, looking like he didn't have a care in the world.

Elian had no idea how he did it.

He didn't turn immediately back to the tent. Life had been challenging enough before Harald's visit, and now it was more so. Better to get his thoughts in some semblance of order before speaking with Samora.

He wandered for a while longer, then returned to the tent, every step heavier than the last. He waited for far too long outside, only jumping inside when some of their neighbors started to shoot him questioning looks.

Samora was inside the tent with her eyes closed, and at first, Elian thought she was sleeping. But as soon as he entered her eyes opened and she sat up.

Harald's question would come soon enough, but for now, there was something more important. He kneeled before her and bowed, pressing his forehead hard against the ground. The tears he'd held back before came freely now. "I'm so sorry."

The suddenness of his apology must have caught her by surprise, because for a long moment, she didn't react. Then she knee-walked over to him, lifted his head from the ground, and embraced him. She held him tight, so hard it was difficult to breathe.

He knelt there, stunned, then hugged her in return.

There were days when he was grateful for his sister's reluctance to speak, because there were times where words simply weren't sufficient, and he never had to worry about her understanding the depths of his feeling. They separated and he wiped the tears from his eyes. "I don't deserve your forgiveness."

She shook her head, but Elian stopped her before she could reassure him. "I understand about the shadow, but you don't understand. It's not as if it created the thoughts. It took my worst thoughts, then consumed me with them. You can say I wouldn't have done what I did if not for the shadow, and you might be right, but it doesn't matter because those were still my thoughts."

Samora watched him for a moment, thoughts churning behind her normally placid eyes. Then she said, "Thoughts don't matter. Actions do. When you had the chance to harm me, you fought back and won."

"I don't deserve your forgiveness."

She shrugged. "Whether you do or not is beside the point. You have it, regardless."

Elian bowed his head, unable to look at his sister. "You're always the strongest, even in this."

She took his hand in her own and squeezed it. He looked up, and he swore he saw admiration, but he must have been mistaken.

He wiped the last of the tears from his eyes. They might not agree on what he deserved, but they had more pressing matters. He didn't believe his apology was over—it had just begun.

"I take it Harald talked to you before he found me?" Elian asked.

Samora nodded.

"I think we should head home with the rest of the Bears," he said. He'd thought it over, and it was the only reasonable decision. He appreciated Harald's kindness in offering him a place with his small group, but joining them was a mistake. Harald and his warriors would move fast, and Elian would only hold them back, and for what - the slim chance he might find someone who could train him to fight?

As he'd walked outside the camp, Elian had realized some-thing. The world had been trying to teach him a lesson for a long time, but he'd been too stubborn to listen. It shouted it whenever Samora was forced to save him, which was becoming almost a daily occurrence.

He was weak, and it was time to accept it.

The truth still hurt, but it was easier to accept the hurt than keep fighting against it. Growing up in his village had made him think that what strength he possessed was something useful, but that was only because he hadn't understood the strength of the wandering clans. Samora fit in better with them than he did, but there was no reason for her to follow Harald. They could return home together, see Mother again, and Elian could do what he could to help, whether that meant working in the fields or hunting for the village.

He was so lost in his own thoughts, it took him a moment to notice Samora was vigorously shaking her head.

"What do you mean? It's obvious that the place I belong is home. The only reason I'm still alive is because you keep saving me."

Samora bit her lower lip and looked away, as though embar-rassed he'd be forced to admit the truth. But saying it out loud made it easier. Bringing the truth to light might hurt, but only because it burned away his delusions. Once they were gone, he'd finally be free.

"You need to go with Harald," she said.

The claim, uttered with such certainty, left him momentarily speechless. His jaw dropped open. "Why?"

She looked away again, and at first Elian thought she was uncomfortable, but when she looked back up, she was as confi-dent as he'd ever seen her. Had she changed so much in the weeks they'd been gone? She looked like their mother.

"These clans need you more than you can guess," she said.

Before he could ask her why, she explained. "When I look

around, I see an incredible variety of powerful warriors, but they're scared. The way we use adani isn't enough to save us, and even if individuals are growing stronger, we're losing too many fighters. One adanist, no matter how strong they are, can't turn away all the Debru. You're different. You're one of the strongest people I know."

"I can't even do a simple—"

She cut him off with a sharp gesture. "I'm not talking about adani. I'm talking about your heart. Your whole life you've wanted to grow stronger to avenge what happened to Father, and despite your inability to bind, you've developed a strength no one understands. You hunt better than most who can bind a spear, you leap into danger for those you love, and you keep pushing forward. That spirit is what the clans need, and you'll lose it if you return home. I can see it in your eyes. You'll settle for something less, and it won't just be you that suffers."

Had the words been uttered by anyone else, Elian wouldn't have believed them. But because they'd come from his sister, who hadn't spoken so much since Father had died, he considered them. Her conception of him seemed so far from reality as to be delusional, but his sister almost always saw to the truth of the matter.

"Is that really how you see me?"

She nodded once, a decisive declaration.

He fell back so he was sitting on his behind. He looked at his sister, then looked around the tent as though his answers had been secretly written upon its walls.

It wasn't reason that changed his opinion. He'd run through his chain of thoughts several times before speaking with Samora, and he wasn't wrong. The reasonable choice was to return home with the clans.

It was how her words made him feel. His soul lit on fire, and he started to daydream what an adventure with Harald might be like. Come to think of it, Harald must view him the same way

Samora did. What Elian had first thought was pity couldn't be. Harald wasn't one prone to pity, and he was too good a leader to invite Elian along if he didn't think Elian could handle the trials of the journey.

In the end, it was as simple as that. Samora's belief unlocked his own, but it came with another bitter truth.

"You'll be going home, then, won't you?"

Samora nodded. "I want to see if we can understand the circles better, and I want to help defend the village if the Debru march toward it. Besides, Brittany is traveling with Harald, leaving the Bears without a healer. I'm happy to help them."

It was the right choice in every way. But it didn't make their pending separation any easier.

Starting tomorrow, Elian would leave his family behind for good.

13

Samora normally welcomed the coming of the new day, but on this particular day she wished the sun would hide behind the horizon for just a while longer. Both the Hounds and the Bears were up early, hoping to be moving by first light. Elian was already with Harald, finishing the preparations for their journey.

Tiafel's tirade against Harald probably still echoed across the plains, but Harald hadn't been disturbed in the least, and in the end, Tiafel conceded to Harald's plan. The older leader hated the loss of even a single strong warrior, but he admitted Harald's plan still left the Hounds stronger than they'd been a few days ago. Warran would remain in command of the Bears as a separate clan, but for all purposes, the Bears had temporarily become a part of the Hounds.

Samora had already packed her tent and supplies into a sled and was helping one of the neighboring families get all their children ready. She kept glancing toward the center of the Bear encampment, where Harald could occasionally be heard booming one order or another. So long as she could hear him, she knew Elian was close. The sky to the east was already starting to lighten, though, so it wouldn't be for long.

She would miss him terribly, and some part of her regretted convincing him to join Harald, but she believed every word she'd said. Most of it was for the reasons she'd mentioned, but there was more to it, too.

Since she'd stopped speaking as often, she'd become convinced there was a deeper order to the flow of adani than anyone else believed. Perhaps even a deeper flow to the order of the world. It wasn't a belief she could articulate clearly, but she held onto it as closely as she did the belief in her family's love.

Right now, she believed it pulled Elian further west. She wished she could point to something solid to defend her belief, something undisputable, but there wasn't. Sometimes, when she let her adani flow around him, it felt as though more of the life-giving strength flowed into him from the west, but the difference, if it existed at all, was so subtle no one else noticed.

Samora's belief was grounded more in a sense of rightness, an extra sense that had become stronger over the past several years. It was that sense that had made her volunteer to leave the village in the first place, and it had guided her in hundreds of smaller decisions before that. She'd come to trust it even if she couldn't explain it.

She didn't think it had ever led her to a more difficult decision than this one.

Questions plagued her thoughts, swarming like grasshoppers during a particularly dry summer. What if she was wrong? What if she'd deluded herself?

The questions weren't new. She'd asked them of herself many times after trusting this new sense that guided her, but the potential consequences had never been more disastrous. If she lost Elian—

She couldn't bring herself to complete the thought.

Samora took heart when she saw Elian weaving his way through the chaos to find her. His steps were fast and sure and the smile on his face came easy. Whatever fears he might have about the future, his posture betrayed his excitement. He'd always been meant for something far beyond the confines of their village. She resolved to hide her doubts from him, to send him off with a smile that matched his own.

"All packed up?" he asked.

She nodded.

"Me, too, though when I look at Harald's pack, I feel like I'm not carrying my weight. I'm pretty sure he could carry the better part of a horse on his back."

Samora grinned at the thought and marveled at the change that had come over her brother. It reminded her that sometimes the difference between giving up and carrying on was as small as a little sisterly nudge. He reminded her of the brother she'd used to know, the one who hadn't burdened himself with so much after Father died.

Their grins faded in unison as they inched toward their farewell. Elian bowed to her. "I could never say 'I'm sorry,' and 'Thank you' enough, but I'm sorry for all I've put you through, and thank you for all you've done for me. Not just this, but always. I'm still not strong enough to protect you and Mother, but when I return, I will be."

She was tempted to argue, as she always was. He focused too much on strength, as though the only measure of a person was how hard they could punch, but she understood all too well why. She hoped that someday he would judge himself differently, but there was nothing she could say or do that would change his opinions today.

Samora loved the confidence in his voice, though. He didn't force her to endure false bravado. He truly believed he would return, stronger than before.

She believed it, too.

"I'll miss you," she said.

His confidence never wavered. He smiled, opened his arms out wide, and stepped forward to embrace her. He wrapped her up tightly and spoke softly into her ear. "I'll miss you, too. I love you. Get home safe and protect Mother."

He stepped back and there were no tears in his eyes. If anything, he looked ready to turn his back to the rising sun and march west.

"I love you, too," she said. "When you get back, we'll see who's stronger."

He chuckled. "Deal."

Harald and the others had already finished their own farewells, and they waited for Elian. He bowed once more toward Samora, then turned to join them.

He never looked back.

SAMORA HAD WATCHED Harald and his small group of hand-chosen warriors leave. They'd set a pace that would have broken her if she'd been forced to maintain it all day, and she was grateful for the much slower pace of the Hounds and the remaining Bears. They didn't even leave their campsite until Harald and the others were over the horizon.

She walked among the Bears for a time, but the ebb and flow of adani around so many people became distracting. She broke away from the column, opting to forge a parallel path a hundred feet to the north.

She'd been so worried about putting on a brave face for Elian, it was only now she realized that he had been the one who'd comforted her. It wasn't that she didn't worry about him, but she no longer had any doubts that their separation had been right. She couldn't guess at Elian's ultimate destination, but his path took him west.

A figure broke away from the long column of Hounds and walked on a path that would intercept her own. The figure was familiar, but Samora had met so many new faces in the past few days it took her a bit to remember who it was.

It was the old healer from Tiafel's tent. The one who'd examined her so efficiently.

Though she wasn't in the mood to speak, she figured she might make an exception for him. She already mourned the loss of Brittany, who'd joined Harald and her brother as the Bears' best healer. The other woman's banter and deep well of knowledge had helped the miles fly by, and she hoped this new healer was no different.

He dipped his head as he neared. "I hoped that you wouldn't mind some company."

Samora smiled and gestured that he should join her, and he fell in beside her.

"I know we've met before, but I didn't have the chance to properly introduce myself. My name is Lenon, and I serve as Tiafel's personal healer."

"Samora."

"If you don't mind me prying, why is it that you walk alone?"

Samora pointed to the long column. "Adani."

Lenon looked as though he'd expected the answer. "You're sensitive to it, aren't you? You sense it, even when you don't try?"

She nodded, impressed with him again. Few understood so quickly.

"There's a great danger to the path you've chosen. Are you aware?"

She narrowed her eyes.

"There are stories of past masters who became so sensitive to the flows of adani they couldn't bear the company of others. At least one took his own life, unwilling to live without the clan."

At her suspicious glare, he dipped his head again. "I don't say this to dissuade you. Your skill should be cultivated. But you should know there is a danger if you follow it too far without caution."

She bowed her head in thanks.

"May I ask you about the circles? Your experiences have me fascinated."

"Harald told my story well. There is little to add."

Lenon wasn't dissuaded. "All he did was tell us briefly about your visions, but he was more concerned about the circle. I want to know about the visions and how they made you feel. I hope there are clues there for us."

She glanced at him. He had an earnest face. "What clues?"

"About the Debru. We've fought them for generations, but we still know next to nothing about them. They've never spoken a word to us, and we've never caught one alive. We don't know where they live or why they keep attacking us. If the rumors circling these recent attacks are true, we know even less than we thought. Your story points to something more, and I'd like to understand it, if I can."

"What do you want to know?"

"To start, would you mind retelling the story? I'd like to hear it from you, if you're willing."

Samora was. Lenon reminded her of Elian. He was observant and thoughtful, and she didn't mind his presence as she did most people's. She nodded and launched into the story. He listened without interruption, and she suspected he remembered every word she uttered.

When she was done, they walked together in silence.

"These feelings and memories, the ones you experienced in the vision - do you trust them?"

"In what way?"

"Do you believe they are or were real?"

Samora had wondered the same question. "It felt as though I was there. I don't know if I was seeing something as it happened or if it was a memory, but I believe it was real."

"Do you think that you were a Debru in the vision?"

"Something else. Something that both feared the Debru and worshipped them."

Lenon thought in silence for some time. When he spoke again, Samora jumped. "Did you know we've never seen a tired Debru?"

She shook her head, both because she'd never heard that, but also because she couldn't follow the conversational leap.

He noticed her confusion, again reminding her of Elian. "I was thinking about if you saw the world as a Debru did in your visions. But you said you were very tired in both visions. It's not conclusive, but I think you're right. You weren't a Debru."

"No one has ever seen them tired?" That was difficult to believe.

"No. When they fight, it's with all their strength. Wounds slow them down, but they never get exhausted. It stands to reason, then, that if you were weary in your vision, you weren't a Debru."

"Why haven't we learned more about them?

"They haven't given us any chance. The farthest west we've ever pushed was before we first clashed with them. Once the fights began, we've only retreated. I've heard legends that in the early days leaders attempted to scout Debru territory, but no one made it far and survived."

Samora's thoughts raced to Elian, and Lenon guessed their direction. "I won't say you shouldn't worry, but if anyone can keep your brother safe, it's Harald."

He moved quickly to his next question. "You said that both times you were in the vision, the world felt cold and dead. Could you describe it better, and do you think the feeling came from the shadow or from the vision?"

Samora gave him a bemused look.

"Sorry to ask so many questions, but I desperately want to understand what's happening. Tiafel and I agree that something needs to change. Humans have been fighting the Debru longer than either of us have been alive, but we're losing, and if we aren't careful, we might lose for good within the next few years. Harald and those like him believe that strength will save us, but I'm skeptical. It hasn't saved us yet, yet knowledge might."

She decided she liked Lenon. He didn't have the gruff, terse demeanor shared by most within the wandering clan, and his pursuit of knowledge resonated with her.

"I'm grateful for them," she reassured him. The question's answer wasn't as easy as many she'd given. "I believe the feeling came from the vision. It's hard to describe, but it felt like one experience. As for how it felt…"

Her voice trailed off as she immersed herself in the memory, seeking the best words that would describe it. Lenon waited patiently.

"Dead."

He raised an eyebrow, inviting her to say more. She gestured to the grasslands they walked through and to the column beside them. "One might say this land is empty, but wild grasses, birds, and more call this land home. Trees grow tall into the sun, and squirrels carry their seeds away. I can hear the children shouting to one another as they race between the sleds. This land teems with life. It's the opposite of everything I felt there. The land was dead, and the people dying."

"And the Debru fleeing," Lenon finished.

She hadn't considered that, but of course that was what had happened. She'd absorbed not just the memories, but the victims' attitudes toward the memories, too, so she'd considered the scene a failed sacrifice.

Lenon's claim convinced her to look at it again, and she saw it for what it was. The Debru were fleeing, leaving those that worshipped them behind.

"Why do you think the shadow so strongly influenced your brother and not you?" Lenon asked.

"Adani shielded me, is my best guess. He struggles to push adani from his body and to shield himself from it. But he has no problem taking it in."

They walked in silence for a while, but it was a friendly one, each of them lost in their own thoughts.

"What ideas do you have about the Debru?" she asked.

"I think they're fleeing something, and that they've now gathered enough space to call our land their home. I think that like the people whose memories you've touched, we're nothing more than an obstacle, or perhaps a means to an end. But maybe, if we can stop any more of them from arriving, we can stop them for good."

Lenon bowed again. "You've given me much to think about, and I'm grateful. I hope we can speak again soon."

She returned the bow and Lenon returned to the column, leaving her alone.

Lenon had tried to leave her with a note of hope, but she'd latched onto something different.

If the Debru were fleeing, what were they running from, and how would the wandering clans stand a chance against it?

14

"Try again," Alec said.

Elian did as he was asked, directing as much adani as he could into his legs. Once he was certain he could push no more, he leaped. His feet reached about as high as Alec's shoulders, but no further. Elian landed gently, having learned to leave some adani flowing through his limbs to reduce the impact.

He shook his head and cursed while Alec scratched at the back of his neck. "You've been practicing?"

"Every day," Elian growled.

"I guess you need to practice more?" Alec offered.

Elian restrained himself from lashing out at the Bear. Alec had been as patient a teacher as he could have asked for, and it wasn't his fault Elian kept failing.

For the first few days of their journey, he'd attacked his training with renewed vigor, inspired both by his recovery and by the journey. He wasn't sure he shared Harald's optimistic view of his strength, but he wouldn't disrespect Harald's invitation by not doing everything he could to grow stronger.

Alec had been a willing partner in the attempt and had given

Elian no shortage of suggestions. Ultimately, though, it had all come to naught, as Elian's jump had just proven. He was no stronger than he'd been a week ago, and he couldn't duplicate any of the feats that had earned him the small amount of fame he'd won in his first battle against the Debru.

Even worse was knowing that all of Harald's group had seen his failure. Elian refused to look in their direction, afraid he'd see them laughing, or worse, taking pity. Alec looked that way, though, and bowed quickly.

Elian cursed under his breath. The last person he needed right now was Harald. If Samora was here, he could have talked to her, but they'd never been farther apart.

"Why don't you join the others for a bit?" Harald asked.

Elian wondered if the giant was talking to him, but Alec bowed quickly and scampered off as though he was being chased.

Harald and Elian walked side by side, because Harald's party only stopped once the sun went down. Elian was no stranger to long distances and longer days, but Harald's pace made even him eager for sleep at night.

"You've been practicing hard with Alec," Harald observed.

"Hasn't mattered much. I'm still worthless."

"I've seen what you're capable of—"

"And that's what's so frustrating!" Elian growled. "I was there, too. I know what I can do, but I can't seem to do it again."

"So, you start by asking yourself what's different," Harald said. He spoke as though he'd already figured out Elian's problem, but he wasn't going to share.

If threatening Harald would have earned anything more than a chuckle, Elian might have tried it, but he was too weak to do much besides tickle the big man. He sighed and thought. The answer was obvious, but it didn't help him. "I was able to use the ability when Samora was in danger."

"What do you think changed between then and now?"

Elian almost snapped that nothing was different, but that was clearly untrue.

"Don't be tempted to think it has something to do with Samora. She's what causes the change, but the change is within you," Harald said.

Elian thought for a while, seeking the answer Harald was leading him toward, but he wasn't sensitive enough to the flow of adani to say what the difference was for sure. Harald walked beside him, as patient a teacher as Alec had been all morning.

Before Elian found his answer, Harald tensed. "Return to the group," he ordered.

Elian frowned, but Harald's tone made it clear he would accept no argument. He ran behind Harald as they returned to the others. Once he was among them, Elian sensed the adani being gathered. He twisted his head left and right but couldn't find whatever had his companions so concerned. "What's wrong?" he asked Alec.

"Otsoa. A large group of them coming at us fast."

Elian's blood went cold. He'd not encountered them since that night, and though he'd sworn revenge on them a hundred times, his commitment fled at Alec's warning.

"What do we do?" he asked.

Alec looked confused by the question. "We kill them."

Of course they did. Before the shame could rise to his cheeks, Harald called his name and beckoned him forward. The group was only six strong, so it wasn't a long walk. "Yes?"

Harald pointed to a spot about three dozen paces ahead of the group. "Give me your sword and take point."

If Elian's blood had been cold before, it froze solid in his veins. "You're—you're joking, right?"

Elian raised his gaze to the giant's face, expecting to see the welcoming smile he'd come to rely on over the past few days. Instead, he saw a hard glare, a side of Harald he'd not seen before. In answer to Elian's question, Harald jabbed his finger in the air.

"I can't take on a pack of otsoa," he argued.

"You'll have to do much more than that before this is done," Harald said.

"But you'll help?"

"Bears!" Harald shouted. "None of you are to lift a finger to help Elian, is that clear?"

A chorus of affirmations answered the order.

"You're going to kill me!" Elian protested.

"You're going to learn to fight." Harald jabbed his finger one more time, and Elian figured he had no choice but to obey. Harald looked like he was about to toss Elian over his shoulder and place him there if he didn't move soon.

Elian handed over his sword and walked to where Harald pointed, feeling more alone than he'd ever felt before. A breeze blew from west to east and he caught the scent of blood. His legs felt weak, and his stomach knotted so tight he feared he'd empty his bowels. He looked behind him, hoping it was all a ruse, but Harald stood still, his arms crossed in front of his chest.

Dark shadows appeared in the distance, and Elian lost what last bit of courage he possessed. The otsoa bounded across the prairie like hungry ghosts, their eyes softly glowing even in the light of day. Elian's legs collapsed and he fell to his knees. He wished he was smaller, so that he might hide from the advance, but he knew their noses would sniff him out no matter what.

Once more, he looked back, expecting Harald to finally take mercy on him. But the man stood, still as a stone.

Elian turned away. Thoughts raced as his eyes darted back and forth.

No place to hide.

No way to run.

The otsoa crested the rise closest him and bore down on him.

He'd never seen them in daylight before, and there was some-thing beautiful in their gait. Here was one of nature's greatest predators.

He was little more than prey.

His despair grew darker and harder, settling like a rock in his stomach. Then his nostrils flared, and like charcoal in a fire pit, the stone in his stomach ignited. He stood before he'd even decided to, fists clenched against the charging otsoa. A glance at Harald confirmed the leader of the Bears still stood motionless.

He snarled at the group.

How could they call themselves warriors if they didn't even protect the weak?

They were pathetic.

Adani raced through his body, twisting and whipping through him like the wind pushed before a spring storm. He pooled an enormous amount in his legs and launched himself at the nearest otsoa. The distance between them dropped to nothing and Elian kicked out with his foot. He connected with the side of the otsoa's head, and it felt no different than if he'd kicked a blade of grass. His foot went straight through, and a moment later the headless otsoa tumbled past him.

The next jumped at him as he landed, and he grabbed, twisted, and threw it at the rest of the Bears. Harald bound a pinprick of adani that hovered over his finger, then snapped the finger at the flying otsoa. The light passed through the otsoa's skull, and it fell, dead, at Harald's feet.

Elian had no time to be impressed by Harald's strength. The rest of the pack was on him, biting and clawing at him as though they hadn't eaten for a week, and he had enough meat on his bones to feed them all. He punched and kicked whenever they got close. Had Master Heinrick been near to judge his form, he would have sighed in resignation as Elian forgot all his training in favor of brute strength.

Against the otsoa, it was enough. Every kick broke bone, and his punches sent them away whimpering. One got its jaw around his right ankle, but he clasped his hands together and brought them down on the otsoa's back, breaking its spine in two. Its jaws spread wide, and Elian kicked the body at another otsoa attempting to sneak around him.

He smashed one to the ground, then spun around to find the next attack.

Only then did he realize he stood alone among a field of dead otsoa. A handful still lived, but not for much longer. They bled into the grass, giving back some portion of all the lives they'd stolen.

He looked at Harald, who had a wide grin on his face. The giant man raised one finger and pointed at Elian.

What was that supposed to mean?

A growl from behind him was his only warning. He twisted, but the adani had fled from his body, and he was so slow. One last otsoa, one leg limp, leaped at his throat.

He was too late in responding. He raised his arms to protect himself, but even that was too slow.

A spear of light blasted over his shoulder and threw the otsoa away.

Elian spun back to see Harald wagging the one finger at him, his grin stretching from ear to ear.

"YOU COULD HAVE TOLD me you would help," Elian complained.

"Do you think it would have worked?" Harald countered.

Elian's exasperated sigh was answer enough.

They'd left the field of otsoa far behind, hurrying even faster than before. Elian didn't understand the rush until Alec explained that the Debru often used the otsoa as scouts. If they hadn't been noticed before, they would be now. Harald wanted to put as much distance between them and the field of battle as he could.

Even as they ran, Harald questioned him. "Now do you understand what the difference is?"

Elian did, but he wasn't sure he knew how to explain it. "When there was no choice, it simply happened. It was less about me making something happen and more about letting it happen to me, to ride it instead of control it."

Harald nodded, clearly pleased. "And the cause?"

"Emotion."

Harald tapped his chest. "Close. It's spirit. Yours soars when your sister is in danger, or when you're pushed to the brink of death, but apparently not before."

"That doesn't seem very useful."

"As it is now, no, it isn't. But spirit can be harnessed. It can be trained."

Harald saw Elian's doubtful look and grinned. "Don't believe me?"

Elian had to admit he didn't.

Harald considered for a moment before answering Elian's doubts. "I suppose it's true there's no way to directly train one's spirit. If we could, our war against the Debru would look different than it does. But the spirit we're born with is not the one we're doomed to die with. It is shaped and molded by our beliefs."

"Even if that's true, how does it help me?"

Harald sighed, making Elian feel like a child unable to learn a very important lesson. He spoke slowly, as though he wanted to ensure Elian heard and understood every word. "The reason your spirit soars when it has is because those are the moments when you've forgotten the beliefs that hold you back."

At Elian's blank look, Harald continued." I don't know exactly why you think you're weak, but you're not. Farmers from the villages don't often seek out the wandering clans, but you joined

Samora, even knowing how dangerous it would be. Even now, when the otsoa attacked, you decided to spend your last moments on your feet, fighting. These are not the actions of a weak man."

Elian stared at his feet. He knew his sister thought the world of him, but she'd love him even if he was a fool. She had often enough before.

Harald's assertion carried a much heavier weight, and Elian wondered if there was more truth to the claim than he thought.

He shook his head. "Father died protecting me, and now Samora risks her life to do the same."

"None of that makes you weak. Even I need friends to pull my tail out of the fire sometimes. None of us survive alone."

Elian understood Harald's argument. Agreed with it, even. Yet somehow, the strength of the argument didn't reach from his mind to his heart. No matter what sweet words anyone used, he'd always needed to be saved.

Harald sensed that he'd said enough. He clapped his enormous hand on Elian's shoulder and gave it a firm squeeze. "The story you tell about yourself is the last thing holding you back from harnessing your adani. If you continue to believe that you're weak, you will be, but if you realize your strength, you might just help save us all."

THE JOURNEY WEST CONFUSED ELIAN. He'd grown up hearing stories of desolation and destruction, but the land farther west seemed much the same as any other he'd walked. If one were to build a few homes here, it wouldn't look much different than home. Perhaps a few more of the Debru's monsters roamed the land, but Harald and his warriors killed all that dared come near.

Elian still tensed whenever a threat approached, but Harald didn't repeat his trial from before. He and the others would bind their weapons of adani and fling them as soon as the offending creatures came in range. If anything, Elian began to take the protection of the others for granted. What dangers could this land hold when he traveled beside such strength?

Then he would remember his home and remember that this strength was in precious short supply. And he would redouble his efforts to break his spirit free from the chains of his beliefs.

Harald had made it sound easy, but Elian soon discovered it was anything but.

Every day after they broke their fast, he wandered away from the group so as to maintain some semblance of privacy. Every day he ran through the long list of techniques Alec had given him, and every day he accomplished no more than he had the day before. This morning was little different.

"I am strong." He pushed adani into his limbs but could tell it was nowhere near what he'd done before.

"I am strong," he repeated, hoping that if he simply said it often enough, he would come to accept it as true. He pulled and pushed more adani into his limbs, but the result was the same.

Who was he kidding? He appreciated Harald and loved Samara for trying to convince him otherwise, but they were blinded by their own kindness. He couldn't even bind a spear. On the battlefield, he was close to worthless.

Except that wasn't true. He had the experience to prove it. He'd killed otsoa with his bare hands. Debru had died from his sword. He took a deep breath and tried to center himself the way Master Heinrich had taught him back in the village.

In the corner of his vision, he saw Harald waving for him to join the rest of the group. If prior experience matched this, it meant the danger approached, most likely an otsoa or something similar.

Normally, Elian would have hurried back at the first sign of trouble. He saw no point in risking his life for a threat so weak the others wouldn't even break a sweat killing it.

He clenched his fists. He'd been wrong about this, just as he'd been wrong about so much else. This was exactly what he should risk his life for, to protect his friends, whether they needed his protection or not.

The fear that normally arose at Harald's gestures never materialized. Elian's heart was encased by a layer of calm confidence. He'd killed Debru, and if he could, he would ensure that no child ever had to lose their father again.

Harald pointed to the western horizon, and Elian saw the three streaks of dark fur bounding toward them in what he now recognized as the otsoa's distinctive run.

Adani bloomed in his chest, and he ran toward the otsoa. Though his strides felt steady and his breath came easy, he covered more ground in less time than ever before. He spared a thought for Gabe, still farming near their home. His one-time nemesis would never catch him again.

He met the otsoa before they were in range of the group's bindings. There were only three, and he moved among them with a calm assurance. In the space of a few heartbeats, all were dead, and he was bounding back to the group. Adani flowed freely between him and the land, and when he met Harald and the others, his smile was almost as wide as the giant's.

He wasn't nearly as strong as he needed to be, but for the first time, it felt like he was truly making progress.

Harald congratulated him with a slap on the back that nearly flung Elian's heart out through his ribcage. Elian coughed as he caught his breath. Alec offered him a quick bow, and even Tera seemed impressed. He joined their loose column as they wandered past, a line of adanists marching forward.

The jubilance of the moment didn't last long, though. They crested the hill the otsoa had just come from and the party came to a standstill.

Elian had never felt further from home than he did at that moment.

No more than a hundred paces ahead, something had sharply divided their world into the living and the dead. Once, the land before them might have been grassland, but nothing grew anymore. Every blade of grass, every plant, and every tree had withered and fallen to the ground.

The land was lifeless for as far as their eyes could see.

15

The Hounds were at rest again, the second time this day. Samora's legs couldn't argue with the relaxed pace, but now that they returned home, she was eager for the journey to end. Tiafel and his Hounds could uncover the secrets of the mysterious circles and coordinate the defense of their land. Samora would help how she could, but with the satisfaction of knowing she'd succeeded in bringing the wandering clans back to defend the village.

She sat in the grass several dozen paces away from the others. If she spent too long among so many powerful adanists her head started to hurt, and now that Brittany was gone there were few people she was interested in talking to. She and Lenon usually spoke once a day, and she appreciated his visits. He'd taught her more about healing in a few short visits than she'd learned from Brittany the entire time they'd been together.

Those visits solidified some of her own ideas. Forming the bindings in the way Rakella wanted had been possible, but unpleasant. It didn't carry the sense of rightness that other choices did. But when she healed with Lenon, that sense was strong. Healing was her path. She was as certain as she was that Elian was supposed to travel west.

The grass here was tall, standing well above her head. Though she could hear the column in the distance, it made her feel as though she was back home, sitting in the fields by herself. When the wind picked up and blew the grasses and her hair around, the sounds of others vanished, as if just for a moment she was truly alone.

Someone blew a horn off to the east, warning the column that they would soon be on the move. The noises from the column increased, and the illusion of solitude was broken for good. Samora didn't rise quite yet. Her pack sat beside her, unopened and ready to sling onto her shoulders when the column finally moved. She only needed a moment or two to be up and walking, so she enjoyed the last of the break as she could.

One thing she'd learned: Hounds didn't move quickly. Or at the very least, they didn't move quickly often.

But they were a large clan, so she understood.

She risked the pain in her head to push out her adani and search the area. She didn't expect to find anything, but it was an old habit and did no harm. As she feared, the pain in her head grew as she sensed the chaotic maelstrom of adani that was the collection of Hounds and Bears. She was grateful so many powerful adanists were accompanying her back to the village, but she thought she'd be even more grateful when she wasn't surrounded by quite so much adani.

She sensed nothing else of interest, though her adani didn't travel as far when she was by the column. It was like trying to look into a dark night when someone held a torch nearby. Everything close was plainly visible, but her senses couldn't penetrate beyond the light of the torch.

She let the adani return to her, but the pain in her head didn't disappear like it had in the past. It grew from a pressure in the back of her head to a pain that wrapped around her skull, as if someone as strong as Harald had tied a rope around her head and squeezed with all his might. She clutched at her head and groaned.

The shouts of children and calls of impatient parents echoed like drums between her ears. The creak of wood and leather scraped the last of her hearing raw, and she would have covered her ears if she wasn't so afraid of letting go of her skull.

What she'd first assumed was because of adani had to be something else. Adani had never done this to her. She rocked back and forth and tried to stand, but her body felt heavy, like Harald sat on top of her. She called out, but her tongue was limp, and her jaw wouldn't move.

When she tried again to stand, her body betrayed her. She pitched forward and could do nothing but curl into a ball. Horses stomped on her head while builders hammered nails behind her eyes. None of the pain she'd experienced before prepared her for this.

She needed help.

Samora let go of her head and tried to crawl, but she couldn't lift the mountains that had settled on her arms. She heard every voice in the column, from the warriors who complained they weren't making better time to the elders who thought the break had been too short. Every voice rang out at once, and though she endured every one of the petty complaints, not one of them stopped to listen for her stifled cries of pain.

Her only comfort was knowing they wouldn't leave her. The Bears had always been kind to her, sharing their food and shelter freely, though such things weren't always easy to come by out here. Someone would notice she was missing, and help would come. Hopefully Lenon could take a look at her and understand what was wrong.

When struggling did nothing but make the pain worse, she ceased her efforts and curled in on herself. It lessened the pain enough to endure it a while longer, though she still lacked the strength to cry out.

Another horn sounded, and this time Samora feared the sound would crack her skull in two, as effective as a sword of adani swung at a Debru. The column lurched forward, picking up momentum like an elderly snake that had just eaten a large meal.

Soon they would come for her.

Soon, now.

She heard every footstep, and every one marched away from her. They were returning home without her.

Soon, though, someone would notice she wasn't with them. They'd ask their neighbor, and the word would spread, and someone would come to check on where she'd been.

But the pounding of the feet grew steadily quieter.

She'd held out a last, desperate hope that their departure would steady the flow of adani, return it to something she could control. That maybe she'd be able to stand and wave for help.

The sharpness of her agony only increased. She tried to push herself to her feet and made it as far as hands and knees before her strength failed her. She collapsed back into the grass, wondering what was happening.

The rearguard approached her next, and one of the mounted warriors would have to see her. She pushed herself up again, but her strength was spent, and she couldn't even sit up.

Samora cried and tried to shout, but her mouth might as well have been stuffed with grass. Even her sobs were choked off, and though the rearguard wandered back and forth, no one rode close enough to see her. Soon, they too were past her, oblivious to the guest of their clan that suffered in silence.

In time, she heard nothing. She'd dreamed of it often these past few days, growing weary of the constant crowd that surrounded her. Now, though, she would have given anything to know she wasn't alone. The wind continued to blow, but now it only reminded her of how empty the grasslands could be.

The pounding in her head refused to fade, even in her stillness. A cold shadow passed overhead, and at first, Samora thought it was a cloud. The pain grew sharper, until she truly believed her head was about to crack open. The shadow passed quickly, and the sun returned. The pounding in her head faded, if only a bit. She rolled onto her back and gasped.

Blackness crawled into the corner of her vision as another band of pressure around her chest joined the one around her head. Breathing became difficult, as if someone heavy was sitting on her.

The shadow passed overhead again, and it was no cloud. Her first guess was bird, but that was clearly wrong. Its wings were long enough to embrace a house, and its tail long enough to knock one down on accident.

The pain reached its apex as the monster passed directly above her. She pushed out her chest with all her strength but couldn't get a breath to enter. The monster circled just to the west of her position, then spread its wings and drifted down.

Toward her.

She cursed as the pain in her skull grew again.

Her headache hadn't just been due to her proximity to the Hounds and Bears. She'd sensed this beast and hadn't realized it.

Ignored and forgotten by an entire clan but spotted from the air by a lone monster. She hoped that wherever he was, Elian had better luck than her. More than that, she hoped he didn't blame himself for her fate. He already carried a heavy enough burden.

As it drew closer, she saw that the monster wasn't alone. A dark figure rode on its powerful neck. A Debru, she was certain, though she'd never seen one that looked quite like it. This one appeared more human than the others she'd encountered. Its glowing eyes left little room for doubt about it's true nature, though.

She soon realized the monster was larger than she'd guessed, which meant it had been flying higher than she thought.

Impressive.

The monster landed with impossible lightness for something so large. It folded its wings up close to its side and the dark figure dismounted.

Not by climbing down, but by floating.

The adani within Samora screamed, but she lacked the focus to perform even the simplest binding. Her vision narrowed further, and her eyelids grew heavy.

The figure raised a hand, and all of Samora's pain disappeared. She gasped for air, taking her first full breath in what felt like days. The darkness receded and she coughed as the cold air hit her lungs. The Debru cocked its head to the side, as if studying an unusual cut of beef.

Samora blinked and tried to focus. She didn't want to fight, but maybe she could frighten it away. She bound one of the globes of light and tightened the weave, shrinking it almost to a point. Then she threw it at the Debru. It wouldn't kill it, but perhaps it would force a retreat.

The Debru swiped with its hand and the light vanished. The binding didn't unravel, it just disappeared, as if it had never existed. Samora gaped, staring at the air where her light had just been.

"What do you want with me?" she asked.

The Debru reached out a hand, which dissolved into advancing shadow. Samora shook her head and bound a dome above her. The shadow crawled over the dome, as though tasting it.

For the moment, she was safe, so she searched for some clue that would doom the Debru. At a glance, there was little about it that was intimidating. It stood no taller than most men, and only appeared a little stronger. It wore a dirty pair of pants but nothing covering its feet or torso. Its feet ended with clawed toes, which spread farther apart than Samora's could.

Beneath the Debru, the grass died, withering away as she

watched. She shivered and realized she could see her breath when she exhaled.

The shadow continued crawling and spreading over her shield, cutting off more of her sight.

If she did nothing, it wouldn't be long before the Debru found a way through and killed her. She didn't want to fight it, but if she didn't, she would soon die. Its power was far greater than hers. It had broken her bindings with little more than a thought.

She needed to catch it by surprise.

She gritted her teeth and wove adani into small bindings of concentrated force. Pinpoints of light danced underneath her shield. She kept them above her, hoping the spreading shadow would block them from the Debru's sight.

When she'd bound all she could, she took a deep breath. The odds of this working were slim, but it was better than waiting passively for death to take her. She brought the bindings down, so that when she let the shield drop, she could launch them from under the creeping shadow.

"Good luck, Elian," she said.

She dropped her shield and launched the bindings in the same moment.

As soon as the shield dropped, the shadow vanished, allowing Samora to watch her bindings catch the Debru by surprise. They hit it in the chest and in the face. One dug into its eye.

The Debru blinked and growled as the bindings spent their strength against it.

None of them so much as broke its skin. Even the one that struck its eye failed to hurt it.

She was tempted to just fall back and let the Debru kill her quickly. There was nothing she could do, not against whatever this was.

The monster behind the Debru roared, and the Debru turned and gestured sharply at it, like a master commanding a dog. The monster roared again, but was otherwise still. The Debru began to turn back to its prey.

Samora stood, an adani dagger in her hand, before the Debru knew the danger it was in. The enemy had left itself completely unguarded, and Master Heinrick had taught her well. All she had to do was thrust. She could see herself jamming the blade in through the Debru's chest, killing it before it killed her.

The vision stole the strength from her arm. She still heard the pained screams of the otsoa she'd lit on fire on that fateful night so long ago. The adani dagger suddenly felt heavy in her hand, and she undid the binding. The dagger vanished.

Her moment of opportunity passed as the Debru turned its attention back to her.

It looked down at her, and though it made no sound, she swore it was laughing at her. As though it witnessed her pacifism and found it more humorous than honorable.

She didn't see its fist move, but she felt it as it lifted her up and sent her flying backward. She hit the ground nearly ten paces away from where she'd been standing, and her ribs felt as if they'd all cracked at once. For the second time that afternoon, breathing became impossible.

At least it was a little warmer the farther away from the monster she was.

The Debru glanced back at the monster it had ridden, which looked as though it strained against invisible bonds. Satisfied, the Debru advanced, in no hurry to end her life. The air froze around her as the grass died at its feet.

It reached out toward her, then looked up suddenly.

She felt the blast a heartbeat before it arrived.

The clear sky crackled with lightning and forked toward the Debru, striking it from four different angles at once. Samora's world went white as she was lifted again into the air, blasted away from the Debru by an incredible outpouring of adani. Dirt and dead grass choked the air, and she cried as she landed on ribs that were now definitely broken.

When the dust cleared, the Debru still stood, but it was staggered. The monster behind it looked unharmed, and it remained still, even as more lightning gathered. A dark cloud of shadow formed around the Debru, racing first around its feet before spinning upward like a small tornado. Freezing wind snapped past Samora, and she pressed herself tight against the ground, her pain forgotten.

The lightning cracked down as before, and when it met the shadow, the world split apart. Something deep in Samora's ears popped and she felt blood trickling down, even as she coughed up more blood.

The assault of lightning didn't stop. It split the air again and again, every blow as powerful as the last. The twisting shadow bent and flexed under the impacts but didn't break.

Then a blazing disc of light flashed overhead, slicing the shadow in half. Lightning struck in the gap left by the disc, and finally the Debru was once again visible.

Its face twisted into a snarl, and it looked far from defeated. It placed its hand against the ground, and all around it the grass started to die.

A wave of warmth washed across Samora's back, but she didn't dare twist to see the source. The sky brightened, and a moment later, dozens of bound spears arced toward the Debru. They shattered before they reached the invader, but the march of dying grass stopped.

The lightning struck again, and this time the Debru was pushed back, clutching at its side. It roared and spread its arms out wide. A hundred shadowy spears appeared overhead, and it flung its arms forward. Samora shivered as they passed her location, but none were aimed her way.

She watched the Debru float back onto the neck of the

monster, which spread its wings and launched itself smoothly into the air.

To her surprise, she felt the creature's adani helping lift it into the sky.

The Debru rode it, but it wasn't like the Debru, or its otsoa servants.

She wished there was something more she could do, some last trick she had to kill the Debru and help her people.

But this fight wasn't hers any longer.

She thought of Elian and Mother and apologized for the grief she knew she would cause.

Then she closed her eyes and prepared to rest.

Except her annoying brother wouldn't let her sleep. Strong hands shook her, forced her back into the world. She tried to grumble, but too much was wrong with her. She opened her eyes, hoping that a glare would send Elian away. It was usually enough.

It wasn't Elian before her. One of the men she recognized, though it took a few moments for the name to come back to her.

Lenon.

She liked Lenon.

He was the one who had his hand on her shoulder, and it was warm. Adani was flowing into her, faster than she'd ever felt.

Beside Lenon was someone else, someone she was sure she'd never seen before. She'd definitely remember the lightning crackling behind her eyes. The stranger was a short woman with long red hair pulled back in a tightly woven braid.

The adani coming off her was beyond belief. Lenon had his other hand around her wrist, and Samora wondered how well they knew each other.

They both looked concerned, though she didn't know why. She was only trying to take a nap.

Lenon's expression eased, and he smiled down at her. "You can rest now. I'll stay by your side."

She wanted to tell him that wasn't necessary, but she was glad. The world seemed dark and cold these days, and he was all warmth and light. But she didn't need to be told twice.

She closed her eyes and slept.

❧ 16 ❧

Harald's group camped that night near the edge of the deadlands. Enough daylight remained that they could have walked on, but Harald unveiled a side of himself Elian hadn't yet seen: that of the cautious leader. Instead of barging in, consequences be damned, Harald sent pairs of scouts both north and south to see if the lands had a boundary. No one was optimistic, but Harald insisted the chance was worth the time spent.

Harald, Brittany, and Elian remained to study the deadlands.

At least, that was what the other two did. Elian's inability to sense the flows of adani meant he was about as useful as a farmer sleeping through harvest.

At the moment, Harald reminded Elian a little of Samora, crouched down with his hand pressed against the dirt. Seeing him mimic her posture sent a pang of longing into his heart. He wished they were together, but at the same time, seeing the endless stretch of deadlands would have broken her heart.

Harald's crouch made Elian think of a predator ready to pounce. He was almost surprised when Harald merely stood and brushed the sandy dirt off his hand. "Adani isn't being pulled," he said.

Brittany agreed. "It's just been drained. I'm not even sure it's possible for adani to flow here ever again."

Her eyes glistened with tears, but Elian wasn't sure why. Dead land was unfortunate, but it couldn't compare to dead humans.

Harald put an enormous hand on her shoulder. "Don't underestimate adani. In time, I believe it will return, and this land will be as rich as it ever was."

Brittany sniffed and nodded. The two watched the deadlands for a moment longer, and then Harald announced he was going to enter. Brittany and Elian protested, but Harald waved away their concerns. "Kati is to the west, so unless the others find a way across, we'll have to walk the deadlands soon. Might as well see if it's dangerous now."

Before they could stop him with objections, Harald advanced into the deadlands.

"Don't you at least want a rope?" Elian asked.

Harald shook his head. His boots crunched against dead grass and sank into the dry, sandy soil. He didn't wander far, and he seemed to suffer no ill effects. He formed a bound spear in his hand, wary of encroaching shadows.

When nothing happened, he nodded as if he'd expected nothing different. Elian didn't relax until Harald's boots bent grass instead of cracking it.

"We'll be mostly limited to the adani in our bodies, but it's not like the circles," Harald said. He gestured for Elian to cross the boundary.

Elian understood that he'd need to walk across the deadlands if he planned on staying with the others, but that didn't make him eager to try. If this failed, he suspected he would be trying to kill Harald within a few nights.

"Brittany will check on you after you return, but I don't think there's anything to fear," Harald said.

Elian exhaled sharply, set his shoulders, and crossed the boundary. The ground felt different under his feet, the dirt loose without a web of roots to hold it tightly together. Besides that, he felt no different than before. He played with adani, and it seemed no easier or more difficult than it had before.

When he'd finished all the tests he could think of, he crossed back over to Harald and Brittany. She checked him and declared him free of the shadow that had tormented him before.

Having learned all they needed, they busied themselves by setting up camp for the evening. That night the two scouting groups both returned and reported what they'd expected: there was no quick way to avoid the deadlands.

Harald wasn't bothered. He declared that come morning, they'd shoulder their packs and cross the deadlands in search of the missing Hawks.

ELIAN GRUMBLED to himself as he hurried to catch up to the others. He carried his pack so that it was against his chest and one of Harald's on his back. The straps dug into his shoulders, he couldn't see his feet over his pack. It was barely midday, and his legs were already burning. The dry, almost sandy soil meant every step was a little harder than it needed to be, and his body begged for a break.

He shouldn't have opened his big mouth.

That morning, he'd asked Harald if there was any way to increase the strength of his spirit. Focusing the adani in his body was useful, but how much more could he accomplish with a larger reserve?

Harald's answering grin still haunted Elian's thoughts. "You want more adani? Then you'll need to get stronger."

Elian had eagerly agreed, thinking Harald had some new practice or technique. Instead, Harald had handed over his pack and told Elian to carry it. When Elian had given him a doubtful stare, Harald had laughed. "Time to get stronger."

Hours later, Elian was cursing to himself. He was already one of the strongest in his village, so why did he need to endure this? And couldn't this have waited for a better time? They walked through deadlands, surrounded by dangers. He needed to conserve his strength, not burn through it.

Harald finally called a stop, and it wasn't a moment too soon. If Elian had carried the dual packs another mile, he would have left Harald's behind and not told anyone.

They found a small collection of decent-sized rocks arranged in a circle, and Elian wondered what story they would tell if they could. Had this once been a camp for the clans, many years ago?

He set the packs down heavily and slumped onto a rock. The top was wide and flat, making it an ideal chair. Harald came by with a waterskin. "Not too much. I don't know when we're going to find good water again."

Elian was tempted to drain the whole skin in protest, but even he wasn't that much of a fool. "When you said I needed to get stronger, I didn't think you meant like this."

That elicited a few smiles from around the circle, which was a rare enough sight these days. Harald's chosen companions were taciturn by nature, but the travels of the last few days had only made them more so.

Harald, Alec, and Brittany were the three Elian knew best. Leland and Gil were brothers who were about as inseparable as two people could be, and the last member of their party was a woman nearly Harald's age named Tera. Leland, the older of the two brothers, said, "One time when we were moving camps, he had me and Gil pull a sled instead of the horses."

Gil jumped in, and it felt as though it were an oft-told story, each of them telling the parts that had been decided long ago. "Might not have been so bad, if he hadn't also insisted on sitting in the sled all morning."

Elian laughed but wasn't sure if the brothers were joking or not. Harald shook his head. "Wasn't even a comfortable ride."

He faced Elian. "It's unpleasant, and it should be, but it's not without reason. The stronger your body is, the more adani it creates. I'll carry my own pack the rest of the day, but tomorrow, when you wake up, I expect you to train. Tell me if you notice any difference."

Elian shook his head. "If getting stronger is what's needed to develop more adani, then I'll carry your pack all day."

"A generous offer, but a foolish one. Breaking down the body is only part of getting stronger. The other is letting it rest and recover. If we were safer, I'd break you until you couldn't move for three days, but I can't allow that here. Your progress will be slower, but you're less likely to end up a corpse."

They finished their quick meal, but before they left, Elian had to satisfy his curiosity. "These stones didn't just appear here."

"We're still well within clan territory. Or at least, land that used to be ours, generations ago," Leland said.

Elian swallowed hard. He knew that the Debru had driven humanity back, but they'd been walking nonstop for days. "This far?"

The others nodded. "How far, do you think, to the edge?" Leland asked Harald.

"Couldn't say for sure. This is the farthest west I've been, too. Several days of travel, at least," Harald said.

They departed on that somber note, and Elian soon decided he was grateful only to be carrying the one pack. Even with only his supplies his legs were exhausted, and by late afternoon he wished for an early end to the evening.

Tera called out a warning and the group huddled close together. She'd been their rearguard, and all eyes turned to her. She pointed east. "Something powerful is coming, and fast."

"Otsoa?" Alec asked.

"Debru. Belog, most likely."

Even Harald's face turned pale at the announcement, and Elian was certain his legs were going to choose that moment to stop working. Belog were the strongest type of Debru that the wandering clans still encountered. Legends spoke of the Vada, whose strength made the Belog look like children, but those hadn't been seen in generations. The Belog were bad enough. Just one posed a significant threat to smaller wandering clans.

Harald and the others looked around. Brittany summed up their predicament well. "About as poor a place to get spotted as possible."

They were in the heart of dead grasslands. Any trees that had grown here had turned to dust and blown away, and even the grass was patchy.

"Dig a hole?" Elian suggested.

Leland shook his head and answered for Harald. "Even if we hid, it would sense our adani. It can probably sense us from wherever it is already."

Harald cursed, then stood straight, a fire in his gaze. "Not much to do but fight, so let's get ready. Spread out wide and keep me in the middle. It'll probably be most interested in me, so see what you can do to wound it while I keep it busy. Don't get close if you can help it."

The others leaped to obey, and Harald focused on Elian. "I want you as far to one side of the line as possible. I'll draw its attention, and the others will do their part as well. But you might be the difference between us living and dying in this fight. No Debru has survived meeting you, so the Belog shouldn't know about you. It won't consider you much of a threat. I don't want you to attack until you see an opening, but once you do, I want you to hit it once as hard as you can, with everything you've got. Then, no matter what happens, get as far away as possible."

"Even if I wound it?"

Harald snorted. "This isn't something against you, but if you even stab it once, it'll be a tremendous success. Even the others won't be much of a distraction, but I'm hoping you'll be just enough of a surprise to give me an opportunity to sneak a killing blow through."

"You've defeated one of these before?"

Harald snorted again. "No, but once I hurt one bad enough, I could run away without dying, and that took everything I had. Now get going."

Elian did, wishing he could sense adani the way the others did. Even now, he didn't have the slightest inkling they were in danger.

He supposed it didn't matter if he chose north or south, so he chose south, in the direction of Alec and Brittany. He passed them both as they set their feet and gazed east. Once he was well past the end of the line he stopped and did the same, watching the horizon for any sign of movement.

He saw nothing, but when he risked a glance at the rest of the party, he saw them preparing their first bindings. What did they sense that he didn't?

Brittany, standing next in line to him, noticed his confusion and pointed up. Elian frowned, then followed the direction of her finger and cursed.

At the moment it was little more than a dot in the sky, but it moved faster than any cloud, and seemed much, much bigger than any bird. *That* was a Belog?

Its tremendous speed gave him little time to wonder. The pinprick of darkness grew, and as it grew, so did his terror. The Debru wasn't just bigger than a bird, it was monstrous, big enough to eat a horse whole.

And it wasn't coming for them. Elian watched as the speeding darkness hurried farther west, passing them well to the north. As it passed, he realized he'd been mistaken before. It wasn't a Debru, but a Debru riding something else. A word came to him, dredged up from a story he'd heard long, long ago.

Dragon.

It flew past them, and Elian wasn't sure if it was just his imagination terrorizing him or not, but he swore the Debru riding on the dragon's back turned to stare at them. Harald's group turned in unison, each following the dragon and its passenger with their eyes.

It never turned to finish them off.

Elian took his first deep breath when it disappeared among some dark storm clouds to the west. Harald signaled the group, and they gathered back together.

"I don't suppose any of you know what just happened?" Harald asked.

No one did.

Harald blew out a long breath. "Well, I'm glad it didn't decide to visit, whatever the reason. Let's get a move on. If we're lucky, we can find a place to take shelter before that storm arrives."

No one asked the question that troubled Elian.

He understood their reason for being out here, but that Debru was strong enough to frighten even Harald, and it had flown west.

Given that, was it wise for them to be following it?

S amora woke slowly, as though sleeping in on a rare rest day back home. Her blankets were warm, and the sun was bright against the tent. She yawned and stretched, only opening her eyes after a few more deep, contented breaths. She felt better than she had in years. The aches and pains that were her daily companions had finally taken their leave.

"I'm surprised you woke so soon," said a familiar voice.

Memory was the last to return, but once it did, it stunned her into silence. She should be dead, not resting in a comfortable bed.

The name of the voice's owner returned with the memories, and once she found her voice again, she said, "Lenon. It's good to hear your voice. Are you the reason I feel so good?"

A soft chuckle came from the other side of the tent. "No one else could have, and had Karla not brought me with her, even my considerable talent wouldn't have been enough. That's the closest I've seen anyone dance with death and live to talk about it in some time."

"I feel wonderful."

"I figured that while I was healing you, I'd fix everything from large to small. Adani is flowing smoothly through you, probably better than even before, considering what you endured."

The bravery she'd felt facing the Debru hadn't come with her into the tent. All she could think was that she was glad she was alive, and she really, really didn't want to die. Tears formed and wet her cheeks, but she made no effort to wipe them away. "Thank you."

A rustle of cloth. "Happy to help, of course. What happened?"

She'd been about to ask him the same question, but since he'd asked first, it was only polite to answer. She told him of the pain that had frozen her in place, followed by the arrival of the Debru on the monster.

"A dragon," Lenon said.

Samora frowned. The name was familiar, but not one she'd heard in many years. "Aren't they legends?"

"Until a day ago," Lenon agreed. "There have been rumors of large creatures in the sky lately, but nothing we could be sure about."

She finished her story, then asked Lenon what had happened since.

"You're right to be upset. The Bears didn't forget about you, exactly. A few claimed they'd noticed your absence, but being as you don't walk with the others, everyone simply assumed you'd gone somewhere they couldn't see you. None was particularly worried, because they all thought you were with someone else. They didn't notice after they left, either, and Warran is about ready to slit his own throat in penance. He swore to Harald he would keep you safe."

Samora didn't think such dramatics were necessary, but Lenon continued before she could say so.

"Truly, you have Karla to thank."

"Red hair?"

Lenon nodded. "That's the one. She's been wandering the area alone, and from the sounds of it, she's been tracking the

Belog that was so interested in you. She was the one that sensed it landing and pulled us into battle. That was when we saw you fighting it. Surprised us all, considering no one even knew you were missing."

Samora's heart skipped a beat. "That was a Belog?"

"In the flesh."

Samora appreciated Lenon's honesty, but the story didn't sit well. She'd been abandoned, and if not for a stroke of luck, would have certainly died. Though she was under so many covers, she still shivered when she thought of the Belog.

She'd heard the stories about the Belog growing up. They were the leaders of the Debru hordes, giants that walked the land nearly unopposed. They were taller, stronger, and meaner than any other Debru. Even the Moka, who led small groups of Debru, were almost nothing in comparison. Only the strongest adanists could stand against a Belog and live to see another sunrise.

"Did it speak to you?" Lenon asked.

Samora shook her head, and Lenon's face fell, but only for a moment. He extended his hand toward her face. "Mind if I check you?"

She shook her head, and he touched her face as he had the first day she'd met him. His adani raced through her body, then returned, and he smiled.

"Fine work, if I do say so myself. I'll leave, because I have strict orders to let Tiafel know when you wake and how you are. Feel free to take some time but be warned that it won't be too much."

At her questioning look, he explained.

"You made a lot of friends yesterday, though you might not know it."

Her confusion made him chuckle. "I'm not sure how it is among the villages, but among the wandering clans, standing up alone against a Belog is uniquely courageous. There are those who might call it foolish, but once I share the details of what you endured, your legend will rival Karla's."

Samora groaned but earned no sympathy from the master healer. "Rest while you can."

With that he stood, bowed deeply toward her, and left her to rest.

HER REST ENDED ALMOST before it began. Warran entered what felt like only a few moments later, bowing and scraping as he did. She shook her head, but it face was pressed too hard to the dirt of her tent to notice.

"I've failed you," he said.

When he finally looked up, she gestured for him to rise. He did, although hesitantly. He looked on the verge of issuing a very long-winded apology when she cut him off with a sharp gesture.

"It's forgiven."

He looked doubtful, but finally acquiesced without complaint. "Tiafel has called a council, and your presence is requested."

Samora wanted nothing more than to return to sleep, but the urge wasn't as strong as it had been before. Although Warran blamed himself, Samora figured there was enough blame to go around. She'd purposefully avoided the others, so when she'd needed them, they hadn't even known.

She didn't want to be surrounded by people day in and day out, but the world had taught her how foolish it was to keep so much distance. She nodded, and Warran was relieved. He backed out of the tent, saying he'd wait until she was ready.

She threw the covers off and quickly stretched. Lenon's healing was remarkable, and it took her a while to simply believe she was whole, that her limbs were all still attached and capable of everything she'd been able to do before the encounter. Of all that she'd witnessed over the past weeks, it was this that left her speechless.

Destruction was simple. Every child with a torch was capable of burning down a house. Most uses of adani were nothing but that childish urge to devastate writ large. As impressive as Harald was, when it came to adani, he was little more than a bigger child with a bigger torch.

Samora shook her head, knowing she wasn't being fair to the giant. He was a caring leader who did everything in his power to keep his people safe. His use of adani might be crude, but it had likely saved more lives than Samora could imagine.

Still, destruction didn't impress her. But to bring back to life that which teetered on the edge of death? Lenon's skill was sublime.

Such were her thoughts when she joined the council. Many of the warriors she recognized from the meetings prior, but it was the new arrival who captured her attention. Tiafel introduced her as a wandering warrior, but Samora already knew her name.

Karla was shorter than Samora remembered, but she'd been lying, broken, on the ground the first time they met. Her fiery eyes matched her vivid hair, but when she looked toward Samora, it was as though she looked through instead of at.

Mother had once told her that those who wielded adani the most were often shaped by it, though Samora had yet to meet anyone who fit the description.

Until now. The unnatural color of Karla's eyes clued Samora in, but that was hardly the most unsettling detail about her. That honor went to her hair, which swayed gently even though there was no breeze. Samora tried to guess Karla's age but failed even at that. Her bearing made her seem ancient, putting Samora in mind of the long-lived elders in her village. But Karla's skin was smoother than her own and seemed to glow when she stared at it.

Samora could have believed Karla was twenty or eighty and would have been unsurprised at any answer in between.

She bowed toward the warrior. "Thank you for saving my life."

Karla shook her head. "I only drove off a Belog. If you're going to thank anyone for saving your life, thank Lenon. Had it been up to me, I would have left you for dead, but the old man was convinced he could save you. Have to hand it to him, though. He's as good as his word."

Samora was grateful she was bowing, so that she didn't have to hide her expression. She bowed a little deeper, then sat upright. Karla's gaze had already moved back to Tiafel.

"Can we get started, now?"

"Please."

"Why are you all heading east, and why are the Hounds joined up with the Bears?"

Tiafel and Warran answered, explaining all that had happened in the last few weeks. Samora ignored their explanation, as she'd lived through most of it. She watched Karla, who seemed unsurprised by everything except for the circles.

When the leaders were finished, Karla said, "You're in for a mountain of trouble unless you turn back today."

The statement landed like a giant boulder in the middle of the council. Tiafel spoke for them all when he asked why.

"There are Belog massing a force larger than any clan, and they are already behind you. In truth, I wouldn't be surprised if they were both to the west and east, ready to crush you the way I might crush a berry between thumb and forefinger."

"How?" Tiafel asked.

"I wasn't sure, either, until I heard your story. You've crossed their path once already."

Samora was slower to understand than the others, but soon she guessed. The Crows had tried to defend the villages and their reward had been death. Harald had wondered what had wiped out an entire clan, but he wasn't here to listen to the answer.

The others in the circle threw half a dozen questions at Karla, but she ignored them as she focused on Tiafel. The clan leader said, "Perhaps it would be best if you told us all that you know."

"I'd just left one of the villages when I came across a pair of Debru using otsoa as scouts. I killed them easily enough, but I was concerned to find them so close to the outer villages. Since I'd heard no word of danger, I tracked them back to their origin, where I found the mass of Debru. I counted about fifty Debru, two of which are Belogs. They don't have as many pets as I'd expect, but still well over a hundred."

Samora's stomach dropped when she heard the count. Numerous as the Hounds were, even with the Bears, they couldn't guarantee a victory in a fight against that many. The presence of the Belogs only pushed the goal farther out of reach.

"Was the Belog we encountered one you counted?" Samora heard a hint of hope in the elder's voice, but it was crushed a moment later.

"No," Karla said.

The council appeared to be on the verge of losing any sense of order, but Tiafel held up a hand. The others quieted. "Do you have any idea what they intend?"

Karla snorted. "I didn't attempt to converse, no. All I can tell you is that when I left, they weren't on the move. They were camped, if you can call standing around doing nothing camping. It felt as though they were waiting for something."

"Or someone," Tiafel added.

"My fear as well," Karla said.

Samora wondered what they meant, then made the connection herself. There was only one entity a Belog would wait for, and that was a Vada. Considering the gulf that separated the Belog from the standard Debru, she didn't want to imagine how much stronger a Vada would be. In legend, each had to be defeated by a clan's worth of humanity's strongest warriors.

As much as she respected the Hounds, she wasn't sure they were up to the task.

She should leave. The wandering clan wouldn't have any place to hide, but alone, she might sneak through and return to Mother. She could sense the Debru before they noticed her, she was almost sure.

But what could she do alone? Even if she snuck through, the only thing waiting on the other side of the Debru lines was a different death.

If all hope was lost, she might consider it. Better to die with loved ones beside you than alone, but hope remained, even if it sputtered and flickered like a candle at the end of its wick.

"What will you do?" Tiafel asked Karla.

"Head west, to see if the Debru gather there as I fear they do. Then I was going to pass the information on to you. Figured you could gather the clans."

"We could use your strength," Tiafel said.

The corner of Karla's lips turned up in a smile. "And if there's a final battle, you can rest assured I'll be there."

Samora expected Tiafel to object, but the elder didn't put up a fight. She ground her teeth together. First, he let Harald leave, and now Karla? Before long they'd be down to half-trained children, every warrior worth their weight wandering the grasslands alone.

Karla turned the question back on the elder. "What will you do? Your position will be known, now."

Tiafel tugged at his beard, but he turned the question loose upon the council. "Thoughts?"

He was deluged with opinions quickly, but they fell into two major camps. One group wanted Tiafel to turn north and find the Wolves. They shared Samora's assessment of their chances and wanted more warriors before attempting to defend the villages.

Others, including Samora, believed Tiafel should attack the Debru immediately. The purpose of the wandering clans was to fight and defend the villages, and any delay might mean the destruction of a village or worse. The battle would be the hardest in a generation, but the risk seemed worth it.

It didn't take long for Samora to understand that her opinion was among the minority. Everyone present agreed they were honor bound to attack the Debru eventually, but there was no point in wasting their lives. The Wolves were another large clan. With their help, they stood a much better chance winning the inevitable battle.

Samora understood the reasoning well enough, and it seemed wise, but she couldn't convince her heart. She'd been to the closest villages and knew the names and faces of people who called them home. Delaying, even for a while, left them defenseless against an overwhelming force.

She didn't speak up, though. It wasn't her place, here among the council, and she doubted her voice would carry much weight. She was here more as a courtesy than anything else.

Tiafel ended the conversation as soon as people began repeating arguments. "Is there anything that hasn't yet been said that needs discussion?" He pointedly looked at Samora, but she looked away.

He waited a moment longer, then said, "Given what I've heard, the wisest course of action is to turn north and seek out the Wolves. Once we do, we'll return to drive the Debru from our land for good."

The decision was supposed to inspire, but Samora was disappointed. Not surprised, though. It had been clear for a bit the way the decision would fall.

The others accepted the decision, and Samora thought that would be the end of the meeting, but Karla surprised her by interrupting. "There is one other thing you should know," she said.

Every eye turned to her, but she stared at Samora, who suddenly wished there was a hole somewhere she could climb into. Karla pointed at her. "I don't know why, but the Belog was interested in her. If you want your movements to remain undetected, you should kick her out of your camp."

❦ 18 ❦

They didn't sight the dragon or the Debru again, but the incoming storm made them just as miserable. A strong wind from the west blew the storm at their faces, and when the rain began, it didn't so much fall as whip straight into Elian's eyes. When it did finally have the decency to land, it soaked into the dry, silty soil, creating a thick, clumpy mud that stuck to Elian's boots with every step.

Harald didn't call a stop, but there was no reason to. There was no place to shelter, and even if they were to all huddle together, all they'd do is sink into the mud as one. Better to keep trudging forward.

If there was one bright light among the dark grey skies, it was that the storm seemed to scatter the occasional otsoa that had troubled them.

There was nothing to do but cover up as much of his face as he could and keep his head down. His footsteps pulled dead grass up by its withered roots, and if he ever rested for too long in one place his foot would sink so far it was hard to remove.

The storm lasted well into the night, and even once it passed, Harald and the others didn't stop. The ground wasn't suitable for resting, so they pushed forward until they found a small rocky rise that wouldn't swallow them as they slept. Elian ate a quick snack of dried meat and sipped at his water, then lay down and went to sleep. The various rocks that poked and prodded his back through his cloak didn't bother him in the least.

The next morning's sunrise was among the most beautiful Elian had ever seen. It cast light pinks and purples against the undersides of the clouds floating peacefully overhead.

He'd woken up before most of the others, but he was in no rush to move. Every shift of his weight reminded him of how rough his sleeping ground had been the night before, and he was content to wrap his arms around his knees and watch the changing colors of the sky.

The ground below was still dead and muddy, but everything above the horizon gave him hope. Beauty existed, even in the midst of death.

The others woke up in their own time, and it wasn't long before they were once again walking through the mud. The going wasn't quite as tough as it had been during the storm, but it wasn't easy. Their previous labors weighed Elian down, too. He didn't think he'd ever gone so far with so little break, but weariness made every limb heavier than it had been before.

At one point in the morning, Harald dropped back and joined Elian. "How are you holding up?"

"Well enough. It's hard to keep up with adani. I'm impressed the others can do it without."

"Do you think they are?"

Harald's simple question almost brought Elian to a standstill. He didn't stop, because he feared getting stuck, but he felt very much a fool. "They're all focusing adani?"

Harald nodded. "It's not as natural for them as it is for you, but yes. It's the only way to survive such long days."

Once his feeling of being a fool had passed, Elian was left once again with the unsettling knowledge that he was the weakest here. Focusing adani within a body was supposed to be the one trait that was his alone.

Harald tore him away from the thoughts that threatened to spiral downward. "Have you kept up with your training?"

Elian nodded. "It works more often than not, though it doesn't come as naturally as I'd like, and I can never hold it for more than a few moments."

"That's a good start. Don't be too hard on yourself. I won't stand here and tell you to take your time, but any level of mastery doesn't come overnight."

Elian was well aware, but he bit his tongue.

Before Harald left to check on the next member of the party, Elian asked a question that had been bothering him for some time. "How are you planning on finding Kati? Tiafel said she'd gone west, and the land is expansive. Now the rain has washed away any tracks that might have helped."

"All true, and if I didn't know the places Kati would check, this would be a hopeless task. But she knows this land as well as anyone still alive, and there are places she'll look first. I plan on reaching the first of these places by this afternoon."

"What kind of places?"

Harald smiled, but it struck Elian as sad. "Places that were once very special to the wandering clans. Places where we gathered and allowed adanists to impress one another."

The sun burned the last, straggling clouds from the sky and dried out the land with impressive rapidity. By the time the sun had reached its midpoint for the day, the land was almost as loose and dry as it had been before.

Elian wasn't sure if he preferred the mud or the loose soil.

Not long after they'd stopped for a brief snack, their journey was interrupted by a corpse.

For the longest time, Elian couldn't believe what he saw. The deadlands stretched for countless miles in every direction, and it looked all the same. There was no reason for them to stumble upon a corpse out here.

And yet they had, and it hadn't been here long. Yesterday's rain had soaked its clothes, and scavengers had already helped themselves to a large part of the flesh and organs within, but there was plenty to learn. Harald squatted beside it, and Elian was surprised he wasn't more distraught.

The corpse was of a woman. Her light brown hair had once reached past her shoulder blades, but now it was tangled and spread around what remained of her head. Her manner of death was easy enough to determine, as at least half her skull had been cut cleanly away.

"Is that Kati?" he whispered to Alec.

His friend shook his head. "Wrong hair."

Harald ran the tip of his finger lightly along the cut edge of the bone. "That's clean. Probably Moka."

"First Belogs, now Moka? What was Kati doing out here?" Brittany asked.

Harald stood. "Unless I miss my guess, we'll have answers soon. We should reach the nearest gathering ground by tomorrow morning."

The giant man stared at the horizon, though Elian couldn't guess what he sought or what he saw. After a moment, he nodded once, sharply. "We'll walk a few more miles, then set up camp early tonight. I want us to be well rested for whatever comes tomorrow."

HARALD WAS BETTER than his word. Not only did they set up camp early, but they also ate more of their supplies than was perhaps reasonable. Elian considered objecting, but his lack of knowledge had him shutting his mouth before he could speak. He didn't know what Harald expected the next day, nor did he know what plans Harald had about their supplies. Game was beyond scarce in the deadlands, and Elian wasn't eager to see if otsoa could be eaten.

Harald didn't seem worried, though, so Elian forced himself to set his questions aside. That became easy as soon as the first bites of food reached his lips. He was hungrier than he realized.

That night, Harald didn't let them take their normal watches. He said he'd spend the night watching them, and the others accepted this without question. "Isn't that backwards? If you're the strongest of us, shouldn't you be the best rested of us?" Elian asked.

"I wouldn't sleep, anyway. Never could, the night before a big fight. Trust me, I'll be fine. I don't need as much sleep as the rest of you."

Elian was hardly convinced, but none of it mattered when he lay down. He was fast asleep before he could form an argument.

The next morning's sunrise came too early. Everyone stretched, readied their packs, then followed Harald west.

As he had the day before, Harald came down the line, speaking briefly with each of them. When he reached Elian he asked, "If it comes to a fight, are you going to be ready?"

Elian tested himself, pushing adani into his limbs. He grunted. Harald had been right. The combination of exertion and rest had done him well. Even without adani flowing through the land, he felt stronger. "I am."

Harald rubbed at his chin. "I'm sorry to press the matter, but I need to be certain. If it comes to a fight, can I count on you, or would it be wiser to leave you near the rear? Just yesterday you were telling me you couldn't focus adani for long."

Elian almost blurted out that of course Harald could trust him, but he wasn't so foolish. Perhaps it would make more sense to have him sit a battle out. He still didn't trust his strength, not when it mattered, and if he failed, if his actions made him a liar, a wrong answer might be the reason some of his friends died.

He couldn't bear that burden, which made the decision easy. Begrudgingly, he changed his mind.

"I suppose it would be wisest if you kept me back. I've gotten better, but I haven't fought with it yet, and I don't want to let you down if you're trusting me."

Harald slowly exhaled his disappointment. "Very well. Keep well behind us as we advance and hold what adani you can. We'll protect you as well as we're able, but depending on what we discover, there might only be so much we can do."

Elian stood straighter. "Don't worry about me."

Harald cleared his throat. "Easier said than done."

He checked with the others and had barely finished when there was a rumbling from the west. Elian's first thought was that another storm had found them, but the day was clear. The sound faded, then washed over them again. It rumbled longer than any thunder, putting Elian more in mind of a dozen drummers all pounding their instruments as loudly and quickly as they could.

"We run," Harald said.

The others spread out in a loose line with Harald at the center. They seized adani, the collective force enough to awe even Elian's dull senses. He gaped as Harald turned back. "Stay well behind!"

Harald ran faster than anyone his size should have been able to. The others kept pace easily, and Elian's jaw almost dropped to the ground. He'd have to focus adani just to stay in sight.

He grinned. Today, finally, that wouldn't be a problem. Adani gathered in his legs, and he sprinted forward. A laugh gathered in his stomach and burst from his lips, his body expressing the joy of such freedom. A dusty wind rushed through his hair. The danger he ran toward was forgotten, at least for the moment.

A louder rumble silenced his laughter.

His pace was faster than his companions, so he slowed and allowed them to draw farther ahead. He listened to the distant thunder, wondering if it would reveal any clues about the battle they were about to join.

The rumbling ended as quickly as it began. Elian strained his ears, expecting the battle to resume at any moment. All he heard was his steady breathing and Harald's heavier footsteps.

After all this travel, were they too late?

The same question must have tormented Harald, because his pace quickened. He pulled ahead of the others. They strained to keep up but couldn't match the strides of his long legs.

Harald crested the rise and was immediately consumed by shadow approaching from the other side.

Elian blinked at the sight. The space where Harald had been was now dark, swirling shadow. Flickers of golden light cracked the shadow for the briefest of moments but were quickly swallowed.

He slowed until he came to a stop. Between him and Harald, the others flung bound adani at the shadows, but it gobbled their attacks with ease. The shadow crashed over the summit of the rise and billowed down the other side. More bound adani followed the first, but it was as useless as trying to stop a wave by throwing pebbles at it.

Elian stood frozen as the shadow threatened his new friends. But what could he do? Even if he gathered all the adani he had in his fist, punching the shadow would do nothing.

He was a fool for thinking he had any part in Harald's expedition.

What adani he had bled away, drained by one fatal cut to his confidence.

Alec and the others formed domes to protect themselves as the shadow swallowed them whole. Perhaps they could fight for a moment or two, but the outcome had already been determined. They'd all known it the moment their attacks did nothing to deter the darkness.

The shadow finished rolling over the top of the rise, and as its tail end dropped down into the depression below, there was no sign of Harald.

Elian swallowed hard, then looked east, the way they'd come. There was no point in him fighting this battle, but he didn't want to die, not here.

He thought of Harald's kindnesses and Samora's insistence he follow Harald west. They were all fools, seeing something in him that simply didn't exist.

He knew, even as he looked east, that there would be no return for him. Assuming he escaped the pursuing shadow, his pack didn't have enough food to support a journey home. Harald had carried most of that burden, and he was gone.

Elian snorted.

He supposed, at the very least, that it made his decision an easy one. There wasn't much point worrying about death when it was a certainty.

He faced the advancing shadow and shouted in defiance. Adani filled his limbs, and he drew his sword and prepared to fight whatever Debru hid within the darkness.

19

S amora sat on the side of a hill and watched the Hounds and the Bears wander away. She'd broken her fast with them this morning, huddled around the cookfire in the way she'd become accustomed to. There hadn't been much conversation, the weight of their impending parting silencing the Bears as though they'd just lost adanists in a fierce battle.

On any other day Samora would have welcomed the silence. She detested the impulse to talk and fill the air with meaningless chatter. Words and language were too valuable to be spent on trivial matters.

Today she missed the conversations almost as fiercely as she missed Elian. She wanted to shout at them, to scream that she wasn't dead, that this was a parting and nothing more. But her own words stuck in her throat, like they couldn't get past the thick stew that served as their breakfast. She sat in silence, as she always did, and wished they would speak.

Then the meal was over, and they finished packing. There were bows and sad smiles, but not a single embrace. Warran promised that once they found the Wolves, they would return to the villages with a vengeance.

After a time, she wandered away, the prolonged parting painful and needless. She wasn't sure where to go. Yesterday, when Karla had announced the Belog was following her, she'd agreed to part ways for the clans' safety, but didn't know where she would travel. A full night of worrying about the problem had left her as confused and hopeless as when she'd gone to bed.

For now, she settled for hiding in the grass, this time willingly, as the Hounds and the Bears left her behind.

She hadn't expected it to hurt so much. She'd only known the Bears for a couple of weeks, and the Hounds less than that. Yet watching them leave was worse than when she'd left home.

Of course, that had been a choice she'd willingly made.

It was more than that, though. She'd felt a kinship with the wandering clans, a sense of belonging she'd never truly felt outside the walls of her home in the village.

She sensed Karla before she saw the woman, but she was surprised how close Karla had gotten before adani sensed her. Karla appeared a moment later and stood beside her. "What are you going to do now?"

Samora shrugged. Today wasn't Karla's fault, but it felt good to assign the blame to her anyway.

She only had one answer, indistinct as it might be. "I want to learn how to heal like Lenon."

"You're stronger than him, by far," Karla said.

"Then perhaps one day, I'll be a better healer, too."

"Girl, you stood your ground against a Belog. The world doesn't need another healer. It needs someone who will protect the villages from those monsters, and you could be that person."

"But I never will be. It's my brother that wants to wander with a sword in hand, not me."

Karla stood in silence for a moment, then shrugged. She said, "Come with me."

Samora rose to her feet and brushed herself off. She had about as much desire to go with Karla as she did to watch grass grow, but it seemed as good a choice as she could make today. If she went home, she'd only endanger her neighbors and her family. She gave Karla a single sharp nod, which was apparently all the answer Karla needed.

Karla led them north, walking a few paces ahead of Samora. She walked quickly, but no more so than Elian, and Samora had long been used to keeping up with her brother. They passed the morning in silence. Samora didn't care where they were going, and Karla was perfectly comfortable with the peace and quiet. She didn't so much as glance back at Samora the entire morning.

They ate lunch on their feet and continued north until the sun kissed the horizon. From the moment Karla had invited her along until the moment they stopped to set up camp, neither had said a single word to the other. It was, Samora decided, one of the most comforting days of travel she'd ever experienced.

She hadn't minded the slower pace of the Hounds and the Bears, but she realized now her time with Elian had prepared her for more strenuous days. She couldn't guess how many miles they'd traveled, but she felt pleasantly exhausted. It was good to be out, walking as far and as fast as her feet could carry her.

She was surprised to hear her sentiments echoed out loud by Karla. The adanist said, "I've lived a long time, girl, and I don't know if I've ever had the pleasure of a more pleasant traveling companion."

Samora agreed.

Karla snorted. "You get a small fire going, and I'll gather some meat. Be back soon."

Without waiting for an acknowledgement, she disappeared into a nearby grove of trees. Samora watched her go, then set about the task of building a small fire. She sensed Karla's adani in the woods, and by the time she had the fire started, Karla had returned with a pair of rabbits.

Karla skinned them both with an expert hand while Samora tended the fire.

"You have some questions," she observed.

Samora gestured to the fire, the rabbits, and herself. "Why? If the Belog are searching for me, you'd be safer anywhere else."

The corner of Karla's mouth turned up in something that almost might have been a hint of a smile. "Most people would have asked where we were going."

Samora shrugged.

Karla said, "If I was anywhere else, I wouldn't know why the Belog are so interested in you."

"And that's worth risking your life over?"

"When you've seen as many years as I have, the idea one must hold on to one's life at all costs loses a lot of its appeal," she said.

"Well, then, where are we going?"

Karla grinned briefly. "To a place where we might find the answer to our question."

Samora arched an eyebrow, unsatisfied with the vague answer.

"There are places in the world where adani gathers. Places where we might find an answer. If nothing else, it'll be the best place in the world to fight a Belog, if it decides to continue its pursuit."

Samora had a dozen more questions, but she sensed Karla tired of their short conversation. She bowed her head. "I can keep first watch, if you'd like."

Karla shook her head. "There's no need. I can sense anything dangerous that gets within a mile, even in my sleep. No reason for either of us to stay up."

From someone weaker, Samora wouldn't have believed the claim, but Karla was stronger than any adanist she'd met before. She didn't think even Harald compared. Besides, she had little reason to lie. If she'd wanted Samora dead, she'd just had an entire day to kill her.

Samora also wasn't about to argue against a full night of sleep. She nodded, and after the meal was finished, she fell asleep, enjoying a quiet night of rest for the first time in weeks.

THE NEXT MORNING Karla was surprisingly conversational. They broke their fast silently, but before they'd walked too far, she started asking Samora questions about her childhood. Samora answered them all but felt as though her answers were disappointing her new companion.

The only stories that piqued her interest were when she learned that Father had been one of the Spiders, and that he'd been killed during the battle many years ago. She seemed particularly interested in when it had happened. Several questions later, she seemed satisfied by Samora's explanation. Samora asked her why she was so interested.

"Unless I'm missing something, it was the same attack that wiped out the Spiders that took your father's life," Karla answered.

"Does that mean something?"

Karla grunted. "Maybe, but maybe not. The Spiders were the wandering clan tasked with guarding your village, so it could be a simple explanation. They're the ones that got run over by the Debru, and one made it all the way to your village. But there might be something more I'm not seeing."

"What clan do you belong to?" Samora asked.

"None."

She didn't elaborate, leaving Samora confused. "I didn't think that was possible."

"You're not part of any clan," Karla observed.

"But I'm from a village."

"You don't know where I'm from."

"Are you from a village?"

Karla's half-smile returned. "No."

"Then you were at least once part of a wandering clan. So why aren't you now?"

"I became tired of watching friends die and grew weary of the burdens of leadership. No matter how foolishly I behaved in battle, death never claimed my spirit, but I didn't want to live any longer among my clan, and so I left."

"You led a clan, and you left, just like that?"

"No. It was a hard process, but one that was necessary for both me and the clan."

That was all she said on the matter, and the rest of the morning passed in silence. Around noon, they encountered two scouts on horseback. Karla waved as they approached.

To Samora she said, "Don't say anything unless they speak to you."

As usual, she didn't explain, but Samora didn't care. The less she had to speak the better.

The riders pulled up short, and the one in the lead scowled when he saw who it was. "Karla, what are you doing here?"

"Nice to see you, too, Aldrick. I came to pass along a warning, among other things."

The rider lacked the courtesy to dismount. "What warning?"

"The Crows have been overrun, and there are Debru between us and the outer villages, accompanied by at least two Belog. The Hounds and the Bears have joined forces, and they'll be seeking you out next. War is on the horizon."

Aldrick scoffed at first, but his stare turned hard as Karla continued. "You're serious?"

Karla's silence was answer enough.

Aldrick didn't debate for long. "Aldo will want to speak with you. Who is your companion?"

"My new apprentice, and no, I won't be speaking with Aldo. At least not right away. I have other matters to attend to."

Aldrick gathered his adani, but Samora assumed it was more an instinctive reaction than a threat. What could he do against someone as strong as Karla? Fortunately, he didn't try anything foolish with it. "You know I speak with Aldo's voice. You're already fortunate you aren't banished from our lands for good, but this is too much."

"I don't care, boy. If Aldo wants to talk, I'll be taking my new apprentice to the gathering grounds."

"You aren't allowed there! Only Wolves can walk that sacred ground."

Karla answered with a defiant glare that Aldrick squirmed beneath. Samora almost felt sorry for the scout. If he'd been more polite, she would have. As it was, she enjoyed watching him seek a way to make Karla obey him. "If I tell Aldo about this, it's likely he marches the Wolves on you."

Karla shook her head. "Ah, he's probably still bitter from my last visit, so you might have the right of it. He's welcome to bring the Wolves to visit, though hopefully by the time he arrives, we'll have found the answers we seek and be on our way. I would pass along one more warning, though, which might change his decision."

"What?" Aldrick demanded.

Karla tilted her head back toward Samora. "My apprentice, here, made an enemy of a Belog, and so now it and its friends are pursuing us. Aldo might not want to get too close until we've taken care of that."

Samora didn't think she'd ever seen a face turn so many different shades due to anger before. Aldrick sputtered and spit, but ultimately, there was nothing he could do. "You're mad! You can't take her to the gathering grounds if she's being hunted!"

"I can and will, and it might just give us the key to pushing the Belog back for once. So, unless you have something useful to add, you should ride off and let us return to our walk. It was much more pleasant before you arrived."

Aldrick sputtered some more, but eventually turned his horse around.

"Oh, and don't forget to encourage Aldo to aid the Hounds and the Bears! They'll need all the help they can get."

Aldrick growled and kicked his horse into motion. Samora watched them go. "Why is Aldo already mad at you?"

"I broke his son's heart."

Samora frowned. "Aren't you—"

She wasn't rude enough to finish the question, but Karla understood it well enough. "Oh, yes, I'm old enough to be his great-grandparent, but I know how young I look to those who can't see past the surface of things. I might have enticed him a bit, too."

Karla chuckled when she saw Samora's expression. "Distasteful, dear?"

Samora shook her head. "The world is a much stranger place than I imagined."

Karla laughed out loud at that, the first time Samora had heard the sound. It was a deep belly laugh, and it made Samora like the woman instantly. "You don't know how true that is, but you're in for a treat tomorrow. Just you wait and see."

***

THE REST of their travels were completed largely in the silence that defined their relationship. Samora kept looking around, expecting Aldrick to come riding over the horizon with the entire clan of Wolves at his back. But either Karla's strength or the implied threat of the Belog was enough to keep the clan well away. No matter how far she extended adani, she couldn't sense another human besides Karla.

It was on one of these searches that she discovered the gathering grounds. Her first brush against them raised her spirits, because it felt almost exactly like Elian.

It was too good to be true, and another push of her adani revealed as much. Like Elian, the gathering grounds pulled adani, but the scale of it was almost beyond comprehension. She and

Karla kept walking closer, which allowed Samora to grasp the distance that still lay between her and her destination.

It was miles away, but it still pulled and pushed adani in jaw-dropping amounts. Her eyes must have gone wide, because her expression elicited one of Karla's half-grins. "You can sense it, can't you?"

Samora nodded.

"I'm impressed. It's nothing more than a slight press against my own senses. You're sensitive."

Though it was daytime, and the sun was bright, Samora swore she could actually see the lines of adani. She feared Debru and pointed it out, but Karla reassured her. "That's the gathering grounds. Have no fear."

It was easier said than done, but Samora followed.

After another mile of walking, the gathering grounds came into view.

Karla didn't have to say anything. There was nothing else they could be.

Samora stood, her mouth wide. Never in her lifetime would she have imagined such a place could exist.

Karla laughed. "Welcome to the gathering grounds of the Wolves," she said.

20

Something shifted in Elian as the shadow raced up the hill toward him. Any shadow that could swallow Harald whole would do the same to him. What would happen wasn't in question, so all that remained was how he would meet his end.

That was an easy question to answer. He'd answered it facing the otsoa earlier in their journey, and he'd answered it when the Debru attacked the Bears what felt like a lifetime ago.

He would meet it standing and smiling, just like his father.

Elian pushed adani into his arms and legs and took a stance that would make Master Heinrick proud. Frigid air surrounded him as the approaching darkness pulled both heat and light within its hungry maw.

Light crackled across the surface of the billowing cloud, like lightning that wouldn't stop. Darkness swarmed against the light and fought to contain it.

The shadow failed. The light grew from cracks into chasms. The cloud expanded rapidly, as though by growing it could once again absorb the light. Smoky tendrils reached Elian, but retreated when he met them with the edge of his sword.

Against threats both within and without, the shadow finally

burst. Separate clouds retreated until they revealed the five Debru responsible for the advance. Three looked like the Debru Elian had been fighting for weeks, but the other two stood a head taller and possessed shoulders as broad as Harald's. These weren't average Debru, but Moka.

He'd only seen one once before. The night his Father died. These were the monsters that had reached his village that fateful night. He'd recognize the red eyes and long limbs anywhere, for the whole span of his days.

Elian had heard of Moka, but he'd never been sure, until this very moment, it was a Moka that had killed Father. They were Debru, too, but were slightly larger and commanded the smaller, more common Debru. At least, that was the best guess of those who fought against them. Without any language that the clans could understand, there was no telling with any certainty. But when an adanist killed one, any Debru in the area lost their coordination.

That explained why the shadow had come so close to overwhelming Harald. A single Moka was stronger than the average Debru, and two of them combined were a considerable force. Maybe not as strong as a Belog, but more than enough to overpower almost any single adanist.

Yet Harald still stood, though the clan's leader wobbled on his feet, exhausted from the effort of breaking the Debru's assault. The other warriors, who'd merely hidden under their domes, looked to be in better condition. They kept their defenses up as they studied the battlefield.

Both Moka turned on Harald while the Debru spread among the others. They ignored Elian for the moment, but it wouldn't be long before he was the only one remaining.

He wouldn't let the Debru reach his friends. He wasn't strong enough to fight against the Moka alone, but if he could help the others, perhaps they had the strength to rid this area of the plague of Debru.

Elian charged down the hill with his sword raised. The closest Debru was twenty paces away and about to stab at Alec's dome with a sword shrouded in shadow. Elian leaped early and prepared to cut through the Debru.

Unlike the one he'd surprised while it attacked Samora, this one sensed him coming. It flicked its sword, threatening to cut Elian in half as he flew past. Stuck in the air, there was nothing Elian could think to do but block the swing.

Their swords met with incredible power. His hands went numb when the sword hit, and it took all his strength to avoid being cut with his own sword, but he blocked the cut successfully. The force of the blow sent him skidding and bouncing through the tall grass for a few paces, but when he came to a stop and looked down, he was remarkably unharmed. He shook out his hand as he stood.

The Debru was looking at him, and though its expression was shadowed by its hood, its head was cocked to the side, as though confused by what it saw.

Alec took advantage of the distraction to stab a bound spear at the Debru's head. It tilted away from the blow so that Alec's attack only grazed it.

The Debru swiped its sword at Elian. The masked blade cut through the grass with a whisper, and although he scrambled away before it killed him, the sword left a shallow gash across his chest.

The Debru dashed at him, leading the way with its blade. Elian parried the first cut, but soon discovered the true challenge of fighting the Debru. The shadow around their blades was harmless by itself, but it embraced and hid the blade, throwing off Elian's timing. It was fast, too, the shadow shifting and crawling around the blade, making prediction of the blade's position nearly impossible.

Fortunately, Alec struck again, this time aiming his spear for the Debru's torso. It spun and shifted to avoid the blow, and

Elian took advantage of the opening. The sudden movement caught the Debru's attention, and it chose to focus on Elian.

Alec's next stab came a moment later, severing the Debru's spine. It shook for a moment, then went still.

Elian turned away before it finished its death throes. Brittany and Leland had lost ground against the Debru that assailed them, but Alec would join them soon. Tera and Gil were moments away from killing their Debru. But neither of those battles would determine today's outcome. Life and death would be decided by their defeat of the Moka.

Before he could see the lack of wisdom in his choice, Elian ran to fight them. Harald maintained a bound shield which was almost as large as the domes that had protected the others from the shadows. Each of the Moka carried a sword, cloaked in shadow, that was probably almost as long as Elian was tall.

Such was their strength that they wielded the enormous weapons like knives. They slammed the weapons down upon Harald's protection, battering him with relentless determination.

Harald was already on his knees. Sweat beaded his brow and his teeth were gritted. Elian had never seen the giant warrior look so small. His dome held but wouldn't for much longer.

Elian shoved more adani into his legs. He covered the distance between him and the Moka in a heartbeat.

The Moka closest to him turned its head at his approach. Without losing its rhythm against Harald, a second bound sword appeared in its other hand.

Elian swore it was longer than the first.

The Moka snapped the blade at him.

Elian leaped over the blade and cut at the Moka's face. The Moka shifted, but the sword still scored a cut across the Moka's shoulder. It wasn't nearly enough to kill the creature, but it caught the Moka's attention.

He scrambled back when the Moka turned to face him. Its eyes burned red, the color bleeding into the dark swords. Its assault forced him to jump back like a hare chased by a wolf. The Moka attacked primarily with its longer sword, and whenever Elian thought he had an opening, it blocked his approach with the shorter sword.

He needed a longer weapon to reach the Moka.

Elian gave up ground quickly, but he couldn't escape the Moka's advance. He saw the blow coming, but there was no escaping the tremendous reach of the long blade. Instinct pulled adani into his arms as he attempted to block the enormous weapon.

The blow launched him a dozen feet across the grasslands. He didn't know how the Moka hadn't just cut through his blade, but beyond the numbness in his hands, he was unharmed. He pushed himself to his feet, and the Moka gave him a look similar to the one the now-dead Debru had given him a few moments ago.

Elian grunted. Adani rushed through his limbs. He was tired of getting hit around. He advanced steadily on the Moka. It cut at him again, but Elian blocked the attack. The Moka's big sword was terrifying, but Elian tracked it easier than the shorter one.

He grinned viciously. When he took another step, the Moka retreated.

From him.

He grunted and shoved more adani in his legs before he leaped at the Moka, swinging his sword with all the strength he could muster. His sword cut into the Moka's long sword, causing it to unravel and disappear.

The one that remained grew darker, pulling in all nearby light. Elian found it hard to look at, but the Moka made no attempt to disguise its intent. It raised the blade high above its head for a killing blow.

Elian didn't flinch. Adani flowed through him easily. The amount wasn't even that much, but it seemed enough. He brought his sword up at an angle, and the attack slid down his blade and away.

Still, the force of the impact drove his feet down into the soft soil until they were covered, but he stood, whole, against the Moka's full strength. He squared his shoulders, then unleashed a flurry of cuts that would have had Master Heinrick rolling his eyes to the heavens.

Elian relied on no technique and no greater strategy than to make his enemy suffer. He cut at anything his sword could reach. Not every cut landed, but those that did were deeper than mere scratches. The Moka fought as though it was unharmed, but its face twisted in agony.

He couldn't kill it, though. He was too slow, the Moka always just fast enough to avoid anything lethal.

At least until bound weapons attacked it from every side. Spears bounced off its arms and back, leaving it open to even more reckless blows from Elian's blade.

Then Tera joined the fight, her strength as great as all Harald's other warriors combined. Even Elian felt her bind the spear behind him. She threw it as he landed a cut, the spear passing just over his head and taking the Moka in the chest. The pressure of its passing made it difficult to breathe, but the spear jutting through the Moka's back was well worth the challenge.

The spear faded a moment later, leaving a gaping hole in the Moka's chest. Its blood, black as night, poured down its chest, but Elian didn't relent. He cut at the monster until it fell against his onslaught.

His arms were heavy and sweat burned in his eyes, but this was no time to rest. Where was the other one?

He looked up and around, but no Debru still fought. Harald was on his back, staring up at the sky, and he hardly looked like a man who had just beaten a Moka on his own.

Elian found the reason a moment later. A dark shadow rolled north, smaller than before.

"You let it get away?" he shouted.

He regretted the outburst as soon as it passed his lips, but it was too late to take it back. Harald's eyes traveled lazily to him, and the force of his gaze was enough to force Elian to study his feet carefully.

For a long time, they stood there, forced to inhale the smells of the dead Debru. Elian understood they were waiting for Harald, but he didn't understand why Harald just lay there. From what he could see, the giant didn't have a scratch on him.

Finally, Harald came to his feet, wobbling as he did. He shuffled over to Elian and forced the younger warrior to look up. "The fact we're alive at all is remarkable, and we owe that, in large part, to you."

The others shuffled behind Elian, as though something Harald said had upset them, but no one spoke out against their leader.

And why should they? Elian had saved them all.

Harald looked like he might say more, but he bit back the words. Instead, he said. "Come. They'll be close now, and I fear what we'll find."

THEIR PACE WASN'T NEARLY AS FAST as it had been before the battle, and it was Harald that held them back. No one spoke out loud about Harald's sudden weakness, and Tera took the responsibility for leading them. She scouted ahead, though she never left their sight for long.

Elian's emotions took time to settle, and he recognized the influence of adani over his thoughts. As it settled into its normal paths through his body, his own temper cooled.

Alec caught up to him. "How are you?"

Elian was scraped and bruised all over, but that was all. He made a show of glancing them over, though he knew all the cuts had already stopped bleeding. He'd always healed quickly, but this time even faster than usual. "Feeling better than I rightfully should, I think."

Something in his answer seemed to put Alec at ease. "You were upset the last Moka escaped."

Elian grimaced. "I was, but it's hard to say what was my own frustration and what was from my adani."

Alec's questioning glance made him explain. "When I use a lot of adani, I notice my emotions often get the best of me. I feel sorry for what I said."

"Are you?" Alec asked.

"What?" How could Alec disbelieve his apology?

Alec shrugged. "I think we've all felt a little of what you're describing. Adani doesn't just strengthen our muscles. It's a powerful force, but it doesn't make us liars."

"What do you mean?"

"It doesn't make you feel anything that wasn't there before. If I'm sad, adani will make it worse. If I'm angry, I'll become furious. You *were* angry that we didn't pursue that Moka."

Elian almost argued, but when he looked back at those moments, he still felt the flickers of frustration. "You might be right. After we'd defeated the first Moka together, I was sure we could kill the other."

Alec nodded. "And you might be right, but now it's beside the point. I'm telling you that you don't need to apologize for your anger. Adani flows stronger when we embrace all that we are."

"Even if I'm frustrated with Harald?"

"Even then, though I think you do him an injustice."

"Why?"

"You weren't in the shadow, so you don't know how strong it was. But it was formed with the combined strength of the three Debru and two Moka. It was all any of us could do to simply keep adani over our heads. That Harald broke that, by himself, is remarkable, and also the reason why he's on the verge of death."

Elian's head snapped around. "He's *what*?"

Alec's face fell, then his eyes widened. "I forget you can barely sense adani. He gave everything he had to free us from that shadow. He shouldn't even be standing now, but he won't stop until he's found the Hawks."

Elian glanced at Harald, who still shuffled forward, his gaze fixed on the western horizon. He swore. "I didn't know."

Alec clapped him on the shoulder. "Now you do, so what are you going to do about it?"

Elian dipped his head deeply to his friend. "Thank you for letting me know."

Alec smiled, then fell back.

Elian walked a little faster and soon caught up to Harald. At the leader's current pace, it wasn't much of a task. "I owe you an apology. I didn't know how much you gave to help the others."

Harald gave him that familiar smile. "Alec talked to you, didn't he?"

"He did."

"Good. I appreciate the apology, but there's little need. There's nothing to apologize for."

"I thought you were being lazy."

That elicited a hint of a grin. "I wish I had been." They walked a few paces in silence, then Harald said, "I'm never sure if your ignorance is your greatest weakness or your greatest strength. There's no doubt it will be something you'll need to be aware of, but at the same time, you haven't grown up in the wandering clans, so you haven't become a victim of the stories we tell."

Elian was confused, and Harald saw as much.

"Our children grow up learning to fear the Moka. Only the strongest of our warriors can fight them, and even then, the odds of success are low. Had they had the opportunity today, everyone here would have run, and they'd be doing no more than we've taught them. You see the world with fresh eyes. I've thought about earlier today, and I'm certain that if you and Tera had pursued, you would have had a better than even chance of winning. Perhaps, in the fights to come, such an attitude is what we need."

Harald's explanation left Elian divided. He was grateful the clan leader thought so much of him, but the idea the Bears should look to him for anything was the height of foolishness. Harald saw the opportunity for change in Elian's ignorance, but he only saw the weaknesses it left him with.

Up ahead, Tera had come to a stop, and was waving to someone out of sight. Harald saw, and almost collapsed. Brittany appeared at his side as though she'd been summoned. "Can't rest yet, but almost."

She took some of his weight, and Elian followed her lead on the other side.

"They're alive," Harald said.

Brittany had her eyes glued to the horizon. "Looks that way. Your faith in Kati wasn't misplaced."

"She's never let me down. She's never let anyone down."

Elian looked up and saw the smile on Harald's face. The expression wasn't the same as it usually was. It would never be accompanied by a jovial laugh or a contented chuckle. This expression reached deeper into the heart than those.

Elian could only remember seeing something similar once before, and that was the smile his father had given Mother after coming home from the fields.

Harald stumbled, but Elian and Brittany kept him upright. They reached Tera and stopped, not exhausted but disbelieving. It had to be a dream, but there was too much dust in his nose and too much weight on his shoulder for that to be true.

A valley stretched out before them, filled with trees that stretched to the sky. Off in the distance Elian could see the afternoon sun reflected off the light of a river. Large birds that weren't scavengers circled above the trees, and Elian could just make out movement within the trees.

His eyes watered, and he blamed the dust that swirled around them.

Two riders rode from the trees toward them, and Harald lifted his arm from Elian's shoulders to wave. He swore the big man was about to cry himself.

Elian took one more glance at Harald. The man's easy smile and ready laugh made it seem like he strode through the world without a care, but Elian no longer believed it.

The riders returned Harald's wave, and Harald stood up tall, his posture making it clear he didn't require their help. Pride would carry him the rest of the way.

He gestured to the woods. "Welcome to the ancient gathering grounds of the Hawks."

Samora knew her mouth hung open, but what else could she do? She couldn't remember a single story about gathering grounds, so she'd had no idea what to expect. Had Karla asked her to imagine it this morning, she wouldn't have come close.

The land ahead was an impossible green. It reminded Samora of the first new grasses that grew after the winter snows melted away, soaking the ground with the frozen water that had been locked within during the short days. It reminded her, but the comparison didn't go far enough in describing the strength of the life that flew through these lands.

At the center of the verdant green was a small lake, less than a mile across at its widest point. The vibrant blue of the water was blended with green, creating the illusion that the wild grasses and lake had somehow blended together.

The land amazed her, but it didn't pull her attention the way the lights did. From a distance, it looked as though a swarm of fireflies danced in the air, thousands of lights that dimmed and brightened but never flickered out. They weren't fireflies, as it was day and their movement wasn't quite right, but Samora couldn't guess their true identity.

When she pushed adani toward the land it returned stronger and brighter, but with little information she understood.

"What is this place?" she whispered.

Karla looked as though she was tempted to repeat what Samora already knew, that this was the gathering ground of the Wolves, but she didn't insult her with that answer. "It's special. There are places across the land where adani gathers. Our ancestors found them long ago, and they've always been sacred places for the wandering clans."

"Why haven't I heard of them before now?"

"I don't think any of the villages are near one. This one is the furthest east we know about, and we've lost many to the Debru. These aren't places we tell stories about. These are places we keep close to our hearts. It's one of the reasons why the Wolves don't want us here. If the Belog is following you, it puts this place in danger."

"So why bring me here?"

"Because it is one of the only places where I might be able to figure out why the Belog has such an interest in you. But it's also one of the only places I can protect you. With so much adani, we are stronger here, so the Debru will be cautious."

Karla walked toward the gathering ground and Samora followed. She noticed, as she drew closer, that the edges of the gathering ground were marked nearly as clearly as the Debru circle she and Elian had discovered. She told Karla as much, adding, "Except this place gives life while those take it away."

"All the more reason to figure out what is happening before it's too late," Karla said.

Karla entered the boundary without pausing, but Samora hesitated. She stuck her hand over the line and felt it tingle. Shaking her head at her own foolishness, she stepped into the Wolves' most sacred space.

Its effects hit the moment her first step touched the grass. Adani rushed into her body, filling her with light and strength. It wasn't as overwhelming as she'd imagined. She held up her hand and stared at it.

Elian had always struggled with his emotions when the adani filled him, but she didn't feel any different than before.

"Do you think this is how my brother feels?" she asked.

"Probably," Karla said.

She frowned. For a moment, it had felt as though she'd finally be closer to her brother, closer to understanding what he endured when adani flooded his limbs. Instead, she found herself confused and further away.

Her disappointment couldn't hold her attention for long. Not in this place. They came close to a cluster of the floating lights and Samora paused to study them. Up close, it was clear each point of light was a well of floating adani, untethered to the world. She thought at first that it might have been some form of natural binding, but when she probed with her adani, she found she was wrong.

The free-floating adani wasn't bound. It was more like it had become randomly knotted. The adani felt like a single web of spider's silk, floating through the air. At times it ran into other threads, and they would run into another. Before long, enough had gathered to release the pinprick of light. She held her palm under one and felt the gentlest warmth brush against her skin.

On impulse, she closed her hand around the light. It entered her body and joined the natural flow of adani.

"If you want to study it, you'll have to come back on your own time. We came here for a purpose," Karla said, pointing to a tree on the other side of the lake.

Samora nodded and followed Karla around the lake. The ground was soft underfoot, but not wet like she would have expected.

Despite Karla's brusque nature, she didn't walk as quickly as she usually did. They kept moving, but Samora had time enough to observe most of what she was interested in.

The healing effect of the gathering ground went deeper than flesh and bone. Samora's weariness fell from her, as though she was a snake shedding its skin. Her spirit felt truly at ease for the first time since Father had died. It wasn't that the grief she'd carried for so long was covered up.

It was more like there was a new, soft voice in the back of her mind telling her that she was fine. That the world was fine, even if it didn't seem that way.

The tree was unlike any near their village. A tall maple tree standing alone, towering high enough Samora couldn't guess its age. All she knew was that it had been old when all the elders she knew had been young. Despite its age, the limbs looked healthy, and though it was almost the season for the leaves to start to turn, this one held onto each of its green leaves as though they were precious children.

The force of adani overwhelmed her. She attempted to extend her adani toward the tree, but it was buffeted back into her body like a leaf suddenly caught in a gale.

"The heart of these lands," Karla said, and even her voice had a hint of awe in it.

Karla reached out and brushed her hand against the tree. "Doesn't matter how much I've seen or done. Whenever I'm here, it's as though all is right with the world."

Samora wasn't sure if Karla wanted company, but the older woman hadn't told her not to touch the tree, so she gently rested the tips of her fingers against its bark. Like the knotted adani earlier, it was warm to the touch.

"I agree," she said.

Karla's head snapped around sharply. "Are you just saying that?"

Samora shook her head and ignored Karla's hard look.

"Explain," Karla demanded.

Samora bit her lower lip. She'd never explained her stranger theories about adani to anyone but Elian and Mother.

But if anyone was in a position to judge her claims, it was Karla. She had a grasp of adani even Harald would be envious of.

"Once I started listening more and talking less, I started to feel something subtle in my interactions with adani. It's not quite a pattern or an order - both words imply more than what I feel, but it's a direction, maybe."

She kept expecting Karla to interrupt and call her a fool, but the woman listened intently, so she continued.

"To me, it feels like a subtle, but still clear, sense of rightness and wrongness. It's the sense that encouraged me to send Elian west, even though I fear it is to his death. Here, it's different than I've ever felt before. It's clearer, and it tells me that everything is as it should be."

Karla didn't speak for some time, but she didn't seem angry. When she finally spoke, it was a far kinder tone than she normally took. "I didn't think there was anyone else who felt it."

"You, too?" Samora asked.

Karla nodded.

She shook herself out of her reverie, then gestured for Samora to sit in a patch of grass beneath the tree. Karla sat down across from her. "There's nothing you need to do for now. Please don't fight as I do this. It will feel odd, but I assure you that you'll be in no danger."

Karla's vague reassurances had the opposite effect than she desired, but Samora stilled her pounding heart and closed her eyes.

They shot open a moment later as she felt Karla's adani mixing with her own. It felt as though a foreign intruder invaded her mind and body, but without the intent to harm. Her body's natural reaction was to push back. With the ample adani flowing through her body, it would have been easy to overwhelm Karla and throw her out.

Samora evened out the flow of her adani and forced it to

ignore the intruder, even as it felt like Karla's adani was emptying her from the inside out.

When it was done, Samora knew she'd have no secrets, but it was of no matter. She had nothing meaningful she wished to hide.

As her adani settled, she listened and noted that the flow of adani went both ways.

She was open to Karla, but the older adanist's history was just as plain to see. She didn't pry, but she took in the enormous span of Karla's years at a glance.

Karla had admitted she was old, but Samora hadn't even come close to guessing how ancient she was. She'd wandered when there was no distinction between the wandering clans and the villages, before anyone had thought to till a field and raise food, tame cows, and feed everyone. She'd been a young warrior when the first outer villages were established.

She'd enjoyed a long string of partners, but none who'd mastered adani in the ways she had.

Samora didn't know how much time had passed, but eventually Karla's adani all returned, and Samora's did the same. Once the connection was broken, she was only herself, sitting beside an ancient maple tree that had appeared in no small number of Karla's memories.

The two sat in silence for a long while, but Samora burned with questions about what she had seen. Only Karla's stern expression kept her from launching them one after the other.

Finally, Karla leaned back, resting on her elbows and looking into the sky. Night had come while they were in the trance, but the gathering grounds were alive with dancing adani, lighting their surroundings almost as if it was day.

"No one's ever done that to me, either," she said. She didn't sound entirely pleased.

Samora wasn't too apologetic. If she was going to open herself up to Karla's study of her past, it was only fair she take a glance at the elder's history.

"The bigger problem, at least for now, is that I have no idea what the Belog want with you. You're as sensitive an adanist as I've ever come across, and with proper training, you could even surpass me. But the Belog have never been interested in me, no matter how strong I've become, so I'm not sure why you should be different."

Though Karla was frustrated, her findings only confirmed what Samora had thought. There was nothing special about her that justified the attention she received. She was grateful Karla thought so highly of her abilities, but right now, she was next to nothing.

Karla thought on it for a moment, then said, "I'm going to sleep on the problem. Maybe something will occur to me. You don't need to keep watch, but don't wander beyond the boundaries of the gathering grounds."

The thought hadn't even occurred to her, but she nodded her agreement and Karla wandered off, soon disappearing into the tall grass on the north side of the lake.

Samora continued to sit with her back against the tree. The sky was clear, revealing countless stars that seemed to dance beside the pinpricks of adani. It was more beautiful than anything she'd seen in a long time, and her gaze lost focus as she took it all in. She wouldn't dare build a house here, but she had no problem imagining living here for the rest of her life. She'd never felt better than she had at that moment.

How much better would the world be, if she could make it all like this?

She smiled at the thought.

More by habit than by design, she pushed a small amount of adani out to examine her surroundings. After last time, she assumed it would all rush back to her, so she wasn't prepared to have it shot like an arrow, far, far away.

Most of it snapped back to her and she blinked.

What was that?

It had been too sudden, too surprising, for her to catch. She pressed her palms against the ground to her sides, then closed her eyes and extended her adani. As before, it shot away, but now that she was ready, it filled her senses with a view of the world beyond her sight.

Adani had always enriched her world. Its insights helped the farmers from the villages raise more crops and healed the cuts, scrapes, and bruises that were an unavoidable part of life. Tonight it widened her perspective further. She sensed the glowing strength of the gathering ground easily, but she found a gathering of humans not far beyond that.

The Wolves, she assumed.

Her adani didn't stop expanding. She found villages and fields, then a patch of shifting darkness that had to be the Debru. Beyond that gathered force, her village, with Mother sleeping peacefully.

Samora would recognize Mother's pattern of adani anywhere. Tonight it flowed peacefully, and she imagined Mother enjoying sweet dreams.

She pushed further. Elian was west, and his adani was so unique there should be no place he could hide. Tears trickled out through closed eyelids when she found him. Danger surrounded him on all sides, but he was well, and Harald remained at his side, though greatly weakened. They were close to another gathering ground.

The sound of someone hurrying through the grass brought her back to herself. She opened her eyes and saw Karla racing toward her. "What did you do?"

Samora explained, and Karla gradually settled. "A fool thing, pushing out that much adani. You might as well light a signal fire, if you want the Belog to find you faster."

Samora shrugged. It was worth it to know Elian and Mother

were alive and well. "There are no Belogs nearby, though it doesn't make the danger we face any less. The Debru gather to the east and west and seek to crush us between them."

Karla's eyes narrowed. "You can sense their intent?"

"No, but they are pinching us between their forces. Whatever their intent, the result is the same."

Karla stroked her chin and gazed thoughtfully at Samora. "This information could be useful, though I don't know how we'd communicate it in time."

"Is this why the Belogs hunt me?"

Karla considered for a moment. "It's possible, but unlikely."

"Why?"

"Because I don't see how us knowing where they are truly hurts them. At best, it seems like a minor annoyance."

Samora wanted to argue the point, but after what she'd just sensed, she better understood. Knowing the exact position of the Debru mattered little. The shadows she'd sensed had a strength that dwarfed entire clans. She was glad Tiafel sought an alliance with the Wolves instead of charging in on his own. They would need the help in the battle to come.

Karla groaned and shook her head. "I'll think better after a full night of rest. You should do the same. Tomorrow we can look more deeply into what you can do."

She put enough force into the last line that Samora decided it was best to listen. She found a comfortable spot to lay and fell asleep with the stars and adani twirling overhead.

THE NEXT MORNING, she awoke to Karla in her face. Judging from the color of the sky, the sun would soon be peeking over the horizon. "Get up," Karla said.

Samora rubbed her eyes and did. Though she hadn't slept that long, she felt more refreshed than normal. If Karla needed her to run all day, she thought she'd be ready.

"We're going back to the tree. I want to see more of what you're capable of."

Samora shrugged and nodded, then followed Karla back to the old maple. The idea of exploring her abilities more deeply appealed to her, too. She sat down quickly, closed her eyes, and placed her hands on the ground. She waited for Karla's instruction.

"How much detail can you sense?" Karla asked.

Samora sent out her adani, reveling in the vast world that opened before her. She roamed far and wide, seeking out whatever might be most useful.

"There are over fifty Debru between us and the villages, but only two Belogs."

Samora frowned as she sensed a faint line of shadow running from the deadlands to the west, near the gathering grounds, to the shadow to the east. "I think I've found some of their tracks nearby."

Karla had her drop from the trance. "How far away?"

"Only a few miles."

"Show me."

Samora did, sad the moment they left the protection of the gathering ground. She still felt better than she had in many years, but she felt the adani flowing slowly from her, gradually returning to the normal balance she was more used to.

"It's rough, leaving, isn't it?" Karla asked.

Samora nodded. "Why don't people just live there?"

"It's too much adani for too long. It poisons most people, unless they have the training and will to endure it."

The miles passed quickly, and soon Samora could feel the tracks of the Debru with her adani. They reached it soon after. Though she'd expected the trail, it was still surprising to see in person. A path, maybe a dozen paces across, cut across the land like an open wound. The grass within was dry, withered, and dead, as if this meandering trail had experienced years of severe drought.

Karla was impressed. "If you can track their movements this closely, we might be able to ambush them, or pick them off in small groups. It's not much, but it's more than we've been able to do so far."

Samora heard but wasn't paying much attention. She'd pressed her hand to the ground and was sending a trickle of adani through it. The path reminded her of the circles, in that everything within was dead, but it didn't feel the same. Her adani traveled more easily here, and though the routes it took were withered and wounded, the paths still existed.

It wasn't that different than how she sensed adani flowing through a wounded body.

"How does this happen?" she asked.

"Debru pull adani from the land as they pass through. We've never understood what they do with it, because their shadows aren't made of adani. Our best guess is that they feed on it, somehow."

Samora wondered.

The adani channels that ran through the soil were no less complex than those that ran through the body, but she was confident she could sense them all. She pushed her adani into the soil as she would a wounded adanist, careful not to send too much into the shriveled ways.

Karla said something, but Samora's focus was too complete. She felt the healing effects of the adani. The roots of the grass caught it like a net, and after some gentle nudging, it regained the barest hint of life.

Starting was the most difficult part. Once she began, the effect cascaded. Healing the grass closest to her made healing the grass further away easier. She couldn't heal all the damage the passing of the Debru had caused, but when she pulled her hand from the ground, a space of about four paces in every direction had recovered.

It was a pittance compared to what had been lost, but Samora felt more satisfied by this small patch of living wild grass than she had the Debru corpses she'd left behind in their last battle.

Destruction was easy. Bringing life was not.

Karla had gone silent, and Samora wondered if she was waiting for a reply. But when she glanced back and up at her newest guide, she saw that Karla's eyes had grown wider.

"What did you just do?" Karla asked, as though the answer wasn't right there in her face.

Before Samora could answer, she was almost knocked over by a sudden wave of pressure against her adani.

Karla swore.

The last time Samora had felt that type of pressure was when she had fought the Belog. At the edges of her perception, she sensed the shadow shift and turn its attention toward them.

Karla pulled Samora up. "We need to run. I think you just discovered why the Belog are interested in you."

22

The Hawk scouts knew Harald by sight, and looked relieved to find him here, even if they were more than a bit confused as to why. Harald was about to launch into the story when one of the scouts shook his head. "It's best we return quickly to the cover of the gathering grounds. Then you can tell your story once to us all."

The last mile passed in the blink of an eye, and soon Elian found himself looking up at the largest trees he'd ever seen.

The scouts rode ahead without hesitation, but Elian wasn't so eager. He noticed the sharp edge of the deadlands and couldn't help but think of the circles. How could it be that life could bloom with such intensity a step away, but fail to find purchase in the dirt under his feet?

"What is this place?" he asked Alec.

His friend's answer was terse. "Someplace safe. For now, that's all you need to know. I'll explain better once we're safely inside and we've had a chance to rest."

Alec's curt dismissal came as something of a surprise, but when Elian looked to the others, he saw Alec's attitude reflected across all their faces. The others shuffled in without him. Tera, who had watched their rear since the battle, paused beside him. "Forgive them. It's easier to stand tall when the road ahead is long. The last miles are always the roughest on weary souls."

"Even on yours?"

Tera offered him half a smile. "Once you've been on as many journeys as I have, one begins to blend into the other. They see only the end of one difficult journey. I'm already looking ahead to the next."

With that, she followed the others in, leaving Elian alone outside the boundary. He shook his head. His caution was needless. No one who accompanied Harald would harm him intentionally. He stepped across the boundary, and though he'd barely moved, he knew immediately that he'd stepped onto a new world.

Adani rushed through his feet and into his core. He gasped at the sudden flow. He first thought it was just him getting used to living land again, but soon decided it was far more than that. Adani gathered here, not unlike how he pooled adani in a part of his body to strengthen it.

Elian squatted down, smiling as he thought of Samora and how she'd always done the same to get closer to adani. He pressed his hand into the rich soil. He couldn't push adani out and sense at a distance like his sister could, but he could feel it rush up his arm and join the extra adani swirling in his core.

His legs felt strong, and the weariness from the long days on the road fell away. He pooled adani in his legs and leaped, bounding halfway up the nearest tree with a single move. He grabbed a limb with his left hand and hung, feeling like a bird looking down on the world. A breeze rustled the limbs of the tree, carrying with it the scents of roasting meat.

Elian dropped down, landing easily.

He felt reborn.

The effect wasn't just limited to him, either. Alec, Brittany, and the others all looked refreshed. The most marked difference was in Harald, who now stood tall with that customary grin plastered on his face. Elian joined the others, his step light and his mood much improved. He'd happily cross the deadlands again, if this was his reward.

His delight dimmed as he followed the scouts and the other Bears into a large clearing. The Hawks were gathered within a circle of protective trees, but they didn't look like they'd be ready to fly anytime soon.

Harald had once told him that the Hawks had never been a large clan, but they still claimed over two hundred powerful warriors. A glance around the clearing only revealed half that number, and a fair number of those were grievously injured. A heavy silence hung over the clearing, only interrupted by the soft conversations of healers with their patients and the groans and cries of the injured.

Harald's grin vanished from his face. His eyes darted left and right through the clearing, then settled on a tall, thin woman with blond hair and blue eyes. He ran toward her, ignoring the stares he attracted from across the clearing. He fell to his knees before her, and though Elian couldn't hear the whispered exchange, the depth of emotion both revealed made Elian turn away.

"Kati?" he asked Alec.

His friend nodded.

Tera took charge while Harald was otherwise occupied. She spoke with one of the scouts that had guided them in, then found a place for the Bears to lay their gear. The scouts began their walk back to the edge of the gathering ground to continue their patrol. The Bears were just getting settled when Harald and Kati joined them. They were holding hands.

Kati struck Elian as a walking mystery. At a glance, she didn't seem much older than Elian, but her eyes reminded Elian of Mother's eyes after Father had died. And Elian didn't think the clans welcomed leaders so young. Years of experience were too valuable.

The pair sat among the new arrivals and Harald spoke for both of them. "The situation is dire. As you can see, the Hawks have suffered tremendous casualties, and they haven't gotten farther west than these gathering grounds."

Kati continued, stepping in so smoothly they might as well have spoken with one voice. "I had hoped that by coming out here we could finally learn more about this silent enemy that continues to drive us back. Unfortunately, every step of our journey has been challenged, and I consider it an achievement to have made it this far. Now we are surrounded, and it seems we've angered the Debru."

Elian's stomach tightened into a knot he feared would never come undone. He'd listened to Harald boast for weeks about the strength of the Hawks, but now they were broken and surrounded by the enemy, and for what?

Nothing at all.

He clamped his jaw tight. It had been foolish for Kati to risk her Hawks in such a desperate bid, and now they all paid the price. Humanity couldn't afford to waste warriors, not for no gain. They might have been the leaders of the clans, but they were fools all the same.

Harald continued the talk, and he sounded as though this was nothing more than what he'd expected. "We'll rest here for a few days. The rumbling we heard was a battle between one of their scouting groups and the Moka who wander this area. The scouts were able to escape back to the safety of the gathering ground, but the rope is growing tighter around all our necks. Once we're as rested and healed as we can be, we'll cross the deadlands and return home."

Elian screwed his fist into the ground but said nothing.

No one voiced any objections. Harald and Kati stood and wandered away from the clearing, still hand in hand. Elian watched them leave, but just before they escaped his sight, he stood to follow them.

They couldn't have come all this way to turn around. They'd been fortunate to survive the Moka attack, and it had to mean more than this. What about the Belog they'd seen flying west on the dragon?

There had to be more.

He hadn't made it more than a few steps when a cautioning hand gripped his shoulder. Elian spun, expecting to find Alec, but it was Tera.

"Nothing wrong about wanting to argue with Harald, but you interrupt him right now and you'll be lucky to escape in one piece," she said.

Elian craned his neck to watch Harald and Kati disappear into the woods. He had his arms around her shoulders and leaned in close.

He forced himself to swallow his frustration, though it burned like a bitter pill down his throat.

"Let's go for a walk," Tera suggested, "but maybe in a different direction."

Elian agreed. If nothing else, a walk would burn off some small amount of his anger.

"How long have they been lovers?" he asked.

"Since before you were born."

"Why aren't they bonded?"

"Both are too bound by their sense of duty. Kati is the strongest leader the Hawks have had in generations, and without Harald, the Bears would have fallen long ago."

"Couldn't the clans come together?"

Tera nodded. "They could, but then there would be one less wandering clan protecting the villages, and all of us are stretched thin as we are."

"It doesn't seem right," Elian decided.

Tera shrugged. "They've made their choices, so who are we to say whether they are right or wrong? No one has forced them to do anything." She paused. "Though I don't think you were so upset because you discovered Harald has a lover."

That brought a smile to Elian's face. He hadn't even been aware that Tera understood humor. "No. It doesn't seem right that we would risk so much only to turn around with so little reward."

"If we push much farther, we risk more for less."

"I understand, but we didn't even discuss other options. What if we sent a small scouting group west while the others rested, just to see what they could learn? It feels like we're retreating from a battle we haven't even tried to win."

Tera challenged him. "Is that what you would do? Send a small force?"

Elian considered. "I think so. I would want to know where the Debru were arranged and see if we can learn anything about what they're aiming for. There's much we could learn. I understand the danger, but if we've already risked so much to get here, why not risk a little more and learn something important?"

They came to a much smaller clearing and Tera stopped to look up at the stars. "How much do you know of the history of the Bears?"

"Almost nothing at all," he admitted.

"Like the Hawks, the Bears used to be a much larger clan before this last Debru push. Harald became our leader almost a decade ago, when the Bears were near the height of their strength. Since then, he's done little except watch his family die a handful of people at a time. He's lost battles and he's lost land, and the few times he's tried launching attacks of his own, the cost was too steep for too little gain. Though he'll never admit this to anyone, he blames himself. He believes that if he was only stronger, or a better strategist, he'd have found a way to reverse our fortunes."

Elian digested Tera's story slowly. It didn't sound like the brave, cheerful commander of the Bears he knew. But he'd seen glimpses of Harald's other side, enough to know there was more to him than what first appeared. He remained silent while Tera continued.

"Anyone else in the clan will tell you that if not for him, we'd already be dead. He's one of the best leaders we've ever had, but he has the misfortune of leading us through our darkest days, and he'll always blame himself. But he hasn't given up."

Elian almost asked if Tera truly believed that, but she anticipated his question.

"He still wants to win. And he'll still throw us into battle if he thinks the time is right. He's not as cautious as some of the other leaders, but he's not as reckless as many believe."

Tera's beliefs churned Elian's certainties and broke them apart. But that molten ember of frustration he'd swallowed after the announcement they were leaving remained, and he couldn't quench it. "Would you have me follow in his footsteps?"

Tera shook her head. "I believe we need some of your courage, and maybe even some of your ignorance. But don't dismiss his ideas out of hand. His wisdom has been earned the hard way."

Elian nodded, and Tera looked satisfied that her message had been heard.

"Talk to him and convince him of your plan. I'll support you, if you like."

A muffled moan snuck through the woods, and Tera smiled.

"Although you probably still want to wait until tomorrow morning."

Elian shook his head, but Tera gestured for him to follow. "Tiafel suggested you meet with Loken, right?"

Tera's mention of the name reminded Elian of why he'd come all this way. While they'd been walking, Elian had thought often about the enigmatic healer. He'd pestered everyone in the group about him, but only Harald had ever heard the name before.

Loken was considered a one of the greatest healers among the wandering clans, but if Elian understood correctly, he didn't belong to any specific clan. He'd joined the Hawks on their expedition west, but he wasn't one of them. Elian hadn't realized such individuals existed, but it made him all the more curious to find out more.

Then the battle with the Moka had happened and he'd discovered a gathering ground, and his concerns had slipped from his mind.

He nodded eagerly. "Do you know where he is?"

"I asked around earlier. He's spent most of his time healing the Hawks since they got here, but he's resting away from the others." She pointed at a faint path through the trees. "If you follow that path, you should find him."

Elian bowed in thanks, and Tera left him alone.

He hadn't gone far down the path before he stopped. Night was falling, but the path ahead was illuminated by tiny points of light. Elian brushed one with his hand and felt a tiny addition to his adani. He stared at the lights, not quite believing what his senses told him.

The forest here was quiet and peaceful. It reminded Elian of huddling deep under a thick layer of blankets in the middle of winter. This silence had a comforting weight to it. He stepped forward gently, not wanting to break the silence.

He found Loken laying in a tiny clearing looking up at the stars. A narrow stream trickled through the clearing, bubbling as it crawled its way through the woods.

At least, Elian assumed it was Loken. He was the first person Elian had found along the path. Given the man's reputation as a legendary healer, Elian had assumed he'd be crossing paths with a white-haired man with kind eyes.

He was wrong on all counts. Loken looked to be only a few years older than him. He had long dark hair, wiry muscles, and a gaze that seemed permanently fixed off in the distance. He didn't look like a healer. The adanist looked like one of the toughest warriors Elian had ever come across.

When Loken sat up and turned, Elian saw that he was missing his right arm. He bowed, both in greeting and to cover up his surprise.

"Are you one of the new arrivals? You don't look hurt," Loken said.

"I am, one of the new arrivals, that is. I'm not injured," Elian said. "Are you the healer Loken?"

Loken gave him the slightest of nods.

"Tiafel said you might be able to help me manipulate adani."

"I don't know what you're doing out here if you can't bind adani, but I'm certainly not interested in taking on a student," Loken said.

Elian interrupted before Loken could lay down again. "It's true I can't bind adani, but I've killed both Debru and a Moka. I don't want you to teach me how to bind it. I want you to teach me how to move it within my body."

Loken didn't answer, but he didn't lay down either, so Elian launched into a quick explanation. Loken listened with growing interest, then nodded. He gestured for Elian to sit across from him. "Show me what you can do."

Elian did, though the demonstration didn't take long. He used all the techniques Alec had taught him, and he sensed the strength of Loken's adani as the healer used all his senses to track his actions.

"I can't help you develop as a warrior," Loken said.

Elian's heart dropped. First Harald wanted to retreat and now Loken couldn't help him? This entire trip was looking to be more and more a waste.

"But I think I can help you focus your adani much better," Loken finished.

Elian's despair turned to joy. "I'm prepared to do anything," he said.

Loken barked something that might have been a laugh. "With any luck, it shouldn't take you more than a few moments. Whoever's been teaching you has meant well, but they aren't good at tracking the flow of your adani, which is nothing more than I'd expect from a warrior."

Loken's words left Elian confused, but he sat silently and waited for the explanation.

"Tell me, when you attempt to manipulate the flow of adani within your body, what do you envision?" Loken asked.

"I envision stuffing a limb full of adani," Elian said, more sharply than he intended. What kind of foolish question was that?

"That figures." Loken came to his knees and smoothly shifted toward him. "May I?"

Elian nodded, and Loken pressed his hand against Elian's chest. It felt warm through Elian's tunic.

"Focus on your adani. It is perhaps most useful to think of it like water that always needs to be in motion. When you attempt to fill a limb, it's like filling a cup. It's easy enough to do, but then you expect the water to be still, which it never will be. It will try to escape."

Elian sensed Loken manipulate the adani within his body. Loken was better at directing Elian's adani than Elian was, but Elian's frustration with that knowledge only lasted a moment. Loken's manipulations were too interesting to observe. The healer stuffed Elian's arm full of adani, and as he claimed, it worked well for a bit, then escaped back into the rest of his body.

"Instead of trying to stuff it into your limbs, circulate it. Keep it flowing, but limit its flow to the desired area, like this."

Loken shifted the adani in Elian's body again. As before, he shifted a massive amount of adani into Elian's arm, but this time, he kept it circulating within the arm. The adani stayed in place. Elian's eyes went wide.

"And, I suppose, if you wanted to develop the technique

further, you could focus the adani in a smaller part of your body, which would feel something like this," Loken said.

Adani shifted again as it swirled in tighter and tighter loops, like a knot being drawn tighter. The adani traveled down to his hand, and when Elian opened his eyes, he saw that his palm was glowing with the same light as he'd seen in the forest on the way to Loken's resting place.

Loken breathed out and Elian's adani returned to its normal loop through his body. Elian kept staring at his hand, as though he'd never seen it before.

"That was incredible," Elian said.

A faint smile crossed Loken's lips. "Can't say I've ever felt anything like that myself."

Elian's questioning look prompted Loken to answer.

"I suppose it might not seem like much to you, but what you just experienced isn't all that different from how we heal. To keep that much adani focused in such a tight loop would normally require all my attention, and I wouldn't be able to maintain it for long. Doing it for you was almost as simple as breathing. Couldn't do that with anyone else."

Elian tried on his own. After having sensed Loken's technique, he found that it was simple to duplicate. He shook his head. All that struggle, and the answer had been so easy. He couldn't tighten the loops of adani as tightly as Loken had, but that felt more like a matter of practice and experience than a permanent problem.

He pressed his forehead to the ground. Adani flowed freely between the new point of contact and the gathering ground. His faded, and there was only adani, and a deep sense of peace, like someone had gathered all his worries and carried them away. "Thank you," he said.

"It was no problem at all. Most interesting problem I've come across in a while, actually. Now, if you don't mind, I'm trying to rest, and your adani is blinding to my senses."

Elian had never heard his adani as being described as blinding, but he didn't doubt the healer, not after what he'd just shown Elian. "Of course. I'm sorry to bother you."

He rose quickly, feeling lighter on his feet. He circulated a fraction of his adani into his legs and bounded easily back down the path.

For the moment he ran as though he were a child again, free from all the concerns of the world.

❧ 23 ❧

E lian had always been faster than her. It didn't matter if they raced around the house or to the edges of the farthest fields. She never beat him. Those times when she thought she was almost as fast, he would glance back, smile, and pull away. She only came close when he let her.

With the Belog behind her, though, Samora ran like she never had before. Her heart pounded against her ribs as her lungs fought to pull in the air she craved. Her thighs and calves burned, and though she pushed adani into her limbs, it was like trying to douse a roaring fire with the water in a small cup.

Karla didn't help. Today she fell into the role so often played by Elian, running ahead of her and casting frustrated glances back at her slower companion.

Samora wanted to scream that she was running as fast as she could, but she couldn't spare the breath.

They were over halfway back to the gathering grounds, and hope surged in Samora's chest. She didn't dare pause to sense the Belog's approach.

Karla had no problem throwing out her adani while running. Samora sensed the pulse as it spread away from the veteran adanist. It was strong enough that when it returned, Samora caught a hint of the shadow it carried past her.

The Belog was close, then.

Samora searched for some hidden well of strength to draw on, but the well was dry. She was one wrong step away from falling, and if she did, she wouldn't rise anytime soon. The gathering ground was visible now, no more than a mile and a bit away, but she wasn't sure she had the speed to reach it in time.

Karla slowed until she ran beside Samora. She wasn't even breathing hard, and when she spoke, it was as easily as if they were sitting across a table from one another. "I'll need the power of the gathering grounds."

Samora nodded her understanding.

"Keep running as fast as you can, and don't waste time looking behind you."

That was hardly comforting, but Karla bounded ahead before Samora could say so.

Samora almost stumbled as she watched her companion. The difference in their abilities hadn't been nearly as small as she thought. Karla's strides covered three paces for every one of Samora's, and the woman still didn't look like she was trying.

Was this how Elian felt when he watched others binding adani?

Samora didn't think she'd ever felt her lack of strength as acutely as she did in that moment, and it gave her a clear glimpse into her brother's heart.

The dark pressure of the Belog pushed any other thoughts out of her head. If it was close enough, she could sense it without sending her adani out, she was in immediate danger. She fought the desire to stop and turn around, though the temptation was sweet. Her body preferred the certainty of doom to the unknown, even if the price of the knowledge was her life.

Karla reached the edge of the gathering grounds and slowed to a stop. She turned and gathered adani, binding it with techniques

Samora had never observed before. The result, though, was comfortably familiar.

Adani grew and swirled over Karla's head, an enormous cloud of potential that dwarfed Karla's previous attacks. Samora sensed it from over a half mile away, and for a moment she wondered if she shouldn't be more afraid of Karla.

The Belog didn't share Samora's worry. Darkness pressed against Samora's senses and made it more difficult to breathe. She was certain that it was just over her shoulder, ready to drop on her like a bird of prey.

Karla didn't release her technique, though.

Samora's left foot tripped over a patch of grass. Her right foot landed hard, and she felt something twist within her ankle. She grimaced against the pain that never came, but her left foot pulled free of the grass, and she merely stumbled instead of fell.

Her pace slowed as her right leg started to refuse to support her weight. She hopped and hobbled, certain that with every half-leap she'd be swept up and pulled into the sky. Less than a hundred paces of flat grassland remained between her and Karla, but it felt as though a chasm separated them.

Karla finally released her technique. The sky overhead started to glow, then exploded in a flash of white-hot lightning. The first flash was followed by another a moment later, and then another, one blending into another until all Samora saw was white.

The air ripped apart as the lightning tore across it. Thunder, louder than any spring storm, shook the air out of Samora's lungs. She fell because she couldn't see, but she pushed herself to her feet as the Belog roared behind her.

The white faded and she could see again. Only a few dozen paces separated her and Karla now, and once again she dared to hope. She risked a glance back and immediately regretted her decision. The rippling shadows of the Belog were only a few paces behind her, and as she watched, snakelike arms extended toward her.

She tripped again, and the sight of the shadowy arms stole the strength from her own. She tried to rise but failed. As the arms descended, she rolled onto her back and bound an adani shield. It wouldn't last for more than a heartbeat, but hopefully that would be long enough. She kicked and scrambled the last few paces toward the gathering ground.

The arms fell against her shield, and she knew she wasn't going to make it. The Belog's power made her grasp of adani seem like that of a child, and her shield cracked as soon as the shadow squeezed.

Lightning flashed once again, and this time it forced the shadow to retreat.

Samora rolled over and crawled on hands and knees over the boundary of the gathering ground.

The flood of adani brought with it sweet relief. It masked some of the pain of her ankle, pushing away the darkness that had pressed upon her from all sides. The Belog was still there, but it didn't frighten her the way it had a moment ago.

With the sudden clarity the lack of fear gifted her, Samora bound the small points of adani that had served her so often before. With the gathering grounds at her back, it was as easy as it had ever been. Her adani was stronger than ever, and she flung the bound adani at the gathered shadow as fast as she could form it.

She didn't believe she could hurt it, and her suspicion was proven soon enough. The cloud of shadow shuddered, as though laughing at her feeble attempts. Still, it felt good to unleash her anger at the creature.

The cloud shrank in fear as Karla's lightning struck. It shriveled until it became something roughly the size of a man, and when that faded, only the Belog remained, standing no more than twenty paces away from her and Karla.

Its glowing red eyes were locked onto Samora. The grass

around its feet died as it stood there, but the circle of death only grew a bit before it stopped its expansion.

Karla lashed out again with the same technique, but Samora thought the lightning lacked its usual potency. The Belog raised a hand and caught the lightning in its palm. Its hand swelled for a moment, then returned to its previous shape.

Karla grunted as the Belog stretched its neck, its gaze never leaving Samora. It paced back and forth, spreading death wherever it stepped.

Samora had another dozen points of bound adani ready to go, but she followed Karla's lead and held them. She used the stalemate to study the Belog. Its human-like qualities caught her attention first, from the way that it walked to the looks it gave her.

Had it been human, she would have called it indecisive, but she couldn't begin to guess what thoughts rolled through its mind, or if thoughts even did.

The sight of the creature so close sent a shiver down her spine. There was something so foreign about it, so inhuman, that her body rebelled at the mere presence of the creature. Its expression looked as though it planned a terrible end for her, but again, it could have been the creature's equivalent of a smile. How was she to know?

All she knew was that it brought death where it walked. No other creature, not even the Debru's pets, killed the very places they stepped. When she pushed out her adani, it came back cold, as though she'd shoved it into a pile of snow and left it there.

Shadow crawled up the Debru's arm, reminding Samora of just how different they were. The shadow coalesced into a long blade.

The Belog shattered the tentative stalemate by leaping forward.

Samora let out an involuntary shout. For some reason, she'd thought it couldn't cross the boundary into the gathering ground, but she remembered now no one had ever said anything of the sort.

It landed on the thick grass of the gathering ground and raised its sword to strike at Samora.

She should have thrown her bound adani at it, but in her surprise, all she could do was notice that the grass here didn't die at its feet the way most grass did. Then the sword came down.

Samora's world went white as the air from her lungs was pushed out by a thunderclap that deafened her to all else. In a moment of panic, she threw all her bound adani forward, not caring what it hit.

When the blinding light vanished and she could see again, the Belog was on the other side of the boundary. Its right arm hung limp at its side, and it snarled at them both, revealing multiple layers of sharp teeth. Samora flinched backward, but the Belog made no move for her.

It paced back and forth, stealing the life from the ground it walked on, but it didn't try to advance, and Karla didn't try to attack it again. It roared, voicing its frustrations to an uncaring sky, and then shadow billowed around it. A moment later the clouds rolled away, moving with a speed even Elian couldn't match.

Samora slumped back into the grass and let out a deep, shuddering breath. She glanced over at Karla, whose pale face and quivering arms made Samora understand how close they had both just come to dying.

❧ 24 ❧

When the next morning dawned, Elian felt as light as he ever had. He practiced his new technique throughout the morning, bounding through the woods like a deer. More than once he scared a Hawk at rest.

Later this morning Kati and Harald were gathering their councils together to discuss their next steps, but for now, Elian was alone, testing himself to see how strong he could be. He stood on the boundary of the gathering ground and the deadlands to the east. For the moment, he stood on the side of the gathering ground and adani flowed smoothly within him.

A creeping dread had slowly spread down his spine as the morning wore on, though. What if this incredible strength was more from the gathering ground than anything he was doing?

There was one easy way to find out, but a surprising fear kept him rooted in place. He didn't want to let go of the way he felt.

He clenched his fists and took a deep breath.

Then he took a step forward. He felt the difference immediately as his body was torn away from the gathering ground's powerful flow of adani. He wasn't as strong as he'd felt a moment ago, but the sensation wasn't as dramatic as he'd expected. Adani still flowed powerfully through his limbs.

He focused a bit of it into his legs, looping it just as Loken had shown him. The technique worked just as well here as it did in the gathering grounds. To make sure, Elian ran, his steps light even in the loose soil. He ran a half-mile in what seemed like no time at all, then decided it was time to return. Scouts hadn't seen any Debru nearby this morning, but there was no point in taking unnecessary risks.

He ran back, then basked in the refreshing flow of the gathering grove's adani. He spent the rest of the morning running through Master Heinrick's sword drills with his newfound ability. The blade moved as though it had a life of its own, and when he felt sufficiently worn out, Elian returned to the main camp, where he was just in time to join the meeting. Warriors gathered around Harald and Kati, who sat shoulder to shoulder on a fallen log. A cookfire warmed a large pot which was already steaming, throwing off wonderful odors.

Elian joined the group, drawn both by the discussion and promise of soup. He took a seat in the circle, greeted the others, then turned his attention to his meal. It wasn't long before Kati began the council, and Elian sipped the broth from his bowl while he listened to the two leaders discuss recent events.

"After we reached here, we had no choice but to stop. I can defend us with the adani from the gathering grounds, but we'd be destroyed if we left. Even with your arrival, our chances are slim," Kati said.

Harald nodded, committing the details to memory. "As we walked, we saw a Belog flying on a dragon overhead. Have you seen it?"

Kati clutched tighter at her bowl. "A month ago, I would have thought you were mad for making a statement like that, but it's been hounding us for a few days. It swoops close and the Belog rains shadow down, but I've been able to defend us with the adani here. After a bit it flies west, but it doesn't go far. Some of my more sensitive adanists have felt it landing a few miles away."

Elian's ears perked up at that, but Harald's mind was on other matters.

"I'm surprised it doesn't attack with more," he said.

"As am I," Kati admitted, "but we are strong here. I could hurt it, and if enough of my adanists were healthy, we might even take it down."

"They've never showed too much concern over self-preservation before," Harald said.

"They've also never ridden creatures from some of our most ancient legends. It stands to reason they can change and adapt as quickly as we can, and I tremble to think of what they might come up with next," Kati said.

Elian couldn't let go of the distance Kati had mentioned. "The Belog is that close?" he asked.

Kati nodded.

Elian faced Harald. "Let me scout farther west."

Harald leaned back and frowned, as though he'd found something distasteful in his stew. "Of course not. Why would I do that?"

"Because there might be something we can learn. It's the whole reason Kati brought the Hawks this far, right? I would make the perfect scout. None of the Debru even spares me a second glance when I'm nearby. I don't want to start a fight, I just want us all to learn something."

"Your assumptions are wrong," Harald said.

"About what?"

"That Moka that escaped saw how you fought against its companion. You might not have earned a second glance a few days ago, but if that Moka has rejoined the others, they'll hunt you down as certainly as they would if Kati or I left the gathering grounds."

Elian growled. "We wouldn't be having this problem if you'd let me kill it!"

Harald's gaze hardened. "Get ahold of yourself, Elian. If you can't control the adani flowing through you, you're no good to any of us."

Elian clenched a fist, but then paid attention to his body. Adani was a chaotic storm inside him. He took several deep breaths, fighting to force it into an orderly flow.

Kati intervened. "Why are you having him try to control it?"

Harald gave a half-shrug. "You can see it yourself. Anger gets the better of him."

"That's not what I see. He's frustrated and angry, but he isn't attacking anyone. When was the last time you got upset about someone merely shouting at you?" Kati's rebuke came with a smile, but Harald grunted as though he'd been punched.

"He's much more pleasant when it's under control," Harald argued, though it sounded like some of the fight had gone out of him.

"Sure, but when have we ever cared about 'pleasant?' I've got adanists I wouldn't allow within ten miles of a village, but there's no one else I'd rather have at my back in a fight." Kati looked at him, and he guessed she was studying him with her adani. "He's strong when he's angry, but he's right, too. When he's calm and I'm outside his pull of adani, I barely notice him."

"I also don't want to get the kid killed because he's too dumb to know better," Harald said.

Kati shook her head, not buying the argument. "You wouldn't have brought him if you'd thought so little of him."

Elian was about to raise his hand and remind them both that he was still here, but the look on Harald's face kept him silent. The giant man looked as though he'd swallowed the distasteful item in his stew whole.

Harald sighed. "When it's just me, all my Bears listen."

"Then your leadership is lacking. If no one disagrees with you, true wisdom will always evade you."

Harald reached out with his hand and took hers. He squeezed it. "I've missed you."

"And I you," Kati said.

Harald looked up at Elian. "You can scout, but you're not going alone."

"I'll go with him," Tera said. "Together, we should be able to stay out of trouble."

Kati stopped Tera. "I appreciate the offer, Tera, but you're among the strongest of the adanists here. Once you leave the gathering grounds, the Debru will flock to you like wolves over a fresh kill. I have someone else in mind. Someone who I think will be a perfect match for this task."

THE YOUNG WOMAN standing in front of him was about as far from the rough, grizzled scout Elian had expected as possible. A thin scar ran down the side of her face, and a matching one adorned her left arm, but otherwise, she looked as dangerous as a kitten.

"Elian, this is Capricia. She's a formidable Hawk but is unique in that she can draw adani from the land much faster than most. It allows her to control the amount of adani she carries, so she'll be less noticeable than anyone else here," Kati said.

Capricia bowed deeply. "It will be an honor to travel with you. Word of your fight against the Moka has already spread."

Harald grunted. "And hopefully that's a fight that won't need to be repeated." He stared hard at Elian. "Right?"

Elian bowed deeply. "Of course."

Harald's tone lightened. "I just want you back, safe, and in one piece."

Elian cracked a grin. "I'd feel pretty bad about myself if it was otherwise," he said.

Harald chuckled and shook his head. "Get out of here, and good luck. I'd tell you that your life is more important than anything you might learn, but I know you'll do as you please."

"I'll be back shortly," Elian said.

After a few more brief farewells, they left the gathering grounds, exiting out the west side. Elian never stopped looking left and right, but he didn't see any Debru nearby, nor shadows hiding them. Once they were about a quarter mile away from the woods, he asked Capricia to extend her adani.

"You can't?" she asked.

He shook his head, and she shrugged, accepting it without complaint. She didn't close her eyes or touch the ground, but her gaze grew distant. "It's hard to say for certain in the deadlands, but I don't think we've been spotted."

He wanted more reassurance than that, but he wasn't going to get it. "Thank you."

"Of course."

As they resumed their journey he asked, "Were you ordered to do this, or was it something you willingly did?"

"Both. Kati told me to, but I'm as eager to find out what's further west as you are."

"Why?"

She shrugged. "Curious, I guess? I'll also be able to claim that I've traveled farther west than any other Hawk, so that'll be nice, too."

Elian almost groaned, but he caught himself. If she wasn't going to take this seriously, they were all going to be in a lot of trouble.

"What about you? What made you so eager to risk your neck?"

"We need to know more about the Debru, and we're closer

than we've ever been. Seemed foolish for us to turn around without at least checking to see if we could learn more."

They walked a mile through the deadlands, their feet sinking into the now-familiar sandy soil. Capricia picked a path westward, choosing higher elevations when she could. The rock and sand still tired their sore feet and exhausted calves, but not as much as the depressions and draws.

When the wind gusted, it picked up the fine sand and flung it at his face. He shielded his eyes as best he could. As the wind became more consistent, he pulled a cloth from a pocket and wrapped it around his nose and mouth.

Abrasive as the sand was, Elian was grateful for the intermittent cover it provided. Nothing taller than a weed grew in these parts, and despite the weight he'd lost trekking across the deadlands, he couldn't hide behind one yet. When he'd traveled with Harald, the lack of cover hadn't worried him much. The space was vast and empty, and Harald was there to fight any monsters that were unfortunate enough to wander near.

Now that he knew the monsters were closer than Harald, and his calm demeanor was more act than truth.

But they had to know. The sacrifice of so many couldn't be in vain.

The blowing dust in the air obscured the horizon and stole Elian's sense of distance. They plodded westward, silent for fear of nearby enemies. Capricia stopped to extend adani regularly, but never issued any warnings. For the moment, only they walked across the desolate lands.

It might have been a mile, but it felt like three when Capricia held up a hand for him to stop. She gestured that he should follow her closely, then dropped onto hands and knees.

He imitated the Hawk, then flattened himself when the wind blew the cloud of dust aside and he could see ahead.

Debru gathered by the dozens, rooted in place like a clan of grotesque trees. Though Elian caught only a glimpse, none moved so much as a claw.

Most of his attention was caught by the motion on the edge of the gathering. Two dragons wrestled shadowy ropes that anchored them in place. Their massive wings were tied tight to their bodies, and a smoky length of rope encircled their snouts.

Then the dust returned and blocked their sight. Elian reached out and grabbed Capricia's shoulders, asking with his eyes if she'd seen what he'd seen.

She nodded.

Elian wiggled his body so he was deeper in the sand.

They'd found the Debru, and with any luck, soon they'd find a weakness they could take advantage of.

🐜 25 🐜

K arla's hands were warm as they wrapped around Samora's ankle. She felt the strain of her recent injury fade away as Karla circled healing adani through and around the ankle.

Samora was grateful, of course, but she couldn't silence the jealousy shouting in the back of her mind. Of all things, she would have expected to be better than Karla at healing, but even that proved untrue. Samora's techniques might have been more refined, but Karla's overwhelming strength, aided by the gathering grounds, worked more quickly.

Samora told herself it was only because it was so much more difficult to heal oneself than it was to heal another.

The statement was true enough, but it didn't make her feel better.

"We'll need to leave as soon as you're able," Karla said.

"You think it will return?"

"If I knew how Belog thought, we'd have won this war long ago. It could march an army of Debru in this direction or never come anywhere near again. It doesn't matter, though. We can't stay.

"Why not?"

Samora hated the petulance in her voice. She knew well enough why they couldn't stay, but the thought of leaving a perfectly safe, life-giving space made her heart thump so hard in her chest it was like she was running from the Belog all over again.

Karla's look made it clear she saw straight through Samora's question, but she answered it with more patience than it deserved. "Gathering grounds are no place for us to hide. They're sacred to the clans, and for good reasons. Retreating to them should be a matter of last resort. But the real reason is because we finally know why the Belog are after you. That's important knowledge that needs to be shared."

"But why does it matter if I can heal the land? Why should the Debru care?"

Karla leaned back and let go of Samora's ankle. The warmth from her touch and healing lingered. "Rotate it and tell me if it hurts."

Samora did and found that it felt great. Karla watched her movements and her expression closely.

When she was satisfied with Samora's healing, Karla said, "Many adanists have worn themselves ragged trying to understand the Debru. I'd suggest you not make the same mistake. We know that when you healed that trail, the Belog leaped to attack us. That's as clear a message as we can hope for. We don't need to understand why."

The argument made Samora feel uneasy. "Just because we haven't understood before doesn't mean we shouldn't strive to understand now."

Karla scooted a step away, so she wasn't so close. "It isn't that I disagree, but I don't want to see you waste your gifts attempting to solve a riddle that has stumped us for generations."

Karla's warning made Samora more curious than anything. "What have other people tried before?"

"There's been a handful of adanists who have sought to learn more about the Debru. One older warrior named Elna, tired after a lifetime of fighting, spent her twilight years attempting to speak to the Debru. Legend has it that she would hunt them down, then talk to them as they tried to kill her. She was an incredible warrior, so she lasted longer than anyone expected, but she still died at the tip of a Debru blade."

"That seems foolish," Samora said.

"Indeed. Others have been more reasonable. I knew one woman who became obsessed with the Debru. Drina. She'd been happily married to a wonderful man, whose name escapes me now. He was killed in a skirmish by a Moka, and it transformed Drina. Most turn to anger or despair, but Drina found her peace in curiosity. She wanted to know *why* the Debru invaded."

Samora found that she was leaning forward. "What did she do?"

"The ability that made her unique was that she could mask her spirit better than anyone I've met before or since. The Debru are sensitive to adani, even though they can't use it, but she could get close and study them. She came back to us once, filled with strange stories like I've never heard before."

"Such as?"

"Oh, things like the Debru don't eat, nor do they move when they don't have to. At times, they appear out of nowhere."

"Is that true?"

Karla shrugged. "Don't have the slightest idea. I'm willing to believe, but I've never seen any of it with my own eyes. Drina returned west after giving her report, hoping to confirm what she was learning, but she was never seen again. No one has been too inclined to follow her lead, at least until Kati decided to take an entire clan west, which was as fool a decision as I've ever heard."

"But how do we defeat them if we don't understand them?" Samora asked.

"They die, same as us. We don't need to understand them to kill them."

"Killing them might make more of a difference if we understood them."

"True enough, but they aren't keen on making friends, and everyone I know who's spent too much time asking the questions you're asking ends up dead, with next to nothing to show for it. I don't mind you asking the questions, but please don't make the same mistakes they did."

Samora accepted the compromise and turned the conversation to their next steps. "I'll try. So, what do we do next? Do we leave here and hope to join with the other clans?"

"We'll need their strength to protect you," Karla agreed.

"Before we leave, can I return to the tree and cast out my adani? Knowing where all our allies and enemies are located will be helpful."

"I was thinking just the same."

Karla stood first, followed by Samora. She gingerly tested her foot, gradually putting more weight on it until she was almost standing on one leg. It held her weight without a twinge of discomfort.

Karla walked with her to the tree, then left Samora so that her adani didn't interfere. It was likely a needless worry, but Samora welcomed a moment to herself. She sat cross legged next to the tree and leaned her back against it. Maybe it was because the sun had shone against the trunk all day, or maybe it was because the tree stood at the heart of the gathering grounds, but whatever the reason, the trunk was warm and welcoming. Samora focused on her adani as she pushed it into the world.

She first explored to the west, seeking Elian's distinctive pull. He'd reached the other gathering ground and felt as strong as he ever had. The nature of his adani was still uniquely his own, but she sensed a subtle change. She wished she was closer so she could sense all that had changed within him.

From the first day she'd come into this world, Elian had been there. They'd celebrated and suffered together, and she'd always taken it for granted that they'd grow old together, too. Now she wasn't so sure.

Change was constant, and she had little doubt she'd grown in ways that would be obvious to him when they reunited. She wasn't frustrated that he'd grown, but that he'd done it without her.

The darkness pulsing west of Elian's gathering ground pulled her attention away from her brother. A sizable force of Debru waited close by, but there were bright wells of adani beside them. Samora couldn't make out what the adani represented, but it and the Debru weren't in active conflict.

What were the Debru doing?

Samora pushed another wave of adani toward them, expanding her new senses as far as they would travel. She found what she was searching for soon after. A perfect circle, larger by far than even the one near where the Crows had died. While the deadlands were dark and cold to her senses, the circle was pitch-black and gelid.

The Debru guarded the circle.

Samora cast her adani closer to where they'd found the fallen Crows. That circle had grown larger, too. The Debru that had been advancing from the west, the ones Samora had thought were coming to crush the clans, had stopped beside it.

Her stomach continued to sink. She cast her adani one last time, flung into the distance thanks to the strength of the gathering grounds. She sent it toward home, digging her nails into the soft soil beneath her.

The last force of Debru were there, and like the other two circles, they were waiting.

Samora didn't want to know what they waited for.

She pulled away from her adani and returned her attention to the gathering grounds. The flickering light of knotted adani was painfully beautiful, and her heart wanted nothing but to rest here forever.

But Karla was more right than she knew. They had to leave, and soon. She hurried to where the ancient adanist was resting and told her everything. It didn't take long for Karla to share Samora's concerns.

They packed quickly, but before they left, a thought occurred to Samora that froze her in place.

"What?" Karla asked, annoyed by the slight delay.

"What if I can heal the circles?" Samora asked.

That brought Karla up short, too. Her gaze stretched past the horizon as she considered the possibilities.

"There's no evidence," she admitted, "but it's as likely a guess as I can imagine. Hurry. We need to reach the other clans and let them know what's happening before it's too late."

"Do you think Tiafel will know what to do?"

Karla shook her head. "I fear Tiafel, wise as he is, is too weak for the decisions that must be made."

Samora took offense on Tiafel's behalf. The leader of the Hounds had never shown her anything but kindness. "He seems strong enough to me."

"There are different kinds of strength, and Tiafel is lacking in the variety that matters most."

At Samora's questioning gaze, Karla elaborated. "He no longer believes we can win. And I know you'll argue that doesn't matter so much, but I'll tell you it does. Once a leader believes that victory is impossible, they aim for a different target. It might be close enough to victory that most don't notice, but I've known Tiafel longer than you've been alive. He'll wait for a perfect moment that will never come. If Harald was here, well, it might be a different story, but he's not, and so I can only hope that Warran and Aldo can sway him."

Karla's face turned grim. "Because if we can't, I'm not sure what hope we have against the Debru."

26

E lian learned more about the Debru in one afternoon than he'd known in his entire life. He and Capricia had both wiggled themselves deeply into the sandy soil and watched the invaders. He feared a single glance would reveal their position, but by the time the wind died, they were halfway buried by the blown dust and lay still as stones.

Capricia was almost shoulder to shoulder with him, so that they could whisper back and forth. She was skilled at concealing the strength of her spirit. He was hardly the most sensitive adanist in the area, but he couldn't sense her at all, even though she was right next to him. There was no way the Debru should be able to sense her.

After some time watching the Debru, though, Elian wondered if their worry was needless. The only two that moved were the Belog. The others remained almost completely motionless.

It wasn't as though they'd been frozen. Elian had seen the Debru stir and shake for a bit before settling down again. If he had to describe the invaders, he would have said they were sleeping standing up.

The dragons regularly tore his attention away from the Debru.

They continued to struggle against their shadowy bonds, and Elian fantasized often about rushing in to save them. If the dragons and the Debru weren't allies, they could be powerful friends to the wandering clans.

"I think we should leave," Capricia said.

"Are you getting scared?"

He'd meant the comment in jest, but she shot him a withering glare that made him want to bury his head in the soil with the rest of his body. "We've been gone for a while, and if we're out much longer, they'll worry about us. And yes, I am worried we'll be spotted."

Her voice was just loud enough to carry to his ears.

"They haven't even looked our way yet. We need to stay to see if we can find a weakness."

"We've already found one. The Debru rest! If we could ambush them like this, we could kill many of them with skilled archers before they even know they're under attack."

Elian hadn't thought of that. Still, he wanted more. There had to be something that would give humanity a fighting chance. "Just a bit longer?"

Capricia grimaced, but she was a victim of her own curiosity. Nerves or not, she was every bit as obsessed as him. They watched and waited, eager to find whatever secrets the Debru hid.

It soon became clear their hopes were misplaced. The Debru remained still and silent. Even the two Belog had settled onto the ground.

"Did you feel that?" Caprica whispered.

Elian shook his head. He'd sensed nothing, but judging from Caprica's expression, he wasn't going to like hearing about it, either.

"Something just passed underneath us."

"Like a monster?" he asked.

Capricia closed her eyes, and Elian felt a gentle pulse of adani flow away from her. She spoke with her eyes closed. "Something like adani, although not adani."

Elian turned his attention to the Debru, worried they'd been sensed, but none of the Debru were in motion.

Capricia's eyes snapped open. "We need to go, now."

Elian didn't question her. He wiggled backward, watching the Debru camp to ensure none of the invaders noticed their hasty exit. None seemed the least interested in him. Once they were out of sight, he asked, "What way?"

Capricia closed her eyes, and again Elian was close enough to feel the pulse of adani. "We're surrounded."

Elian looked around but saw nothing. "By what?"

"Otsoa. Hundreds of them."

Elian let out the breath he didn't realize he'd been holding. "Then we'll fight our way through them."

"The instant one of them dies, the Debru will know, and they'll catch us before we get far."

Elian cursed. He hadn't thought of that. "There's no gaps we can slip through?"

Capricia pointed back toward the Debru camp. "No otsoa that way."

Elian blew out a long breath. "Right."

His thoughts raced for a bit, then slowed as they kept running into the same walls. They couldn't fight their way through the Debru. They could fight their way through the otsoa, but then they'd have the Debru on them anyway. Their journey had taken them too far from the gathering grounds' protection. They couldn't outrun the Debru, especially not if they had the dragons in the air.

The dragons.

"You'd say we're doomed, right?" he asked.

She nodded, her lips tight.

"You want to free a dragon and see if it will give us a ride out of here?"

Capricia looked at him like he'd gone mad.

And maybe he had, but what did it matter? If they were dead one way or the other, they might as well go down swinging. He saw the same decision playing out in her eyes, and then she smiled.

It might have been the most beautiful smile he'd ever seen.

"Sounds like as good a time as any," she said.

They hatched their plan, if it even deserved the name, quickly. The rise in the land that hid them from view curled around the camp, which would allow them to get reasonably close to the dragons without being spotted. They'd have to run across a short stretch of open field, though, which Elian wasn't looking forward to. The Debru hadn't seemed too concerned about their surroundings, but he assumed they would care about two humans rushing for their bound dragons.

Assuming they reached the dragons alive, they'd try to break the bonds and somehow convince it to give them a ride.

At the very least, Elian figured he could throw the camp into chaos for a bit.

They hurried around the rise. Capricia hid near the end, but Elian pulled on her arm. There was no point in delaying. The longer they remained, the more likely their discovery.

When Elian emerged from the cover of the hillside, he was surprised to see how close he was to the captive dragons. Their size was such that he had judged them farther away. Now that he was close enough to hit them with a stone, there was no denying their enormity.

The closest point of comparison he could find was the size of the ancient trees back in the gathering grounds, but even those majestic oaks didn't do the dragons justice. He had no doubt the dragons could have stretched their powerful necks to the top of any tree in the sacred wood, but comparing a dragon to a tree robbed the dragon of its overwhelming vitality. Both tree and dragon shared a sense of deep peace, the patient wisdom Elian always associated with elders, but the dragons' adani burned with a ferocity that put the village's occasional bonfires to shame.

Even at a hundred paces, Elian felt as though the proximity to the burning spirits of the dragons would singe his soul. He ran forward before he questioned the wisdom of his choice. Capricia followed right behind, and Elian swore he glimpsed a grin on her face.

They made it almost halfway across the remaining distance before Elian knew the Debru had spotted them. They didn't shout or point as Elian would have expected from a human scout. Instead, those closest to him shivered. That shiver rippled outward to their neighbors, and in its wake, the Debru came alive. Heads turned toward him, and claws extended.

As Elian watched the great awakening, he knew fear like never before. Every drop of blood in his body froze as he and Capricia became the sole focus of the most dangerous enemy humans had ever known. For a few long moments, the Debru shook themselves awake but didn't attack. He didn't know why, but he wasn't going to waste the moment.

His blood may have frozen, but his limbs carried him ever closer to the dragons. Their soaring spirits gave him a sliver of hope, which shone brighter than a full moon on a cloudless night.

Then the Debru charged.

By the time they did, Elian was only a dozen paces from the closest dragon, who had also turned its attention to him. Elian shoved as much adani into his arm and hand as he could. He was still flush with strength from the gathering grounds, and he swore he saw his arm glowing. He drew his sword and cut at the dark binding that surrounded the dragon. His blade hit hard and true, and the darkness *thrummed* as though it were a string held tightly between the two hands. It vibrated but didn't break.

Elian cut at the same spot again, suddenly feeling very much the fool. Had he really thought he could free a dragon?

It looked as though the dark rope might be weakening, but it might as well have been his imagination.

"Let me," Capricia said.

Elian raised his sword to cut at the rope again. He wasn't strong compared to many of the warriors he'd met, but he hadn't sensed any useful strength from her.

He reconsidered the moment she stopped hiding her spirit.

Adani flowed through her, not like a rushing river, but like a deep well of water being gently stirred. She raised a hand, and at first, Elian thought she bound adani similarly to Samora. At a glance, it looked like she held a pinprick of light in her hand. But when it shot forward, he realized it was closer to a needle. The adani she poured into it was considerable, even if it wasn't nearly as much as someone like Harald was capable of. Its focus, though, was unlike anything he had sensed before.

The needle sliced through the dark rope as though it was an illusion. The rope vanished, blown away by a wind Elian didn't feel.

The dragon stood and snapped its wings open, the force of its adani almost driving Elian to his knees. Its wings were wider than any tree's branches, and when it leaned forward and roared, it brought all the Debru to a halt.

Only the Belog stirred, rising from its slumber as though to discipline a misbehaving child.

The dragon roared again, and though the sound vibrated Elian's bones, it didn't cause the Belog to falter.

Dread creeped through Elian's spirit. The Belog had captured this creature once before, and it seemed confident it could do so again. He turned to Capricia and gestured toward the second dragon.

Comforted by the Belog's presence at their backs, the other Debru moved forward again, cloaking themselves in shadows to prepare for their assault.

Elian looked up at the dragon that now towered over him. If

there was a way out of this mess, it was on that dragon, but he couldn't guess how he was supposed to get from here, on the ground, onto the dragon's neck. Somehow, he didn't think asking politely would work.

Capricia flung another one of her needles at the black rope restraining the second dragon but failed to snap it. She muttered something to herself, then launched another needle. It hit in the same place as the first, and this time the rope snapped. The second dragon followed the lead of the other, standing and roaring at the approaching Debru.

In answer, tendrils of darkness stretched from the cloud to wrap around the first dragon's neck.

Elian swore. He hadn't gone to all this trouble to fail to rescue even a single dragon. Adani pooled in his legs without a thought, and he leaped. The jump carried him up and over the dragon, and he landed on the dragon's broad back. Its scales were so warm Elian could feel the heat through his boots. He ran forward, attacking the tendrils with his blade, careful not to cut the dragon.

Unlike the rope, these scattered as soon as he cut them. More tendrils reached out, wrapping higher up the dragon's neck. Elian prepared to launch himself at them, but the dragon leaned back and snapped the tendrils as though they were old and weathered string.

The attack did nothing to capture the dragon, but it encouraged the dragon to leave sooner rather than later. Adani shifted underneath Elian. It reminded him of Capricia's calm and deep reserve, except much, much more expansive. Adani surged as the dragon flapped its wings, and then Elian sheathed his blade because he knew he would need both hands.

A moment later, he was flying.

More accurately, he was clutching desperately to the dragon's scales as it turned to fly away. The dragon seemed completely indifferent to Elian's presence. It beat its wings faster as the

Belog started to run, shadows gathering around its clawed hands.

The dragon surged away as dark tendrils stretched toward it.

It was too slow.

The Belog caught it with a single tendril that wrapped around the dragon's hind leg. Elian wondered if the dragon would simply pull the Belog along, but the rope froze the dragon in mid-flight. Adani fought against shadow, the sight of freedom so close.

The second dragon took off after the first, aiming for the Belog's rope. It wouldn't make it in time, though. The second Belog had arrived and gathered the same tendrils in preparation for its attack.

Elian's dragon screeched a warning and the second dragon banked away, releasing a mournful roar. The Belog launched his shadow, but it didn't reach far enough. The second dragon floated high overhead, no longer in danger but too far away to help.

Capricia had been left behind, though, and if Elian didn't think of something quick, the first dragon would be just as trapped as it had been before. No brilliant solutions presented themselves, but when in doubt, there was always the option of cutting something.

He stood on the dragon's still back and let his limbs fill with adani. He opened his eyes wide.

It was as if he stood inside the gathering grounds. Adani flooded his hands and feet, and he felt as though he'd just woken from a long nap. He looked up at the open sky, sad that he wouldn't fly higher than this.

It was another foolish decision, the last in a long string of them, but it was easy enough to justify. He couldn't leave Capricia, and if it was a choice between neither him nor the dragon escaping or one of them, well, that was easy enough, too. He offered a slight bow of his head to the dragon, then dropped off the side.

He cut at the rope as he fell. Alone, he wouldn't have had a chance, but the dragon was already pulling with all its might, and Elian did nothing but add a little extra force to the dragon's efforts.

The rope snapped and Elian fell back to the land, where the shadows of the Debru were quickly advancing. His adani-strengthened legs absorbed most of the fall, but he felt one of his ankles twist and pop, and he didn't think that he'd be running anytime soon.

Not like there was any place for him to run to.

The dragon he'd just been riding shot upward like an arrow launched from the bow of a giant. It roared as it rose, and its cry was joined by the second dragon much higher.

Elian looked up and smiled.

He was glad they were free. It was something, at least.

Capricia came and stood next to him. Though he'd kept them here and gotten them surrounded, and his best idea to save them was flying away, she didn't seem angry. She gave him half a smile, and though it seemed impossible, he believed it was genuine.

"Sorry," he said, though it sounded pitiful.

She shrugged. "It was exciting for a while."

Without another word she prepared to meet the advancing Debru. A slender bound needle formed above each hand, and she waited for the smoke to come closer so that she might more clearly sense her targets.

Her acceptance strengthened Elian's will. He'd never met anyone like her and was sad he wouldn't have a chance to walk back to the lands of the wandering clans by her side. He looped his adani into his fists and ankle, hoping he would last long enough to make the Debru regret this fight.

The wave of shadow crashing toward them slowed, as though the Debru were no longer interested in their prey.

"Elian!" Capricia shouted; her voice filled with sudden hope.

He looked at her but couldn't guess what inspired her. Had Harald and Kati rode to their rescue? He twisted to search the horizon but saw nothing except the endless deadlands. When his gaze returned to her, he saw that she was pointing up at the sky.

He followed the direction of her finger and saw another shadow racing toward them, so fast it blurred.

A moment before it was too late, he realized one of the dragons had returned. It plunged toward the ground, moving so fast Elian was sure it would send up dust and dried roots for hundreds of paces. In the instant before it hit the ground, it snapped its wings open, and the bloom of adani that resulted almost lifted Elian off his feet.

Instead, he stood, rooted to the ground as the massive creature raced at him and Capricia, claws open.

Better that, he supposed, than a Debru shadow. The dragon moved so fast he imagined he wouldn't feel a thing. He shifted so that he faced his fate head-on. The Belog extended their ropes once again, but because they had to reach over their own Debru, they were too slow to reach the speeding dragon.

A moment before the dragon crushed them both, it slowed again, expending more adani in that heartbeat than Elian had used in his entire life. It grabbed him and Capricia, each in a separate claw, then launched itself and its unprepared passengers into the sky.

27

Their problems began less than a day after they left the gathering grounds. They'd barely been gone for the morning when they came across a fresh track of dead grassland left by a wandering Debru. Samora hadn't sensed any near earlier that morning, so it had either moved a considerable distance, or her sense wasn't as reliable as she believed it to be.

Neither thought comforted her.

They both extended their adani, Karla now skeptical of Samora's claimed abilities, but neither sensed a Debru nearby. They continued along the path they'd agreed on earlier, but they hadn't gone more than a mile when they came across a pack of kettu.

Karla sensed them before they sniffed out the pair and shifted their path so that they were downwind of the creatures. They squatted in the grass and ate some of their dried meat while the kettu wandered in a different direction. Samora ignored the constant doubtful looks Karla shot her way.

It was possible she couldn't sense something as small as kettu from such a vast distance, but combined with the Debru's tracks, it seemed more likely that the Debru were on the move in the area. If so, the reason was likely her. They were being hunted.

Once the kettu were safely away, they returned to their feet and hurried northwest. Several days separated them from the assembled clans, and those miles seemed much longer now than they had when they'd planned the journey in the safety of the gathering grounds.

More kettu appeared within the next mile, and then again the mile after that. Karla sensed them both times and guided the pair safely around. By the time they reached a place Karla decided was safe to camp, Samora was exhausted from the constant tension.

That night, she was woken early by Karla's rough hand. When she cracked open an eye, she saw her companion had a finger to her lips. Samora nodded, sleep easily slipping into frustration. Did Karla think she was going to start babbling?

She rubbed her eyes and looked for the moon. It had been just over the horizon when she'd lain her head down and it wasn't much higher now. She stifled a groan as she rolled up into a deep squat.

Karla leaned over and whispered softly into her ear. "Two kettu, not far to the west. But there are otsoa in the distance."

Samora nodded. She'd decided it was wiser to follow Karla without question, so she didn't ask for further clarification. The adanist had lived for decades on her own. If anyone could guide Samora back to the safety of the wandering clans, it was this woman.

She felt Karla send out her adani, but even after it returned the elder adanist remained still. Time passed slowly, and Karla didn't move a muscle. She sent out another pulse of adani, pointed southwest, then raised her finger to her lips again.

Their progress was painfully slow. Karla moved through the tall grass with so much care they made less disturbance than a snake sliding across the ground. Samora followed as best as she was able, but she lacked Karla's experience. She felt like a cow rolling around in the grass in comparison.

Karla held up a hand to stop them. Samora had been following so closely behind, Karla's gesture almost accidentally slapped her. Karla sent out her adani, then whispered into her ear, "There are three otsoa just south of us. Maybe a hundred paces. I'll take the two to the east. You take the one to the west. Don't kill it, but make sure it can't follow us."

Samora frowned at the instructions, but Karla was already forming two bound spears. After seeing the adanist fling lightning, the handheld spears seemed rather pitiful. She was glad Karla only wanted the otsoa wounded. Despite the suffering the animals had caused, Samora wasn't sure she could bring herself to kill one. The idea of wounding one made her stomach churn, but she recognized the need. She followed suit, opting to create four spears instead of one.

Karla gave her a strange look but didn't ask any questions.

Samora nodded that she was ready, and Karla counted them down with her fingers. When she formed her fist, they both stood and flung their adani.

Guiding spears wasn't quite as simple as guiding the small points of adani she usually used, but there were only four and they were small. She struck true with three out of the four spears, each taking the otsoa in one of its powerful legs.

The otsoa took half a step and collapsed, letting out a painful wail that made Samora want to cover her ears. She feared the cry would bring the Debru, but Karla's otsoa made similar cries, and she didn't seem bothered. At Samora's questioning gaze, Karla said, "The Debru don't usually care when one of their pets gets hurt. If they did, they'd be rushing all over the place for no good reason. They only care when the creatures die, as that usually means an adanist is nearby."

Samora gestured to the otsoa, who continued their plaintive wails. Her heart went out to the wounded creatures, even though she knew that if she healed them, they'd thank her by snapping her neck in their jaws.

Karla shrugged. "I haven't sensed any Debru close enough to listen."

That hadn't been the entirety of what Samora had meant, but it was answer enough. The otsoa might be their enemy, but they were still just animals, and she'd been raised to only harm animals when necessary.

This was necessary, but it seemed kinder to give the otsoa a quick death than the slow suffering they would endure now. There weren't other predators in the area that would pick them off, so they wouldn't die until they bled out, which might be quite a while.

If Karla cared at all, she didn't show it. She sent out adani to scout their way, then continued to lead them roughly northwest.

THE SUN BURNED BRIGHTLY OVERHEAD, and Samora wished it would hide behind a cloud, or better yet, hide behind the horizon and ease the pounding behind her eyes. The journey that was supposed to take three days was now in its fifth, and Samora couldn't remember the last time she'd slept.

Truly slept.

She was so tired she sometimes lost entire miles of memory, and she wasn't sure if she'd just fallen asleep walking, or if her mind had become so tired it simply couldn't be bothered to remember even the most recent past.

She was far too tired to care about the answer.

Karla was in better shape than her, but not by much. The adanist had taken on the bulk of the responsibilities the last few days. She scouted with her adani and guided them through the ever-tightening noose of animals and Debru that hunted them. Three times more they'd had to cripple animals, but the last time, the Debru had learned. They'd shown up not long after, and it was fortunate Karla had sensed them coming from a distance and forced Samora to run until they were safely away.

They'd had to shuffle downstream through a muddy creek, and only Karla kicking water in her face prevented her from falling asleep and drowning in the shallow water.

Karla stopped at the top of a rise, but Samora didn't notice until she ran into the other woman's back. She mumbled something incoherent and tried to focus bleary eyes on the endless prairie.

A rider approached. Karla waved, and the gesture was returned. Karla took one look at Samora, then sighed. "Last time I agree to escort a pup through the wild."

Samora didn't even take offense. She was too glad to have stopped walking.

The scout's cold greeting cut through the warm blanket of exhaustion surrounding Samora. "What are you doing?"

Karla grunted. "Just fetch Tiafel, and quickly. He should bring some strong warriors with him for protection, too."

The scout raised himself to his full height, which struck Samora as being terribly funny. He was already sitting on a horse and towering over them. What good did sitting taller do? Especially against someone who stared down Belogs.

She snickered but silenced herself at Karla's sharp look. "We've figured out why the Belog are pursuing her. We could hurry straight to the center of your camp, but we don't want to endanger Hounds unless they agree to it. So go and summon Tiafel. We don't have much time."

Karla's explanation caused the scout's expression to drop into a deep frown.

"I could just order you to turn around," he said.

Karla nodded, and she revealed the full amount of adani she controlled. The air didn't quite crackle as it did before she attacked, but all of Samora's hair stood on end.

"You could," Karla answered.

The scout's horse whinnied and stamped around, and the color drained from his face. He nodded, then rode northwest without another word. Samora couldn't tell which was more eager to be gone: the horse or the rider.

Karla grunted. "Didn't even have the manners to say 'farewell.' I'm going to have to ask Tiafel how he's raising the young ones these days."

With that, Karla sat and pulled out some food. She offered some to Samora, who accepted it as she sat down beside the adanist.

"Thank you, for everything," she said.

She didn't want to imagine what would have happened if Karla hadn't intervened. More than likely, she'd be dead somewhere, torn apart by forces she didn't understand for a reason she'd never have discovered on her own.

"Happy to help," Karla answered.

Samora raised a skeptical eyebrow, but Karla didn't explain herself. The corner of Samora's lips turned up in a smile. If this was Karla willing to help, she pitied anyone near if Karla was forced to do something she didn't want.

It took longer for Tiafel and the others to show than Samora expected, and she hoped it wasn't because of some disagreements within the camp.

Eventually, though, Tiafel appeared, and he brought most of his greatest warriors. Samora saw all the warriors who made up Tiafel's council, as well as Warran and a handful of Bears. They were joined by a few other warriors Samora had never seen before. One older warrior stared at Karla with such venom Samora assumed he was Aldo, the leader of the Wolves.

She broke out in a genuine smile when she saw Lenon riding behind the warriors. Of all the Hounds, he was the one she missed the most, and was most eager to share her adventures with. If anyone could help her understand the abilities she'd developed, it would be him.

Tiafel ordered the horses to a stop several dozen paces away. A handful of the younger riders kept an eye on them while the rest of the Hounds and Wolves gathered around Karla and Samora.

Karla gestured for them to sit, and Tiafel eventually did, though he didn't look pleased. As soon as he sat, he cut straight to the heart of the matter. "Our scout says you know why Samora is being hunted, but also that the pursuit for you has only intensified. We came across kettu on our way here, too. Explain yourself."

The question was directed at Karla, and the adanist was more than happy to answer. She spoke briefly of their experiences since they'd left the wandering clans, from the discovery that Samora could push her adani farther than anyone Karla had met to her ability to heal the lands the Debru destroyed.

Lenon's ears perked up at that, and he shot Samora a questioning glance. She nodded and he stroked his chin as he smiled.

Tiafel was less impressed. "If we could find a way to send messages quickly back and forth over long distances, her ability to sense the Debru would prove invaluable. But as it is, it hardly makes a difference."

Aldo focused, though, on what mattered. "I don't think we need to worry about Samora's ability to sense so far away yet. Instead, let's focus on what it has taught us. The Debru are gathered around the circles, including one forming near a village. How will we respond?"

"If we attack, we leave our borders undefended," Tiafel said.

Samora forced herself to bite her tongue, but Karla didn't bother with restraint. "If you don't attack, you'll allow the Debru to do whatever they want *within* our borders."

Tiafel paled at that but didn't argue the point.

He wasn't given much of a chance, either. An otsoa howled off in the distance, followed by many more. The warnings from the scouts followed right on the heels of the howls. A young woman rushed up to their circle and bowed. "Otsoa are gathering but haven't attacked yet," she reported

"Any sign of Debru?" Tiafel asked.

"Not yet, but we fear they aren't far behind."

Tiafel shook his head as he looked at Karla and Samora. "You always bring trouble wherever you go."

Aldo snorted derisively. "You speak the truth there, old friend."

Karla paid them their insults little mind. "Will you welcome us in, or do we run?"

Warran spoke for the first time since the impromptu council had been seated. "I gave my word to Harald that the Bears would protect Samora. I was willing to let her travel in Karla's protection, but now that she seeks to return, I welcome her with open arms."

Samora felt a lump form in her throat, but she nodded her thanks.

A growl escaped from the back of Tiafel's throat, and after a moment's hesitation, he nodded. "Fine. Let's return to camp and prepare our defenses. If the Debru want these two, they'll have to fight to get them."

28

Had Elian been given a choice, he would have much preferred to fly on the dragon's back than in its claws. Riding on a dragon's back made him feel as though he and the dragon were partners. In its claw, he felt very much like a piece of meat, even if he was being carried away from the slaughter instead of toward it.

He took solace in the views. The dragon's claws gently pinned his arms to his side, but his head was free, so he could look around and watch both land and sky.

When he had been younger, he had dreamed about being a bird and taking flight. The dreams had returned after Father's death, when he'd spent every night flying as far away from the village as his wings would carry him. His wildest imaginings didn't come close to comparing to the reality.

Once the dragon had leveled off and Elian was reasonably certain he wasn't going to die soon, he gaped at the endless expanse of wild grassland. The deadlands were an enormous dark smudge against the green and browns of the living grassland. He lost himself in the rolling hills and the expansiveness of it all.

He'd always known, somewhere in the back of his mind, the

endless nature of the land, but in his daily life the world was much smaller. On a hard day he might only wander ten miles away from the village, and he'd wandered that area often enough there were landmarks everywhere he turned.

Flying stripped those landmarks and any sense of distance from him, forcing him to confront the vastness of the land directly. It stunned him into a temporary, wondrous stupor.

Capricia returned him to the paths of reason. Her head was only a pace away from his, but she still had to shout to be heard. "Where do you think it's taking us?"

The question hadn't yet occurred to Elian. He'd been so lost in wonder and gratitude for escaping the Debru he hadn't worried about their destination. He'd just assumed, without any reason, the dragons would take them someplace safe.

Elian craned his neck to catch a glimpse of the sun. The dragon was too large, and it blocked out his view, but he could see the shadows of trees and hills far below, and he quickly determined they were flying west.

Deeper into Debru-controlled territory.

His heart pounded faster. "West!"

Something tickled his thoughts, something that didn't seem right, but he didn't see anything that worried him.

"Are you sure?" Capricia called.

Elian looked down again and took note of the shadows. It was closer to evening than morning, so shadows would fall to the east, and they were heading the opposite direction.

"Yes!"

"There's no deadlands!"

Elian's eyes widened. Capricia was right, and it was that detail that had been worrying at his own thoughts. The wandering clans had accepted that everything to the west was deadlands, but that wasn't true. The grasslands below were as healthy and fertile as anything closer to Elian's village.

The wandering clans needed to know, and they needed to

return to their families and friends. Elian craned his neck, though it did nothing to bring him closer to the dragon's face. "Hello! Thank you for saving us!"

The dragon kept flying, as though it hadn't heard anything.

Elian didn't know what to say to a dragon. He wasn't even close to certain the dragon could understand a word he said, but he didn't have a better idea, so he said, "Could you take us back to our friends? They'd be willing to help you, too!"

The dragon flew on, oblivious to Elian's attempts. Capricia tried after Elian, but her luck was no different than his own. When her spirits waned, he gave it one more try, simply because he didn't know what else to do.

Eventually they both gave up. Elian kept his spirits up, though. He was flying with a dragon, and he was alive. He'd expected neither not that long ago. "We'll find a way back!" he promised Capricia.

She said something in response, but he didn't catch it. He lifted his head to look at her, but she was looking down and the wind blew her hair in such a way that he couldn't catch the slightest glimpse of her expression.

He let his head fall. The dragon didn't seem as though it was going to put them down soon, so he turned inward, pushing adani through his body. It was already working on healing his ankle, but with his attention, the efforts sped up. Elian wasn't sure he'd be in fighting shape when they landed, but at the very least he should be able to walk.

He bit his lower lip. He was making the same assumption he'd made before, that the dragons somehow had good intentions. Perhaps the only reason they'd been saved was because Debru didn't taste good, and the dragons needed a snack before continuing their journey.

Being able to walk was a start, but it wasn't enough. He needed to be able to fight.

Hopefully, the dragon wouldn't mind if he stole a bit more of its adani. He opened himself up fully to the dragon's power, and it flowed through his body as though he was resting in the gathering grounds.

Adani washed the aches and pains from his limbs. Weary muscles felt well rested, and the weights fell from his eyelids. He pushed more adani toward his ankle, hoping it could heal even faster. It grew warm as strength straightened the ankle and sucked the swelling away.

He didn't think he'd pulled the dragon's strength for long when he tested the ankle by rolling it around. It felt as good as it ever had, and he said a silent thanks to the dragon. He was about to cut himself off from the flow of adani when he noticed something unusual.

Though he didn't want to miss a moment of this flight, he closed his eyes to focus on the sensation. The torrent of adani was so great that it caused some of his own adani to spill out. It was as if he was a half-full cup of water, and someone kept pouring pails of fresh water into him. Most of it spilled out, and most of what spilled out was from the pail, but a little had started in the cup.

His adani reached the dragon, dwelled there for a moment, then returned.

It was a pale imitation of what Samora or Capricia was capable of, but it was the same technique. The biggest difference was that his happened by accident instead of by intention. Still, it made him feel like a proper adanist.

He followed the flow of adani into the dragon and paid careful attention to it as it returned to him. It returned slightly changed from when it left, and in that change, Elian discovered a brand-new world.

Emotions hit him first. He could name them as they passed through him, but they weren't his emotions. These went painfully deep, striking into his soul like a hammer forging a sword. He named the first emotion anger, but it was a burning inferno compared to the dim and flickering candle of his own anger.

At first, he thought the anger was directed toward him, but that wasn't quite right. The anger wasn't at him, but for him. The dragon raged at the Debru for attacking Elian.

Elian's heart leaped. First, it meant that he was much less likely to be a dragon meal soon, but it also meant the dragons stood against the Debru, just as humanity did. Once again, he considered the tantalizing possibility of allying with the dragons.

Anger wasn't all he felt. The dragon was also filled with compassion, and this *was* directed at him and Capricia. There was something else lurking beneath anger and compassion, but it took him a while to understand what his adani told him.

The dragon carried with it a deep well of sorrow, deeper even than the adani it could call upon. Elian probed further, seeking the reason for such sorrow, but a dark veil hung between his spirit and that of the dragon's, and he couldn't see what lay beyond.

His attempts stirred something within the dragon, and Elian soon realized he had company. In his eagerness he lost his focus, and the presence faded for a moment before he recovered it.

What came to Elian weren't words, exactly, but the meanings that lay behind words, the truths that language could do nothing more than point at. The dragon was taking him home, someplace safe, in gratitude for saving the dragon's life.

Except the dragon's lands were far from the lands Elian called home. From what he sensed, this dragon called a mountainous land countless miles away its own. The dragon would take him far away from the Debru and their invasion, but even farther away from all he'd ever known.

The dragon showed Elian its range, and it was a beautiful land, as far removed from the plains of his youth as fire was from water. Towering waterfalls dropped so far, the streams that fed them turned to mist before they reached the bottom. Walls of gray stone rose to heights that made the majestic trees of the gathering ground seem as small as saplings. Caves within the stone served as home for the dragons, sheltering them from the elements and prying eyes.

It was the sort of land Elian had only heard of in legends, a place he could easily explore for the rest of his life and still not understand even a small part of its secrets.

A place away from all the problems that haunted him.

His heart soared as high as the dragon that carried him, but it fell to the dirt even faster. The dream, tempting though it was, wasn't real. The dragons had been caught, hadn't they?

He formed the question without words, imagining the Belog catching the dragon and asking how.

The dragon grumbled but showed Elian a memory. It had flown toward a circular patch of barren land. Through the dragon's vision, Elian saw not just the desolation of the surface, but the darkness that churned underneath. The dragon extended adani into the Debru circle in an attempt to shatter its hold on the land.

It hadn't sensed the danger until it was too late. The Belog had hidden its spirit and launched itself from the shadows of a nearby tree. When the shadowy tendrils had wrapped around the dragon, they'd entrapped both flesh and spirit.

The feeling of the barbs digging into the dragon's soul, shared with perfect clarity, reminded Elian of an experience he would much rather forget. It was the same shadow that had dug its way into his soul and turned him against his sister.

A shiver ran up his spine. He'd touched those shadows again. He searched his body for sign of the infection but sensed none.

Connected as they were, the dragon understood his efforts. It revealed another memory, much more recent. Of Elian, carried in the dragon's claw, but with a fragment of shadow within. Elian sensed himself cleanse his body of the fragment, pushing it out when he borrowed the dragon's adani to strengthen his own.

He hadn't even noticed.

The dragon's generous offer tempted Elian in a way he wasn't prepared to resist. The new land and freedom promised endless opportunities, a chance to see more than he'd ever dreamed of.

All he had to do was sacrifice his family.

He figured it was a mark of how tempted he was that he even considered it.

Instead, he imagined the gathering ground where Harald, Kati, and the others waited for them. He tried to locate it as well as he could, trying to show the dragon where it was. He imagined returning on the dragon's back.

The dragon didn't respond, but Elian sensed another flow of adani, one he wasn't included in. He caught flickers of brief thoughts, but they were foreign to him.

The dragons silently spoke to one another.

He wanted to interject, to find some way to take part in the conversation, but he guessed he'd been excluded for a reason.

Whatever passed between their rescuers ended quickly. The dragon's presence returned to press against Elian's senses, and it said that it agreed.

Elian's heart soared even as the dragons descended. He and Capricia were gently released onto the ground. He put his full weight on his foot and was pleased to find it held him without complaint.

The dragons settled next to them and waited expectantly.

"What do they want?" Capricia asked.

"They're going to take us home."

Capricia looked at him as though he'd lost his mind, and he scratched at the back of his neck.

"I think I can speak with them, at least a little. They were going to take us to their home, which is even farther west, but I asked them to return us to the gathering grounds. They agreed."

He couldn't tell if her eyes were wider when she looked at him or the dragons.

Elian climbed up the one he'd helped save from the shadowy rope, the same one he'd "spoken" with. It didn't fling him off, so he assumed their agreement held.

Capricia climbed on the other dragon with only a little hesitation. Once they were both securely mounted, the dragons spread their wings and leaped into the sky.

Elian almost cried. From the tension of this morning's hunt to the creeping dread of observing the Debru forces, his spirit had endured a wide range of emotions. He'd surrendered to certain death, only to find himself flying with dragons.

He tried to extend his adani into the dragon so they could converse some more, but it rebuffed his efforts, not unkindly, but firmly.

Elian took note. The dragon didn't have to share its adani if it didn't want. Or, at the very least, Elian wasn't strong enough to force the matter.

His conversation stymied, he took joy in watching Capricia ride her dragon. Her smile was so wide it was as if the wind had pulled her face back into a permanent grin. She shifted her position every few beats of Elian's heart, as though no single view could satisfy her.

Before long, he had a matching smile on his face, which only fell when he wished Samora could be here, too. He didn't think she'd experience quite the same delight Capricia did, but she'd love it all the same.

It wasn't all that long before they passed over the deadlands, the sight of which caused Elian's stomach to knot like it had earlier in the day. He saw no sign of the Debru but wasn't sure what that meant.

Soon after the vivid green canopy of the gathering grounds came into view. Elian felt a pressure against his adani, so he extended once again to converse. The simple act of extending his adani made him want to leap and shout. It might be nothing compared to most adanists, but it remained a great success for him.

He asked the dragons to drop him and Capricia near the edge of the gathering ground, and the dragon seemed to accept. They banked and lost altitude, coming to a gentle stop just inside the border of the gathering grounds. Elian couldn't say with any certainty, but it felt to him as though they were as pleased to be upon the gathering grounds as he was.

Harald, Brittany, and Alec soon emerged from the trees, advancing as though they weren't sure if they faced a new enemy. Kati and a band of her Wolves were right behind.

Harald spotted Elian first, and Elian waved. The enormous warrior stood, slack jawed as he stared at the impossible sight.

Elian slid off the dragon, then approached Harald. "Well, we've had quite the day. How about you?"

29

The assembled leaders and warriors beat a hasty retreat to the relative safety of their camp. In their haste, Samora and Karla were largely forgotten, left to make the journey on foot while the others rode to safety. Only Warran spared a handful of his Bears to ensure they reached camp in one piece.

Tiafel's and Aldo's casual dismissal added one more coal to Samora's growing frustration. The Debru were camped by her home, standing guard only a few miles from where her mother slept. The wandering clans should be sounding the horns and mounting their horses, not retreating to their camp to decide their next steps.

When she'd first met the wandering clans, she'd finally felt as though she'd found a home of her own. But the more she got to know of them, the more unsure of that first impression she became.

Her thoughts must have been written on her face because Karla said, "Don't judge them too harshly. The answer may seem obvious to you, but for these men, all our futures ride on their shoulders. They won't make this decision lightly."

"Waiting to decide is a decision too, and it's one that might kill my mother."

"And everyone else you've ever known." Karla agreed. "But that doesn't necessarily make it the wrong decision."

"How can you say that?" Samora snapped.

"Because I've had to make those decisions too," Karla said quietly.

It wasn't her words, so much as it was the weight of sorrow behind them, that silenced Samora. She'd glimpsed all too briefly a handful of the moments that Karla spoke of. It was easy to forget sometimes the burden of experience she carried.

Karla waved away the apology Samora was about to utter. "It's not that you're wrong either, but if you don't see the world as they do, you'll never sway their opinions."

The words settled heavily on Samora's shoulders. She wanted to argue it shouldn't be her place to convince the leaders. While her complaint might be true, it didn't matter. She was letting her opinions of how the world should be get in the way of changing the world as it was. That had been one of the first lessons about adani Mother had hammered into her. Too many adanists tried to weave the force in ways they believed should work. They lost themselves in attempt after attempt when all they had to do was observe how adani actually behaved.

She remembered Karla's words about Tiafel in the gathering grounds. "You said Tiafel was waiting for a perfect moment that will never come. Why?"

Karla inhaled deeply. "It's hard to explain to one so young."

Samora's expression encouraged Karla to try anyway.

"You need to understand how so many years of leading a clan changes a person. Tiafel has ordered hundreds of friends and family to their deaths, and for what? What success have we seen that in any way makes our sacrifices worth it? That's the question he asks deep in his heart. I have little doubt that if you were to ask him, he would tell you he's fighting to win. I'm sure he even believes it. But he's not looking to win. Not anymore. He's fighting not to lose."

"So how do I get him to help?"

Karla turned the question back on her. "What do you think?"

Samora sat with the question for a time, pondering as she walked. Howls of the Otsoa followed them but seemed farther away than before. They were distant enough that they didn't interrupt her thinking.

"I need to make him believe that doing nothing is more dangerous than attacking the Debru."

Karla's slight nod of approval made Samora feel like she'd just completed a difficult binding. But her excitement quickly faded as the next question came to mind.

"So how do I do that?"

Karla shook her head. "That, girl, I don't know. But we'll have to figure it out by the time we reach their camp. Otherwise, your village might never receive the help it needs."

It felt as though Karla had dumped a pile of stones on top of her head, and the weight was overwhelming. Karla saw her distress but did nothing to help.

The camp of the Hounds, Bears, and Wolves came into view and Samora slowed her pace. She needed more time to think and to plan. More time to work up her courage. This was beyond her.

But she had no choice except to put one foot in front of the other.

Too many people were counting on her. She couldn't afford to fail.

———

BY THE TIME THEY ARRIVED, the council was already halfway gathered near the center of the camp. Almost everyone who had rode out to greet them was present, and many more beside.

Samora took one look at the gathering of warriors and turned around, fear forming a lump in her throat.

Karla stopped her before she could find a corner to hide in. "Just where do you think you're going?"

Anywhere but here. Samora couldn't say the words, but was sure Karla felt her terror. Her heart thudded against her chest.

It wasn't just the number of people, though that was a large part of it. It was their strength and their expectation of her. The gathered council weren't just warriors. They controlled a blinding amount of adani that made her head spin. To step inside that circle invited a splitting headache, an agony so strong she wouldn't be able to hear herself think.

And in that maelstrom, she'd be expected to persuade them to send their loved ones into a battle they had little hope of winning.

She couldn't.

She didn't belong anywhere within miles of this place. When she'd left their village, it had been with the expectation that the wandering clans would know about the circles and know how to heal them. She'd looked forward to seeing more of the world and possibly meeting masters who would teach her more about her abilities.

Now she'd seen more of the world, and she'd met masters who had been able to help her. All she wanted today was to return home.

But to do so, she'd have to go through the Debru, who were hunting her.

The unfairness of it all made her want to curl up in a ball.

Karla leaned close, so she could speak without being overheard. "There's nothing to fear."

Samora looked at her as though she'd gone mad. Her expression softened, though, when she saw the compassion on Karla's face.

Karla said, "You're thinking that you don't belong here. You don't want this, right?"

Samora nodded, grateful not to have to explain how she felt.

"None of this is about you. That council needs to know what we know, and I think it's worth them knowing what we believe. But what happens after is their responsibility. If they decide not to fight, that's on them. You can't take responsibility for a decision that isn't yours."

"But why should they listen to me?" Samora's voice was hoarse.

"Because you've got a gift that none of them possess, at least not yet. It doesn't mean that you're right, but they'd be fools not to listen."

"It hurts to be among them." Samora hated the petulance in her voice but couldn't control it.

"I know that better than most, but you'll suffer a much greater pain if you don't try. Then you will bear some responsibility for what happens, and it will eat at your spirit until there's nothing left."

Samora stood, rooted in place, torn between advance and retreat. When she thought of entering that circle and having every eye on her, her knees felt weak. She'd rather face another Belog than the combined councils of three wandering clans.

Thoughts of the Belog calmed her racing heart and focused her attention. If she didn't speak to the councils, the Debru won, and if they won, she suspected her warm world would someday look like the one she'd visited in her visions.

She nodded.

"Good," Karla said. The older adanist kept a firm grip on Samora's arm as they completed their long journey. They sat in the grass as the other adanists gathered. Everyone moved with a quick step, so it wasn't long before Samora was sitting in the heart of the largest council she'd ever witnessed. Most of the adanists were from the Hounds, with the Wolves close behind.

Warran only brought a few warriors to the council, but all of them together made the otherwise large space feel small.

Tiafel spoke first. "Everyone here knows what has happened. The Debru have broken through our lines, wiping out the Crow clan in the process. As we speak, they have set up camp only a few miles away from one of the outer villages, standing guard around one of the mysterious circles. We don't know what those circles are or what they mean to the Debru, but they care enough about them to defend them, which doesn't mean anything good for us."

Tiafel paused to measure the reaction to his words. He'd said nothing that wasn't known by all, but his summary was met with grim looks. Samora wished she knew these leaders better so that she could guess what thoughts ran behind their stony faces.

Tiafel continued. "After some discussion, two ideas are our best, though 'best' is perhaps too generous a term for the choices we face. The most straightforward option is that we attack the Debru with our combined forces. We outnumber them substantially, though that isn't taking into consideration the two Belogs. Victory would be anything but certain."

A few heads nodded around the gathering, but Samora didn't know if they were agreeing with Tiafel's declaration that victory wasn't certain, or if they were eagerly awaiting a fight.

"The second option is to retreat and reform our lines on the other side of the Debru. If we did, we would likely abandon the outer village. We can plan our retreat so that we pass by the village. If we all work together, we can get their tools and necessary possessions loaded into our sleds. We can take all the stored food, as well. The villagers can join us on our retreat, and when we have the time, we can escort the villagers to new homes or absorb them into our ranks if they wish. However, it makes no sense to attempt to protect the village with so many Debru so close. Better to help the villagers abandon it before the fighting begins. If the circles keep expanding, it wouldn't be long before the village was consumed, anyway."

Samora's hands had become fists, and she was halfway to standing before Karla pulled her back down. Tiafel probably hadn't meant to be as dismissive of her village's fate as he had been, but he certainly acted as though the loss of Samora's home was nothing more than a temporary inconvenience.

Karla's grip was firm. She leaned over. "Hold onto it for now. Your time will come."

Tiafel again looked around the circle, but his gaze never came close to where Samora sat.

"I believe our best hope for survival is to retreat and reform our lines on the other side of the village," Tiafel concluded. "Our lines were stretched thin before the loss of the Crows, but now that they're gone, contracting is our only hope of maintaining a solid defense against the Debru. Hopefully, as we come into closer contact with other clans, we'll be able to push back and retake the land that we've lost. The Serpents patrol their lands as well as the Hawks', and though they are far away, if we send word the Red Foxes might answer."

Tiafel might believe his claims, but Samora knew it for a fool's dream. They would retreat and retreat, always being whittled down by the unrelenting pressure the Debru crushed them with. The clans would wither and weaken as the Debru grew in strength and numbers.

Fortunately, Samora wasn't the only one who felt that way. One of the warriors stood. He rose from among the Wolves, but Samora had never seen him before. "We can't keep retreating. If we surrender one of the outer villages, it won't be long before we're fighting for one of the inner villages."

There were a few muttered agreements to this, but not as many as Samora would have liked to see.

Tiafel nodded along with the concern. "I share your fear, but the time to strike isn't right. This gathering is evidence enough.

With all of us here, how many miles of our land is now unde-fended? Abram taught us to strike from a position of strength, but right now we are as weak as newborn lambs."

"That isn't true," Karla said, raising her voice so that all could hear her clearly. "Yes, we've been hit hard, and even more so as of late, but we are not weak. The youth among us are some of the most talented adanists we've seen in generations, and there is another part of the story that needs to be heard. We might finally have a weapon that can strike hard at the Debru."

Tiafel nodded, giving Karla permission to continue. Karla, in turn, gestured for Samora to rise. "Now's your turn."

Samora stood, but her legs quivered, and she was certain she would either faint or collapse in front of the gathered warriors. She tried to swallow the lump of fear in her throat that made it hard to breathe, but it remained firmly lodged. Just as she'd feared, every eye in the gathering was on her, waiting to hear of the weapon Karla promised.

Her throat was dry, and she would have done almost anything for a skin of water. One warrior across the circle cleared her throat, clearly impatient, but Samora didn't even know where to begin. Her head pounded with every beat of her heart, making it difficult to stitch her thoughts together into an argument.

The silence stretched, and Samora swore she could hear the disgruntled warriors start to mutter under their breath. She almost sat back down, but she knew too well the consequences of failing here.

She forced herself to take a deep breath and relax her body. All she had to do was speak, and then it would all be over. But she couldn't do it.

She sought refuge, as she often had in the past, in adani. Her first brush against the timeless force pained her, the gathering of strong spirits blinding her to all else. She didn't flee the sensa-tion, though, but sat with it. After a heartbeat, or perhaps several, her senses adapted, and she marveled at the web of adani that connected the warriors here.

Her attention wandered to the connections between her and the others. When she stood, she had felt all alone, but now she saw through that illusion. The warriors here were legends, but they shared her worries and her fears. They looked to her, a nobody from one of the outer villages, for any shred of hope.

Adani flowed between them, but it seemed to her she had more to give. It was, she thought, a clear as sign as she'd felt from adani in many days.

She found her voice, which rang out loud and clear across the gathering.

"When I traveled with Karla, we discovered I could heal land the Debru had passed through. As soon as I did, the nearest Belog attacked, and we still aren't sure why. The longer we thought about it, the more we became convinced it might have something to do with the circles. Whatever they are, they're important to the Debru and they're growing. Perhaps this ability to heal the land extends to healing the circles, as well. It's the only reason we could think of why the Debru would react so strongly. But to be sure, I need to visit a circle and test my new abilities against it."

She took another deep breath, not daring to look around the circle. "I know what I ask, and I know that I have no right to do so, but an attack on the Debru opens up possibilities for me and Karla to investigate the circles and maybe even break their hold on the land."

Samora bowed deeply and sat. Sweat poured from her armpits and down her back, and she was sure those sitting next to her could smell the stink of her fear.

It was worth it, though. Several of the council spoke up, agreeing that an attack on the Debru gathering was their best plan. Samora could do nothing but stare at the ground in front of her, but as she heard one councilor after another speak in favor of the attack, her spirits lifted. Not everyone agreed, but she felt the majority were with her.

She had done it. The satisfaction, combined with the nerves leaving her body, caused her to shake.

She barely noticed when Tiafel stood up and the increasingly agitated crowd grew silent. She only noticed when Tiafel called her name. When she looked up, every eye was once again on her.

All her worries and fears came crashing back upon her, stronger than before because they were unexpected.

"You say that you and Karla believe the Belog attacked you because of your healing of the land. Do you have any proof to support your claim?"

"The Belog launched itself into motion the moment I healed the land," Samora said.

"But isn't it just as possible that the Belog was searching for Karla, and your healing allowed it to find you?"

"No Belog's ever moved that fast just for me," Karla spat.

"So far," Tiafel countered, his voice a gentle rebuke to Karla's sharp tone. "I believe everything you said is what happened, but I can't help but question the conclusions you arrived at. Do you know you can heal the circles?" he asked Samora.

She had to shake her head.

"Indeed, you've been inside more circles than anyone here. Was there anything in those past experiences that would lead you to believe you could heal them?"

Samora remembered the feel of the circles, the way that adani unraveled within them. She wanted to argue her case, but she wouldn't lie, not with so many lives at stake. She shook her head again.

"So, you want us to risk all of our lives, simply because you *believe* you can heal the circles, absent of any real evidence?"

"It's the only rea—" Karla began.

"It's the only reason you can think of!" Tiafel thundered,

surprising them all with his vehemence. His outburst silenced even Karla.

His voice returned to its typical gentle volume. "I want to believe that what you're telling me is true. That Samora has a gift the Debru finally fear. I've wanted to believe something like this since I was a child. But it's for exactly this reason that I need to be skeptical. Every life here is precious to me, and if we get this wrong, there's a good chance it's all of humanity that pays the price. I'm sorry, but I simply can't believe you. Not without proof you can share."

A long silence fell over the council, and Samora felt the tide of sentiment turning against her. She searched for something that would convince the council, persuade them that she and Karla's guesses were right.

But they were just guesses, and Tiafel was right to doubt.

"I still believe our best course of action is to reform the lines and abandon the outer village, at least for now. Once we've strengthened ourselves, we can send a group with Karla and Samora to seek out proof. We're not giving up. We're just planning to strike at the best possible moment."

The argument sealed the decision. Even Samora was almost halfway convinced it was the right and reasonable course of action.

Slowly, a handful of voices rose to agree with Tiafel. The agreements came faster and faster, until the final decision was nearly unanimous.

The wandering clans would retreat, and Samora had failed. Her home, built by her father's hands, would soon be abandoned to the ever-growing threat of the Debru.

❧ 30 ❧

Seeing the surprise on Harald's face was worth all the suffering Elian had endured in the past day. The giant warrior, calm even in the face of massive Debru assaults, looked as though he were contemplating running back into the cover of the trees.

The effect was even more pronounced when the dragon Elian had been riding roared. Even Elian jumped. He spun around and reached his hand to his sword as he sought some new enemy.

None presented themselves, and it seemed to Elian the dragon's roar had a different quality than it had when they'd freed it from the Debru.

"Do you have something to say?" he asked.

In response, the dragon lowered its head. Elian walked up to it and placed his hand next to the snout. The dragon's breath felt hot enough to singe the hair on his arms, and he was all too aware of how close he was to the dragon's sharp teeth, but he couldn't understand the dragon unless he touched it.

And although he knew it was petty, he was also well aware that he was being watched by a group of warriors who didn't think much of him yet. This was as good a time as any to change that.

He wouldn't learn what the dragon needed from him if he was thinking about impressing Harald, though, so he dropped those thoughts and focused on his adani. He looped it through the hand that touched the dragon, then pushed it just beyond.

As before, he sensed the connection with the dragon, though as before, it felt more like he was pulled in by the dragon instead of being in control of the process himself. He didn't fight the pull, though, and a vision floated before him. It was of the dragons, circling the Debru high above their camp. He recognized the shaped contours of the land. It was the same place they'd encountered the Debru.

The dragon pulled his attention away from the Debru toward a spot to the west. Elian saw nothing that caught his attention, but he sensed a difference in the land through the dragon's senses. A perfect circle of deadlands that pulled all adani away, protected by a much vaster deadland that didn't.

The vision faded, but the dragon's next message was so clear it was as if it was spoken. The Debru and the circle both needed to be destroyed.

"How?" Elian asked.

His eyes widened at the answer.

The dragon gently shoved Elian's adani away and he stood alone, his hand resting on the dragon's snout. He pulled it away, took a few steps back, and bowed. The dragon waited, as patient as a mountain.

Under any other circumstance, there was no chance Harald would believe him, but with a dragon at his back?

It might just be possible.

Elian squared his shoulders and turned around to face the others. They all looked eager to shower him with questions, but the presence of the dragon made them as quiet as Samora. Elian gulped, then said, "I can tell you the full story later, but Capricia and I freed these dragons from the Debru. I've been able to speak with them, after a fashion, and they've shared with me some of their information."

Harald and the others didn't look to be in any more disbelief than before, so Elian continued. "The Debru seem to be protecting one of the circles that Samora and I first saw, and then you witnessed, Harald. The dragons believe they are a great danger and need to be destroyed."

Harald had the same question Elian had asked a moment ago. "How?"

"The dragons believe they are capable of the deed. But to do so, they'll need to focus their attention on the circle. Their previous attempt was what got them captured by the Belog, and the same is certain to happen if they try again. They want us to fight the Debru while they break the circle."

Harald cracked his knuckles, and to Elian's surprise, directed his first question at him instead of the dragons. "You saw the Debru camp?"

Elian nodded, not sure where any of this was going.

"They all just standing around there, like Drina once told me?"

Elian didn't know who Drina was, but he nodded.

Harald turned to Kati. "What do you think?"

She proved to be the more cautious of the two. "How many Debru are there in the camp?"

"Three dozen, plus two Belog," Elian said. He'd counted often to make sure.

"That's a lot," Kati said to Harald.

"Wouldn't be fun if it wasn't," Harald replied.

"Are there more dragons that could help?" Kati asked the dragon.

Elian thought he would have to connect with the dragon again, but to his surprise, the dragon nodded its head.

"And this is something you think we need to do?" Kati asked.

Another nod.

Kati and Harald shared a look, but it seemed as though they'd come to an agreement. "Then you'll have us at your side. Can we launch the assault at dawn, the morning after tomorrow?" Harald asked.

The dragon nodded again.

"We'll see you there," Kati said.

The dragon gave one last roar, then spread its wings and shot into the air. Elian joined Harald and the others in watching it speed into the distance. Once it was gone, Harald clapped Elian so hard on the shoulder it felt as though the joint was going to pop out of its socket. "You are without a doubt one of the most interesting people I've ever met," he said.

"It feels like I'm mostly in the wrong place at the wrong time."

"Seems to be doing you good so far. Loken must have really helped you, too. I can feel the change in how adani flows through your body."

Elian and Capricia joined the others as they retreated into the wooded sections of the gathering grounds. They told their story in bits and pieces, frequently interrupted by the others. They'd only been gone a day, but it felt as if the whole world had shifted around them in that time.

No longer did he feel like an outsider looking in. Though they asked question after question, not one had to do with his abilities. Capricia downplayed her own involvement and made no mention of Elian's inability to bind adani like the rest of them.

Sitting around the Hawk's fire was as comfortable as sitting down to eat with his family, and when he finally fell to bed that night, it was with a contented sigh.

HARALD FOUND him training by himself early the next morning. "I was hoping to get a word with you."

"Of course." Elian released the adani focused in his legs, marveling at the way it returned to the rest of his body without hesitation, like a small stream of water returning to its course after the children's dam broke. After so many seasons of fighting the wrong battle, it was as if endless vistas of possibility now stretched out before him.

His greatest regret was that he hadn't discovered the truth earlier.

"Why the long face?" Harald asked.

Elian made a fist, then released it. "I was just thinking how much stronger I would be if I'd learned the truth about my abilities earlier. I spent years trying to bind adani, thinking I was useless. You and Loken guided me to the truth, but now I must start all over."

Harald's face was impassive, and Elian felt as though the enormous adanist didn't sympathize. "Few prey are as elusive as truth. Instead of regretting the time it took you to discover it, you should celebrate the fact you found it all."

When Elian didn't respond, Harald said, "Think of all the different paths you could have followed. You grew up in a village, so no one would have judged you for putting adani aside and throwing your strength into the fields. Instead, your choices have led you here. You're stronger than before and you're about to take part in a battle that villagers will be singing about before the end of harvest."

Elian wished he could share Harald's enthusiasm, but he couldn't so easily let go of the memory of all those wasted years.

Harald, sensing that his arguments were failing, said, "It's actually about the battle tomorrow that I wanted to speak with you."

Elian looked up sharply. "You want me to stay behind?"

Harald frowned. "What? No. I want you by my side when the

attack begins. I've promised Kati that I would bring her a Belog's head as a gift."

Elian almost choked on his next breath. "You did *what*?"

The sheepish grin on Harald's face looked out of place. Harald scratched at the back of his head. "It's possible I got carried away, but now that I've made the promise, I intend to see it through. The Belog needs to die, anyway, so we might as well be the ones to do it."

"Just you and me?"

"Tera is going to join us, too."

Elian knew he should be honored that Harald wanted him, but a powerful wave of doubt drowned any pride he might have possessed. Who was he, to think he belonged by Harald's side?

Hadn't he just said he was just starting to learn? He would help in the fight, but not against a Belog. He stared down at his feet as he shook his head. "I don't think that's a wise idea."

"Why not?" Harald's vehemence startled Elian and made him take a step back. "Your sword has ended more Debru than most of my warriors have, and you've shown no lack of courage in the short time I've known you. So why wouldn't I want you to help me with one of the most important parts of tomorrow's battle?"

"You know why," Elian said.

"I really don't," Harald answered. Elian expected him to continue, but Harald went silent, offering the statement as a challenge. But Harald had to understand. He might act like a fool at times, but he wasn't one.

Elian's insides squirmed under the weight of Harald's gaze, but eventually he had no choice but to answer, to confess his shame. "I want to fight and help. Truly, I do. But I'm still learning how to use my strength. I'm nothing like you or Tera. If anything, I've been more lucky than strong. If I join you tomorrow, you're going to have to worry more about protecting me than fighting the Belog, and I won't be the reason you have to hold back."

Elian's cheeks flushed with shame. He couldn't raise his eyes to meet Harald's, but he saw the giant's fists clenched so tight the knuckles were white. For a moment, he feared Harald was about to hit him, but the legendary warrior simply turned on his heel and walked away without another word.

HE DIDN'T JOIN the others for that evening's supper, claiming that he wanted to continue his training. No one questioned his story, for which he was grateful. Training would have done him well, but he'd been next to useless since Harald's visit that morning. Bitter thoughts intruded frequently, robbing him of the focus he required to shift the flow of his adani. He spent twice as much time cursing himself for his foolishness as he did training.

He was sitting on a fallen tree, doing exactly that, when Capricia found him. She carried a pair of bowls in her hands, which she balanced perfectly as she sat down beside him. She extended one of the bowls to him.

Pride almost made him refuse her offer, but his stomach growled loudly. He blushed, bowed his head in thanks, and took the bowl. He ate slowly, the only sounds the laughter of the others in the distance and the scrape of their spoons against the sides of the bowl. It didn't take long for the bowl to empty. He put it down beside him.

"Thank you," he said.

"You're welcome. Were you the one who infuriated Harald?"

Elian nodded.

"Wondered if that might be the case. Everybody but Kati has been staying out of his way since this morning."

She didn't ask for an explanation, but Elian felt as though he owed her one. "Harald wants me to join him and Tera to join the attack against one of the Belog tomorrow. I told him that would be a mistake, that he would spend more time trying to protect me than fighting the Debru."

Capricia looked up at the night sky, barely visible through the trees. "When Kati asked me to join you, she told me that you didn't use adani like the rest of us. The implication was that I was supposed to protect you, which I agreed to."

Elian felt some of the weight lift off his shoulders. Finally, someone agreed with him. He needed too much protection to be useful in such an important battle.

She continued, "But then, when the battle found us, it was you who came back to rescue me. You could have flown off on the dragon, and I wouldn't have even blamed you. But you returned, and somehow convinced the dragons to join our fight. I was much more of a burden on you than you were on me."

Capricia stood and held out her hand to take Elian's bowl. Elian handed it to her, offering another slight bow of thanks. His insides turned as her words created a maelstrom in his chest.

"Sometimes, it's easier for others to see the truth about us."

She took the bowls and started to walk away but stopped before she got too far. She didn't turn, but she cast her voice in his direction. "Harald hasn't asked anyone else to join him tomorrow, either."

ELIAN DIDN'T SLEEP well that night, but few of the warriors did. It would take time to reach the battlefield by dawn, and it was just past the middle of the night when the combined forces of the Hawks and the Hounds started to form.

Elian had tossed and turned as his mind tumbled over what Harald and Capricia had told him. When word came that it was time to gather, he wiped the bleariness from his eyes, stood, and stretched. He strapped his sword to his hip and drew it to ensure it cleared the sheath without a problem.

The sword felt good in his hand, as though it had always belonged there. It was, without doubt, the most generous gift anyone had given him. After all the tossing and turning, the final decision was surprisingly easy.

Elian followed the others, and it was no problem finding the place where he belonged. Harald and Tera were near the front of the assembly, standing alone. He came, stood by Harald's side, and locked his gaze onto the darkness stretching out ahead of him.

Harald glanced down and grunted softly. Elian saw the leader's smile in the corner of his eye, and knew it matched his own.

                         ❧ 31 ❧

T   he Wolves, Hounds, and Bears began their retreat the next
        day. The combined council had argued long into the night
about what their new boundaries would be, and from what
rumors Samora had heard, none of the clans was particularly
happy about the resulting compromise. Enormous swaths of land
were about to be given up without a fight, and even the gathering
ground of the Wolves was at risk of being abandoned.

   None of the disagreement changed the leaders' decision to
retreat, dashing the last of Samora's hopes. Now they walked, not
just away from the land they'd once guarded, but away from the
Debru as well. Their plan was to make a large half-circle, avoiding
any conflict with the Debru by retreating south first, then circling
around farther east to position themselves between the Debru
and the remaining villages.

   "Samora!" Karla was practically shouting.

   She blinked, realizing after the fact that Karla had been trying
to get her attention for some time. "Sorry."

   "Your head looks so full of thoughts I'm a bit worried it's
going to pop. Care to share?"

The two of them were on foot, wandering apart from the main column. Their position had been a compromise, much as everything else had been the last few days. Tiafel didn't want them too far from the column in case their presence tempted the Debru to attack, but Samora and Karla didn't want to be too close and blind their adani.

Fortunately, it seemed that so long as they retreated, the Debru had little interest in them. Even the otsoa and kettu sightings had declined since they began their march.

Samora wet her lips and cleared her throat. "I can't disagree with anything Tiafel said during the council, but it still feels like we're wrong for retreating."

"What bothers you most?"

"The wait. Tiafel's plan will eventually bring us close to the circles, which is good, but I don't think we have enough time to wait as long as he expects us to. The Debru could move at any moment."

Karla's soft gaze seemed to look through her. "Is that what bothers you most?"

She hadn't wanted to bring it up, but it seemed as though Karla knew her complaint even before she voiced it. Samora grimaced. "Adani pulls me north and east. Toward the circle."

"Then why are you walking south?"

Samora gestured to the long column snaking its way south. "I can't do anything alone."

"Why not?"

Samora stared at Karla as though she'd lost her mind. "I'm only one person. I can't fight an entire clan's worth of Debru."

"Why do you need to fight? Isn't your strongest gift, the one the Debru fear most, healing?"

Samora scoffed. "I can't do much healing if I'm busy being killed by the Debru, either."

"I would protect you," Karla said, as though it were the most natural decision in the world.

Samora shook her head, not believing what she heard. If Karla was so set on visiting the circle, why hadn't she said something more during the council meeting? She was a respected adanist, and they would have given her words more weight than Samora's.

But more than that, Samora couldn't understand why this woman was so willing to risk her life for Samora's sake. They hadn't even known each other that long, but she didn't blink at the idea of walking alone into the heart of Debru-controlled territory. Nothing she did made sense.

"Why?" Samora asked. "Why would you help me heal, especially after spending so much time telling me I need to fight?"

Karla looked off into the distance, the barest hint of a smile on her face.

"You say that adani pulls you toward the circle, and I believe you. Adani has been pulling me toward you since before we met."

LEAVING the rest of the clans was an easier task than Samora had imagined. She'd thought of the scouts as both far-seeing warriors and an unbreakable line of defense that would keep her and Karla close to the column. Even her first experience with the Belog hadn't disillusioned her about the usefulness of scouts.

She questioned their worth a lot more that night. Karla and Samora slipped away from the camp without anyone questioning them. They'd prepared a simple story about wanting to train away from the camp, but they didn't need it. They masked their spirits while questing out with their own adani. Scouts and guards glowed against their senses, and they were easy enough to avoid. Their escape involved plenty of crawling and lots of waiting for the right moment, but no luck. Long before dawn they were beyond the sight of the scouts, and no shouts of alarm carried over the plains after them.

"I wish I had Elian's courage," Samora said.

Karla raised an eyebrow. "You seem plenty courageous to me. I've seen many people break under much less."

"I nearly fainted speaking to the combined councils."

Samora had meant for Karla to laugh, but the adanist didn't so much as crack a smile. "True enough, and many would find the task easy. But I see your fear. Speaking before that gathering was every bit as terrifying for you as facing down a Belog, and you did it anyway. Courage isn't about doing what others find hard. It's about doing what *you're* terrified of doing."

"Elian would be marching toward this circle without hesitation if he thought it would save Mother."

"So are you."

Samora finally worked her way toward saying what she had wanted to at first. "It doesn't seem wise to be following me. You should return to the clans. There's no reason for both of us to die."

Karla didn't respond, and Samora figured she was considering her choices. Samora didn't want to make this journey alone, but she didn't want to risk Karla's life because of some vague feelings. Eventually, Karla sighed.

"I've already told you that I've lived long enough, and I travel of my own free will. My death, if it awaits, rests on my shoulders and my shoulders alone. Are we clear?"

Samora swallowed hard. She hadn't expected such a rebuttal. "Yes."

Karla's voice softened. "Do you trust adani?"

The simple question left Samora stumped for some time. Her first instinct was to say that she didn't. Why should she trust such a vague feeling, something that couldn't be explained to most people?

Her actions said otherwise, though. She'd been more than willing to part with Elian when he went west because she believed it was right. She'd left the protection of the clans because of the same feeling, even though reason called her a fool. The truth left her feeling uncomfortable.

"I guess I do?"

For some reason, that brought that familiar thin-lipped smile to Karla's face. "I was once like you, at least in this way. I felt the influence of adani. Sometimes I listened to it, other times I ignored it in favor of reason, or the arguments of friends. If I'd been asked the question, I'd have answered in much the same way. But now that I've been paying attention for more years than I care to count, I've become a true believer."

"What changed?"

"Mostly, it was nothing more than experience. I trusted it often enough and found myself where I needed to be enough times that it proved itself. Which is why I'm here. It pulls me toward you, and so I'll stay by your side. As soon as it pulls me in another direction, I'll follow it that way."

Samora shook her head. "I can't imagine being so trusting. Doesn't it ever pull you toward something that makes no sense?"

Karla snorted and gestured to their surroundings. "Today seems to fit that description, and yet here I am."

Samora supposed, but it still seemed hard to believe.

"You know the problem with humans?"

"They're loud, obnoxious, and prone to foolishness?"

"Sure, but their real problem is that they're so convinced they've got the world figured out. Every year adanists learn new techniques and discover new secrets, but we still think that we understand everything. Girl, I've lived long enough that I know there's nothing farther from the truth. I think it's more like we're staring at a single tree and thinking we understand everything about the forest. I understand your doubt as well as anyone, but don't be afraid to trust adani."

"What if it leads me someplace I don't want to be."

"That's still where you belong."

Samora shook her head. She couldn't bring herself to see the world the way Karla did. Not yet. But she respected the woman too much to dismiss her as a madwoman.

Perhaps she was the one who saw the truth no one else could.

FREED from the slow pace of the combined clans, they made good time. For the first two days, Samora kept glancing over her shoulder, expecting to see scouts on horseback chasing them down. But the horizon remained clear, she never heard hoofbeats, and her adani never picked up another soul nearby.

By their fourth day of travel, they'd reached land Samora was familiar with. The rolling plains took on familiar shapes. Twisted oak trees and waist-high cairns pointed the way home. Though only weeks had passed since she and Elian had left, she felt as though she'd been gone for most of her life. The landmarks sparked memories that felt as though they'd come from another person, a child whose worries, fears, and dreams seemed so much smaller.

She stopped at a tree that marked the southwest corner of a field that had long since been abandoned. No one had farmed this far from the village since the Debru had attacked. Wild wheat fought a battle against other advancing grasses, losing more ground with every passing year.

Something it had in common with the humans that had once planted it, she supposed.

"Is something wrong?" Karla asked.

Samora nodded in the direction of the village. It was the same worry she'd obsessed over since they'd decided to stop by and visit Mother.

"It's still your choice, but I haven't sensed so much as a single kettu since we've parted ways with the clans," Karla said.

Neither had Samora, but that didn't make the decision any

easier. If anything, the lack of knowledge only increased her doubts. If the otsoa and kettu had been obviously hunting her, she would have known to stay away. Instead, she'd had to weigh unknown risks. She and Karla moved much faster, and in a more direct line, than the clans. They could warn the village earlier. But if the Debru still hunted them, their presence would only bring that much more attention to the village.

Karla stood beside her, waiting in silence for her decision. The older adanist's lack of advice sometimes annoyed Samora, but knowing the woman was only following her sense of adani took some of the edge off her irritation.

Samora still couldn't fully wrap her understanding around Karla's complete trust in adani, but it provided her a way to think about this decision. She closed her eyes and sensed the flow of adani, listening for any direction it might give.

The pull was subtle, so much so she wasn't entirely sure she wasn't imagining it, but it pulled toward the village.

Or perhaps it pulled toward the circle and the village was just in the way.

She couldn't tell.

But they hadn't been attacked yet and she wanted to warn Mother. It would be foolish to walk right past her village on their way to the circle. She ran her hand against the weathered bark of the oak and started walking home. Karla followed without question.

They didn't get much farther before their arrival was noticed by a group of farmers working out in the fields. They exchanged friendly waves, but once the farmers saw who it was, they rushed to meet her.

Had Elian been with her, the reunion would have been filled with warm embraces and loud laughter. Instead, the farmers stopped awkwardly a few paces away and asked how she was. They didn't look like they expected much of an answer, and eyes went wide when she said, "I need to speak to Henk. Where is he?"

The farmers cast worried glances between one another. One said, "He's home."

Samora frowned. It was near harvest. This was no time for Henk to be sitting around the house. He should be out in the fields, lending a hand. "Why?"

More worried glances, and Samora's stomach twisted. They spent more time looking at their feet than looking at her.

A growl escaped the back of her throat and she stood tall. "What's happening?"

She wasn't sure if they were more surprised by her question or her tone, but she shocked them into answering. Laird, the eldest of the group, answered her. "Been strange happenings, since you left. Most of them swirling around Henk. He wasn't feeling good for a bit, then seemed to get better. But he started giving orders and staying home, like he was better than us. Some strange orders, too."

"Such as?"

"Ordering us to abandon all the fields to the east, at least for now. And he keeps trying to send your mother after you."

Samora shook head. "Why?"

"He won't explain and won't have anything to do with your mother. Things have been tense, and we're not sure what's coming next." Laird looked up, hope in his eyes. "Don't suppose you know anything that can help us?"

"Nothing yet, but I'll find out. You and the others need to prepare to leave. There's danger close. The Debru are gathering."

She didn't have time to answer their questions, and she didn't think they'd listen to her without the support of at least one of the village elders. "I'll speak with Henk. For now, just be wary."

They didn't look like they needed to be told twice. After a brief set of farewells, she continued toward the village. Her heart ached when she caught sight of her home, but she set her course toward Henk's small place near the center of the town square.

A tall woman intercepted them before they reached the outskirts of the village. Samora smiled wide when she saw her mother for the first time in ages, and she finally received a warm embrace, though it was broken off far too soon. As she always seemed to, Mother looked through her and understood. "You're here to see Henk?"

"There's Debru gathered to the east, by the circle Elian and I found. You'll need—"

"How is your brother?"

"Alive and well the last time I sensed him, but he traveled into the deadlands with a group of powerful adanists."

Mother shook her head, her expression both proud and resigned. "Of course he did."

"What's wrong with Henk?"

Mother looked defeated, as though the last few weeks had sapped her vitality from her. "I don't know, he won't let me see him. You've heard?"

"Laird told me. I was going to see him now."

"Then I'll come with you," Mother said. She took Karla in with a glance. "I remember you from when I was a child. You don't look a year older. You've been traveling with my daughter?"

"More like following her around, but yes."

Mother thanked Karla, and the three women marched toward Henk's home. It felt like they were marching to battle.

When they came close to the front door, Mother spoke loudly. "Henk, Samora has come back with news! We need to speak with you."

The door didn't open, but Henk's voice carried through the shuttered windows. "She'll have to come back later."

"Henk!"

Samora didn't think she'd ever seen her mother so frustrated, and she shared the feeling. She'd come too far to be turned away by Henk's cowardice. But it was Karla who solved their problem. With a flick of her hand, she sent a small spear of adani at the door. It shattered into small fragments.

Mother glared at Karla, but her stare had little effect on the adanist. "We don't have time for this pettiness," Karla said. She strode into the small home like a conquering hero. Samora and Mother had little choice but to follow.

Though the day was warm and bright, Henk's house was cool and dark. All the shutters were closed, but that alone didn't explain how cool the house remained. The hairs on Samora's arm prickled.

In the corner of the room two red eyes glowed with murderous intent. Samora gathered adani, ready to meet an attack, but Mother opened one pair of shutters to let light into the room, revealing Henk squatting in the corner. His skin was pale. He snarled and covered his eyes from the light that invaded his space.

Karla also gathered her adani to attack, but Samora held out her hand as she extended her adani toward the village's leader. The sensation that came back to her was painfully familiar. She'd felt the same shadow in Elian after he'd been hurt in the circle.

Samora reached for Henk, but he punched at her. She avoided the blow but retreated a few paces. "Can you knock him out?" she asked Karla.

"They're coming, and there's nothing you can do to stop them," Henk said.

"With pleasure," Karla replied. A rod of adani appeared in her hand, and she stepped forward and snapped it across Henk's head. He collapsed into a heap and Samora knelt next to him. She trickled adani into him just as Brittany had into Elian when he'd been infected.

The shadow had penetrated deeper into Henk's spirit, but it fled with a fraction of the effort. Samora wasn't sure if it was because of Elian's unique relationship to adani, or if Henk's shadow was different in a way she couldn't sense.

Regardless, it wasn't long before the shadow was purged from his body. Samora healed the bruise on his head as well, impressed with how easy the technique came to her. When she was finished, she pushed one last swell of adani into Henk's body and his eyes fluttered open.

He blinked and shielded his eyes from the light of the window, but his eyes no longer glowed, and he frowned as he looked at them. "What are you all doing in my house? Samora? What are you doing here?"

Mother guided Henk to unsteady feet. "You haven't been feeling well, and it sounds like your memory has been affected. What's the last thing you remember?"

Henk stared off into the distance. "Yesterday I went north to seek out the circle that Samora had told us about. When I found it, I stepped inside. After that, my memories get fuzzy. I'm not sure what's real and what I dreamed."

Mother squeezed the upper part of Henk's arm. "You went to visit the circle weeks ago, Henk."

His face paled. "What happened?"

Mother told him of all that had happened in the village, of all the questionable decisions he'd made and all the flimsy justifications he'd offered. Henk accepted Mother's explanations without much question, and Samora wondered how much he actually remembered. When the shadow had taken Elian there had been no memory loss. Eventually, Mother reached Samora's arrival.

"Thank you for saving me, but why are you here?" Henk asked.

"An entire clan's worth of Debru have taken up a guard position around the circle. Three of the wandering clans have joined forces, but their plan is to abandon this village and reform the front to the east of here. Karla and I came to give you advance warning and to see if anything can be done about the circle."

"What can *you* do?" Henk asked.

Samora winced against the sting of his words. The question was a necessary one, even if it came barbed. "I'm not sure, but I've had success healing the land after the passage of the Debru, and we have some reason to believe I might be able to slow the growth of the circles, or maybe even heal them."

Henk looked at her with the same amount of skepticism he'd use if a child had come up to him and proudly announced they'd vanquished all the Debru. She didn't fault him for his doubt, but it wormed its way toward her heart and became her own.

Who was she to think she could do this?

She might not respect Henk much, but he'd known her almost as long as anyone.

Karla grunted, interrupting the meeting. "If it's all the same to you, we need to get moving. The Debru haven't been too active the last few days, but there's no telling how much longer that's going to last. One way or another, your village is going to be evacuated, so you can run now or prepare yourselves to leave when the wandering clans arrive. But I'd suggest earlier, because Samora and I are about to poke an enormous beehive of Debru, and I'd rather you not be anywhere close when we do."

Karla's words carried a weight Samora's didn't. Henk didn't question her but looked to Mother. "What do you think?" he asked.

"We should do as they ask," Mother said without hesitation. She turned to Karla and Samora. "There will be much for us to do, but you two should be on your way. I'll escort you to the edge of the village."

They said a quick farewell to Henk and followed Mother out of the house.

"Will you need anything?" Mother asked.

Karla said, "We're well provisioned, but thanks."

At the edge of the village, Mother stopped. She pulled Samora into a tight embrace. "I'm proud of you."

The farewell stirred a storm of emotions within Samora's chest. She wanted to sit with Mother and talk to her for days about her journey and what she'd learned. But the only way to earn that privilege was to stop the Debru. "Thank you," was all she could force past her constricted throat.

There were tears in Mother's eyes when she stepped away. Samora wiped her own away with the back of her hand, nodded one last time to her mother, and followed Karla toward the circle.

D awn hadn't yet broken, but the sky closest to the eastern horizon turned subtle hues of pink and orange as the sun approached. For most of the night the clans had marched through the deadlands like silent, shadowy wraiths. At times, when Elian's attention wandered, he would start and imagine that he was surrounded by Debru. Then his focus would return, and he was by Harald's side.

They weren't far now from the Debru position, and Elian admired Kati and Harald's sense of timing. The clans would arrive just before dawn, perfectly positioned to launch an attack with the help of the dragons.

A pair of scouts rode toward them from the west, and Harald and Kati advanced to meet them. The procession never stopped, but the scouts fell into an easy walk beside them.

"The Debru are where Elian said they'd be, with the strength he claimed. We counted more than two dozen Debru and two Belogs," the first scout said.

"What about otsoa or kettu?" Elian asked.

"Didn't catch sight of anything but Debru," the scout answered.

Harald didn't say anything, but it was clear the report didn't set well with him. They'd halfway expected the Debru to strike out at them the moment they left the gathering ground in force, but they hadn't seen so much as a kettu.

Elian wasn't sure if it was his place to speak up, but he needed to remind them of what had happened to him and Capricia. "Pardon, but when we were here last, we also thought that we'd advanced unobserved, but then we were encircled by otsoa."

Harald nodded in agreement. "It's seemed too easy so far. Any sign of the dragons?"

The scout shook his head. "None yet, but the sky is dark. If they're flying high, we might not have seen them."

"I don't like it," Harald said. "There's too much we don't know."

Kati shrugged. "I'm guessing Elian is right. The Debru have been too wary of our advances for me to believe that we're sneaking up on them. If we turn around, we're only going to have the Debru at our back."

Harald agreed. "Only way forward is forward, then. We just have to hope the dragons are as good as their word."

Elian couldn't imagine they wouldn't be, but they knew so little about the dragons Harald was right to worry. "They'll be here," he said, hoping he sounded more confident than he felt.

The scout described the Debru's arrangement, which was largely unchanged from when Elian had seen them. Harald was most interested in the placement of the Belog, who were west of the main force, closest to where the dragons had indicated the circle was.

"How do you want to get to them?" Kati asked.

Harald stroked his chin. "Straight through. Our adanists won't be able to stand long if the Belog aren't killed, and I don't want to risk complicating everything further by trying to work our way around them."

"We'll attack with bows first. With any luck, we can bring down a few before the fight begins in earnest," Kati said.

She left to pass the orders to her clan. Harald watched her for a long time before turning his attention to the challenge before him. "Good luck," he whispered, so softly that Elian was certain he was the only one who heard.

THEY REACHED the small rise where Elian and Capricia had watched the Debru from just before dawn. Harald, Kati, Tera, and some of Kati's commanders walked to the top to scout one last time. They scampered quickly down and ordered the archers to the front.

Elian had been confused by the presence of physical bows among the wandering clans when he'd first heard of them. They seemed almost as useless for an adanist as the sword he wore at his side.

Harald had set him straight. "There are times when we don't want to unleash our full adani, and there are hunters who simply enjoy having a bow. Adani is useful, but it can't and shouldn't do everything for us."

Whatever the reason, Elian was glad they had the archers now, even if it was only about a dozen. If each arrow struck true, that was a dozen less Debru that would join the upcoming battle.

The archers waited for their order, and Kati looked to the sky. It was as clear a day as they could ask for, without a wisp of a cloud overhead. Elian joined Kati in looking to the sky, but there was nothing to see. He even looked to the east to see if the dragons approached from behind.

The sky was empty as far as his sight could reach.

Kati didn't give the order to launch. They all waited, and again Elian couldn't help but compare them to the Debru. The adanists stood still, ready to fight the invading clan on the other side of the rise, but not moving.

It felt to Elian as though he was a bowstring that had been pulled taut. He wanted to snap forward, to charge forward and face the Debru. But Kati held him back, waiting for the promised dragons.

Movement from the rear of the clan caught Elian's attention. A pair of adanists had thrust their hands up in the air, signaling Kati. Elian hadn't learned all the signs the wandering clans used, but he recognized the one for otsoa easily enough.

Just like before, the Debru tried to encircle them.

The report stirred Kati to action. She looked toward Harald, who nodded his agreement. She raised her hand and signaled the archers to prepare. Wood creaked as a dozen bows were pulled back at once. Kati brought her hand down, ordering them to launch.

They did so, sending a flight of arrows into the rapidly brightening sky. Before the arrows had even reached the highest point of their flight, each of the archers had another arrow nocked to the string and pulled back to their cheeks. They released again without any order from Kati.

Kati and Harald signaled the charge, and the adanists followed the arrows over the rise. Elian reached the summit just in time to see the first volley of arrows streak down. He bit back a yell as he watched, but exhilaration turned quickly to disappointment. A handful of Debru threw up bound shields of shadow, and the arrows slid off them like rain down a roof.

Elian didn't pay any attention to the second volley. As always, the fight would be between adani and shadow, and hopefully his steel tilted the balance in their favor.

Elian looped adani through his legs, but even so, he had to sprint to keep up with Harald's long strides. Harald formed a spear of adani that crackled with pent-up force and flung it as he ran. It punched through the thin Debru shield and struck one of the creatures in the chest. The spear exploded in a flash of blinding light, sending a wave of force out that punched the air out of Elian's lungs.

The air suddenly filled with dozens of varieties of bound adani, hoping to make the most out of Harald's disruption.

A dark cloud spread rapidly from the Belog, covering the Debru in darkness and absorbing the bound adani with ease. Elian cursed, but Harald didn't bat an eye. "Keep a close hold of your adani in there," Harald said.

Elian only had time to nod before the cloud was upon them.

Harald formed a glowing sword of bound adani, as long as Elian was tall. He swung at the cloud, and it parted before the giant warrior, revealing a small group of Debru waiting for him.

Harald swung at the nearest, cutting through the shadowy blade that the Debru raised to block the blow. His sword continued through the Debru, slicing it nearly in half before he pulled it free and turned his attention to the next opponent.

Tera's sword wasn't strong enough to cut through the Debru like Harald's, but she moved into a second cut the moment her first was parried. The Debru clawed at her but lost its hand in the process. A final cut took its head, and she was on to the next, doing her part to keep Harald safe.

Elian was positioned behind the other two, but plenty of Debru attempted to flank them, keeping him occupied. Elian's sword felt like an extension of his body, and though he lacked Tera's experience or Harald's strength, his sharp blade always seemed to catch the Debru by surprise. He didn't land any killing blows, but he cut at limbs and shadows and kept their flank safe.

The Debru fled from his sword, but once they were beyond his reach, they turned their attentions once again to Harald. Even when Elian cut them, they ignored him in favor of the Hound's leader.

He couldn't much blame them. He'd considered Harald impressive before, but Elian had never seen a display like this before. Harald's techniques were some of the earliest taught to all adanists, but executed with a power and focus few students could even dream about matching. His spear thrusts made the ground tremble, and his swords cut through Debru as though they were stalks of wheat.

Their advance through the shadow rarely faltered for more than a moment. The shadow fled before Harald and Tera. When Harald eventually stopped, Elian almost bumped into him. Dark clouds surrounded them, and Elian couldn't see more than a few paces in any direction. He heard fighting, but nothing close.

A few spears of shadow stabbed at them, but Elian had no problem parrying their lazy attempts. He sensed no bloodlust behind the strikes.

Harald's breathing slowed as he centered himself. "They're guiding us toward the Belog."

His prophecy came true almost as soon as the words were out of his mouth. Even Elian sensed it, more as a pressure against his chest than anything his adani shared. The cloud before them darkened and took shape. The Belog was twice as tall as Harald and made of nothing but lean muscle and disdain. In its right hand it carried a shadow bound as a whip.

Even Elian's dull sense of adani and shadow felt the bursts of darkness emanating from the monstrous opponent. It cried no orders that Elian could hear, but all the Debru danced to its commands all the same.

The Belog raised its hand and snapped the whip forward. Elian prepared to move, but the whip wasn't long enough to cover the distance between them, so he didn't fear.

Harald bound a shield of adani anyway.

At the last moment, the whip stretched, racing toward them faster than lightning.

Harald's shield absorbed the blow. It stopped the whip, but the force of the impact knocked Harald to his knees. The whip snapped forward again, but Tera cut it with a thin disc of adani, dissolving it before it could remove Harald's head from his neck.

"Best get yourself up before I have to drag pieces of you away," Tera said.

Harald grunted and used his hands to support himself as he stood. "I forgot how hard they hit."

"Even you'd be a fool to go toe to toe against one."

"Might not be much avoiding it if there's two of them."

Their short rest ended when the Belog formed a spear, a dark mirror of Harald's technique. Harald cursed under his breath, then shouted, "Move!"

Tera ran left while Harald ran right, leaving Elian alone between them. The Belog turned to track Harald, leaving the space between it and Elian undefended.

He wasn't going to waste the opportunity. Elian looped all the adani he had into his limbs and sprinted forward, covering the ground between him and the Belog in two long strides.

The Belog thrust its spear at Harald. The giant adanist dodged the thrust and formed a spear of his own. Before he could stab at the Belog, the monster's spear melted into a sharp sword, and it cut across the battlefield. Harald was forced to use his spear to deflect the sword into the air.

Elian had eyes only for the Belog's unprotected knee. If he could bring the Belog down, Harald and Tera would have no problem killing it. He was about to swing when a ball of shadow formed between him and the Belog. It shot a shadow spear at his chest. He blocked the spear with the flat of his sword, but the force of it lifted him off his feet and tossed him back like a rag doll.

Elian kept his feet and looked left and right to see if any Debru thought to attack, but with the Belog toying with the three adanists, they were free to focus their attention on the Hawks. Elian couldn't tell how the greater battle was progressing, but the sounds of fighting hadn't come any closer, which didn't seem like a great sign.

It didn't matter. Once they brought the Belog down, the rest of the battle would be theirs. His hands still vibrated from the Belog's last attack, but he'd survived.

He quickly shook out his hands, then rejoined the fight. Harald and the Belog traded blows, faster than Elian could see. Waves of force buffeted Elian, but the strength of his legs didn't falter. Tera threw a powerful spear from behind the Belog, but it skipped harmlessly off a dark shield the Belog formed with a thought. When Elian got close, another shadow appeared to strike at Elian. This time, he was prepared, cutting through the shadow before it could impale him. The sphere responded by shooting two more dark threads at him, but Elian cut through those as well.

A seed of hope bloomed in the darkness that surrounded him. Combined, he was certain one of them would reach the Belog and land a fatal blow.

The Belog moved, so quickly it almost seemed as though it had disappeared in one place and appeared in another. Harald and Tera followed the movement without problem, but Elian lost a step against the monster. It had backed up several paces, putting all three of its opponents in front of it.

A wave of shadow erupted from the Belog. It struck Harald and Tera's shields first and threw them back. Elian thrust out his sword, but the shadow crashed over and around it, striking him undefended.

The blood in his veins turned to ice, and fresh rage beat in his heart. He recognized the sensation a moment before dark thoughts overwhelmed him. It was the same as the shadows in the circle, corrupting him from inside. He looped his adani, but without the aid of the dragon, he could do nothing but hold it back for a moment.

It was a stronger flood of shadow than he'd dealt with the last time, and even though he was more capable than before, it didn't matter against the Belog's incredible strength. Elian resisted a moment more before shadow burst through his defenses and made his mind its own.

As soon as his resistance stopped, so too did the pain. The shadow passed over him like a gentle summer rainstorm.

He looked for his true enemies. Harald and Tara had dragged him all the way out here, even though they knew it was unsafe. He would make them see the error of their ways, no matter the cost.

For the moment, their meager adani was overwhelmed by shadow, but they would soon emerge.

And when they did, he would kill them for their crimes.

Samora sat in the grass and rubbed each of her shoulders in turn. The afternoon's walk had only covered a handful of miles, but each had felt like five. She and Karla had made slow progress throughout the day, and now the sun raced them toward the horizon. They'd been dodging kettu and otsoa since they left the village, taking turns casting out their adani for any sense of the creatures or the Debru.

Their enemies had remained remarkably consistent. While the grasslands felt flooded with Debru allies, the Debru themselves hadn't moved a muscle.

"Have they moved?" Samora asked.

Karla frowned and shook her head. "Still in the same place. But I'm not sure I should cast again today. I'm losing focus, and a couple on the outskirts stirred when my adani passed over them."

"That's no problem. We're close enough I'm happy to cast adani for the few times that remain."

"You've got a gentler touch than me, anyway," Karla said.

"Any guesses why the Debru aren't closer to the circle?"

Karla's frown grew more pronounced, which was answer enough.

It was one of the questions that had been frustrating them since they left the village. Now that they were closer to both the Debru and the circle, they realized that the Debru were almost a mile away from the growing monstrosity. It allowed Samora and Karla to sneak closer to the circle by walking in a wide arc that kept them plenty distant from the assembled Debru. Their plan added several miles to their journey, but the reward of not having to fight was well worth the price of sore feet and tense shoulders.

Still, the positioning of the Debru left them both uneasy. If the invaders were guarding the circle, as they had guessed, why were they so far away? And why did they only position themselves to the west of the circle? Karla and Samora were about to approach the circle from the east, where there were no Debru.

It seemed a simple oversight, but with the Debru, there was no telling. Samora joined thousands of adanists throughout history when she wished they understood their enemy better.

She supposed the Debru might count on the kettu and otsoa, but that still seemed a poor second choice to simply establishing a perimeter around the circle. The relative ease of their advance made them both think they were walking into a trap, though neither of them had sensed anything that raised their alarm.

"Ready?" Karla asked.

Samora nodded, and they continued south. The circle was only about a mile away, but they advanced as though in the middle of an enemy camp. They paused once to ensure they avoided a roving pack of kettu, but they didn't come to a stop until they'd covered half the remaining distance. They took cover among a thick growth of trees while Samora cast out her adani.

"Nothing's changed," she said.

Karla didn't say anything, but her unease was easy to see. She looked out and around their cover, but the gathering darkness made it difficult to see anything well. "How close do you need to get?"

Samora had been wondering the same. "Should I try from here?"

Karla nodded. They didn't want to risk giving away their presence unnecessarily, but they were close enough and protected enough by the trees it seemed worth the try.

Samora put her hand down against the ground and pushed a slim thread of adani into the world. Until she was certain it would work, there was no point announcing their presence too loudly. She sent the adani toward the circle and listened closely to all the stories it shared with her. Every animal that could have fled already had, but that had been true back when she and Elian had first discovered the circle.

It wasn't long before the pull of the circle grabbed her adani and yanked it deeper. She didn't resist the pull but followed the adani where it led. As soon as it struck the edge of the circle, it started to unravel. She followed the individual threads, allowing her attention to drift between the various strands.

Samora wasn't sure what had changed between her first attempts and this one, but she sensed her adani right up to the moment it vanished closer to the center of the circle. She breathed out slowly and opened her eyes. Something lurked in the heart of the dead land, a darkness deeper than any night. It pulled adani relentlessly toward itself, turning it into something else and eating it whole. It grew with the circle, a malignant growth upon the beauty of her world.

"Can you do something?" Karla asked.

Samora ignored the question, closed her eyes, and sent another thread of adani into the world and toward the circle. She let it drift. Allowed it to get caught in the vortex of the circle's pull. Once again, her adani unraveled, but this time she tried to control the individual strands. It wasn't that dissimilar to healing, where her adani was broken down by the patient's body and made its own. It was eerily similar, in fact, the difference being

353

that when the presence at the center of the circle stole her adani, it didn't use it to heal but to grow and consume yet more adani.

She found she couldn't control the threads. The pull the presence exerted was stronger than anything she could accomplish from this distance. She severed the strand of adani, then cast out a wide net to ensure her activities hadn't brought them more attention than they wanted. She released a small sigh of relief when she found the Debru and their creatures remained in place.

There wasn't much time to waste. The circle was already larger than the one she'd encountered at the site of the Crow's destruction, and the sense she had of the presence was that it was growing ever closer to contentment. Every strand of adani she sent toward it brought it one step closer to completion.

She didn't want to live in a world where she knew what that completion meant.

One more option remained to her, though she was doubtful it would work. Without shifting her position, she sent a last thread of adani toward the circle. She let it drift along the natural currents of adani until it found the circle, which pulled it ever closer. Once it struck the circle she kept her full attention on the thread, resisting the circle's ability to unravel it. She gently knotted it, reminded of the glowing points of light in the gathering grounds. The knot unraveled as it drifted toward the center of the circle, but she kept gently tugging on it, pulling it tight even as the circle did its best to unravel it.

The thread made it halfway through the circle before she lost control. She severed herself from the adani, opened her eyes, and leaned back. She was surprised that night was almost over, and that the first hints of dawn could be seen on the eastern horizon. "I'm not sure if I can do anything, but I know I can't do it from here. The circle's too strong."

She leaned back against one of the trees and closed her eyes. Her body was tired, but her mind jumped from thought to thought. She'd learned more about the circles this night than they'd yet known, and it seemed there had to be a way to stop the presence. But how?

"Then we get closer," Karla said, her voice betraying only a sliver of nerves. "Are you fit to travel?"

Samora nodded. "Tired, but good. We don't have time to rest, though. Whatever is happening in the circle is nearing completion."

"Then get your scrawny tailbone out of the grass and follow me. We've got a village to save."

Samora grunted and pressed her palms against her eyes, rejoicing in the moment of relief. "Seems more like something you should be doing than me."

Karla offered Samora her arm, which Samora gratefully took. The woman pulled her up as though she didn't weigh more than a handful of seeds. "I would if I could, but I get the feeling this isn't work I'm cut out for. I could sense you working with adani, but just barely. Your skill, at least in this domain, is far beyond my own."

"Doesn't feel like enough."

"And maybe it won't be, but that doesn't mean you weren't our best chance."

Samora appreciated the older woman's confidence, but her head was pounding from the last effort. She squeezed the sides of her skull, earning a very brief reprieve. But as soon as she let go, the pounding returned. She understood now what Elian had meant when he said it felt like Harald was playing war drums on top of his head.

"Gently loop some adani through your head," Karla suggested.

"Mother told me never to do so."

"And generally speaking, she was right. But you've got a gentle touch, so it will do you no harm."

It was probably a sign of her exhaustion and suffering that she obeyed without another shred of hesitation. She sent an additional sliver of adani from her core through her head, and the pain vanished as though she'd just woken up from a full night of sleep.

"That's incredible, thank you."

Karla grunted. "Consider it something to use only in crisis. A gentle brush of adani can cure much, but it's an easy matter to destroy the mind."

Samora bowed, both thanking Karla and expressing her understanding.

She felt refreshed as they left the copse of trees. The rest of the journey to the circle was an easy one, and there were none of the Debru's creatures nearby. They stopped on a small rise overlooking the circle, and Samora gasped.

It was one thing to sense the circle with her adani, but entirely another to see it in person. She knew it had grown large, but to see the swath of destruction it had brought with her own eyes horrified her. Dead brown grass lay on its side, joined by trees that had fractured under their own weight. She thought she saw dead fish floating on the mirror-smooth surface of the pond in the center of the circle.

"You said it yourself that we don't have time to waste, so I'm not sure why you're standing around staring," Karla said.

The reminder brought Samora back to herself. She took a few steps down the rise so that she wasn't so conspicuous against the horizon, but she didn't dare approach any closer. The pull of adani this close was already intense. She took a seat and pressed both of her hands against the ground. As before, she sent out a single thread of adani. It was pulled from her the moment she released it from her body, unraveling as soon as it struck the edge of the circle.

Samora strengthened the thread, not to hold it together, but to track the unraveling more closely. As it had before, the thread unraveled the closer it came to the darkness lurking at the circle's center. She tracked the various wisps of adani, fascinated by the feelings it passed back to her. She exerted more of her will, holding the wisps of adani closer together. This close to the circle, her control was great enough that she succeeded. The wisps converged, fighting against the currents of power that pulled them apart.

As they converged, adani passed more information back to her. The darkness at the heart of the circle wasn't something that thought. It had been created for a purpose, and only reacted to the threats it faced. It almost felt as though someone had bound it, given it instructions, and then left it behind.

If it could be done by shadow, could it be undone by adani?

The thought was intoxicating, but not one to pursue now. Adani kept feeding her more information about the darkness. Something about the way it felt was familiar, but the reason why eluded her, like a word on the tip of her tongue she couldn't find.

She pushed the wisps further together, almost tight enough to weave back into a full thread of adani. This work was even finer than the healing techniques Lenon had shown her.

In that moment, as the tips of the unraveled thread came closer together, she sensed the darkness more clearly than before, and she understood what it was. A power, greater than even the Belog, waited on the other side, ready to step through and lay waste to the land.

The circle was a gate, and a Vada prepared to enter.

Samora cursed under her breath, but before she could consider her next move, the circle finally reacted to her presence. A wave of shadow shot from its heart. It caught her by surprise, shredding her adani and consuming it in an instant.

She severed herself from the thread before the shadow rushed back into her, but the wave of power wasn't meant just to destroy the adani. The circle pulsed with the same dark power as the Belog, but it ran through the ground without affecting either her or Karla.

The veteran adanist understood before Samora did. She cursed. "I think the circle just called for help."

Samora agreed, but the Belog that would soon be approaching seemed downright quaint compared to the danger the circle held. "The circle is a gate. A Vada is preparing to enter, and very soon."

In the days she'd traveled with Karla, she'd never seen the woman lose her composure, but she did now. Her eyes went wide, and she cursed up a storm that burned Samora's ears. Karla didn't try to hide her presence as she sent out a powerful wave of adani. When it returned with news of their surroundings, her face went pale. "Every Debru and creature within miles is racing toward us. I'll hold them off as best I can, but I won't last long. If you're going to stop that Vada from arriving, you're going to have to do it fast."

❧ 34 ❧

E lian had never known that rage could be so freeing. He'd spent so much of his life trying to contain his emotions so that adani couldn't make them too strong to control. But now that the Belog had blown the seals off his heart, he basked in complete and utter freedom.

Adani looped through his limbs faster than before, making him as strong as the legends he'd grown up dreaming about. He would make that giant fool suffer for everything. For separating him from his family. For taking him so far away from his home. In the contact with the shadow, he glimpsed some of the Belog's plans. He understood the circles would serve as gates to bring the Vada and their countless Debru to this world, eager to devour its adani.

The growth of the gates was almost complete, which meant it wouldn't be long before a Vada strode into the grasslands outside his village.

And Elian wouldn't be anywhere close, helpless to aid his mother or the farmers who had watched over him since he was a child.

Harald was no better than a bug that needed to be squished

under the heel of his boot. He certainly possessed more adani than almost every other living thing on this wretched world, but compared to the Belog and Vada, he was nothing.

A small voice shouted in the back of his head, but Elian brushed the irritation away with a growl. He looked down at his arms, and they felt powerful, as though he could seize control of the world with his bare hands. He looked up and looked around. The shadow remained, but now his eyes had no trouble seeing through it.

He found Harald with little problem. He cowered under his shield, gathering his strength for his next assault. Elian brandished his sword and strode toward the enormous fool. Why didn't he see that his struggles amounted to nothing? That there was nothing he could do?

The shadows no longer affected him, so Elian strode through them, the master of both light and dark. As he neared, the shadows around Harald cleared and he saw Elian approaching. At first, his face lit with that familiar and frustrating smile, but then he saw something he didn't like. His face fell, and Elian's heart soared at the sight.

"Elian, what happened?" Harald asked.

The Belog attacked Harald before Elian answered. It lashed out with twin spears of shadow, forcing Harald into a defensive stance.

Elian approached, unconcerned about the shadow spears that ripped the air apart before him. He leaped forward with all his newfound strength, stabbing the point of his sword straight at Harald's exposed side.

Fast as he was, Harald had seen enough to be forewarned, and somehow, he found a way to slip between the Belog's spears and Elian's sword, giving up ground fast to avoid being impaled. Unspeakable joy brought laughter to Elian's lips. He was fighting Harald, one of the greatest supposed heroes of the age, and he was winning!

A pressure against the shadow warned him of a threat coming from his right side. He twisted and brought his sword up to block a bound knife thrown at his leg. His sword cut through the adani as though it were as thin as hair, and he laughed at Tera's clumsy attempt to slow him down. Before she could attempt another strike, the Belog aided him with a barrage of spears. She danced back, too far away to help her precious leader.

These were the best the humans could field? They were contemptible and had no idea how much strength separated them from their future masters. He sensed all of the battlefield through his master's senses. Across the field the humans desperately fought the battle they couldn't win. Their vicious and hungry pets slipped through the small gaps in the human's weak defenses, sowing chaos wherever they went.

The humans had focused most of their forces on the master's companion, but it handled the onslaught without difficulty. Only a few of the humans had any inkling of the strength available to them, and they died like insects.

Laughable.

Elian's attention narrowed back on Harald, his sword seeking blood with the speed of a snake's tongue. Aided by another barrage of Belog spears, Elian pushed Harald back even farther.

Impressive as Harald's ability to evade Elian was, it was only a matter of time before Elian broke through his defenses. Small cracks in Harald's defenses began to appear, nothing so large Elian dared thrust his sword into, but ones that promised to become larger as he exerted more pressure.

A roar from the skies above stabbed cold fear into his heart. The old masters of this world were here, summoning what meager strength remained to them. The Belog's attention turned toward the sky, leaving Elian to fight Harald alone.

He didn't need the Belog to fight Harald. He lashed out, but the small cracks in Harald's defenses healed, and it wasn't long before Elian was retreating closer to the Belog.

Another roar preceded a blast of adani that slammed into the shadow, returning it to the Belog's keeping. Elian looked up at a clear blue sky, the sun shining on his face, and hated it. The only blemish against the sky were the dragons, and they were even more disturbing than the burning sunlight. They bound adani and dropped it on the battlefield, where it destroyed Debru and strengthened the Hounds and Hawks. One such binding exploded close to the Belog, and while it did no harm to the masterful Debru, it washed over Elian, too.

Adani grasped the shadow gripping his heart and pulled. The shadow clawed for purchase, but the dragon's adani overwhelmed the Belog's curse. Shadow shredded under the assault, pulling some of Elian's spirit with it, leaving his legs weak. He felt empty inside, as though the shadow had hollowed him out as it died. Some still remained, poisoning spirit and flesh, but for the moment, reason returned.

Shame rushed to his cheeks, and he almost dropped to his knees. It had happened again. Harald watched him closely as he stumbled backward, but didn't press his advantage. Even after this, Harald treated him with the kindness of a parent loving their wayward child.

Elian didn't want it. He wanted to be respected, not merely loved. He couldn't bear to see the lack of judgment in Harald's eyes.

Elian turned and ran. He had no destination in mind, he just knew he couldn't be here. If he stayed, he might hurt Harald, and he couldn't live with that shame. As he ran, he saw a few of the dragons break off and drop adani down on the circle, and he hoped they had the strength they claimed. The circle couldn't stand.

His thoughts turned darker, and though he fought the infection of shadow with what little adani remained in his spirit, the Belog's hooks were too deep in him. He looked at the edge of his sword and wondered if it wouldn't be better if he just took his life now, while the decision was still his to make.

A shadow passed overhead, accompanied by a familiar pattern of adani. He looked up and saw the dragon he had rescued from the Belog earlier. It dropped a small binding of adani that landed close to his feet, washing over him and giving him the strength to fight the encroaching shadow for a moment longer.

Elian gulped hard. He couldn't win against the shadow. That strength didn't yet belong to him, but his choice remained. Take his life now, before he could harm those he cared about, or keep fighting and hope his allies would rescue him yet again?

Put that way, the answer was perfectly straightforward. He turned the tip of his sword so it pointed at his throat. He grimaced as the shadow within him screamed, and he forced himself to think of more pleasant times. Of racing Samora back home, always keeping just ahead of her so that she would push herself to run faster. Of working with Father in the garden, a task he'd hated at the time but would give anything to go back and experience again.

He gripped the sword tightly and tensed his muscles but was stopped by the growing pressure of adani. He looked to his left just in time to see his dragon rush toward him and scoop him up in its claw.

For the second time that week, he found himself rescued and close to helpless. He dangled high in the air, and he very briefly considered stabbing his sword into the dragon's stomach. He wasn't sure it would penetrate, but it was no more than this dragon deserved for taking him away without his permission. It was no better than Harald.

Elian shook his head to clear the shadow from his thoughts. He didn't have much time, and the dragon, again, had given him another chance. He looped adani in his core and pushed it gently toward the dragon, sighing with relief when it connected to the dragon's much larger well of spirit.

Finally, he had the strength to push the shadow from his heart.

It felt like extricating himself from a bed of thorns. The shadow had sunk its claws in deep and refused to release him without a fight. Elian worked the shadow free, looping his dragon-aided adani and tearing the shadow strip by strip from his soul. The work felt as though it took an age, and he was painfully aware there was a battle being won or lost below.

The dragon sensed his distress but sent nothing to him to increase or relieve his worries. That silence carried its own message, which was that Elian needed to focus on his own health first before he could bother himself with the needs of his friends.

The knowledge of the battle below made every heartbeat feel like a day, but Elian kept his focus tight, and soon he felt the last shred of shadow surrender to his healing. He laughed at the lightness of his spirit, and the dragon roared to match his mood.

His mirth was short lived, though. He looked down to the battle below and saw that the humans didn't fare well. The Hawks had taken severe casualties as the second Belog had focused its attention on the clan. Kati's tremendous use of adani was all that kept her people from complete annihilation. Otsoa attacked the back ranks, and while they weren't strong on their own, they were devastating as a distraction from the waves of Debru that broke upon the front lines of the clan.

Elsewhere, the dragon's attacks aided the adanists greatly, but they were as impotent against the circle as the humans.

Harald and Tera fared little better. They faced the full fury of a Belog, and it was a testament to their strength and skill that they were still alive. But the Belog's judgment of the humans, which Elian had been all too privy to, wasn't wrong. Strong as they were, they couldn't do more than annoy the Belog.

Elian's fears and worries started to overwhelm him. He sensed adani responding, even stronger now because of his connection to the dragon. He clamped down hard on his emotions, stuffing them deep into his chest. His friends needed him in control.

The dragon rumbled, and Elian turned his attention to his newest ally. "We need to rescue them," he said.

The dragon rumbled again, as though ignoring Elian. A tight knot of frustration bubbled in his chest, and he wished the dragon could just speak.

A vision swept away Elian's sight, and the surprise of it brought his thoughts to a standstill. Only then did he pay attention to the flow of adani between him and the dragon, and the vision became sharper. It was of a small dragon, roaring as it flew beside a larger one.

Every small roar was echoed by a giant one. Elian didn't understand until he extended his adani further, sharpening the vision.

The roar wasn't just a sound made by a dragon's throat. It came from the very center of their spirit. The elder taught the youngling how to reach deep and unveil the spirit buried within.

When the dragon sensed Elian understood, the vision faded.

Kati had said something similar to Harald about him. Had she been right? When he'd been under the control of the shadow, it had unleashed his emotions and made him stronger than before, so maybe.

In the end, it wasn't a rational decision. He watched in horror as Harald was driven back hard by a powerful series of blows from the Belog. The big man swayed on his feet, and from up high, he seemed pitifully small.

He deserved far more than the weaknesses Elian had shown him thus far.

The dragon swooped down at Elian's request, and he pulled from the dragon's seemingly endless reserve of adani to strengthen his limbs and rejuvenate his tired mind. The dragon—his dragon—roared, calling others to it. Adani dropped on the

Belog from all sides, staggering it before it could land the killing blow.

His dragon flew straight down, leveling off perhaps a half mile away from the Belog. They flew across the battlefield, so near the ground there were times Elian thought he could reach out with his sword and take a head or arm from a Debru. But his focus was on the Belog. If it fell, it might shift the momentum of the battle in their favor. At least, he hoped it would.

When they were close, his dragon sent him a message through their connection, a feeling Elian interpreted as *Good Luck*. Then the dragon bled off most of his speed and tossed Elian straight at the Belog.

The maneuver was as surprising to Elian as it was to the Belog, but the Belog's attention was being torn in half a dozen different directions, and so Elian recovered from his surprise first. He cut wildly at the Belog's face, his sword cutting deep into the monster's cheek. He landed and rolled, coming up behind the Belog as it roared its displeasure.

Adani looped through his limbs faster than he could track, powered both by the dragon's assistance and his own fury. Twice now the Belog and their manipulation of shadow had tried to make him hurt those he cared for.

Now, finally, he had the strength to do something about it.

He raised his sword and charged forward, ready to end the Belog forever.

35

"If you want full use of your adani, you'll want to move farther away from the edge of the circle," Samora told Karla.

The other woman scoffed. "Sure, but the farther away I am from you, the easier it is for what's coming to reach you. I'll need to be close if you want me to protect you for more than a moment."

Samora considered arguing, but they didn't have the time to waste. Belog moved fast, so they didn't have more than a few moments before the Debru reached them and Karla was overwhelmed.

So how did she destroy the circle?

The entity at the center of the circle didn't like adani too close. It unraveled the adani, turned it into something different as it was consumed. When she'd tried to bring the adani back together, it had sent out a call for help.

It was slim, but it was all she had. She took a deep breath to steady her racing heart, then pressed her hands firmly into the ground on either side of her. Adani slid from her hands into the soil and was immediately pulled toward the circle. She sent more of her adani into the thread, strengthening it for the battle to come.

As she'd come to expect, the adani unraveled as soon as it struck the edge of the circle. She allowed the unraveling, hoping that as the individual threads of adani made it closer to the presence at the heart of the circle she could bring them back together. That seemed easier than fighting the circle the entire way toward its core. She pushed even more adani into the thread, causing it to glow bright against her senses.

The circle eagerly pulled the adani toward it. The tip continued to unravel, spiraling out into ever thinner threads. She squeezed her eyes as she fought to keep track of the ends, to keep them under some semblance of her control. In many ways, it wasn't that much different than keeping track of the small spheres she liked to bind, but the difference was the incredible force on the other side trying to rip them from her grasp.

She thanked Mother for the practice as she followed the binding as its ends split again. The tips weakened as the circle hungrily pulled them closer. When the tips were on the verge of winking out and transforming into something else, she reinforced the threads of adani with strength from her own body. The tips glowed bright against the darkness, and she began to bind them back together.

The presence at the heart of the circle responded violently. A storm of razor-sharp shadow assaulted her adani. She sent more of her strength into the threads, and although a few strands fell to the blades, most endured the assault.

Though she focused most of her attention on the battle she fought, she couldn't help but notice the one developing around her. Karla had bound half a dozen spears of adani, none of them very strong, that she launched into the distance.

Samora couldn't spare the attention to sense what was coming, but given the weak power of the spears, she assumed the otsoa grew close.

Her moment of distraction was almost enough to doom her entire effort. The heart released another cloud of cutting shadow and half her remaining threads vanished before she had the presence of mind to reinforce her bindings with more adani. She could already feel the strain on her spirit as she battled the presence, but she wasn't yet close to striking it with adani.

Samora had no choice but to turn the whole of her attention to her own fight. The circle would demand everything she had. She hated leaving Karla alone, but the risks of failure were too great.

KARLA CAST her adani one last time toward Samora, more to satisfy her own curiosity than because of any need. She wondered if the girl had any idea how rare her talent was. The adani Samora ran into the circle was barely thicker than a strand of hair but glowed like a second sun to Karla's senses. That combination of strength and control was incredibly rare, and the girl hadn't yet tapped into the full power of her spirit. Karla could sense the thread of adani well into the circle, which was impressive by itself. She felt the way the circle tore up adani and ate it, but Samora's thin thread resisted.

If anyone could find a way to defeat the circle, it was that girl. She just needed the time to do so.

Karla tore her attention away from the circle and to the threats converging on them. The otsoa would be the first to arrive, so she bound a handful of spears to welcome them. She hurled the spears as soon as the creatures were close enough that she was certain of her aim. The spears arced through the sky and fell to the ground. Each had been thrown near the center of an advancing pack, and the force of each was enough to kill most of a pack.

She formed a handful of small darts and picked off the few

otsoa that remained. By themselves, they were barely dangerous, but if she didn't kill them by the time the Debru and the Belog arrived, they'd be trouble.

As if summoned by her thoughts of them, the Belog rushed over the horizon. As the cowards preferred, they were covered by roiling clouds, but there was no mistaking the darkness of their presence within. The shadow served to protect them both from the light of the sun and the adanists.

She breathed in deep, her weavings as familiar to her as the sound of her laugh or the sight of the stars in the sky. She bound adani high above her, knotting it into the beautiful destructive patterns she was so fond of. The air crackled as she wove additional layers on top of the existing ones. It was a shame she didn't have the strength of a gathering ground to take advantage of. With one of those, she thought she might be able to hold off the Belog long enough for Samora to succeed.

As it was, well, it didn't pay to worry too much about that. She'd lived more than long enough.

Lightning bolted down from the sky, causing the ground beneath her feet to tremble. Two, three, then four bolts struck the lead Belog in quick succession. The roiling shadows that covered it vanished, present one moment and gone the next. The Belog wasn't too large, as far as Belog went, but it was still half again Karla's height.

She didn't care. It's size only made the monster an easier target.

More lightning struck the Belog, burning across the hastily erected shields it used to protect itself. It staggered under the blasts, but Karla kept hitting it, never giving it a chance to regain its balance. She weaved lightning as fast as she ever had as she opened her spirit up wide. There was no point in holding anything back.

Karla wondered if Samora had thought their plan through to the end. Even if, by some feat of incredible fortune, they were able to break the circle, their own lives were forfeit. One way or another, this ended with them being surrounded by an angry clan of Debru, and Samora didn't want to kill.

Not that it would make a difference at that point.

Karla kept up her assault, hoping that just one of her bolts would get through the Belog's defenses and strike it dead.

The other Belog didn't seem disturbed by its companion's struggles. It rushed forward without its partner. Adani screamed a warning, and Karla spared a single bolt of lightning to strike down the shadow spear that launched out of the cloud.

She was already halfway through her spirit's reserve and the battle hadn't even reached its peak. Why wouldn't the fool Belog just let one of her bolts through?

Thirty Debru crested the hill behind the assaulted Belog, ignoring it in favor of attacking Karla.

She supposed that figured. In her experience, the Debru really didn't like her.

But it wouldn't be long before all of them were on top of her, and not even she was strong enough to live long through that.

Samora needed to hurry.

SAMORA FELT THE GROUND RUMBLE, but it was as if it was some distant thing, happening to a land far, far away.

Her world had condensed into a single contest of skill, strength, and will. The tighter she bound the strands of adani, the closer she came to touching the center of the circle with it, the more the circle fought her. It was like trying to tie a knot in a piece of rope while a dozen farmers stood on each end and tugged it taut. Just as she would bind two threads together, they'd come undone with a snap that almost caused her to lose her tenuous grip on them.

When binding the adani together failed, she tried simply

forcing the threads toward the center of the circle, but it felt like trying to thread a needle with a rope as thick as her wrist. She pushed and pushed, but the sheer power of the circle was far beyond her own. It seemed to possess a limitless amount of shadow, which it flung against her meager efforts with abandon.

The vibrations of the battle beyond she felt through her bottom told her she didn't have much time, but no matter how she tried to force the threads closer to the center of the circle, she wasn't strong enough. She pushed as much as she had into the thread, but the circle had no trouble batting her efforts away.

The Vada grew closer, too. She felt the darkness as a physical weight against her chest, pushing harder and harder until it became difficult for her to breathe.

With a last, desperate effort, she flung everything into the thread and tried to bind the adani.

It didn't advance her even the smallest amount.

Her focus broke as despair took over. The constant attacks of the circle broke through and sliced her thread into pieces, unraveling it further and converting it into the food it so desperately sought.

The attack traveled back up the thread, and though she severed it before it struck her spirit, she felt a sudden, sharp cold in her chest.

She wanted to sob. The more she gave to the fight, the more the circle took from her. She already felt lightheaded. She wasn't even sure she had the focus to bind another thread and send it into the circle. But the Vada was almost here. She had no time.

Samora cracked open her eyes and immediately wished that she hadn't. Debru flowed over the nearby hill, charging toward Karla with burning eyes. Her friend stood alone against the advance, lightning falling from the sky in a continuous stream of fire.

Her glance didn't reveal the location of the second Belog, but the first was almost upon them, barely slowed by the glancing blows of lightning that occasionally snaked down from the skies toward it. Samora rose to help, but before she could get to her feet, the Belog threw a spear straight at her.

Karla raised a shield that deflected the shadow spear, but it still landed no more than a dozen paces away, the force of the impact lifting Samora off her feet. Her arms and feet scrambled for anything to grab, but she hit the ground hard. She heard her ribs crack a moment before her torso turned into a raging fire of pain.

KARLA SWORE LOUDLY, though she couldn't hear herself over the rumble of thunder and the attacks of the Belog. She held a bound shield before her as she manipulated the lightning above, but neither would last much longer.

And Samora had failed.

Karla hadn't felt any of it, too consumed by her defense of the girl. But she'd seen the girl rise to her feet and try to help against the Belog. The sudden movement had distracted her, and she'd almost let a Belog spear kill Samora. It had landed close enough that it might have anyway.

Samora lay just outside the edge of the circle, but her eyes were closed, and she wasn't moving.

Karla's shield shuddered as the closest Belog finally reached her and brought a giant shadow hammer down on it.

It held but wouldn't for another strike. She was at her limit.

If she was going to die, though, she planned on bringing as many of those ugly monsters with her as she could. She had one last trick that she hadn't shown them yet. Something special she'd been saving up for just such a moment.

She began weaving adani, giving the Debru one final farewell gift.

Samora kneeled next to one of the wounded from the Debru assault. Brittany kneeled beside her, guiding her through the healing techniques she knew. She had a smile on her face as she sensed Samora's flow of adani through the wounded man.

"When we say 'push' adani into the wounded, we mean something a little less…intense," Brittany said.

Samora gave her new friend a questioning glance.

"You're pushing too hard, trying to exert too much of your will over the adani. Instead, think about trickling it in and letting it heal on its own. Our work as healers is less about trying to tell adani what to do and more about directing it to the right place and letting it take care of the rest."

Samora's eyes snapped open, and she coughed up blood. She tried to move, to rise, to roll over, but every time she so much as shifted her weight, she regretted it. Her breathing sounded wet and raspy, and she worried that her left leg was broken.

Not like there was anywhere to run.

The circle pulled adani from her, stealing the warmth from her body.

She grunted, surprised she wasn't more afraid. She had failed her family, failed her village, failed everyone. More than afraid, she was ashamed. Elian had always believed himself the weak one, but in the end, she'd been the one who hadn't been strong enough to matter.

It's more about directing it to the right place and letting it take care of the rest.

Why wouldn't the memory leave her alone? She'd been trying to direct the adani to the center of the circle, exactly where it was needed.

She might as well try it one more time. Her body was already pressed against the ground, so she extended the thread straight from her navel. Without much adani to spare, the entire thread was thinner than the unraveled tips of her last attempt. She couldn't imagine it would do much if it made contact, but the attempt was better than just laying here and waiting to die.

As she expected, the circle pulled the thread, still eager for any shred of adani. She followed it as it unraveled, but she didn't fight the process like before. She just kept herself connected. The tips of the adani grew fainter and fainter, to the point where she almost wasn't sure they existed.

But she was sensitive enough to feel them still, and remembering Brittany's advice, didn't push any more adani into them. It went against every instinct she'd developed as an adanist, but she'd tried everything else, and the faint wisps of adani, still connected to her core, didn't yet alarm the presence at the heart of the dead circle.

She came closer than she ever had, and through her connection, she felt the Vada growing closer, eager to step through. With all the fighting happening around the circle, there was more adani to consume than ever. It wouldn't be long at all, now. It just needed the gate to finish forming.

Her adani grew closer yet to the center, still her adani, though almost impossible for even her sensitive spirit to find.

The center of the circle finally noticed the wisps, and it launched its blades to cut at the adani. Her instinct was to send more adani down the thread, but she had little to spare, and she'd already tried it. Instead, she just kept tracking the ends of the unraveling thread, watching as they danced of their own accord.

The circle's defenses became more frantic. It sent out more of its shadowy force, but the threads wove between them with ease, growing ever closer to the heart of the circle. The presence sent out another call for help, and Samora felt the Vada on the other side of the gate gathering its own force to help.

Shadow rained down on her body from the nearby Debru, but none reached her. Karla gave the last of her strength to serve Samora, to give her a few more precious moments.

Samora's adani finally touched the presence that lurked deep in the circle and penetrated it easily. The light reached into the darkness. To Samora's senses, it was as if the adani had entered a wounded body and was rushing up and down the blood vessels. The whole body was diseased, but there was no place the light didn't reach, so long as she didn't interfere.

The presence unraveled, slowly at first, then quickly. It fought its dissolution, but against adani's gentle and persistent pressure, it surrendered, surprisingly fragile despite all the defenses that surrounded it.

The last moment of unraveling was violent. The presence vanished, replaced by a massive well of adani.

Samora assumed it was all the adani it had stolen since it had been formed, returned to its original form. But with so much in one place, it reminded her of her brother. It pulled adani toward it, just as the circle had, but the flow was no longer one way. It returned adani to the world even as it pulled from the surroundings.

The dead grass of the circle sprang to life, a vivid green that was achingly familiar.

The circle's destruction had become the seed of creation for a new gathering ground. It was, she thought, one of the most beautiful sights she'd ever seen, even if it was surrounded by angry Debru.

Samora smiled as the last of her consciousness slipped away.

KARLA LAUGHED as the weight of the past few weeks fell off her shoulders. She shifted a few steps to the side, basking in the familiar feeling of a gathering ground. She couldn't begin to guess how it had shown up, but it was here, and she still hadn't shared her gift with the Belog.

Adani refreshed both her depleted spirit and her tired limbs. She allowed a trickle into her mind to restore her focus.

The weaving of the gift was easy, and her supply of adani seemed endless. Her first target was the Belog she'd finally wounded earlier. She cast the lightning down, a concentrated weaving several times more powerful than any she'd created before. When it struck the Belog it scattered off in all directions, piercing Debru as it jumped from creature to creature.

She laughed again, ecstatic like she hadn't been since she was a child. The Belog slumped over, dead, surrounded by nearly a dozen of its minions. No one had ever landed such a blow before.

Granted, she'd almost killed herself to wound the Belog earlier, but that didn't take away from the enormity of what she'd done.

She wove the adani again. Against the fresh Belog, she wasn't sure it would be enough, but it would certainly clear the area of Debru and otsoa. Her body burned, not used to so much adani passing through it in such a short period of time.

They were probably still dead, but she'd make the Debru pay dearly for the privilege of taking her life.

Before she could cast the weaving, shadow erupted from the Belog and its spirit diminished. She'd never felt a Moka or a Belog do anything similar, but she couldn't sense it as easily as she usually could.

It rushed away, carrying the surviving Debru along with it.

Karla held onto her weaving, certain it was a trap she didn't yet understand.

But when she cast out a web of adani, it told her that she was alone with Samora and that the Debru were fleeing west, back to the deadlands.

Samora's wet cough brought her back to her surroundings. Karla let go of her adani and grinned. The girl had done it.

But she had paid a steep price. Karla picked her up as gently as she could, though she heard the broken bones shifting as she did. Then she laid Samora within the protection of the gathering ground and set to work.

There was still much to do before she could rest.

36

The Belog cut at Elian with an enormous shadow sword. Elian didn't try to dodge. He'd seen the speed and control the Belog had over its weapon, and if he tried something foolish like jumping over the sword, his limbs would land in different places. Instead, he angled his blade, just like Master Heinrick had taught him when he was younger.

The Belog's sword scraped off his, but even the glancing blow was nearly enough to lift him off his feet. He stumbled to the side but regained his balance quickly.

On the other side of the Belog, Harald took full advantage of the distraction. He formed a spear and threw it at the Belog's unprotected back.

The Belog threw up a shield of shadow, but the impact of the spear knocked it forward. Elian launched himself at the off-balance monster. The Belog blocked with his shadow sword, but this time, when Elian cut, it sliced the shadow sword in half.

He'd been expecting his blow to be blocked, so cutting through the shadow made him land awkwardly. The Belog regrew its sword and cut down, leaving Elian no choice but to block. He grimaced as the sword came down, expecting the impact to bring him to his knees. But again, when their swords collided, it was Elian's steel that triumphed over the Belog's shadow.

The unexpected result again left Elian unprepared, but Harald saved him by occupying the Belog with another spear thrust. Tera contributed a brace of bound knives to the cause, whipping them at the Belog's face.

Elian's mind shouted at him to retreat, but he was close to the Belog now, and its weapons seemed no match for Elian's steel. His spirit demanded an attack, and he was done containing it. He stepped forward and cut at the Belog, aiming for its thigh. The Belog brought its sword down, but Elian's blade cut cleanly through.

He came close to cutting off its leg. It leaned back, but the tip of Elian's sword cut deep into the thigh. It wasn't fatal, but the Belog stumbled back, appearing for the first time to not be in control of the fight. Harald, still behind the Belog, struck at it with spears, each one releasing a wave of force that Elian felt in his bones. He couldn't imagine how the Belog stood so long against such an assault.

It was likely a mistake to think of the Belog in human terms, but Elian swore he saw fear in the Belog's eyes. It retreated against the onslaught of attacks, but they left it no place to hide.

Instead, it lashed out with blinding speed, sending a dozen spears of shadow at Harald. It was the greatest attack they'd seen from it yet. Elian lost sight of Harald under the sheer volume of spears, but he trusted the enormous warrior would survive. He had to.

Unfortunately for the Belog, such an attack left it exposed and undefended. Elian stepped into the space and cut at the Belog's knee. The edge of his sword glowed as it sliced cleanly through the joint. As the monster fell, Tera threw a handful of knives into its chest.

The Belog roared in pain, but before it could recover from the blow, Elian brought his sword down on the Belog's neck, now at a height he could easily reach. It sliced clean through, ending the Belog's call.

Elian stood tall, the adani rushing through his limbs making him feel like there was no challenge he couldn't overcome. He surveyed the battlefield again and was pleased at the effect of the Belog's death.

No dragons attacked the circle anymore. Most dropped bound adani on the heads of the Debru, thinning their ranks as they battled against the Hawks. The extra support from the ones who had been fighting the circle tilted the balance of the battle, and the Hawks pressed forward through the Debru that remained. A handful of dragons flew behind the front line of the battle, scaring away the otsoa with adani, tooth, and claw.

The Hawks acquitted themselves well. Kati and her best fighters battled against the other Belog, and at the moment, the battle seemed even. But as Elian watched, the Belog realized it wasn't winning. Hawks and Dragons picked off the Debru that supported it. Each of the Belog's allies that fell freed an adanist or three to join the fight against the commander, and before long the Belog was retreating under a constant barrage of bound adani. It was only a matter of time before it fell.

Once it did, the rest of the battle was as good as over. Elian's gaze was torn away, though, by Tera's horrified cry. He turned around and swore.

In the rush of all that had happened, he had forgotten about Harald. The giant warrior was on his knees, bleeding from multiple wounds. His right arm hung limp at his side, a chunk of muscle missing from the upper part near the shoulder.

Elian rushed toward Harald as the man tipped forward, catching him before he smashed face-first into the dirt. Blood covered his arms and made the giant difficult to support, and his breathing was ragged. Tera joined him on Harald's other side, eyes pleading with her leader to stay.

"Did we win?" he asked.

Elian nodded. "When the Belog focused on you, Tera and I were able to kill it. Kati and the Hawks have overwhelmed the other, and the dragons are picking off the surviving Debru. We won."

Harald coughed up blood. "A good day, then. I'm glad to hear it."

Elian halfway expected Harald to rise and brush his grievous wounds off, but instead his body suddenly went limp. Elian panicked for a moment, but Harald's chest continued to rise and fall, each breath sounding like Harald was trying to move a mountain. The legend lived, but Elian wasn't sure for how much longer.

Elian motioned for Tera to help him lift Harald. They each positioned themselves underneath one of Harald's arms, and on a shared count, lifted him high enough they could drag him back to the Hawks.

By unspoken agreement, they hurried, hoping they weren't too late.

ELIAN PACED BACK AND FORTH, then stopped when he worried he was about to wear a new path in the thick grass of the gathering ground. The Hawks had made a stretcher for Harald, and Loken and Brittany had fussed over Harald the entire journey back to the relative safety of the old woods. Elian had carried one end of the stretcher the entire way while a string of Hawks took turns carrying the other end.

Once they'd reached the gathering grounds, Loken had taken Harald away and given orders that they weren't to be disturbed. Elian had tried to rest in the woods, but memories of the battle and worries about Harald's fate made the towering trees seem like walls that were closing in. He'd retreated to the western edge of the gathering ground where there was more grass than trees.

A shadow passed overhead, and Elian looked up. His dragon circled high above, bringing a weary smile to his face. He waved and it bled some of its altitude, coming in for a soft landing in front of him.

"It's good to see you again," Elian said.

The dragon brought its head down and Elian approached, gently laying his hand upon the snout. He closed his eyes and allowed the adani that looped through his limbs to extend into the dragon. It was easier than in the past, the connection forming more naturally. He tried to express his gratitude but was quickly overwhelmed by the dragon's own.

Visions flashed before him. The first had the dragons circling triumphantly over the battlefield. It had been many, many years since they'd experienced such a victory. Some of their younglings hadn't even believed it possible anymore. They roared in celebration and Elian's heart echoed their joy.

The next vision was of a few dragons flying near the circle. Despite their best efforts, the circle remained whole. The dragons' silent concern turned Elian's insides to water. They'd won a great victory here today, but it wasn't complete, and the dragons feared the circle.

It troubled him, too, but questions about the circle would have to wait. They had wounded to attend to and dead to honor. For now, the Hawks and Hounds would remain in the gathering ground. In a few days, perhaps, they might visit it again and seek answers.

The visions ended with one of the dragons flying above a column of humans and fighting by their side. Elian wasn't sure if the vision was of a memory long lost to humanity or a dream of the future. The intent behind the message, though, was clear.

"We'd be honored to fight beside you," Elian said.

The dragon's head shifted under his touch, and Elian swore the dragon nodded. It broke contact and rose to its full height, blocking the setting sun and casting a long shadow over Elian. It roared with satisfaction, shaking the air out of Elian's chest, then took off into the sky.

Elian watched it leave. He was pleased to know that he would soon see it again.

Hurried footsteps behind him brought his attention back to the present. It was Brittany. Her face was pale and her gaze downcast, and for a moment, Elian feared the worst. Before he could ask, she blurted out, "He wants to see you."

She turned and hurried away, forcing him to chase after. His lips burned with questions, but suspected she wouldn't answer. He forced himself to be patient. She led him through the thick trees until they reached a fallen log that had its top carved flat to serve as a bed or a table. Harald lay across it, and he didn't look that much better than when Elian had carried him off the battlefield.

Bandages covered his arms and chest, and the one around his right arm was particularly bloody. Harald was pale, and Elian feared he'd been summoned for some sort of deathbed confession.

Brittany turned and left as soon as Elian entered the clearing, and he watched her go. He could think of half a dozen reasons why she was so upset but hadn't the slightest which reason it was.

When Harald spoke, his voice was stronger than Elian expected, and it made him jump a little. "Forgive her. She's lived her entire life seeing me in one way, and I can no longer be the leader she looked up to."

Elian frowned at Harald's choice of words. "How are you?"

"I've felt better, but I will live, and Brittany and Loken tell me that's mostly thanks to you."

Elian brushed away the praise. "Tera did just as much to help carry you off the battlefield."

"Perhaps, but you were the one who sent adani into me, keeping me alive, even as you did so."

"I—," Elian stopped. He had no memory of sending any adani into Harald. "I did? Are you sure?"

"Loken is. He claims I had more of your adani in my spirit than my own when he first laid hands on me."

"I didn't know."

Harald gestured for Elian to come closer, which he did. "Regardless, you have my thanks, both for killing that Belog and for saving my life."

"Both tasks I'd happily do again."

Harald nodded. "I'll get to the point. Thanks to you, Loken, and Brittany, I'll live to see another sunrise, and hopefully plenty more after that. But I won't be able to fight again, not the way I have in the past."

"You don't need an arm to bind adani."

"No, but I won't be able to fight up close like I did today. I won't be able to wade through the thick of a battle. I still plan to lead the Hounds, but it won't be like I used to. I'll need someone strong to take my place on the battlefield, someone my adanists will look up to and follow."

"Then Tera is your best choice."

Harald shook his head. "Tera is an incredible warrior. One of my best. But she didn't ride a dragon into battle today, and she didn't charge a Belog armed with nothing but a sword. She will always be treasured among the Hounds, but she isn't you. Swear your loyalty to me and become my strong right arm, my sword in the battle against the Debru."

Elian considered for a moment, surprised to find how certain he was. It was barely a choice at all. For the first time, he felt like his steps were light. He knew how strong he was. The dead Belog was all the proof he needed.

He dropped to a knee and bowed to Harald. "I will."

EPILOGUE

Samora opened her eyes as adani returned to her after making its incredible journey. She breathed in deep and didn't fight the smile that grew across her face. She nodded, and even Karla had a hint of a grin on her face at the gesture.

"He survived, then?" she asked.

"He feels stronger than ever. The way adani flows through his body has changed."

"And what of the Belog?"

"Gone, but the circle remains."

Karla's face fell. She leaned back until she was laying in the grass. She stared up at the clouds. "I suppose it would be too much to ask that someone there figures out the secret of the circles, too."

Samora agreed. "We were fortunate to figure it out here."

Karla snorted. "Don't know what you're saying 'we' for. I didn't do a thing when it came to that circle."

"You kept me safe."

Karla waved away the comment. "Can you tell what stage the other circles are at?"

"Not easily. The one closest to where the Crows were slaughtered is the most developed, now, and if I had to guess, it's on the verge of becoming a gate within the next few days."

"Too soon for us to reach?"

"Probably."

Karla kept staring up at the sky, strangely calm despite the news.

Samora didn't judge. She felt much the same. That last battle had taken more out of her than just adani. Ever since she'd woken up from Karla's healing, she'd wanted to do nothing more than lay around and rest. Unraveling the circle had left her more weary than a full day in the fields, and no amount of sleep could wash the exhaustion completely away. She'd spoken of it with Karla, who said she felt the same, though neither of them tried to explain why.

There was no way to do so, of course, but she wondered, if she were to jump from here to the next circle if she could duplicate what she'd accomplished here. The way she felt now, she wasn't sure.

When she closed her eyes to sleep, the weariness reminded her of what she'd felt in her visions of that other place. She and Karla had examined each other carefully for lingering traces of shadow, but neither of them were infected. Samora suspected it was simply contact with the Belog that sapped her will. Right now, all she could hope was that the weariness would fade in time.

She lay down beside Karla and closed her eyes, eager for a nap.

"Don't get too comfortable. They're getting close," Karla said.

Samora grunted. She wasn't sure what worried her more: the battles she would have to wage with the other circles or the discussions she would have to lead with the combined clans' councils. She imagined standing in front of the council and recounting the last few days.

The familiar fear she expected never arose. She'd still rather be by herself, but after facing a Vada about to enter their lands, speaking to a crowd seemed as simple and straightforward as hunting with Elian.

The thought of her brother made her chest ache. With the Belog gone from his location and the sense of his adani, she knew he'd been through a fight that had changed him. It hurt that she hadn't been by his side, and she wondered if he felt the same. She, at least, had the benefit of being able to find him. He wouldn't know anything about what had become of her.

Soon, though, she'd find her way to him. They'd fought the Debru back this time, but if she had truly sensed what she thought she had, their war was far from over.

Thinking about Elian banished some of the lingering weariness from her bones. She pushed herself to her feet and turned to meet the scouts just now laying eyes upon the new gathering ground for the first time. They stopped and stared, uncomprehending, and Samora waved to them.

There was much to be done. She and Karla would have to explain what had happened here and work with other healers to see if anyone else could perform the techniques Samora had learned. So long as the knowledge of the circles was hers alone, all of humanity was in danger.

She needed to seed her knowledge in as many places as she could and hope that it would take root in others. She couldn't fight the battles to come alone, despite Karla's continued insistence they could take on the rest of the Debru by themselves.

She thought of Elian, always ahead of her, always charging forward. He never tired and never faltered.

Despite the generous praise Karla had heaped on her since her battle with the circle, Samora didn't feel like she'd grown strong enough. The adani that she'd sensed from him made her realize how much stronger he'd become in her absence. No matter how fast she ran, he always seemed to be a little bit ahead of her.

She didn't mind. Wherever he was and whatever had

happened to him, she was going to catch up to him, so that when the Debru launched their next attack, they'd find a more prepared humanity than before.

Samora didn't welcome the responsibilities that awaited her, but she didn't feel like she had to run from them, either. Her answers wouldn't be found in the silences of empty grasslands.

They'd be found together, with friends, family, and allies by her side.

ALSO BY RYAN KIRK

The Legend of Adani

Born of Light and Shadow

From Shadow to Flame

The Ascension of Light

A War of Light and Shadow

Waterstone

The Rise of Shadow

The Shadows Beyond

The Last Sword of the West

Last Sword in the West

Eyes of the Hidden World

A Sword Named Vengeance

Wraith's Revenge

Frontier's End

Song of the Sagani

Legend of the Sword in the West

Nightblade

Nightblade

World's Edge

The Wind and the Void

Blades of the Fallen

Nightblade's Vengeance

Nightblade's Honor

Nightblade's End

Saga of the Broken Gods

Band of Broken Gods

Fall of Forgotten Gods

Rise of the Resurrected God

Oblivion's Gate

The Gate Beyond Oblivion

The Gates of Memory

The Gate to Redemption

Relentless

Relentless Souls

Heart of Defiance

Their Spirit Unbroken

The Sentinels Saga (with Taylor Crook)

Path of the Eternal Sun

A Path Divided

A Path Reforged

Primal

Primal Dawn

Primal Darkness

Primal Destiny

Song of the Fallen Swords

These Fallen Swords

Standalone Novels

The Last Fang of God

Blades of Shadow: A Nightblade Story

ABOUT THE AUTHOR

Ryan Kirk is the award-winning and internationally bestselling author of over thirty fantasy novels spanning nearly a dozen worlds. He lives in Minnesota with his family, where he enjoys long, meandering walks outside even when the snow is high enough to cover his legs. When he isn't glued to his keyboard, he's usually in the woods, either on foot or on bike.

facebook.com/waterstonemedia

instagram.com/authorryankirk

bookbub.com/authors/ryan-kirk

www.ingramcontent.com/pod-product-compliance
Lightning Source LLC
Chambersburg PA
CBHW020014120726
47903CB00004B/1284